THE **BURIED** AND **THE BOUND**

ROCHELLE HASSAN

ROARING BROOK PRESS

NEW YORK

Published by Roaring Brook Press
Roaring Brook Press is a division of Holtzbrinck Publishing Holdings Limited
Partnership
120 Broadway, New York, NY 10271 • fiercereads.com

Our books may be purchased in bulk for promotional, educational, or
business use. Please contact your local bookseller or the Macmillan Corporate
and Premium Sales Department at (800) 221-7945 ext. 5442 or by email at
MacmillanSpecialMarkets@macmillan.com.

Library of Congress Cataloging-in-Publication Data is available.

First edition, 2023
Book design by Samira Iravani
Printed in the United States of America

ISBN 978-1-250-82220-8 (hardcover)
1   3   5   7   9   10   8   6   4   2

For those of you fighting battles and facing monsters of your own.

May you be victorious.

CHAPTER 1

TRISTAN

WHEN THE LIGHTS in the house went out, Tristan pushed through the gate with a nudge and left it swaying open behind him.

A homemade bird feeder hung in the corner of the tiny yard; a set of wooden wind chimes knocked together softly, as if they, too, had secrets to keep. His footsteps landed soundlessly on the grass. Back door, kitchen window, living room with curtains drawn—these he flinched past, half expecting an accusing face would loom out of the darkness and stop him.

Half hoping.

But no one did. Before long, he found a bedroom. Huddling in the shadows with his back against the wall, he drew his master's silver knife in a line down his palm. Blood welled up, and he pressed it into the window frame. His hands were littered with cuts—some fresh, others scarred over—from a year of this work. The blood of a bondservant was a signal. It would guide his master to this home, this window, and to the person inside.

The first time had been the hardest.

"Please don't make me do this," Tristan had begged, voice choked with humiliating tears, after their contract was sealed and his master had described the errand he was meant to complete for her. "Not yet, not tonight—"

A pitiful attempt to stall, and it did him no good.

"Yes." Her voice seeped, sludge-like, through the woods. "Tonight."

Tristan had never been a brave person, and he didn't want to die. So he'd obeyed.

There were no tears anymore. Now there was nothing but the task at hand.

He slept uneasily on a park bench with his backpack for a pillow and his worn-out coat for warmth. As he dropped off, she woke. From her prison in the woods, she sent her magic after the call of Tristan's blood. Without him, it would have drifted, lost and directionless. Instead, it found the window and slinked inside. It skittered through the dark like a filthy, many-legged thing, sensed its victim fast asleep, and crawled inside their head.

Her voice echoed through their dreams, and Tristan's.

Come, she told her victim, conjuring up the deepest desires of their heart. *I can give you what you want. Whatever you want.*

It might not be tonight. It might not even be tomorrow. But, sooner or later, they would go stumbling into the woods and never return.

ALONE, TRISTAN VENTURED deep into a part of the woods where no light penetrated, not even starlight. If he'd cared to consult a map, it would've told him he was in Blackthorn, Massachusetts. But as he walked, he drew further and further away from the world he'd grown up in, the safe human world of tidy suburbs, inflatable Santas, and Walmart supercenters. He skirted past fairyland's boundary and entered a third realm—a pocket of space and time that bulged cancerously between human and fae territory. Those worlds had edges; this one didn't. Entering it wasn't a matter of crossing a border, but wading into the cold and dark. The forest, here, was gnarled and gray and dead. He picked his way through the withered roots and animal graves with only a flashlight and a stolen pair of hiking boots to aid him.

After a while—he had stopped paying attention to how long it took, since it was different every time—he came to a wide clearing where the ruins of an old cabin stood. The roof had caved in. The walls had moldered away to low stumps. A tree grew from what remained of the cabin's floor, the trunk so swollen it had all but consumed the foundations. Its sickly gray-green bark was veined with noxious black sap, and its roots spread into the surrounding forest like an infection.

Tristan laid a hand on the trunk. In response to his touch, it split open at the fork, its branches peeling apart with a wet crack and exuding the distinct, rotten stench of black magic. From this gaping hole in the world crawled the creature to whom Tristan had signed his life away.

He wasn't permitted to look at her; with relief, he averted his eyes. One time had been enough.

"I have a gift for you, my ward," she croaked. Her voice was the rattle of wind in dead winter branches. She rarely spoke; she didn't need to. The bond made her demands plenty clear enough.

He suppressed a shudder. A gift from the hag would be no gift at all.

"You understand, boy, that you have disappointed me. Too often." He bowed his head. "Yes."

A year ago, the hag had offered him a simple bargain: ten years of servitude in exchange for a magical favor. Desperate, he'd agreed. But it was clear to him now that he wouldn't last ten years; he had barely made it through one. She was always furious with him, for his ineptitude. His reluctance. His weak heart.

"What am I to do for ten years with an unsuitable bondservant?" she asked, and the bond ached inside him with an emptiness beyond anything he had ever known. It was the insatiable hunger of an immortal devourer, and her way of telling him, wordlessly, what she had not the energy or inclination to say aloud: *My patience is not without limit. And I am starving.*

"But just yesterday, I—" His throat was so dry he could hardly get the words out. "I've been . . . obedient."

"He was *ill*," she snapped.

"I didn't know that."

He really hadn't. He hadn't looked—he never looked beyond a cursory glance here and there, because he couldn't stomach the thought of evaluating the hag's victims like produce at the grocery store.

The moment lingered, his childish admission of ignorance hanging damningly between them. She was in no hurry. Time, to her, was meaningless.

"No matter," she said. "I have found a remedy that will serve us both."

"Please," he said. "I . . ."

What could he say? *I'll do better?*

He couldn't do better. But she knew that already.

She cackled, and her laugh was whitewater crashing against stone. His breath came short and shallow; his heart fluttered against his ribs like a trapped moth. He couldn't run. There was nowhere to go.

"This gift requires a living spirit. I cannot wield it," she said.

But Tristan could. Tristan was a living spirit, and hers to do with as she wished.

She did something new to the bond, then. She had used it to hurt him before, but this was different, a pain that saturated his skin, pain that was everywhere, burning him up and breaking him down. It was in his bones and in his head, and it made everything *wrong*, from the way the clothes scraped against his skin to the way his mouth tasted to the colors on the inside of his eyelids to the sound of his own voice—

All at once, it stopped.

Tristan curled into himself, his head pressed against the base of the tree, its roots digging into his side. At some point, he must have fallen. And his throat was raw like he'd been screaming. The bark was cold and sticky, so he forced himself to pull away. He almost felt like himself again, but there was a—a residue. It wasn't on him. It was *in* him.

The sound of a wet, inhuman panting filled the clearing.

"What—what is—"

"Be quiet."

His teeth clicked together. He didn't move.

"Can you feel them?" she asked.

What he felt was—a breeze carding through his fur (he did not have fur) and dry soil under his claws (he did not have claws) and his tongue against the back of his fangs (he didn't have fangs) and a hunger that almost matched the hag's. The urge to chase and catch and kill beat inside him like a pulse—

And they weren't *his* feelings at all. With a gasp, Tristan wrenched away as if dismissing an intrusive thought: cutting it off before it could take the landscape of his mind and reshape it, give new names to its peaks and valleys, own it more than he did. "What did you do to me?"

"I have given you a gift of magic," she said.

The knowledge came to him then in bits and pieces; some of it she said aloud, some of it he learned from the bond, and later it would be so muddled in his head that he wouldn't be able to tell the difference. The hounds were his familiars, she told him. They belonged to him, and he belonged to her, and when they hunted their nourishment would be hers, too.

"I don't understand," he said. The hounds pawed at the ground or snapped at one another; others paced, their immense forms swaying in and out of the shadows. Some just watched him with unnervingly intelligent eyes. They were tense, unhappy, restless. He didn't know how he knew. He just did.

"You understand power," said the hag. "All living things do. All dead things, too."

"Power? So I'm supposed to control them?"

"Try."

He extended his hand toward one of the hounds. It approached slowly, reluctantly—but it did approach, looming over him, closer in size to a bear than a dog. Its obedience was fragile, his control tenuous. If he wavered, it would resist.

"Like this?" he asked the hag, when the hound stopped a few feet away from him.

"Go on," she whispered.

He got to his feet, reaching this time with his thoughts. His hand curled reflexively as he grasped, in his mind, the fresh link between him and his so-called bond-sibling. Again he felt what the hound did, but the hound felt him, too, his fear and desperation, and what a year's worth of suffering had done to him. With all the resolve he could muster, he pushed a single command through the bond:

Attack.

The hound gave a full-body shiver, from the tips of its ears down the arch of its spine. It shook its head, jaws snapping, and its claws raked the ground. At last, it whipped its head up, and its black eyes locked on the decrepit old hag in her perch.

With a growl like an engine revving up, the hound lunged over Tristan's head and onto the gateway tree, clinging to the bark with its claws. It climbed with deadly speed and heaved itself up onto the branches at level with the hag.

Keep going, Tristan thought. He stoked its most base and potent instinct. *Kill.*

The hound sprang at the hag with jaws gaping wide, and then— and then—

It twisted away, fell from the gateway tree, and landed on its side atop a raised root with a *crack* that reverberated through the clearing. At the same time, pain drew a searing line of heat up Tristan's back, there for only a brief, terrifying instant. The hound was bent almost in half. A few weak, piteous whimpers escaped its panting mouth. Its spine was broken; it was dying.

Tristan watched, stricken, as it shuddered and jerked.

Then—the hound rolled to its feet. Gruesome snapping noises filled the air as its crooked back popped into alignment. It shook out its fur, shot Tristan a reproachful glare, and loped away into the woods.

The gateway tree creaked, though there was no wind. Laboriously, it bowed, lowering the cup of its branches until the hag hovered before Tristan. Her putrid stench, like rotten meat, suffocated him. Blind though she was, her face was angled toward his, as if she *could* see him. He didn't dare turn to check.

"Do you know why that didn't work?" the hag said.

Shivering, Tristan shook his head.

"The hounds are only as strong as their master," she said. "It didn't fail. You did."

She stroked a finger down his cheek. Her touch was leathery and so hot it stung his skin, like candle wax. Tristan flinched and screwed his eyes shut, giving in to cowardice.

"But you have a vicious streak," she whispered. "I intend to nurture that."

CHAPTER 2

AZIZA

"You can't stay there," she said. "You'll starve."

The Christmas tree towered over her, a three-story-tall monument to its corporate sponsors, whose logos had been etched on glass snowflakes, stitched into ribbons, painted in gold on red baubles. Standing beside it with her hands in her pockets, quiet and intent, she gave every appearance of caring deeply about which fitness brand or retail chain had paid to put their name on a tiny plastic reindeer. But Aziza was more interested in what was under the tree than what was on it.

"There's nothing down there for you," she went on, her back to the scattered crowds. "No campers or lost children. Nothing with fingers or ears for you to bite off."

Light poured down from the lampposts lining the park trails. Ropes of flashing rainbow bulbs crisscrossed the walkways and studded the vendors' stalls. Here, though, at the heart of the fair, under a mountain of tinsel and fake pine needles, was a pocket of darkness. When people walked too close, their shadows met the base of the tree and briefly merged with that dark place. She tensed.

Shadows were vectors for certain beings. Get two shadows to touch, and you had a bridge.

Under the pretense of tying her shoelaces, Aziza knelt to study the shade—this cunning little predator that had taken such pains to blend in.

There.

Past the tangle of the bottommost branches and the cords of the fairy lights, the darkness turned dense and oily black. She inhaled the sharp-sweet smell of pine needles and caught an unmistakable sour note underneath.

"You can either let me take you back to where you came from," she said, "or I can drag you there. Last warning."

This was what passed for festive in Aziza's world: corralling dangerous magical beings while "Blue Christmas" warbled in the background.

The winter solstice coincided with the annual fair at St. Sithney's Park, which made it one of the most dangerous times of the year for Blackthorn, whether most people knew it or not. Every night for twelve nights, Aziza paid the dollar entry fee and did a sweep of the fair and its surroundings, watching for telltale signs of unwelcome visitors. Not the rowdy, drunk ones from Boston, here for a night or two—the *other* visitors.

Unhurriedly, she picked up the cup of hot chocolate she'd set on the ground, drained it, and tossed it in the trash can a few paces away. In the time it took her to leave and return, the shade neither moved nor showed any sign of surrendering.

She got on her hands and knees and peered into the dark. Behind her, the sound of passing footsteps slowed. Strangers always wanted to know whether she was all right, and if she was lost, and why was she bleeding? It was exhausting.

"Dropped something!" she said, with a forced smile. Once he moved along, she tore open one of the salt packets stashed in her pockets—bought in bulk, ten dollars for a thousand of them, and restocked three times already this year. She dumped its contents on the ground and blew, scattering salt under the tree.

The shadows spasmed and bulged like a blanket tossed on top of an irate cat. Everywhere the salt landed, the shade burned, tendrils of steam rising off it. It hissed, not a serpentine sound, but a whisper of the sort your mind might trick you into hearing when you were alone and it was too quiet—an untethered, fleshless sound. Aziza removed one of her gloves and held out her hand, waggling her fingers.

"Go on, then. Take a bite."

A shadow lashed out at her like a whip. Aziza snatched her fingers away and closed her other hand around the shade's head.

Gotcha.

She shoved her bare hand back into its glove, tugging it into place with her teeth. The shade writhed, shrinking, trying to get small enough to escape through the cracks between her fingers, but Aziza clasped her hands together and willed them into a prison.

Hold, she thought fiercely, and in her mind, her hands became a living cage. She stood and made her way out of the fair. No one noticed her; she didn't *look* very magical, even if she did have the arched nose and frizzy hair of a cartoon witch. At seventeen, she cleared five feet by a handful of inches. In her uniform of jeans, boots, a sweater, and a military-green coat, her one concession to holiday spirit was the candy cane pin on the flap of her bag. She spotted people she vaguely recognized, maybe classmates, maybe folks who lived on her block. St. Sithney's wasn't close to her neighborhood, but Blackthorn wasn't very large, either, and *everyone* attended the fair. But she didn't make eye contact.

She passed vendors distributing handmade ornaments, tacky

coffee mugs, cupcakes iced in red and green, and hot chocolate dosed with generous shots of liquor. Skipping children and their sedate parents wove through the stalls. Couples bobbed past holding hands and sharing packets of candied peanuts or caramel popcorn. This was no place for a shade. It would've been miserable if she'd left it here.

Shades liked cold, dark, quiet places, and often lurked on the border between Elphame—fairyland—and the human world. This pocket-sized pain in the neck had strayed too far from the boundary, gotten overwhelmed by the noise and the warmth, and didn't know how to get back to the safety of the woods.

You should be thanking me, she thought, and was rewarded with an insistent pressure on her palms as the shade tried to claw through her gloves.

But this mistake wasn't entirely the shade's fault. In a normal year, it wouldn't have been so easy for the shade—or anything else—to slip out of fairyland. Only, something was wrong with the boundary these days. Since last winter, Aziza's weekly patrols had turned into daily patrols as she did damage control and bought information from the pixies with their preferred currency: colorful hard candies and rainbow sequins. But not even pixies, the nosiest of all fae, had any idea what was going on.

The fair took place on the flat lawns in the middle of the park. But St. Sithney's was vast. Its lawns rolled into low hills with deep banks of snow between them and no space for ring toss games or photo booths; these she navigated with ease, having made this walk too many times to count. Beyond the hills lay the forest, shrouded in the shadow-silk of twilight and well removed from the din of the crowds. This forest spilled into a state park, sprawling on and on, nothing but wilderness for miles. The tree line at St. Sithney's marked Blackthorn's physical and magical boundary. The solstice weakened that boundary; it thinned the veil. So did the colorful string lights, tinsel, and pieces of paper scribbled with holiday wishes they put up on the first day of the fair, literally marking out the seam between worlds with a trail of revelry.

The *veil* was only a metaphor, of course. The boundary she sought now mostly couldn't be seen—except every now and then when she looked closely, she'd glimpse a wavering in the air, like heat haze. She was a hedgewitch, and hedgewitches could *feel* the boundary. But it helped her concentrate sometimes if she pictured a veil in her mind's eye.

She stopped beside one of the blackthorn shrubs for which the city was named, its spiny branches white with frost and laden with clusters of berries. The music from the fair was just a rhythmic hum, not even loud enough for her to make out the lyrics.

"Time for you to go home," she told the shade, speaking into her clasped hands. It had gone still, as if the proximity of the woods had soothed it.

The other side of the boundary was Elphame. There were places where Elphame and the human world overlapped, and the forest here at St. Sithney's was one of them. Strange and wild places, where you could cross between the two realms without even knowing it. The boundary was a force of nature, not a wall, and in its shifting magical currents, gaps would form, allowing things to pass through from either side. As a hedgewitch, Aziza could use her craft to seal those gaps. It was hard, never-ending work, even in the years when the boundary was stable—because the boundary could never be *completely* closed. But she did it anyway, because it needed to be done, because it kept Blackthorn safe, and most of all because she loved magic more than almost anything else. Even when it meant freezing her ass off in the dark when she could've been drinking cider and picking out a garish knit hat for her grandpa. Part of her even loved the ridiculous shade.

Open, she thought, and peeled back a corner of the veil to create the smallest doorway, a portal to fairyland the size of a letter box. A gust of honey-sweet air wafted over her face. The heady warmth of Elphame beckoned her, but she paid it no mind. She unclasped her fingers and tipped the cup of her hands as if to pour out water.

A sound broke her concentration. The shade wriggled free, dropped to the ground—it was no larger than a thimble now—and, remaining firmly in the human realm, slithered away into the trees where even Aziza would be unable to find it, at least not right away.

She swore, but her voice was drowned out by the sound she recognized, now, as the baying of a pack of dogs.

The ornaments on the barren branches jangled dully as one, two, three—maybe half a dozen shapes streaked out of the forest, south of her. The glow of the fairy lights soaked into the snow and painted the creatures in psychedelic colors, warping their profiles so she couldn't make out exactly what they were. Vaguely canine in the shape of the snouts and ears, but much too big to be dogs after all. In a flash, they crossed the lawn, and she lost sight of them as they plunged into the fair.

A scream cut through the cheerful lilt of the music. And then another. And another.

Without thinking, she ran back toward the fairgrounds and ducked into the outer row of stalls. The crowd had transformed into a stampede, and when she moved closer, it swept her away through alleys of glittering displays. People shoved at her from both sides and stepped on her heels, everyone trying to get in front of someone else; she almost fell. Over the shouting and the crying and the crash of something breaking, the baying of the too-big-to-be-dogs came again and again from every direction.

But when one of them leapt into the crowd, it was soundless. People scattered, bowling each other over. Those in front of Aziza stopped, and those behind crushed into her—and someone was howling in agony, their voice soaring above the chaos. She elbowed her way forward and caught a glimpse of something massive and four-legged and covered with black fur; a man was crumpled beneath it, fragile as a paper doll caught under a tank. All she could do was watch helplessly through the gaps between people's shoulders as a pair of enormous jaws clamped down on the man's throat, and—there was no way anyone could have their neck bent at that angle and still be alive. No way they could gush bright red arterial blood like that and survive. Aziza lurched to a stop, paralyzed with horror. And then the beast was gone, bounding away with its kill before she could get a better look at it.

Someone shouldered past her, nearly knocking her flat. A blow from the other direction spun her around, and she barely knew which way she was going anymore. Desperate for air, she broke free of the crowd and staggered into the square with the Christmas tree. Barely ten minutes ago, she'd taken the shade from here, and everything had been fine. Now the fair was a disaster scene and it didn't even feel real. A person had just *died* in front of her.

The path to the exit made an arc around the square before veering away. She stayed on the sidelines and watched people surge past. Their fearful faces and shouts—for help, for missing loved ones, for the person in front to go *faster*—were vivid to her now that she stood apart. Their shoes trampled over a bloody smear on the ground, the only remaining sign of what had just happened.

She took a few seconds to catch her breath. Had that thing come out of Elphame? She'd never seen anything like it, but its speed and size couldn't *not* be magical.

Aziza loved magic, but she loved it like you'd love a pet boa constrictor: with cautionary measures, a healthy respect for its dangers, and a full awareness of the fact that the thing you loved could turn on you at any moment.

That was when she realized she wasn't alone. There was someone else in the square, too, a boy about her age standing so close to the Christmas tree that the shade would've been able to nip at his ankles. He was tall, with curly hair, a baggy Star Wars hoodie under his coat, and an expression that said, very plainly, *Oh shit*. He cupped his hands around his mouth and shouted, "HAZEL!"

His girlfriend? His dog?

She didn't know or care. What Aziza wanted to know was what the *hell* he was thinking, standing out there in the open like that when every rational person in sight was running for the exit.

The crowd had thinned out enough that she could have rejoined it without getting crushed again. But shadows moved at the edges of her vision. Not daring to look, she *sensed* more than saw the shape creeping behind the stalls. Stalking them. They'd wandered away from the herd, and now she and this boy were easy prey.

She took off at a sprint, caught the boy by the arm, and dragged him along, not slowing.

"Hey!" he said, digging in his heels.

"We have to move!"

"I can't—"

Aziza changed course, swinging around in the direction he'd been pulling, unbalancing him, and using her momentum to propel them back into the fair and beyond, toward the forest. There, at least, they could hide.

"You can look for Hazel later!" she said. "There's something following us."

He stopped resisting, so she let him go. They raced across the snowy lawn, fought their way into the woods through tangles of prickly brambles, and finally broke into a clearing.

"Great," said the boy, eyeing their surroundings. "I feel super safe now."

"People who stand around looking clueless during emergencies don't get to have an opinion," she snapped.

The string lights back at the tree line twinkled through the gaps in the branches; their glow filtered weakly into the clearing. The boy put his hands over his face, pressing down on his eyes, and groaned. "Oh my god. I let her out of my sight for one minute—"

"Who?" Aziza pulled out her phone with shaking hands to use as a flashlight. Its white glare shone on the frost and turned the shadows into streaks of charcoal.

"My sister. She's thirteen and can't stand still for more than twenty seconds at a time." He swiped at a cut on his cheek where a stray branch must have nicked him. "I should go back."

If that thing was still following them, he'd get himself killed wandering off on his own, based on the total lack of vigilance he'd shown before. She scanned the trees with her light.

"What's your name?" Aziza asked, stalling.

"Seriously?" he said.

"What?"

"We're in the same English class and lunch period," he said awkwardly. "I transferred in September from Fairview."

"Oh. Okay," she said. Part of her made note of that—Fairview was close, same school district even—but mostly she was too distracted to pay much attention. What was that, moving over his shoulder—a bough wobbling in the breeze, or something else?

He sighed.

"I'm Leo Merritt," he said. "I think we should get out of here."

"Maybe we should give it another minute," she said, unconvincingly.

"I hear sirens. Come on."

She wavered. Maybe he was right. But before she could make up her mind, a growl cut over the distant keening of the sirens.

Leo froze. He took a slow, deliberate step backward.

Another growl. Louder, closer.

Aziza's flashlight bounced off a pair of eyes as bright as the decorations in the fair, electric. As the creature padded out of the forest and into the clearing, Leo swore.

Even on four legs, it was taller than either of them and broader than the two of them combined: a wolf blacker than black, as dark as the space between the end of a dream and the moment of waking. It flowed more than walked from place to place, solid and at the same time insubstantial, like the wind could have blown it away—a motion that was closer to the undulating of steam than the stalking of a canine. But its fur bristled. Its fangs dripped saliva. Frost crackled under its weight.

"Do we run?" Leo whispered. He backed up until he stood level with Aziza. The wolf twitched its head, eyes flickering between the two of them—black, she thought, with no pupils or whites, but reflective in the dark as if possessing a tapetum lucidum, flaring with a hellish glow when her flashlight passed over its face.

She didn't answer. She didn't even dare to breathe.

A crashing in the forest: the unmistakable sound of someone running very fast, shoving aside branches and trampling foliage. Her phone's light caught a glint of platinum blond hair. A boy, ghostly pale and wide-eyed.

The noise he made must have startled the wolf, because its lips drew back from its savagely sharp teeth, and it snarled, its body tensing like a spring before it leapt—

At Leo.

Aziza's phone dropped to the ground, and the light went out. She knocked Leo aside, swung her bag off her shoulder, and—in a move that felt both instinctive and completely absurd—slammed it into the wolf's face.

It let out a yelp no different from an ordinary dog. But then it whirled around, a rattling growl emanating from the back of its throat. Up close, it radiated heat so powerfully Aziza felt it on her skin like sunburn. Its eyes looked into hers, and it lunged, snapping its jaws shut around the bag. The fabric shredded.

Aziza wheeled backward, boots skidding dangerously over the frost. The wolf advanced on her—the smell of sulfur and wet dog filled her nose—its jaws opened wide—

Her back hit a tree trunk, and she was cornered. She screwed her eyes shut. The last thing she saw, beyond the gleam of white fangs, was the phantom boy as he reached the clearing, his skeletal hand outstretched—

The growling ceased. The oppressive heat withdrew.

When she opened her eyes, the wolf had vanished, and so had the boy.

"Shit," Leo breathed. "Where did it go?"

She slid to the ground as her knees finally gave out on her. Leo knelt and steadied her with a hand on her shoulder.

"What happened to that guy?" she asked roughly.

"What guy?"

She started to answer, stopped, and shook her head. The boy had been mostly hidden by the trees and moving fast; she'd only glimpsed him by chance because the light from her phone had hit him dead on for about half a second. No wonder Leo had missed him. There had been more pressing things to worry about.

Leo helped her stand. "Come on. There might be more of them. We need to get out of here."

CHAPTER 3

LEO

THE FAIR STANK of blood and sugar, and Hazel was nowhere to be found.

Parts of the park had been cordoned off; ambulances were being loaded up with the wounded. Leo averted his eyes from the sight of lacerated flesh and mangled limbs. He wove between upended stalls, darted past smashed displays, avoided the remnants of string lights that had been slashed clean through and now dangled listlessly. Cops were taking statements from witnesses, but Hazel wasn't with them. His heart clenched tighter and tighter with every second that passed.

He hadn't gone to the fair last December. Hazel had embarked on a campaign of pleading, bribery, and no-holds-barred shrill yelling to make him reconsider, starting three days before it opened and ending two weeks later, on closing night, with Mom gently ushering her out of the house so they could go without him. Leo hadn't had the willpower to get out of bed, let alone process Hazel's teary-eyed disappointment.

This year, he was better—not entirely well, but better—and he was trying to make it up to Hazel. That was why he'd volunteered to take her to the fair on his own.

And then he'd lost her.

He was on the verge of true panic—breathless, dizzy, falling-apart panic—when a plaintive, perfectly familiar voice said, "I've been looking for you *everywhere*!"

Behind him was his total brat of a sister, glaring fiercely with her fists propped on her hips, like she was a matronly old substitute teacher instead of a skinny seventh grader with braces. Or their mother. Leo took after Mom, too, but not like Hazel did. They both had Mom's dark curls, her cheekbones, her smile and her brown eyes. But you could still see Dad in Leo's features—in the shape of his jaw and nose, and in his expressions and mannerisms, sometimes. Not Hazel. Hazel was entirely their mother's daughter.

He resisted the urge to shake her. "Where the hell were you?"

"I was here," she said, with a flap of her arms that could have meant either *here in this very spot* or *somewhere within a five-mile radius of here, but who cares about those little details anyway?*

"Mom won't let me take you anywhere if you won't stay where I can see you—"

"You're going to *tell* her?" Hazel gasped.

Of course he wasn't going to tell.

"Maybe," he said.

"Leo!"

"*Unless*," he added, "you promise me something right now."

"What?"

"I'm giving a friend a ride home." If you went to the same school and had a shared near-death experience, then you were friends. "She almost got bitten by a—"

Hazel's eyes doubled in size. "You *saw* the *wolves*?"

"Listen," he said, slowly and clearly. "I'm helping my friend get home. You know what we say about new people, right? You can't ask her invasive questions, and you can't say anything about—"

"That was *one* time," she said.

Leo took her by the shoulders and steered her back to where he'd left Aziza. She monologued about every piece of wreckage they passed and volleyed questions at him until Leo said, "That's her," and then she shut up. Hazel was weirdly shy around strangers.

Leo had entrusted his unlikely savior to the care of a paramedic. It didn't seem right to leave someone alone after a traumatic experience, but Aziza hadn't even wanted the shock blanket. And he had to admit, she didn't look like she was in shock. Right now, she mostly just looked pissed off. She was fiddling with her phone, which must have hit a rock when she'd dropped it, because the screen was completely shattered; it was probably no use as anything other than a paperweight now. With a disgusted grimace, she dropped it into the pile of rags at her feet that used to be her backpack.

"Hey," he said. "Found her."

Hazel hung back, fidgeting, but managed a nervous wave when Aziza looked up. He knelt to help Aziza gather her things, which spilled out of the tears in her bag.

"Thanks," she said. "And for the ride. I'd take the train, but—"

She winced. To get back home, she'd have to take Blackthorn's dinky little two-line subway system, switching from the east-west to the north-south at Champlain, getting off at Green Street, and taking the bus from there. The trains were a mess coming out of the fair even on a normal night; now, with everyone leaving all at once? Forget it.

"Don't worry about it. You're, like, ten minutes away from my place anyway," he said, snagging the corner of a notebook. It fell open. Righting it, he caught a glimpse of one of the pages, which contained a meticulous sketch of something winged. Something he *recognized*.

His heart flipped over. He snapped the book shut and passed it to her before she could notice how he'd lingered on it.

When they got to the car, she laid the tattered remains of her bag in the well of the passenger seat. His hands shook so hard he almost couldn't get the key into the ignition. The night trickled away either too quickly or not quickly enough, depending on whether you asked Leo's anxiety or his agonizing hope. He dropped Hazel off at home first, and then it was just him and Aziza, and he had ten minutes to either make a total ass of himself or find the answers he'd been searching for all year.

"Spit it out," she said.

"Huh?"

"You want to say something," she said. "Just say it."

Her eyes were startlingly intense when she really looked at you; if they'd been standing, he would've taken a step back.

"I saw your notebook."

"What notebook?"

"The one with the drawings."

"And?"

He couldn't blame her for being evasive. But he'd spent the last year doing his research, sorting out the nonsense from genuine fact, and he knew the real thing when he saw it.

At least, he thought he did. Maybe he was just desperate.

"Let me start over." His hands tightened on the steering wheel. The view outside the window was all black and gold, the asphalt and the streetlights filling his vision. Out here in the quiet part of Blackthorn—away from its historic district and its burgeoning corporate sector—the icy roads sprawled, languid and rambling. Bland shopping centers and sleepy tree-lined neighborhoods faded to murky irrelevance on either side of them. "Do you believe in magic?"

She shrugged, like she'd never given it much thought. "Why?"

"I do. I have good reasons to believe in magic," he said. "On my sixteenth birthday, I lost my memories. Not all of them. Just the ones that matched a—a really specific set of criteria."

"Everyone forgets things," she said, after a beat.

"Not like this. Not overnight. I knew it was coming, so I wrote down everything I wanted to remember. But when I woke up, I couldn't read it. I asked my mom to read it to me, and I couldn't understand her. She wasn't surprised because, uh, she's cursed, too. So is my dad. We all are. Except Hazel. Firstborns get all the bad luck." Leo glanced sidelong at Aziza, quick, and then away again. "Doesn't that sound like magic to you?"

"Why are you telling me this?" she said. Her voice was so low that the drone of the engine almost drowned it out.

"Because I need help," he said. "I need to break the curse."

"And you think *I* can help."

"I think you're a witch."

"How dare you," she said, deadpan.

It took him a beat to figure out she wasn't being serious. Probably.

"Okay, yeah, no labels. I totally respect that," he said cheerfully. She made a derisive noise but still hadn't actually told him to fuck off, which he found encouraging. He pressed on. "But I mean . . . someone tells you about a literal, magical curse, and you're not even a little bit curious?"

"*If* that someone was telling me the truth," she said, looking out the window as if barely interested in the conversation, "I'd want to know *how* they were cursed before I even considered believing them."

"I—I don't know how," he admitted. "I was maybe six years old when it happened, and the only thing my parents will tell me is that it had to do with a malicious spirit."

"A *spirit*?" Her tone was scornful.

"But not what kind, or why. I used to try guessing, but it never got me anywhere."

One time, he'd asked Mom if it had followed her from Italy. It didn't seem so far-fetched that she might've run into a malevolent, curse-casting ghost back in the tiny European town where she'd grown up, tucked away in the countryside, with its orange trees and centuries-old churches. All sorts of things might exist in a place like that. Dad, meanwhile, had lived in suburban Massachusetts his whole life.

She got *so* mad at him for even suggesting it, though.

You think America doesn't have monsters? That was what she'd said. *You think there's less evil here than anywhere else in the world?*

He must've sounded like he was blaming her. Like he was ashamed of where Mom came from. He hadn't meant it like that, but there was no telling her anything when she was angry. Still, he'd felt bad about it. So he stopped guessing.

"Spirits can't curse you," Aziza said flatly. "That's bullshit. Either you're not cursed, or your parents are lying about how it happened."

He'd known that; he'd just wanted to see whether Aziza knew it, too. The lack of hesitation in her response was vindicating. He'd been right about her.

"The curse is real," he said. "Trust me."

"Yeah? What kind of curse does an imaginary spirit cast? Why would a spirit want to take away your memories?" She scowled. "Lots of things besides curses can do that, you know. Are you sure you didn't hit your head?"

He *really* didn't want to say it out loud.

It had been a while since he'd talked about it. The loss still over-whelmed him. Grief was all-consuming; it had torn him up inside until, for a while, there had been nothing left. This time last year, Leo had been locked in his room trying to sleep away the terrible empti-ness. Fall and winter, he slept. When spring and summer came, he was either running from the grief or searching for a solution, depend-ing on how you looked at it. Maybe both at the same time.

Not knowing what—*who*—he was grieving only made it harder to let go. He couldn't even mourn properly. Closure was nowhere near the realm of possibility.

"I was cursed to forget my true love," he said finally, hating how simple it sounded and at the same time grateful it didn't sound the way it felt, corrosive and violating.

She didn't laugh at him, at least—just gave him a long, unreadable look before facing the windshield again. "Who has a true love at sixteen?"

"I did. I *do*."

He didn't say: *I had to have been in love, to miss a ghost this badly.*

"I'll take your word for it," she said. "Look, I can't help you."

His heart plummeted.

"Why not?"

"For one thing, it happened years ago, and you don't even know for sure what did it."

"And if I did know?"

"Even then, it would depend on . . ." She hesitated. "It would just depend, okay? If I could help you, I would. But I don't think I can."

It was so—anticlimactic. He had been so *sure* this time. He couldn't be right back where he'd started, at another dead end.

They turned onto a block of cramped row houses, the stoops packed with snow, and he pulled up at her place.

"Thanks for the ride," she said, scooping up her belongings and opening the door. "And . . . I hope you find your true love. I guess."

"Right. Thanks," he said. "See you in January. Merry Christmas."

"Happy solstice," she returned, with a wry smile.

She stepped through the gate, unlocked her front door, and disappeared inside.

All right, she couldn't help him. So what? He was no worse off now than before. He'd just have to keep looking for a way to break the curse on his own. And he *would* keep looking. Even if it took the rest of his life.

Curse or no curse, you don't just give up on true love.

CHAPTER 4

TRISTAN

EVERY INCH OF Tristan hurt.

After the sirens had died off and the searchlights were snuffed out, he climbed down shakily from his hiding place in the crook of an old elm.

He wanted nothing more than to curl up on the ground and let the forest take him. He would crumble into the leaf litter, until lichen crusted over him and he disappeared under the bracken and the bluebells come spring. It would be quiet, he thought, except for the skittering of insects over his brushwood shroud, and there would be no smell or taste of blood, just the earthy comfort of moss filling his throat.

But the bond had pulled taut with the hag's impatience, so he set off. The way from St. Sithney's to the hag's territory was treacherous; there were places where the thicket grew so dense he could hardly walk, and as he crossed into her boundarylands, that unnatural, moonless dark shuttered the world. He fumbled for his flashlight—pointless, since his eyes were blurry with tears. But he didn't need to see, not really, when he was here. The bond told him everything he needed to know about the hag's territory; he could navigate because *she* could. No matter what condition he was in.

He found her waiting for him. In the corner of his eye, she was a sickly off-white blur, like a fungus growing over the gateway tree's branches. But even the revulsion he usually felt in her presence failed to manifest tonight. He didn't have the energy for it. He knelt.

"I did what you said."

"Did you?"

Already, the hag's voice was stronger. The gateway tree had grown incrementally taller, barely enough to make a visible difference—it was more like he'd caught it in the middle of a languid stretch after a long nap. It had always had a presence that registered in his mind, in an unsettling way, like a person; his eyes habitually searched it for a face, expected it to feel warm like flesh when he touched it. Sometimes he was convinced the hag was only an extension of a greater beast, like the lure on an anglerfish.

He couldn't think straight. The hag had asked him something. What was it again? Right—the question of what he'd done. And what he hadn't done. The hounds had sensed the crowds and the revelry at St. Sithney's, and they'd taken off, leaving him behind. He hadn't been able to control their hunger in the slightest. As the hounds had fed, their victims' life energy had soaked into the bond between them and Tristan—their would-be commander—and then flowed from Tristan to the hag through *their* bond. He was nothing but a conduit, a glorified rain gutter.

As his futile attempts to contain the hounds sent him ricocheting in and out of their minds, he had seen the massacre unfold through their eyes. He wouldn't soon forget the texture of bone between his teeth, or the ease with which flesh had torn under his claws. His muscles had burned in time with the hounds', and though he bore no visible marks, he ached with phantom scratches and bruises from where the victims had fought for their lives.

"I did what you asked and more," Tristan said to the gateway tree. Unwillingly done was still done.

"Yes," she rasped. "But something has changed."

Uselessly, he wiped at his eyes with his filthy sleeve. He was beyond shame. What else could she possibly want?

The hag couldn't hunt on her own. She was blind and unable to leave her grounds. That was why she needed a bondservant to find her prey. They shared a magical contract, which was a complex binding spell with terms they each had to abide by. There had to be an exchange, for one thing, or else the magic wouldn't take. It didn't have to be an equal exchange, but she had to promise him something for his servitude. Her promise was protection. He couldn't die or sustain serious, permanent injuries—unless she chose to inflict them herself. As long as he served her, and once his term was complete, he would never have to suffer the same fate as her victims. And, of course, he earned one magical favor of his choosing, to be awarded on the final day of his tenth year and no sooner.

Should he prove himself truly unworthy of serving her, though, she'd order him to recruit someone new to take his place in the bond and finish what was left of his contract—someone healthy and young, who wouldn't be missed, and who was foolish enough to make deals with her. Tristan would resist, but she would use the bond to torture him until he broke. Then, when she had what she wanted, she'd kill him. Death by her hand was his only way out of their agreement. But she wouldn't demand a replacement except as a very last resort. Starting over took a lot of energy—a precious and limited resource for the hag—and came with no guarantees. The next bondservant might turn out to be no more competent than Tristan. If she ended up with no servant, even for a short time, the broken, incomplete bond would take a toll on her. She would prefer to wring as much use as she could out of him instead.

This was going to be his life from now on, the bloodshed from last night repeated over and over until the hag was satisfied.

And she would *never* be satisfied.

"One of the hounds," she said, "found a witch."

Tristan tensed. His mind shied away from the memory of that awful moment in the clearing. Was she about to punish him for calling off the hound and taking away a kill? But she left it there, let him sit with it, parsing out her desires through the bond, reading her greed and her wrath.

"You want . . . her," he said. "As your next victim."

He should've seen this coming. Life energy kept the hag alive, but magic was true nourishment. As far as Tristan knew, no other creature had the ability to steal and devour magic the way she did. Even a spirit could only absorb small shreds of energy and perform minor charms—while the hag could take a witch's craft in its entirety and reflect it back like a cursed mirror.

Tristan's "gift" had once belonged to a necromancer. One who had come to the hag willingly. Why, Tristan couldn't have said. He could only speculate. Before Tristan, the hag had been imprisoned, slumbering—until something or someone had woken her. Why not a necromancer? The hag herself had admitted she was no living spirit; like the hounds, she existed somewhere between life and death. Maybe this necromancer had woken the hag last year, but once she'd grown strong enough, she'd turned on him. But Tristan might never know for sure.

"Find her," the hag commanded, with a covetous exhale that ran through the whole of her territory. The gateway tree shuddered; the woods sighed.

"But—" Tristan said. It wasn't fair. So many people had died tonight already. The hag was more than well-fed—she had gorged herself on the hounds' kills. Now she wanted another? Not an anonymous kill, either, but a girl with a name Tristan would have to learn and a face he could see all too clearly in his memory.

"You want the favor I have promised you, do you not?"

"Yes, but—"

Not like this, he thought. *Maybe you should end this. Maybe* I *should end this.*

He wasn't afraid to die anymore. But he was terrified of what the hag would make him do *before* he died. He was so careful to choose the hag's victims randomly; he couldn't bear the thought of sizing someone up, searching them for the same weaknesses he himself had, and handing them over to the hag to take his place.

"Careful, boy," the hag said, softly. "You are not entitled to my continued patience."

Mutinous words clawed at his throat.

The hag waited him out. She must have sensed it, what was going on in his head. How badly he wanted to turn on her.

Briefly, he saw himself doing it—telling the hag *no*. And then, when she ordered him to find his own replacement so that she could be rid of him at last, saying *no* again, a magic spell of his own. This fantasy version of himself could withstand everything the hag would throw at him: the agony she could send through the bond to make him feel like he was being skinned alive, the nightmare visions that could last for days on end, until he was certain his mind would break before his body did. He'd survive it all for as long as he needed to, until the hag got tired of the struggle and ended it. And once she got rid of him, she'd have no one to pick up where he left off. She'd have to wait for someone to stumble into her neck of the woods, like she had with him, while suffering the wound left by the broken bond. Since it was winter, maybe it would even take some time before she found her next servant—weeks, or even months. Maybe Blackthorn would get a small reprieve from the hag. That would be his parting gift.

But he wasn't that person. The one who could outlast the hag. He was weak, and in the end, he'd give in and do just what she wanted. Let other people suffer to make his own suffering stop.

And maybe that made him an even bigger monster than she was.

A laugh rattled out of her. She didn't need to wait for his reply; she knew she had him. She left him there, and the gateway tree sealed up behind her, leaving Tristan alone in the dark.

THE NEXT EVENING, he stole a shovel from one of the groundskeepers' sheds.

St. Sithney's was closed to the public. He had to jump police barricades and sneak past wildlife control to get to the forest. The lights from the fair still hung there, dim and lifeless.

Tristan should not have been standing before a threshold to fairyland at the moment when day crossed into night. Of course, he hadn't gotten to where he was in life by having good judgment.

The hag had taught him a little about Elphame—just enough so that he could get in and out of her territory without stumbling into that realm by mistake, where he might accidentally forfeit an organ or his ability to see the color blue to some crafty fae entity. She said that last time, in the time before her yearslong slumber, her territory had infringed on Elphame. But the hag was more powerful and deadly than all but the rarest, most reclusive of fae—the ones she called the Fair Folk. Blackthorn's fae couldn't do a thing to her.

"Your connection to me will shield you, too," she had told him. "But you must know what to say and what to do, and you must always mind your manners around the fae."

It was because of the hag that he knew what conditions would make it possible for him to get to Elphame. Timing was important. Midnight, midday, sunrise, and sunset were the witching hours— never actually an hour long—when the boundary between worlds thinned. The ebb and flow of Elphame's natural magic made the boundary porous for seconds or minutes, during which one could cross over from one realm into the next. Though he couldn't predict exactly where and when the boundary might open up, he had to be at a natural border—like the tree line at St. Sithney's—during one of those times of high magic. Ideally, he'd find a fairy door, which was an arch formed by the woven branches of a pair of trees. Not a literal door. But it symbolized a threshold, and symbols held power. He had found one today, a stroke of questionable luck; now all he had to do was wait.

The sun dipped below the trees as he went through the fairy door, and the air changed. It smelled sickeningly sweet as it washed over him, prickly and clinging like static electricity. That was how he knew it had worked; he was in Elphame. The last rays of sunlight trickled away, and night sealed the threshold. He wouldn't be able to return to Blackthorn until the next witching hour at dawn.

The hounds belonged to neither the human world nor fairyland, and they could pass between the two at will, traveling through the shadows. Last night, they had ended up on *this* side of the boundary. Following his new instincts, he took a winding path through the wilderness. The forest was a labyrinth of black pillars. Brambles caught at his clothes; he fought through winterberry thickets and stepped gingerly over fallen leaves. Unidentifiable sounds made a disorienting backdrop to his journey—not crickets, not raccoons, but something *else*. Things with voices that murmured in a language he didn't understand; things that dogged his steps, laughing almost too softly for him to hear, until they got close enough to smell the hag on him and left him alone. They watched, though. He was certain they watched.

He came to a gap in the woods, a crescent-shaped sliver of a clearing. When he shined his flashlight in a low arc over the ground, its bumps and shapes and shadows revealed themselves for what they were: five victims of last night's massacre. The bodies had been mostly stripped of flesh, but hair and clothes and even skin still clung to them. Even the quickest glance robbed them of anonymity. He couldn't see the bodies as a group of indistinct strangers. They divided into specific tragedies: a clenched fist, the curve of a small shoulder, the pattern on a pair of socks.

One of them was in a private school uniform, not all that different from the one he used to wear. For a split second, he was another Tristan, one who lived in a world of white button-ups and haircut regulations, and *that* Tristan could've screamed from the shame and guilt.

Swiftly, he locked that person away. The old Tristan wouldn't be of any use here.

The smell was overpowering; his knees nearly buckled at that alone. He got as near to the bodies as he could bear and set about digging a trench.

The ground was frozen and hard. He had to wedge the blade of the shovel into the dirt and then stomp on it to break the surface, again and again until he'd cleared away the top layer. He abandoned his coat and pushed up his sleeves, and he started shoveling in earnest, determined to make the pit as deep and secure as he could.

Hours after he'd entered Elphame, he pushed the bodies into the trench using the shovel, wincing each time he heard a thud or a crunch. It felt wrong to toss them in a mass grave like this, abandoned in fairyland. But it was better than leaving them in the open to be further desecrated by scavengers. They deserved to rest.

At the last body, he paused. This was a man no older than thirty. One of his arms was gone, and there were deep gouges on his torso, chunks torn from his thigh. Up close, the wounds looked as if they'd been cauterized; Tristan almost gagged on the smell of cooked meat. The man's face was mostly intact, the limp brown hair darkened with blood, the eyes wide open in a final expression of horror.

Fighting down the nausea, Tristan crouched beside the body.

If he was stuck with these powers, then he might as well see if anything good could come of it.

With two trembling fingers, he touched the place where the man's pulse would have been. The new magic within him still felt foreign and deadly, like an invasive species. But instead of shying away from it, he let it loose, flooding his veins and flowing down to his fingertips. It didn't make him feel powerful, though. It made him feel possessed.

Live, Tristan begged in his mind—and was answered by movement under his hand.

The man shifted, not like a person waking up, but like his muscles were spasming. His limbs jerked, his fingers tearing at the grass, his head lolling on his neck. His eyes found Tristan, and blinked.

Tristan swallowed. "You're going to be okay," he said, as if he had any right to promise such a thing.

He reached over to get an arm under the man's shoulders and help him sit up—the wounds would kill him again unless Tristan could get him to a hospital—but the man stopped him; his remaining hand flew to Tristan's wrist and latched on.

His skin was colder even than it had felt when he'd been dead. Tristan gasped in pain. Where the man touched him, Tristan's skin seared as if he'd gotten an ice burn. A gray tinge crept up his arm from that point of contact, and he felt *something* within him being drawn into the undead man.

Tristan ripped his hand away. There was a crack, as if the man's fingers had broken. The corpse reached for him again, grasping, and now Tristan knew he wasn't imagining it—the eyes were empty as glass marbles, the lips blue. Tristan's skin was bright red and blistering in finger-shaped bands that marked where the corpse had gripped him.

As it struggled to its feet, Tristan grabbed the shovel, gave a mighty swing, and bashed the cadaver's head in. It fell to the ground, motionless.

He used the shovel to push the body into the trench with the others. After, he leaned against the handle, pressed his face into his arm, and swallowed a few deep lungfuls of air.

Why don't I know better by now? he thought bitterly.

He filled the grave back in. When he was done and all traces of the victims were gone, he hesitantly attempted a prayer for them. He wasn't religious, but maybe some of the victims had been, and . . . it was the least he could do. His parents used to insist on his going to church every week, so he was able to mumble a few remembered lines. But those memories were bad ones, and filled him not with grace but with hurt and resentment and something approaching hate. He shook his head to dismiss those feelings, abandoned the remembered prayers, and made up his own.

He didn't apologize. It wouldn't have felt honest.

Overhead, the sky had lightened to a washed-out, predawn violet, which meant his time was running short; he picked up his coat and hurried back to the tree line. His muscles were sore, and it hurt to run, but he didn't want to spend even one more hour in fairyland.

Almost there, he told himself. Through a gap in the woods, the edge of the park was visible, the grass shiny with dew. He checked his footing as he stepped over a root, and when he looked up, some-one was watching him.

He froze. A humanoid shape, wood-skinned and smelling of pine needles, barred the way.

"There is a price for passage," it creaked.

I'm broke, he thought hysterically. But his mouth was smarter than the rest of him.

"Nothing I have is mine," he said. "I belong to the hag of these woods."

Its thorny head tilted.

"These woods are not *those* woods," it said.

Tristan spread out his hands, palms up, feigning disinterest. "Will you steal from a hag?"

After a moment, the figure melted into the bark of a tree. He crossed over the boundary at daybreak without any more trouble.

CHAPTER 5

AZIZA

THE WARDS CRACKLED faintly when Aziza stepped through the front door, returning from the catastrophe at St. Sithney's and her uncomfortable conversation with Leo Merritt. Jiddo had warded the perimeter of the property and every threshold inside it; a necessity, when your granddaughter was a hedgewitch who'd started practicing her craft long before she'd learned how to stop fae from following her home, either to wheedle for more tokens or take vengeance for some offense she hadn't known she'd committed. Aziza used to bring home pixies the way other children brought home stray cats, and they would steal all the keys and spare change. She had tried to put a collar on a pooka, and it had shapeshifted from a hare to a python and slithered away, nearly sending Jiddo to an early grave when he found it in the hamper. She had invited the Man at the Bus Stop over for dinner—he looked a little different each time you saw him, except his eyes were always the cloudy grayish blue of a distant sky, he wrote in a notebook that never ran out of pages, and he only appeared when it was raining. He was a spirit who could grant good fortune during travels, but if you refused to converse with him, your fortune would be poor, and you'd probably slip on ice next time you left home or get rear-ended during your commute. Jiddo, who was not the most talkative on the best of days, had not been amused.

Thus, the wards. Raising Aziza had made Jiddo paranoid, and rightfully so. Tonight, she couldn't blame him.

Merry Christmas, Jiddo, she thought, as she locked the door and dropped her things. *I got you hours of stress and worry. Just wait till you see what I do for New Year's.*

She hung up her coat, stepped out of her shoes, and continued down the hall in her socks. The living room was cramped and cozy, with more seating than necessary for two people who never had company. The windows on the back wall overlooked a small, over-grown yard, which would be bursting with flowers come spring. Their modest Christmas tree stood in the corner. Aziza decorated it each year while Jiddo passed over the ornaments one at a time or held the end of the string lights, slowly feeding out more as she wound them through the branches. When she was little, he'd hoist her up so she could place the star on top.

She found Jiddo—her grandfather, Professor Khaled El-Amin—in his armchair, mug of tea in hand and an old-fashioned cast-iron kettle on the side table as he graded exams for the ancient history course he taught at Blackthorn Community College. He was tall and thin as a cypress, and wore his usual khakis, cable-knit sweater, and wire-rimmed reading glasses. Prominent crow's feet tugged at the corners of his eyes, which traveled over her weary face and dirt-streaked jeans as if checking for injuries.

"Hi, Jiddo," she said, with forced nonchalance. Maybe he'd been so preoccupied with his grading that he didn't even know anything had happened at the fair. Maybe he hadn't noticed she'd been gone longer than normal, and maybe he hadn't tried to call her—

The news played on the muted TV, she saw then: a shot of the deserted fair from above, a composite sketch of the wolves, a body count in the chyron at the bottom of the screen.

"Please tell me you left as soon as you realized there was trouble," Jiddo said. His voice was a low growl, gruff with age and stiff with concern. "I've been choosing to believe you were only late because of the trains, and that you weren't answering your phone because it was dead, and not because you decided to meddle in whatever *that* was."

He jabbed his pen in the direction of the TV.

"My phone *is* dead," she said, and he groaned, hearing what she didn't say.

"I told you to be back before dark," he said.

"It's December! It gets dark practically before I wake up," she argued, and it was an old argument, one they'd been having back and forth all year. She detoured to his chair on her way to the kitchen to plant a kiss on his cheek. She hadn't seen him since this morning. If her parents had been around, they could have kept him company while she was gone. But they weren't. She and Jiddo only had each other.

"And it's almost the solstice," she went on, opening the fridge and going for the Tupperware that contained last night's leftovers. "There was a shade. So I trapped it and took it to the forest. But then . . ."

She hesitated. The first few months after she'd noticed something wrong with the boundary, she hadn't mentioned it to him. He worried about her too much already. In Lebanon, up in the mountains where Jiddo had grown up, there were ghouls and wights; there were beasts that looked like hyenas until they caught you alone and transformed into men who would force their victims to make impossible, deadly bargains. Jiddo's wards had helped protect family homes, the little villages in the hills where the human population was sparse and the land still belonged to the wilds, and to Elphame. Ward-keepers like him, and others with protective magics, were highly respected. He had never practiced alone the way Aziza did; his family had been his coven, though they weren't all ward-keepers. He'd worked with his cousins, and distant aunts and uncles, and with his daughter and her husband—Aziza's parents. Her mother had had a gift for locking—anything, not just doors—and her magical locks were not easily picked or broken. Her father could create secret chambers out of nothing, miniature pocket realms for hiding things or using as bunkers and escape routes in emergencies.

Aziza, though, had no coven. Her parents had died when she was a little over a year old. And Jiddo was no longer young enough to teach his classes and then go walk with her through the woods for hours on end, or to spend his evenings in the cold at St. Sithney's. He didn't practice much at all anymore, other than renewing the wards he'd placed on the house almost two decades ago. When her parents had died and he'd stepped in to raise her by himself, he'd let his craft fall by the wayside.

You were all the magic I ever needed, he'd always said.

Jiddo had made his peace with the fact that she would be a lone witch, and that there was no stopping her from practicing her craft, but that was when things were *normal*. This year was not normal. This year, not a day went by without some problem or other that she could trace back to fae mischief. The beetle infestation at the hospital. Sailboats crashing in the shallows and the survivors—when there were survivors—swearing they'd heard the most beautiful music just before they went under. Shades at the holiday fair. It had gotten so bad that even Jiddo had noticed, and that was when the arguments had started.

But she couldn't stay home, and she couldn't stay out of it. As he well knew.

She didn't want him to worry more than he already did. But— she glanced at the news, which now showed police officers taping off the entrances to the park—it was too late for that. So she told him everything while she reheated her day-old pasta and took it to their tiny two-person table in the corner to eat. Between bites, she recounted how the creature had cornered her and Leo, trying to describe the indescribable—its size, the blackness of its eyes and fur, the way it had moved.

Jiddo rubbed one hand over his white mustache. "Those were blækhounds."

"Bleak hounds?" she echoed. "Very . . . accurate."

"*Blækhounds.*" He searched for a piece of paper, realized all he had were exams, and reached for the notepad on the coffee table instead. There, he wrote the word out shakily—his arthritis was acting up, but he'd no sooner take a break from work than she'd stay home during a solstice week. "They are undead beasts, shadow beasts. They're not immune to silver, but it won't kill them, either. Nothing does."

"Where did they come from?" she asked eagerly. "Are they—"

"They're not fae," he said. That meant her hedgecraft was use-less against them. Despite that, she couldn't suppress the familiar, faintly awestruck fascination she always felt when she discovered something magical that she hadn't met before.

As a hedgewitch, Aziza could strengthen the natural boundar-ies between the human world and Elphame. She was immune to many kinds of fae enchantment, especially the sort that addled the mind and made humans more easily tricked or trapped. And she had ways of sending back most creatures that strayed across the boundary—she knew which tokens could be used to bargain with them, when to use physical force and when to persuade, what repelled them and what attracted them. This knowledge had come from years of dedicating all her free time to protecting Blackthorn.

But now, when it really counted, it seemed she couldn't do a thing.

"That boy I saw at the end—he must have called it off somehow, right?" she asked Jiddo, as she got up to rinse out her empty Tupperware. "Do you think he's a witch?"

Behind her, Jiddo hesitated, his silence oddly strained. "I'm not sure."

She dried off her hands on a dishrag and dropped into her chair at the table again, lost in thought. The scrape of the other chair startled her. Jiddo had joined her, wearing a grave expression that put her on her guard.

"Your compassion has always made me proud. But you walk a thin line." When his voice went low like that, it sounded like the rumble of shifting earth, an impending rockslide. She usually found it comforting.

"What do you mean?" she asked warily.

"I know your craft is important to you, but it almost killed you tonight."

"The blækhound almost killed me," she argued.

"And you were only out there because you think that it's your job, and yours alone, to protect Blackthorn," he said patiently.

"It is, though. You're the one who told me that Blackthorn is the reason I'm a hedgewitch."

"And the sea shapes the coast, but is the coast the keeper of the sea?"

"I'm not *sand*," Aziza said, exasperated.

Witches couldn't perform any craft they wanted. The magic decided how it would manifest without the witch's input. They could learn techniques to advance their craft, but they could never change the nature of their magic. Jiddo built wards. These were intricate, powerful wards, but that was it: his one ability, his craft. And hedgecraft was Aziza's. But hedgewitches were unique, compared to other kinds of witches, in one crucial way. The gift was hereditary only in part. Aziza had hedgecraft somewhere in her ancestry, but there was another condition that had to be met before a hedgewitch would appear in the family line. Hedgewitches were born where they were needed—in uncommonly magical places, places where the veil was thin. Blackthorn, caught between woodland and coastline, forest and sea, walled in by major natural boundaries—the same kinds of boundaries that tended to align with Elphame's magical ones—was one such uncommonly magical place. Blackthorn had needed a hedgewitch, and so Aziza, born in this city to her immigrant family, had been born a hedgewitch. It was a natural phenomenon, the way ecosystems self-regulated.

She would have been a witch either way, but if her parents had settled in some other city, she probably would have inherited her mother's or father's craft, or maybe even Jiddo's ward-keeping. Blackthorn had *made* her a hedgewitch, and in doing so, it had given her a connection to its most secret and fantastical places and beings. Aziza had watched selkies shimmy halfway out of their sealskins to sunbathe at the base of the cliffs at low tide. She'd unscrewed strangers' headlights to coax young pixies out from the innards of cars parked too close to the forest. She'd obtained awful scratches up her arms after wrestling a rogue imp back into Elphame; wasps had followed her around vengefully for days. That hadn't been one of her better moments, but it was worth it for the other times, like when she spied colonies of teacup-sized lesser fairies mingling with the string lights in the park during the holidays. (She always let that one slide.)

In making her a hedgewitch, Blackthorn had given her *purpose*. It had given her a way to put down roots. She couldn't cook the food Jiddo had grown up eating, or speak Arabic, which was his and her parents' first language. She had never visited the place where they'd been born. Her roots weren't there; they were here in Blackthorn, not only because she'd been born here, not only because her parents had chosen it, but because *it* had chosen *her*.

And Aziza chose it back. That was how you made a place your home: You put work into it. You carved out a role for yourself. You made yourself belong even if you weren't sure you did. She returned the favor Blackthorn had done her, in making her a hedgewitch, by doing everything she could to be worthy of this gift.

Jiddo reached out and laid his warm hand over hers. The veins stood out on the back, and the knuckles seemed swollen in the heavily lined skin.

"When I taught you what I could teach you about magic," he said quietly, "I did it to keep you safe. Fae would always be drawn to you, even if you never sought them out, and being ignorant would have left you vulnerable. But you're still a child. I can't stand by while you put yourself in danger."

"I'm fine. I've been fine all year."

"Things are getting *worse*. It's not your job to fix it."

"Who else is going to do it?"

"I don't care who, as long as it's not you!" he snapped, and then rubbed a hand tiredly over his eyes. He was tired most of the time. He wasn't that old, but already he talked of retirement, even if only in that half-hearted grousing way of his. She'd told him he could at least let down the wards—maintaining them used up energy. But he wouldn't hear of it. "If there are blækhounds here, none of your tokens or your silver or your bargains will keep you safe. The only safe place is behind these wards. Aziza, listen to me: No more meddling with fae. No more trips to the park during solstice or equinox nights."

"You're telling me to stop being a witch," she said.

"I'm telling you to lie low for a little while." His hazel eyes gazed steadily at her over the rim of his glasses, as sharp as they'd been a decade ago. "If I can't be sure you're safe here, I will take us someplace else. There are people we can stay with out of town, if we must."

Aziza recoiled—*leave* Blackthorn? At a time like this?

He sighed. "But I would rather it didn't come to that. For once in your life, you are going to put caution above your curiosity. You are going to start listening to me when I tell you to be home before dark. Do you understand?"

It should have been an easy question to answer.

Blackthorn needed her now more than ever. The boundary needed her constant attention. It was bad enough she'd let the shade go earlier. If she just *quit*, things would only get worse.

But Jiddo had never threatened to *flee*. She hadn't even known he *knew* anyone out of town, other than the relatives they still had back in Lebanon, with whom he spoke only intermittently. And she couldn't bring herself to fight about it. Not when he couldn't fight back. He didn't have the strength to argue or yell at her. She had no car for him to ban her from, and no allowance, either—she worked on the weekends and during the summer, mostly gardening and walking dogs, to make the money she spent on food and public transportation. If Aziza rebelled, there was little he could do to control her. Their relationship depended on trust, and he was the only family she had; losing that wasn't an option.

So she said, "Yes, Jiddo. I understand."

But understanding didn't mean obeying.

CHAPTER 6

LEO

"I met a witch who said you're lying about the curse."

"Excuse me?" Mom said, or started to; she caught herself after the first syllable, but it was too late. A frog squirmed from her lips and dropped into her lap, where it hopped to the ground and out of sight before anyone could make a move for it.

"Ghosts *can't* cast curses like ours," Leo continued. He set his fork down on his plate. "I was pretty sure about that already, but I wanted to hear it from someone else."

It was him, his parents, and Hazel at the table. Every now and then, Spot—his dad's poltergeist—would make the lights flicker; his attempts to knock Dad's water glass off the table had so far been unsuccessful.

"I thought you were done with internet witches," Dad said mildly.

"She's not an internet witch. I'm talking about Aziza. You know, the girl who saved my life the other day," Leo added, because he thought maybe his parents would soften at the reminder that he had almost *died*, right before Christmas and everything. When he'd gotten home that night after dropping Aziza off, Mom had swept him into a rib-cracking hug. Then she'd tried to tell him and

Hazel off for not calling as soon as they were safe, but Dad had gently pointed out that they had done well by sticking together— Leo and Hazel had exchanged sheepish looks but nodded along as if that were absolutely correct—and helping a classmate get home safely, too. Leo could've used some of that energy right about now, that tearful, doting, grateful-our-eldest-child-isn't-dog-food energy.

But Mom's expression only darkened.

"Anyone can tell you she's a witch and pretend to be special and magical and wise," Mom said, producing a trail of neon-blue poison dart frogs. "You can't believe everything people say."

Leo had always held on to the hope that his parents weren't lying to him, not on purpose. Maybe they really did believe a spirit had cursed them. Pushing them for more information always turned out like—well, like this conversation right here. So he'd done his own investigating into the subject of curse-breaking and left them out of it. But he'd hit a dead end. Aziza said nothing could be done unless he knew what had cursed them. If they were hiding something crucial, he had to find out what it was.

"You're always so vague when I ask you about what happened," he said. "About how we got cursed. Or you change the subject, or you get mad at me for even asking."

Composing herself, Mom raised her hands to sign. "This conversation is over. Mind your business," she told him, palm out and fingers pinned together, each gesture stiff and tense.

His business? Nothing had ever been more his business.

"I lost someone I loved because of this," he said.

"What do you know about love?" Mom signed. "You're seventeen. Grow up and then talk to me about love."

That wasn't exactly what she said—ASL had its own grammar, different from English—but that was pretty much the gist of it.

"Maria," Dad murmured, reaching out to touch her shoulder lightly.

"I have a right to know how this happened to us!" Leo said, covering his hurt with anger.

"If you'd spent this much time thinking about school," Mom signed rapidly, "you wouldn't have been kicked out."

"I wasn't kicked out," Leo shot back, stung.

(He sort of had been, though.)

"Let it go, son," Dad said. His glass inched toward the corner of the table; he caught it and put it back down next to his plate. "The curse can't be broken. We talked to every single self-proclaimed witch in the state, and plenty outside it. They all said it was hopeless." Leo opened his mouth to respond furiously, but Dad held up a hand. "I know it's hard to lose someone. Trust me, I know. But the best thing any of us can do is move on."

"Exactly!" Mom put in.

"We're lucky nothing *worse* happened to you," Dad went on. "At least this won't stop you from getting a job or accomplishing anything you want to accomplish in life. Not like my curse, or your mom's."

Mom had been cursed so that toads fell from her lips when she spoke. She thought it was a silencing curse—that it was designed to take away her voice. She hadn't been back home in over a decade, terrified of what her family would say if they found out. And Dad had been cursed with Spot, who had gotten him fired from every office, banned from a host of shops and restaurants, and publicly humiliated on countless occasions. He didn't dare set foot on a plane.

"I know," Leo said reluctantly. "I know that—in a way, I got off lucky. But—"

"The curse doesn't mean you can't be happy with someone else,"

Dad said, pressing his advantage at the first sign of weakness. "Your true love is the one you *choose*. So . . . discussion over, all right?"

"But—all this time—why would you lie about—"

"Discussion *over*," Mom snapped, out loud. The last syllables were muffled by the exceptionally fat toad that slid from her lips and plopped into her hands. It offered an indignant croak for punctuation.

Leo got to his feet.

"Okay. This was . . . informative," he said. Dad gave him a warning glance sidelong. Hazel chewed slowly on what was left of her chicken, eyes wide.

"You didn't lie about me, right?" she asked worriedly. "*I'm* not cursed, am I?"

The glass of water tipped over the edge of the table and crashed to the ground.

Dad heaved a sigh. Leo walked away without looking back.

HE DIDN'T REMEMBER much about the time before they were cursed. Just fragmented images, like his dad holding him above the waves at the beach, or falling outside and scraping his hands, or the lullabies he'd help his mom sing to Hazel.

As for day one of being cursed, he remembered things flying across the room—Spot had been extremely volatile then, and Dad hadn't yet worked out the routines that would keep him in check—and a lot of crying. And the thing he remembered most vividly was picking up a frog that was hopping across the kitchen floor, not knowing where it had come from or why it was inside, but being fascinated by how slimy it was. Yeah. Out of all the things he could have noticed or overheard that day, *that* was what he'd chosen to focus on—but, in his own defense, he'd been six years old and frogs had ranked above grown-up yelling on his priority list.

But he also remembered the voice. He had dreamed it the night before, and he dreamed it again sometimes even now, and the words never changed, so he knew them by heart.

Son of the wicked, your curse is this: My heart was stolen from me, and so shall I steal yours. You will know true love, but when the clock strikes midnight on your sixteenth year, you will forget. Let no word, no touch, no day or night linger in your memory. Let reminders go unseen and unheard. Let your love be lost to you in name and in being, and let each passing moment take your love farther from your reach.

Grim stuff. Not that he knew it at the time. Actually, life was *great* for him. Frogs kept turning up all over the place, to his delight. His dad had to get a new job working from home and Leo got to see him *all* the time. They moved to a different house, one where the neighbors were a little farther away and they had more privacy, which also meant a yard with *tons* of space for him and Hazel to run around. For him to run and Hazel to toddle along after him, anyway, or for her to flop down when she got tired and for him to dig up interesting bugs that he then presented to her with much fanfare. It was weeks, maybe months, before he told his parents about the dream he kept having, the voice, the words. He didn't think his parents had even known that Leo was cursed before that.

He didn't exactly remember the conversations that had followed. How his parents explained magic and curses and true love to a first grader. But he'd slowly pieced together everything else he knew by asking questions as he got older. When he was maybe twelve or thirteen, his questions grew more insistent. Desperate, even. It was as if, before, his curse had been an abstract concept, something he dreaded but couldn't fully comprehend, but all of a sudden it had become concrete and terrifying in an acute, immediate way.

Was that when it had happened? Had he fallen in love at age twelve? He didn't think so. But maybe he'd found them—the one he was *destined* to fall in love with—and maybe the curse had somehow pointed that person out to him. Maybe the voice from his dreams had whispered something new for the first time, whispered a name, and Leo had just *known*.

But that was speculation. All he knew for sure was that his memories from about age eleven to age sixteen had—gaps.

There was plenty he'd forgotten over the years, normal things like history lessons and episodes of TV shows and any number of days where nothing remarkable happened. That kind of un-remembering felt different, though, from what the curse did to him. The un-remembering of the curse was like standing at the rim of a crater. A big, jagged hole. Something ruined. Something that should've been there, but *wasn't*.

It was you. You *were there,* Leo thought pointlessly, as if his true love could hear him. That was the part he had never figured out how to explain to his parents, didn't have the words to explain to Aziza, either. His true love felt *real*. This wasn't a theoretical person, like a dream girl, or some unattainable, idealized crush, like an actor. Recognition and familiarity were a kind of historical record. Past interactions, even ones you'd forgotten, stayed in your head, influencing how you read another person's body language and how easily you talked to them, and whether you thought they were funny or annoying, and whether seeing them made your day better or made you want to run the other way. The person in his head that he could only refer to as *you* was familiar in that exact same way, even when Leo couldn't see them. He *knew* them without knowing them.

In the last year, he had learned that absence was unmistakable, even if you couldn't name what was missing. Love was unmistakable.

It suffused him, like light. It had changed him. He couldn't remember being changed. But he had been.

He had spent a lot of time thinking about the words of the curse. Some of it was pretty clear-cut. Like the part about forgetting. And how he couldn't be reminded—people could try to tell him about his true love, but he'd forget that, too. What bothered him the most, though, was the last bit: *Let your love be lost to you in name and in being, and let each passing moment take your love farther from your reach.*

It sounded as if, somehow, the curse had done something to physically *take* his true love from him. Whoever or whatever had cursed his family . . . had it gone after his true love, and hurt them? What else would've stopped his true love from just reintroducing themselves on Leo's sixteenth birthday, as painful as it might've been to lose their history together? Had they not wanted to start over? Or had they not had a choice in the matter?

The idea that he might have endangered someone just by falling in love with them made him sick.

That was why he couldn't give up. There was more at stake here than just his feelings. Even if it turned out his true love wanted nothing to do with him, he had to know that they were okay.

Your true love is the one you choose, Dad said. But he was wrong. Knowing what was to come, knowing what would happen on his sixteenth birthday, Leo wouldn't have *chosen* anyone. He wouldn't have put himself or anyone else through this if he'd had a choice.

Would he?

He woke up earlier than he needed to, no alarm, just too restless to stay in bed. Mom was up, too, even though she usually slept in when Hazel didn't have school. He found her camped out on the couch, one leg folded under her, her laptop on the seat next to her and sheafs of sheet music spread over the coffee table. She wrote curriculums for music courses—and did a few other things on the side, like sold handmade jewelry through an online shop, but that was her main thing, the music. She used to sing. Went to school for it and everything.

She looked up at the sound of his footsteps and pointed at the second mug next to hers on the table.

"How did you know I was awake?" he signed, and picked up the mug, taking it with him to the other end of the couch. He and Hazel tended to use ASL with Mom, partly out of solidarity, partly so they wouldn't get rusty. Dad too, though he wasn't as fluent.

"Your mom knows everything," she signed, light and easy in the way her hands spread open and out.

He took a sip. It was some kind of milky, spicy concoction—cinnamon, turmeric, ginger. A few other flavors he couldn't place. Mom wanted to discourage the coffee addiction he'd picked up recently, so she was always trying out recipes for natural alternatives. For a while it was matcha, then chicory root. This one was sweeter than her usual, a peace offering in several spoonfuls of honey.

"'S good," he muttered. She glanced over at him with a flash of a tired smile. Something in him that had gone tight and defensive last night relaxed now, like a fist uncurling.

He sucked at staying mad at her. She was still his mom.

"I'm, uh, probably taking a drive next week. After Christmas," he said aloud, and then switched back to signing with his one free hand. "I'll be back before the New Year."

Taking a drive was the euphemism he'd adopted for when he left town, sometimes for days, looking for an end to their curses. He'd found someone online who'd told him about a family curse—an especially gnarly one, where all firstborn boys for generations lost their left eyes in strange accidents before they turned twenty—which he claimed to have broken by drinking water from an allegedly magical spring in Vermont. Mostly, anything that involved eating or drinking something that had been lying around outside did nothing but give him a stomachache, but he'd found that people's stories and superstitions often stemmed from a truth. A misunderstood truth, but a truth nonetheless. And snooping around sometimes led him to evidence of *real* curses, broken and otherwise. Real magic. A glimpse of it, at least.

Mom didn't look at him as she said, "Fine." Hand open, quick tap of her thumb against her chest, not happy about it but not willing to argue today. The ceasefire was still in place.

"Unless," he added, in his most innocently hopeful tone of voice, "you wanted to save me some time?"

"Good try."

He gave her an exasperated look over the rim of his mug. He was pretty stubborn when he wanted to be, but he had nothing on her. It was weird, though. Despite everything, he'd never thought of his parents as particularly secretive people. It kind of made him uneasy, that he'd missed something like that. Because what else was he missing?

But he could keep secrets, too.

Mom had a few orders to ship out today, so he volunteered to take the pile of them to the post office. Driving helped him think, and his car was his favorite thing in the world. He'd worked for years to save up the money for a beat-up old Chevy, little more than a heap of scrap metal when he got it, and then he'd spent months fixing it up himself. It had given him something to do in the bleak period of time immediately following his sixteenth birthday.

But as he wiped the condensation off the windows, he glanced into the passenger side and spotted something on the floor in front of the seat. An unassuming black notebook, so generic it could've belonged to anyone in the world. But it didn't. It belonged to Aziza.

It must've fallen out of her torn bag, and she wouldn't have seen it in the dark. He climbed in, blasted the heat, and then swiped it off the ground to flick through. He wasn't going to *read* it, because what if her bestiary doubled as a journal? But it couldn't hurt to skim through the pictures.

The pages were covered in sketches of blurry dark shapes hiding in shadowed nooks, figures that seemed to peel themselves out of tree bark and river currents, stubby creatures with sharp teeth and beetle wings. Leo forbade himself from reading the notes that accompanied the drawings, but if he happened to glimpse dates and times and other scribblings with details of what sounded like real encounters, well—he couldn't really help it, could he? The notes often ran right into the sketches, a wealth of information just lying there on the open pages. He lingered over the one he'd recognized, the short, mantis-like thing with the iridescent wings veined like leaves.

The right thing to do was return the notebook straightaway—which gave him the perfect excuse to talk to her again. All he needed was a lead. She didn't think she could make a difference, but she was his best chance.

His *only* chance.

CHAPTER 7

TRISTAN

THE GUEST ROOM window was unlatched, the way he'd left it over a year ago.

He dumped his coat in the trash bin outside. After months of near-constant wear, it was mottled with holes and tears and stains, and the zipper had broken yesterday. He stole things sometimes, when he really needed to—like his boots, which he couldn't have done without. He needed a coat now. But upstairs—on the second floor of this pretty white house with the white picket fence—there was a bedroom no one slept in anymore and a closet full of clothes no one had worn in a year.

Tristan climbed through the window and left it open behind him. Even this—a guest room as bland and inoffensive as possible—sent a pang of longing through him. He didn't miss this house or the way he'd felt when he lived here, but the simple notion of a bed and a roof and a door you could lock . . . the presence of unneces-sary things, like tailored curtains and the landscape painting on the wall . . . it all seemed unbearably luxurious to him now.

The first thing he'd learned about being homeless was that it was time-consuming. If he wanted a bed or a shower at one of the shelters he used to cycle through, he had to wait in line for hours, so he mostly slept outside. Even in the cold; even in the snow. If he wanted to wash up or use the bathroom, it was a matter of finding a business that wouldn't toss him out on sight. Cops were a mixed bag: Some would point him to places where he could get free food, and others would threaten to charge him with vagrancy or loitering for, essentially, daring to exist in front of them.

The second thing he'd learned was that being homeless was *humiliating*. He'd huddled on street corners and begged for change. He'd pissed in dark alleys after three shops in a row had kicked him out before he could use their customers-only restrooms. He'd watched people's eyes skate right over him as if he were invisible. This, though? Coming back to his parents' house after they'd sent him away? This was the most humiliating of all.

He wasn't going to take any money. He just wanted a decent coat.

The guest room opened onto a short hallway. All Tristan had to do was cross the living room and get to the stairs.

But he hadn't known what it would be like to return here. He wasn't the same person he'd been a year ago, and being back in the world of sixteen-year-old Tristan made him feel claustrophobic somehow; he didn't fit here anymore. He walked the halls of this house like a stranger. Like he hadn't sat at that dinner table biting his tongue at age fifteen because he never knew what innocuous comment would trigger one of his father's towering rages. Like he hadn't hidden in that bathroom and pretended to be sick to avoid getting dragged to church at age thirteen, when the sermons had started to make him hate himself. Like he hadn't stood frozen around that corner listening to screaming arguments at age eight, when he'd first become conscious of the fact that marriage didn't have to mean liking each other.

By the time he made it to his bedroom, his head was buzzing with remembered anger, with the fear and hurt he'd suppressed all the time he'd lived here.

His mother hadn't gotten around to redecorating his bedroom yet; it was just like he'd left it. He'd never bothered to hang anything on the walls. When he was twelve, his father had thrown out his sketchbook because, he said, Tristan wasn't a child anymore and he needed to find hobbies that were appropriate for a grown man. After that, Tristan always kept his sketchbooks in his locker at school rather than risk bringing them home, so they were probably rotting in some landfill by now. But his tattered paperbacks lined the shelves. His chemistry textbook and half-finished notes lay spread across the desk, as if waiting for him to come back and pick up where he'd left off.

The closet door stood ajar, full of mostly school uniforms, but the coats hung at the end, untouched. He took his heavy down coat along with a lighter one. He could give away the former once it got too warm to wear, or hide it someplace until next winter rolled around.

Still planning on being homeless next year? he thought, and then: *I might not even be alive next year.*

He sighed and reached for the light switch, but a flash of red caught his eye: a scarf, silky-soft and long enough for the ends to brush the ground. Tristan's eyes burned as he tugged it off the hanger.

I don't deserve to take this with me.

But his hands were already draping the scarf around his neck and knotting it.

He threw on the down coat and stuffed the lighter one into his backpack. That was all; he didn't have room to carry much else, and he didn't want to linger here.

His hand was on the doorknob when, downstairs, a lock turned with a weighty clunk, a set of keys jangled, and a pair of high heels clacked across the tiles.

Shit. Trust him to show up on the one day his mother decided to come home early. She ran a wedding-planning business and pretty much set her own hours—but between the holidays and Valentine's coming up, shouldn't she be inundated with newly engaged couples? What was she doing here?

It was fine. She wasn't coming upstairs. He could wait her out.

Her presence had a greater effect on him than he could have anticipated, though. For a split second he wanted to come out of hiding, go downstairs, throw himself on his knees, and tell her he was sorry for everything. He would beg her to let him come back home.

But this *wasn't* his home. Not really.

His father had been bad-tempered and scornful, quick to criticize every decision Tristan made, able to pick at Tristan's insecurities and target them with sly insults. He'd liked the idea of having a son. Just not the reality of who Tristan became. He had wanted an upstanding Christian boy, big and broad-shouldered like he was, who liked to talk about sports and politics. Instead he got Tristan, who'd inherited his mother's delicate features and wanted to spend all his time drawing his silly pictures. At her best, his mother was rational, smart, ambitious; if she was in a good mood, she would tell him all about her latest projects, eyes sparkling, and get his opinion on venues and floral arrangements. At her worst, she was teary and snide, and gave him the cold shoulder if he upset her. She needed everything to be perfect, including and especially Tristan. She was bitterly unhappy, obsessed with appearances, and, eventually, unrecognizable from the woman who had put his first sketchbook into his hands and had a stack of her old watercolor paintings stashed away in a closet somewhere.

When they were angry, they'd say the cruelest things to him and then, later, deny it had happened. If he argued, he was disrespectful; if he felt hurt, he was too sensitive; if he stayed quiet, he had an attitude, and if he avoided them then he was probably up to no good. They were emotional, volatile, controlling. They'd treated love as an obligation. It came with conditions, and God help him if he stepped out of line. If they could've cut him up into pieces and kept only the parts they found acceptable, they would've done it in a heartbeat.

No, they hadn't loved him. They hadn't even liked him.

And when he'd needed them most, they had let him down in the worst way imaginable.

Downstairs, the house slowly filled up with all the familiar sounds he associated with his mother: the television turned on to HGTV, silverware clinking together as she emptied the dishwasher, and even—he flinched—her voice as she spoke to someone over the phone.

It was all so normal. His life had basically ground to a halt after they'd kicked him out, but his mother had gone on like nothing had happened.

He missed her as much as he hated her.

Rage built in him like a headache, right behind his eyes, so that he could hardly think around it. The hurt and resentment and bitterness that had been stirred up just by being in this house again surged past the barriers he'd tried so hard to erect in his mind. He should never have come here.

A resounding clatter jolted him from his thoughts; the silverware had landed on the floor, and his mother was screaming.

Tristan flung the door open, ran to the top of the staircase, and stopped. From his angle, he could see a sliver of the living room and the kitchen.

His mother must have been on the phone again, because she was saying, "Come home, come home, please, it's those—those wolves—from the news—"

Tristan brought his nagging background awareness of the hounds into focus, and the bottom dropped out of his stomach. The hounds were *here*, five of them, circling the house. He knew, without seeing, that they clawed at the walls, that one had leapt onto the roof and was tearing shingles out of it, as if it meant to rip open the ceiling.

"Okay, I will," his mother said, the words barely coherent through her tears. He hoped his father was telling her to call 911 and not directing her to the gun locked away in their closet. Bullets wouldn't even slow them down.

Then the lights flickered out, the TV shut off, and—judging by his mother's sudden wail—the line went dead.

Tristan jogged down the stairs and stood at the entry to the kitchen. She'd hidden between the island and the kitchen sink; all he could see were a few strands of white-blond hair, the side of her arm, the outline of her leg. She'd wrapped her arms around her knees like a child and was crying.

One of the hounds snapped its jaws at the window above the sink. Its teeth left scratches on the glass and long streaks of saliva from its lolling tongue. Two more flung themselves at the living room windows. The others could not be seen, but made themselves heard. When they barked, it was thunderous, deep and explosive, with the rough edge of a growl, and there was a banging that came over and over again—like a screen slamming open and shut during a storm. It was the sound of their bodies ramming against the doors. They were frothing at the mouth, enraged. One of them hit the window so hard it bashed its lip open against its own teeth, leaving a smear of black blood on the glass before the wound stitched itself up.

Tristan couldn't breathe. He had done this. It hadn't been on purpose, but the hounds were tied to him. They had sensed his anger, and they were here to do his bidding. If they'd come of their own accord, doors and walls wouldn't have stopped them; there was no locking out a shadow. But it wasn't enough for them to just get into the house; they wanted to wreck it in the process.

So what? a part of him thought. *Maybe the hounds can scare a little decency into Mom. Let her be afraid, like I am. Why should I protect her? She never protected me.*

And then another voice whispered through his mind: *I intend to nurture that.*

No, he thought. *Stop. STOP!*

They didn't stop, even though Tristan was meant to be their master. In the days since the massacre at St. Sithney's, he'd gotten *worse* at controlling them, not better. He'd failed in this as he'd failed in so many things.

Then he remembered something that made his whole body go cold: He had left the window open when he'd come in earlier.

He dashed through the living room and down the back hall. In the guest room, a hound was squeezing its enormous body through the window. Its huge paws scrabbled at the frame. Its head rolled on its neck. Its back pushed the window open as wide as it could go, and the frame strained until the wood creaked; its heaving mass overflowed into the room like tar spilling out of a pipe.

"GET OUT!" Tristan roared. It snarled at him, baring its teeth.

He'd had enough of things he couldn't control.

He *was* their master, and they would know their place.

Tristan slammed into the hound at full speed, knocking it and himself out the ruined window.

By the time the lights went on again and the police sirens finally came wailing around the corner, Tristan and the hounds were gone.

CHAPTER 8

AZIZA

WHEN AZIZA WAS little, Jiddo had taught her the basics of hedge-craft. Not being a hedgewitch himself, he could only tell her what little he'd gleaned from the hedgewitches he'd worked with on rare occasion in the past. It had been Jiddo who'd first instructed her to visualize the boundary as a veil. He'd taught her how to identify certain fae, and he'd gifted her the silver pocketknife she kept in her bag. When other children were learning to speak to their elders with respect, Aziza was learning the etiquette of human-fae interaction: how to be both polite and firm at once, how to make bargains without leaving a loophole for the crafty ones to exploit, what could be given away and what should never be. And he had told her that if she must meet with the fae, she should stick to the woodland folk. The fae of the sea were deadlier by far. At least in part because if something cornered you in the woods, you could run away; but if you were caught in the sea, there was nowhere to go but down.

Aziza shivered as she zipped her coat up to her chin and shoved her hands deep into her pockets. A bitter wind lashed at her cheeks; she blinked, her eyes stinging, and squinted out at the deserted path ahead. To her right, a broad stretch of shore sloped unhurriedly to the frothing ocean. The winter moonlight turned the rippling sand gray and hard, like cement.

She had to wait until Jiddo had gone to bed before she snuck out each night. He was a heavy sleeper, and as long as she was back before six or seven in the morning—when he usually woke—he'd never know she was gone. This had been her routine for the past week, ever since the attack at the fair. It was the 27th now. The hounds lurked in the woods still; a few hikers had been picked off in broad daylight.

Whatever was happening to the boundary, it had gotten worse since the hounds had appeared. Was that just a bizarre coincidence, or were the hounds connected somehow . . . ?

Focus, she told herself.

During a normal year, days and times of power—like midnight—thinned the veil; *this* year, they threatened to split the boundary apart like a broken seam. But her magic tended to the boundary as the minutes dragged by, plugging the gaps and sewing shut the invisible tears. Midnight passed. She walked a straight line down the boardwalk, letting the murmur of the sea lull her into a state of relaxed concentration as she worked. It was a kind of ritual, this patrolling, that made it easier to hedge. Like a spell, but one that she wove with her actions and not her words.

She had almost reached the pier when something around her— changed. Goose bumps crept over her skin, despite her many layers. She looked hard into the shadows under the pier, dreading the ghoulish smile of bared fangs or the glassy reflection of moonlight on black eyes. But nothing was there. Nothing came toward her from the road, or the ocean. She checked her surroundings, turned back the way she'd come—and her gaze caught on a flash of white.

It was a mare with a coat of flawless ivory, standing in the shallows of the sea. She watched, rooted to the spot, as it nickered gently at her. A wave swept in. The glittering black water washed away the sand at its feet, revealing backward hooves.

A kelpie.

Another one surfaced, a sedate chestnut with a thick dark mane like clumps of seaweed, water sluicing off its neck as it climbed up to the shore. Their eyes tracked her.

They must have slipped through right before she got done mending the boundary. She would have to undo her work, create an opening for them to return to Elphame, use her magic to urge them through, patch up the boundary again . . .

Her head throbbed. Magic had an energy cost; she couldn't use it indefinitely, not without her body feeling the strain. If she took it too far, she would pass out. But she couldn't leave them here. She drew out her magic again, and her vision blurred from exhaustion. Moonlight skimmed the surface of the ocean and cast a halo over the waves.

Open, she thought, and when the briny scent of the wind turned sweet and its clawing cold gentled into a caress, she knew it had worked. The pull of Elphame was tantalizing and inexorable. She reached out to the kelpies, her magic into theirs, her magic the call and theirs the response. Kelpie magic filled her mouth with the taste of blood, like she'd bitten her tongue. It stung like invisible teeth on her throat.

Go back, she thought. *Go home.*

The kelpies froze, ears ticked forward, nostrils flared. Their hooves stomped at the shallow water, restless; the chestnut tossed its head, as if to throw Aziza's influence off.

Why was it resisting?

Against her better judgment, Aziza looked away from the kelpies, eyes scanning the deserted beach, the pier, the dimly lit street, and—*there*. A taxi was parked at the corner. It hadn't been there a few minutes ago. The driver had climbed out, a middle-aged man in a jacket and beanie, his keys clutched in his right hand, his sneakers sticking in the sand so that he had to tug them free with every uneven step he took across the beach. Toward the kelpies.

"HEY!" Aziza yelled at the top of her lungs. "STAY BACK!"

But it was no use; he was spellbound, that was clear from the glazed look on his face and his total lack of response to her shouting. A long stretch of sand and two hungry kelpies separated her from him. Every drifting step took him closer to the water.

Her boots sank into the sand as she stepped off the sidewalk, and her hand rose to her backpack strap. If she dropped it and ran full-tilt, she *might* get to him in time. But the second kelpie, the chestnut, it wasn't even looking at the man. It was watching *her*.

Since when are you brainless meat-grinders this bold, huh? she thought, unsettled. She did the mental math, and she didn't like her odds of getting to the man before the kelpie intercepted her. Let alone getting them both back to safety while he fought her every step of the way. No silver knife would be enough to save her from two kelpies in a feeding frenzy. But to leave him—she couldn't stand it. He was *right there*.

The taxi driver was within arms' reach of the white mare now, hand already extended, fingertips descending over the mare's neck in a light, reverent touch. It bent one of its front legs and extended the other, lowering into a bow. The man drifted along its side, to where a saddle would've rested.

Aziza lashed out with her magic, striking at the kelpies as if with a metaphysical sword. But her magic wasn't *meant* to be a sword. Its blade broke against the kelpies' hunger.

And the man was climbing onto the white mare's back: awkwardly, hands fisted in its mane, hunched over as though, even in his bewitched state, he was afraid of falling. As the kelpie turned and waded into deeper waters, Aziza's feet moved almost without her permission, carrying her forward—there had to be something else she could do, this couldn't be *it*.

But the white mare was neck-deep already, the man clinging to its mane as the waves sloshed around him. Swimming, a kelpie was faster than a land horse in full gallop. When the mare dove, he didn't even scream; the water closed over his head, and they were gone.

Aziza stood there, unblinking, until her eyes burned. But nothing surfaced. There was only the moon's white-faced reflection out there in the deep.

The chestnut ascended, trailing reverse hoofprints as it left the waterline behind and started for Aziza. Its nostrils flared as it caught her scent. If the kelpie couldn't bewitch her into climbing on its back—and a hedgewitch was immune to such magical compulsions—it would happily rip her apart on dry land.

Her time had run out. She took off at a dead run.

The soles of her boots dragged in the sand, kicking it up behind her, but then she was on the sidewalk again and speeding up. The storefronts were dark—boutique clothing stores, surf shops, the vegan burger place Aziza had broken into last month to kill a sand wight made of driftwood and dead fish that had been hiding in the cellar. But there was a 24-hour CVS a block down. If she could just get there and hide until the kelpie lost her scent and went back to the water—

The sound of hooves striking the pavement and an equine scream of rage almost made her stumble. It was *leaving* the beach to come after her. She couldn't risk leading it to other people.

Changing course, she darted down an alley, weaving around a

cluster of overflowing trash cans and recycling bins until she came out on one of the main thoroughfares. A clatter sounded from behind her as the trash cans were knocked over.

Just get to the train, she thought. Her boots slid over patches of frost that clung stubbornly to the pavement. If she slipped, she was dead.

The gaping mouth of the staircase that led to the underground was situated beneath a streetlamp. She all but threw herself down into the station, and it was a miracle she didn't fall and break her neck on those muddy steps, coated with the grimy remnants of the morning's light snowfall. The light inside the station had a filmy quality; that and her frantic heartbeat made her feel light-headed, detached from reality.

She turned the corner past the stairs. Behind her, hooves struck cement as the kelpie bounded after her. She jumped over the arm of a turnstile and onto the platform, but the kelpie was right behind her, cantering past the ticket machines and through the sick half-light and up to the gate. Here it hesitated, snorting and shying away from the metal barriers.

Determinedly, it reared back and struck its front hooves against the metal arm of the turnstile with a thunderous crack. Sparks flew, and it let out a pained shriek. Its white marble eyes rolled in their sockets; its lips were specked with foam and drawn back to reveal cruelly sharp teeth.

The turnstiles wouldn't stop it for long. Aziza ran to the far end of the empty platform, gasping for breath, eyes glued to the darkened tracks.

Please hurry. Please hurry.

Her lungs burned. The increasingly frantic calls of the kelpie echoed down the platform.

A light appeared in the mouth of the tunnel, and the groan of the approaching train shook the air. It barreled into the station, drowning out the bang of the kelpie's hooves as it finally leapt over the turnstiles and onto the platform.

The train slowed; the kelpie galloped toward her; Aziza threw herself against the doors before the train had even fully stopped, banging on them uselessly as if that would help—the clatter of hooves and a trumpeting scream like a battle cry filled her ears—

The doors slid open and she fell into the train car, sprawling onto the faintly sticky floor.

She twisted into a sitting position. The kelpie stood framed in the train's open doors, dripping onto the platform. Here, at last, it had reached its limit. Not even the promise of fresh prey would compel a kelpie to enter a tube of solid metal, stinking of humans.

The doors slid closed, and the train rolled away, shaking over the tracks as it accelerated. Aziza pushed to her feet and watched the kelpie out the window until the platform was replaced by the darkness of the tunnel.

THE FIRST DAY of the new semester, Jiddo was already at the table when she came downstairs. It was still dark out. She normally left before him, especially since the university wouldn't open back up until mid-January.

Had he figured out she'd been gone all night? Had he heard her slip inside a couple of hours ago?

"Good morning," she said, shuffling to the fridge. Her voice was hoarse with exhaustion, but hopefully it sounded like the exhaustion of a person who'd just woken up rather than one who'd barely slept.

Aziza had not gone to bed at a normal hour since her run-in with the kelpies. She'd had longer patrols and fewer breaks. When she did sleep, she dreamed of drowning.

"Come here," Jiddo grunted. He had something laid out on the table in front of him—a fountain pen and an inkpot, a square of cotton, small piles of herbs, a sewing kit. His hands were clasped together in what may have looked to an outsider like prayer, but which she recognized as a sign that he was concentrating.

"Jiddo!" she said. "You already spend too much energy on the wards! What are you doing now?"

The cloth was covered in Arabic script—she couldn't read it, but she recognized Jiddo's handwriting. The ink still shone, only half-dry. As she sat down next to him, he packed the herbs into the cloth and folded the corners over it. Mugwort, verbena, moss. A spell pouch.

Spells were a more advanced sort of witchcraft than what Aziza did. There were three parts to a spell: the language, which didn't have to be verbal and didn't even have to include words, strictly speaking; the offering, which could be something physical, like the herbs Jiddo was using to fill the pouch, or could be a ritual action, or could be something else entirely; and the magic, which was innate. Different classes of witchcraft required different kinds of spells, and Jiddo couldn't teach her a hedgewitch's spells. Aziza got by using sheer willpower and the ritual of her patrols to direct her magic, and while that method got the job done, spellwork took witchcraft to a level of complexity that was inaccessible to her.

"This will protect you," Jiddo murmured, as his stiff fingers finished wrapping the herbs into the ink-marked cloth. "I need to know that you have something to keep you safe when you leave the house every day."

She shoved down her guilty thoughts of her nighttime excursions.

"Will it protect me from the blækhounds?" she asked.

"No," he told her. "But our wards on the house would keep the hounds out, if they ever tried to enter. The spell pouch is a more . . . concentrated form of protection, one that will not work on them."

He slid the sewing kit over to her and held out the pouch, his fingers pinching the top of it closed.

"So is it for the fae, then?" she asked, threading a needle before taking the pouch from him to sew it shut.

"No. Hedgecraft is the only kind that works on fae."

She paused over her first messy stitches.

"Then what's it for?" she asked, exasperated.

"Something is happening in Blackthorn that I don't like." He rubbed a hand over the white stubble on his jaw. He'd be clean-shaven by the time the semester started for him next week; for now, though, he looked grizzled and weary, and she thought she saw shades of who he might have been in another life, if he'd been a ward-keeper still instead of a history professor who lived in a quiet suburban neighborhood with his granddaughter. "There are many magical threats worth guarding against besides hounds and fae."

"Like what?"

She said it offhand, hoping that if she slipped the question in while his guard was down, he'd answer without thinking too hard about it. This was her usual tactic for getting him to tell her anything about her parents, a subject that Jiddo didn't like to talk about. They had gotten sick around the same time, unexpectedly, and died barely months apart. Not even twenty-five years old. Jiddo had never completely recovered from the loss.

She didn't want to make things hard for him. And she'd never felt like she needed any other parent. She wondered about them, though.

They were a mystery, and sometimes she felt—irrationally—that there were parts of herself she couldn't understand without understanding *them*.

Which was nonsense. She was her own person. Jiddo had done more to make her who she was than her parents had.

But she still wondered.

"More than I could count," he said grouchily. "Just keep it with you. And don't go to the park. Some young fools are wandering around the woods with guns and making bets on who will be the first to bring home a wolf pelt."

At Mary Towne Estey High, it was as if the holidays had never happened. There was no room for discussion of presents or vacations; all anyone wanted to talk about were the "wolves" and when they'd strike next. For not a single one of them had been caught yet. There had been two more confirmed sightings of the hounds since the attack at St. Sithney's, and each time, someone had died.

Aziza didn't take part in the speculation or listen to those who claimed they'd seen the hounds in person—in parking lots late at night, through sewer grates, scaling the roof of a neighbor's house looking for a way in. The authorities held firm to the claim that the "wolves" were in the woods, and *only* in the woods, and any other sightings were the product of fearful imaginations.

She snuck off campus during lunch period and went to the local library a few blocks away. Bridget Bishop Memorial Library was one of her favorite places in Blackthorn. In a past life, it had been a church, and half the people who went in still expected to find rows of pews instead of bookshelves behind its polished double doors and stained glass windows. Its spires jutted into the sky, castle-like, and the steps out front were flanked by pillars.

She found the librarian balanced on a rolling stool, one hand braced on the bookcase in front of her and the other busily sliding a history text back into a gap on the top shelf. Her long skirt fluttered around her ankles.

"Got a minute?" Aziza said.

"For you? Always." The stool rattled as Meryl let go of the shelf and hopped down. She brushed her hair out of her face—it was cut short and combed into a neat bob, but it tended to curl into disarray at the slightest provocation, floating up in defiance of gravity. Her round glasses magnified her blue eyes so that they looked about twice their actual size.

Since the library was a block away from the elementary school, Aziza used to stay there and do her homework until Jiddo showed up to walk her home. Meryl would sneak her plantain chips and packets of dried cranberries. Now, she was still one of the only people in the world Aziza could talk to.

She followed Meryl to the circulation desk and recounted a heavily abridged version of recent events, starting with the fair.

"You were there that night?" Meryl's eyes went even wider behind the glasses.

"I'm always there around the solstice."

"Of course," Meryl said, with an indulgent smile. Aziza had learned that if she spoke openly of witchcraft, Meryl took it as a kind of elaborate game of pretend that Aziza had been keeping up her whole life, a joke they were both in on. When Aziza was maybe nine or ten years old, she used to try and bring Meryl proof. She'd turn up at the library with lesser fairies hidden in her backpack or wind sprites in empty water bottles. But the lesser fairies refused to come out if Meryl was around, and when the wind sprites plucked curiously at her skirt and her bangs, she only smiled and said that she'd better go turn down the AC because it was getting chilly.

So Aziza talked to Meryl about everything: school, current events, whatever she'd done over the weekend. The things she would have talked to an older sister or a mother about, she brought to Meryl. And she talked to her about witchcraft, too, because Meryl didn't believe, but she didn't mind, either.

Today, she hadn't just come here to talk—she'd come to do research, and Aziza's research always started with Meryl's recommendations.

But as Meryl pulled an ever-growing stack of books off the shelves and dropped them into Aziza's arms, the sheer magnitude of the task ahead began to dawn on her. Something resembling the hounds existed in just about every type of mythology around the world. Barghests, church grims, werewolves. Huay Pek in Yucatán; inugami in Japan. Hellhounds, guardians of the land of the dead, and the Cŵn Annwn, a ghostly pack that ran with the Wild Hunt.

But she had to start somewhere. Because if she was right that the hounds were connected to whatever was wrong with the boundary, then they might be the key to fixing it, too.

"Thanks, Meryl," she said, wobbling under a tower of research material.

Meryl laid her palm flat on top of the stack before Aziza could walk away.

"I'm encouraging you to *learn* about the hounds," she said, "because learning is always good. I'm *not* endorsing field research. It's one thing to run into them by accident at the fair. *Looking* for them would be something else entirely."

Aziza donned her most innocent expression. "You think I'd do that?"

"I think it wouldn't be the first time I've caught you getting up to things you shouldn't. I think you look exhausted right now. If there's something wrong . . . If you're in trouble . . ."

A taxi parked on the corner of a dark road. A hand reaching for an ivory mane. The taste of sea salt mingling with the iron tang of kelpie magic.

Aziza blinked, and the images were gone.

"Meryl," she said, "I'm an antisocial virgin who's obsessed with witchcraft. How much trouble can I really get into?"

Meryl did not seem comforted by that sentiment.

Aziza hobbled away and almost collided with Leo Merritt outside. He was bundled up in a coat and a scarf, his nose red from the cold, but he broke into a grin at the sight of her.

"Hey!" he said. "Here, let me help."

He scooped up half of the stack before she could object. She scowled at him. If he needed a library, there was one on campus. The only reason for him to be *here* was if he'd followed her.

"I told you I can't break your curse," she said. "If that's what you want, you can leave now."

"I know! I just, uh. I still don't really know anyone at school, so I thought . . ." He glanced down at the stolen books he held. "I guess you're busy."

Aziza battled with herself. She had work to do.

But he was so . . . sad. And pathetic.

"Over here," she said, and led him back inside, to one of the study tables. And it *wasn't* because he looked cold and she wasn't about to let someone whose life she had personally saved die of pneumonia. She'd simply decided she didn't feel like working outside today. They sat down, tossing their jackets over the backs of their chairs, and he shuffled through the mountain of texts, scanning the titles.

"So the wolves *are* magical," he said. "I knew it."

"Keep your voice down," she said, checking to make sure they were alone. She filled him in on what Jiddo had told her: that they were blækhounds and were not, under any circumstances, to be screwed with.

"Did your grandpa say how to get rid of them?"

"I don't think he knows how," she said, and grudgingly added, "Not that he'd tell me if he did."

She stopped—she'd already said too much. It was just that she'd never had anyone but Jiddo she could talk to about real magic and be believed. In fact, it had been years since she'd spent her lunch period with anyone other than Meryl. It was hard to make friends and even harder to keep them when strange accidents always seemed to happen around you—things knocked over or stolen, trees uprooted. That one time with the wasps. At age ten, she'd vanished during her first and only sleepover and climbed into the attic, where a sandman had been hiding in a broken wardrobe, his long limbs folded together and his pale face staring out at her from the shadows as she'd bartered away last night's dreams so that he'd leave. Her friend's mom had found her covered in dust and pouring salt on the windowsills so that the sandman wouldn't come back, and no one realized that Aziza was the reason their youngest stopped sleepwalking after that night; all they knew was that there was something off about her, something maybe a little bit frightening.

So Leo's unquestioning belief in magic and his desire to know more—even though he'd witnessed how dangerous it could be—kept taking her by surprise. But that was no reason to confide in a stranger.

He watched her sort the books into three piles: Maybe Useful, Maybe Bullshit, and Definitely Bullshit.

"Why did you transfer?" she asked.

"I felt like a change?" Avoiding her eyes, he picked one of the books off the Useful pile, even though she hadn't told him which pile was which. "Actually, I might've lost my scholarship to my fancy private school."

Scholarship, huh? Smarter than he looks, she thought unkindly.

"Was that curse-related, too?"

"Kind of," he said. "My curse kicked in right around the start of sophomore year. September before last. It—I couldn't—" He cut himself off with a humorless laugh. "I lost it. I didn't recognize the inside of my own head. I would know things and not remember how I knew them. I'd have opinions about things and not remember why. Something funny would happen, and I'd think, *I should tell . . .* and then I'd *feel* the name slipping away from me."

Aziza listened intently. "That's incredibly powerful magic."

"Why do you sound so impressed?"

"It *is* impressive," she said defensively. "And then?"

"And then . . . I stopped talking to people, and I quit the soccer team, and my grades fell off a cliff. The scholarship was gone by the end of the year."

"So now you're here."

He opened the book to the table of contents, glancing down at it absently. "I don't really care where I go to high school. But when I got the news about losing the scholarship for good? God. For once I was happy my mom doesn't talk." At the look on her face, he added, "She *can* talk. She just doesn't like to. It's her curse."

"What is?"

He told her about the toads, and about Spot.

"Wow," said Aziza. Now, *that* was real magic.

"Wait a sec," he said. "I almost forgot—this is why I was looking for you."

He opened his backpack and pulled out a familiar notebook. Her bestiary. She reached for it unthinkingly. "Where did you—"

"You left it in my car the other night." He handed it over. "I didn't read it . . . but I might've flipped through some of the pictures. You're not a bad artist."

"It's not art," she said. "Just observation."

"Are all those things real?"

"Yeah."

"And you've seen them? You . . . make them go away?"

"Mostly," she said. "You can't keep magic out of Blackthorn completely. Or anywhere. You probably wouldn't want to. I just make sure the dangerous ones stay clear."

Mostly, she added, only in her head this time. She swallowed against the sudden taste of salt in her mouth. Her hands flicked through the pages of her bestiary, feeling the texture of the paper and the faint ridges where she'd dug her pen in too hard, and letting it ground her.

When she looked up, his eyes were on the bestiary, too, with an expression of cautious hope. "That night—you said spirits can't cast curses. So what can?"

"Witches, sometimes," she said. "And fairies. But there aren't any of those around Blackthorn, luckily for us."

"Any in there?" He gestured at the notebook.

"No. I've never gotten a good enough look at one to draw them, and I hope I never do. How did you even—" She snapped the notebook closed and held it up. "What made you look at this and think it was real? There are a million explanations you could've jumped to other than *she must be a witch*."

"For, like . . . six months after my sixteenth birthday, I barely spoke to anyone," he said. "I didn't do much of anything except sleep. It was, uh . . . bad." From the look on his face, that was an understatement. But he continued, "Then I decided I wasn't going to let the curse win. Since my parents said it was a spirit that cursed us, I started contacting paranormal investigators. Most of them only talked to me after I sent them videos of Spot making spooky shit happen around the house."

"Does Spot perform on command?" she asked, intrigued.

"No, but I know how to provoke him." By now he was leaning over the table with a conspiratorial air, and she found herself leaning closer to listen. "But, uh, paranormal investigators? Turns out they're not very helpful. Even the good ones. The one thing they all agreed on was, ghosts don't do curses. Like you said. But anything that *seemed* like a curse was probably the work of a demon."

He looked at her meaningfully, as if waiting for a reaction.

Aziza scoffed. "Please."

"Okay, good, because the demon shit *terrified* me," Leo said, with feeling. "All right, so I didn't think an exorcism was going to help me get my true love back. You need magic to break a magic curse, right? So I started looking for magic instead of ghosts. I found a Wiccan group online—"

Aziza stifled a laugh.

He gave her an exasperated look. "They're very nice people!"

"I'm not laughing at the Wiccans."

"*Anyway.* Most of the ones I talked to, when they say they're witches, it's more of a spirituality thing. Instead of a magic-is-real thing. But if you *ask* them about real magic, a lot of them have stories. So I just started . . . following leads. Drove my parents a little nuts, because I'd take off and be gone for days. Cut school if I had to. I only came back so I could work, because my parents definitely weren't funding any of it. Summer break, I was gone for maybe . . . two months?

And I'd just pick up random jobs along the way. Sometimes I almost didn't come back at all." Leo's eyes went distant, remembering. "I went to Boston, New York, Georgia. Louisiana, Maine. I'd sleep in my car. When I came home, there were reminders everywhere. Like, *everywhere*. Whoever my true love is, we must have been attached at the hip, because I can't even go to the post office without getting that weird, fuzzy, *almost-remembering* feeling I get when my brain's trying to fight with the curse. My car is the only place I *don't* have to worry about that, because I didn't get it till after I turned sixteen."

"And did you find it? Real magic," she said, trying not to show how interested she was in the answer.

"Almost, but . . . no." He shrugged. "Anytime I got close—or *thought* I got close—I'd hit a dead end. No one with anything real to hide wanted to talk to me, because . . . why would they? But sometimes, when I was on the road, I'd see things. Like—here, let me see that."

She passed the bestiary back to him, and he flipped through it until he found what he was looking for. He turned it around and showed it to her. It was an entry about pixies, illustration included. They looked a little like foot-tall praying mantises, blending easily into the woods and grasslands where they mostly lived, with long, slender bodies, bulging eyes, and wings that fanned open to reveal entrancing patterns.

"I saw this page when I was helping you pick up your stuff at the fair," he said. "That's when I started thinking you could be the real deal."

"You've seen a pixie before?" she asked. "Where?"

"A few months ago, when I was on my way back toward Blackthorn. I stopped right after the exit to get some coffee, and when I came back, one of these things was under my car. But it ran away before I could get a closer look. And this." He flipped to the page on sandmen. "Like I said, I slept in my car a lot. I woke up one night, and I swear to *God* I saw this thing watching me through the windshield. What is that? Slender Man?"

"It's a sandman. They're fae that collect dreams. When you're in transit . . . When you're in between places . . . you're more vulnerable to supernatural forces. Closer to Elphame, where things like this live," Aziza said. "And Blackthorn in particular has been—more active. Lately. It doesn't surprise me that you saw something. Especially if you were out there looking for it."

"So all of this—" He tapped the notebook. "This is what you do? You're like a . . . beast tamer?" His eyes went very wide, and his voice dropped to a whisper. "Are dragons real?"

"A *hedgewitch*," she said. "And they were once. I don't know if they still are."

"Whoa." He sounded impressed. "Vampires?"

"Come on."

"I don't know if that's a *yes* or a *no*," he said nervously.

She glanced at the time on her phone. Lunch was almost over. She had gotten no research done at all and felt unaccountably annoyed about it, even though it was all her fault for humoring Leo Merritt.

"Don't look for fairies, Leo," she told him seriously. She felt compelled to stop this fool from getting himself killed, like he'd almost done at the fair.

Sure enough, the humor in his expression faded. There was the glint of something hard and serious in his brown eyes, something that told her looking for fairies was exactly what he'd had in mind.

"I know you want to get rid of the curse," she said. "But one wrong move, one tiny mistake, and they could ruin your whole life.

They could do so much worse than what they've already done to you, *if* they're really the ones responsible."

"And that's why you protect Blackthorn from them. And from other fae." Far from being deterred, Leo looked at her like she'd single-handedly restored all his hopes and dreams. "Think you could use some help with that?"

She blinked at him, astonished. "Are you kidding?"

"Nope!" Maybe he'd spoken off the cuff, but he was clearly warming to the idea already. "I could be, like, your assistant."

She opened her mouth to say, *Like hell you could*, and then stopped. "Did you know—"

Did you know some fae like the taste of human flesh? Did you know that a kelpie could make you forget your true love's name as fast as any curse could? Did you know their victims wake up underwater right before they drown, once the kelpie decides they're deep enough that escape is impossible and it doesn't need to bother keeping them bewitched anymore?

"Did you know," she said, with no tremor at all in her voice, "that fae hate cars? Also trains. Anything that involves being enclosed in metal. Airports are crawling with fae, but get on a plane, and you're in the clear."

"Really?" He beamed. "You know, *I* have a car."

"Right . . ." She hesitated. She didn't want to bring anyone on her patrols—he'd just get in the way, and she worked best alone. But then, *alone* hadn't been good enough the other night. *She* hadn't been good enough. Maybe it was time to try something new.

And it would be nice not to stake her life on the trains being on time.

"Just tell me where to go and how to help," Leo said. "And if things go wrong, or something comes after us, you'll have a getaway car."

"And in exchange, I—I don't know. I won't take you to the fairies, and as for curse-casting witches . . ." She hated to admit it, but he had to know what he was getting into, and how little he stood to gain. "It's not just that I don't know any. It's that the *only* other witch I've ever met is my grandfather. If you're looking for information, I'm as much of a dead end as all the other leads you spent last year chasing."

"But you can tell me about magic, right? You can help me get better at seeing what's real and what's not," Leo said. "Just teach me whatever you know. Tell me about witchcraft and all those things you drew in your notebook. *Anything* could help me."

"That's all?"

"Sure." He shrugged. "I need to do *something*. The curse won't break itself. Uh . . . I think."

She eyed him thoughtfully.

"I stay out most of the night. Now that the new semester's started, I'll have to take naps after school, do homework between classes and during lunch. My grades are average at best, and I'll be lucky if I can keep it that way," she said. "You're up for that?"

"I don't care," he said. "I want my memories back."

"No promises. First, we'll do a test run."

"When?" he asked.

"Tonight."

CHAPTER 9

LEO

LEO WOKE IN the guest room.

His phone alarm blared from the pocket of his jeans. Grimacing, eyes still shut, he fumbled for it and turned it off.

He'd fallen asleep in his own bed a few hours ago, wanting to get some rest before going to meet Aziza. The sleepwalking wasn't new—that was why he'd kept his phone in his pocket instead of leaving it on the nightstand. This was far from the first time he'd ended up in the guest room. Other times, he had the overwhelming urge to unlock the back door in the middle of the night; he'd wander downstairs and only come to when he stood in the open doorway, the cool night air on his face and his hand resting loosely on the knob.

Now, he crept into the hall, taking care not to wake Hazel—she slept in the room across from his. When she talked in her sleep, her voice carried through both their doors. She mostly spouted nonsense. Sometimes she laughed, which—Leo was not too proud to admit—scared the absolute shit out of him. When she had nightmares, he could hear her crying, and he'd get up and wake her. Tonight, though, nothing was louder than Leo's thoughts.

The night before his sixteenth birthday, Leo had wanted to stay awake more than anything. If he didn't fall asleep, he could guard his memories. If he held his true love's face in his mind's eye, if his true love's name still rang through his head at the stroke of midnight, could the curse really take it from him? He'd stayed up for hours, writing down everything he wanted to remember, so that—if he failed to fight the curse—he'd have a record of his lost memories. He'd use his notes to find his true love, and it wouldn't matter if he couldn't remember them. They'd start over, together.

None of his plans had mattered in the end. Before midnight—despite being on his third cup of coffee since dinner, and the fact that he was sitting up fully dressed at his desk with the lights on—he'd passed out. He'd slumped over and landed on his notebook face-first. When he woke up, the notes were useless. He couldn't read them. He recognized the shape of his own script, the slant of the capitals and the hurried scrawl of the vowels. But the letters wouldn't coalesce into words. They slipped from his mind as soon as his eyes passed over them.

Mom had stayed up waiting for him, with two cups of tea and the curtains pulled back so the soft dawn light could spill inside. She'd known he'd be there. She'd known, even when he had refused to believe, that there was no fighting the curse. He'd stumbled downstairs and shoved the notebook into her hands, begging her to read it to him.

"To my future self," she'd started. Raindrop-sized frogs spilled from her mouth, chasing the words into the shadows surrounding their circle of light. But it was a wasted effort: He couldn't understand her.

On his seventeenth birthday, he'd burned the notebook. He didn't want to read about his memories. He wanted to remember them. As he grabbed his backpack and headed out to meet Aziza, he felt like he had that night last September. A little reckless. Wondering if he'd regret this later. Determined, in that wild, nothing-to-lose sort of way. But mostly, he felt like he was waking up after a long, dark dream.

"How do you know that he's not just drunk?" Leo asked.

He hurried to keep up with her as she jogged to where they'd seen a lone stranger wandering into the forest. Addled, she'd said. Walking unsteadily. Which, in Aziza's world, didn't mean *drunk*. It meant *being lured into the woods by the fae*.

"I just have a feeling," she said.

They'd met up at St. Sithney's, parts of which were still cordoned off with yellow tape. Aziza ducked under it, and Leo—after a moment's hesitation—followed. Phones held aloft, flashlights on, they followed the man's boot prints a short way into the woods. There, the tracks stopped abruptly, as if he'd been plucked off the ground by an oversized bird of prey.

"A fairy door," she said. "He's in Elphame."

Before them stood a pair of trees that had grown together in such a way that their branches braided into a graceful arch. It was a doorway into Elphame that opened not at the urging of a hedgewitch, but during the natural thresholds in time. Like midnight. Aziza had explained that she broke down fairy doors when she found them, but another always popped up sooner or later. That was just the nature of the boundary.

"Huh," he said. "I guess that means we've got to go get him."

"You don't have to come with me for this part. In fact, you shouldn't."

"And miss out on a field trip to fairyland? No way," he said, and then held up his hands in a pacifying gesture. "Don't look at me like that. I'm taking this seriously, I swear. I just want to help."

She was so tense and preoccupied that his reassuring smile—which worked on most people—was completely lost on her. But he was sure everything was going to be all right. He wouldn't have come here if he didn't think Aziza knew what she was doing.

"All right, but stay close," she said. "If we get separated, you won't be able to get out of Elphame without me."

"Where would I even go?" he called after her.

She strode through the arch, Leo close behind, and just like that, they were in Elphame. Blackthorn's ambient noises hushed, as if a literal veil had fallen between them and the city: There were no screeching tires, wailing ambulances, dogs barking; no voices or music in the distance. Though their flashlights bleached the world of color, the dark seemed richer somehow, velvety and touchable. The scents of moss and damp soil and unseen flowers wove together, cloyingly sweet, and twined around him like rope, even now in midwinter when most things were dead. The air itself moved more softly against his skin.

Now he understood her warning to stay close. There was something treacherously alluring about this place. It would be all too easy to just . . . wander away, follow the warmth and sweetness wherever it wanted to take him.

Aziza grabbed his arm. "You with me?"

"Yeah." He shook his head. "It's, uh, it's intense."

"You'll get used to it. Just stay focused."

"Why does it feel like . . ." He waved his hand in a vague gesture, unable to put the feeling into words.

"Magic," she said. "Pure, ancient, wild magic. You don't need to be a witch to sense it."

"Wow," Leo breathed.

She pointed. "See those lights?"

A trail of them, phantomlike and winking gently, shone through the darkness. An unsteady figure chased them, entranced, and as he neared each ghostly blue light, it vanished, leaving the next one in line to draw him deeper into the woods.

"Are they dangerous?" he asked.

"Not if you ignore them," she said. "They'll hypnotize you and lure you away from home. If you're lucky, you snap out of it in some clearing miles away from where you started and manage to find your way back home. If you're unlucky, no one ever hears from you again."

"Or if you're *very* lucky, the local witch comes to your rescue?"

"Or that."

They caught up to the man, took hold of his arms, and turned him around. He struggled weakly.

"I need to go that way," he mumbled. "I'm supposed to follow them. I'm supposed to . . ."

Aziza shushed him gently.

"No," she said, more softly than Leo had ever heard her speak to anyone. "I think you're supposed to go *this* way."

"I am?"

"Definitely," said Leo.

"Oh," he said. "All right, then."

A few more steps would bring them back to the fairy door. Through the arch, the familiar yellow glow of the lamps in the park guided them back to Blackthorn.

Something creaked. Aziza stopped, bringing Leo and their dead-weight of a companion to a halt as well. It took him a long moment to identify the fairy door as the source of the noise. As he watched it carefully, one side of it shivered.

Aziza inched backward, and Leo followed her lead. "A nymph," she said in an undertone.

It was like the trunk of the tree had gone liquid; something was sliding off it, peeling away, a humanoid figure disentangling itself from a wooden embrace. When Aziza had said *nymph*, he'd pictured something benign, a beautiful girl with pointy ears and sparkly green magic. This figure was more forest than girl, her body made of woven roots and coarse, furrowed bark. There *was* beauty in the graceful curve of her neck, shaped by wind and sunlight, and the intricate braiding of the supple branches down her head and back, but it was a harsh and forbidding beauty, the beauty of an untamed wilderness when you were delirious from starvation and knew that no one was going to find you. Her limbs creaked with every move, and something skittered off her as she emerged. At last, the creature freed her hand from the arch and peered at them with eyes of gleaming, hardened sap.

"You trespass, gatewalker," said the nymph, her voice a wintry crackle.

"I'm leaving now," Aziza said.

"There is a price for passage."

Without dislodging the man's arm from around her shoulders, Aziza tugged the candy cane pin off her backpack and held it out in her palm.

"A token," she said.

The nymph's ragged mouth stretched wide in what might've been a mocking smile. "One token for three trespassers?"

Aziza turned to Leo. "Do you have a pin, or anything shiny?"

He checked his backpack, rooting around one-handed. His fingers closed around a pin from his old private school, still in the plastic slip it came in, buried deep in an inner pocket of his backpack.

The nymph plucked the pins from their outstretched hands, her tree-bark flesh scratching Leo's palm, but she refused the spare Aziza offered for the half-conscious man.

"It must be *his*," the nymph insisted.

He looked at Aziza blankly. She translated: "Things that belong to us have value. The belonging is what *gives* them value."

That didn't really make things any clearer, but he helped her check the man's pockets anyway. He had some loose change, but the coins were scuffed and dull. He wore no belt buckle and carried no weapons or mirrors. He had a phone, but Aziza shook her head at it.

"You don't offer electronics to fae," she said under her breath. "It'll only offend her."

"Okay. In that case, watch or wedding band?" Leo asked.

"Watch."

"Hope this doesn't have sentimental value." He unclasped it from the man's limp arm.

"Hope it does," she said, looking back at the nymph. "Then our debt will have been paid in full and more."

The nymph's rough-hewn features leered at her. Her brittle wooden fingers accepted the watch from Leo; clutching her new treasures close, she sank back into the grain of the tree from which she'd emerged. The change was so smooth, so seamless, that when she was gone, he was half convinced he'd imagined her.

"Whoa," Leo said, but Aziza was already dragging him and the man through the arch, nearly sending them toppling out the other side. The air lost its sweetness, and the overwhelming presence of potent magic receded. He checked his phone; it was well past midnight. The fairy door was closed, and there would be no more wanderers crossing into Elphame by mistake. Not until dawn, anyway.

Aziza was breathing hard, her fingers tightly fisted on the man's sleeve. But when she looked up, her expression was lighter than Leo had seen it yet.

"We made it," she said, laughing.

"Were you, uh, not sure we would?"

"No, but—" Her smile faded. "There's been a few . . . mishaps, lately. Come on."

They left the man under a lamppost, where—she assured Leo—the light would wake him up soon and he'd recall only dreamlike snatches of what had happened to him. Then they returned to the fairy door, where Aziza climbed up into the trees to separate them; it was newly formed, so all it took was untwisting some of the smaller branches. Otherwise she would've had to come back with a saw.

Leo was fine until they climbed back into his car, and then he found he couldn't quite bring himself to drive away yet. He turned in his seat to look through the back windows at the dark, distant forest.

"I can't believe that just happened," he said, very quietly.

"I know," she said. She sounded resigned. "I understand if you don't want to—"

"That was *amazing*."

"What?"

"We just *talked* to a *tree*. And she was so—And you weren't even afraid of her."

"Some fae are hardwired to kill," Aziza said. "Nymphs aren't. They're dangerous, but they can be bargained with. You don't have to be afraid as long as you can pay."

"Guess I'll have to stock up on pins."

He started the car.

"That's it?" Aziza said. "That's all you have to say?"

"Yup. So. Same time tomorrow?"

A beat of hesitation, and then she said, "I guess so."

Leo grinned at the steering wheel. He'd done it.

They had a deal.

CHAPTER 10
TRISTAN

LAST WINTER, HE used to snag a bed at the shelters every now and then. They were crowded and not always safe, but at least they were warm. He could get a shower, a meal he didn't have to skin, and a bed to sleep on, if he made it before all the spots were full and the doors closed.

One night, he was in a bunk near the back corner of a dorm with two rows of beds: simple cots with metal frames, thin mattresses, and barely a foot of space between any pair of them. His neighbor was a kid maybe a year or so younger than him, emaciated, his pupils reduced to pinpricks and his bruised hands clutching a raggedy old pack.

Tristan had ignored him, closing his eyes against the harsh fluorescent panels in the ceiling and waiting for lights-out. He'd been only a few months into his "contract," the worst few months of his life, and a long winter stretched before him. It had been a feeding night. His hand smarted from the newest cut he'd made earlier with the ritual knife.

The weapon had been given to him by the hag, and it had belonged to her since *before* she became a hag, from the days when she was still only a witch. That made it over two centuries old. Back then, she'd been no more than a hearth witch—a craft of small household magics, lighting cookfires and brewing natural remedies for minor ills the townsfolk suffered. She'd been the local wise woman in a time when medicine and magic might as well have been one and the same, the closest thing to a doctor that her village had. The knife had been a gift, but the charm upon it was her own. The spell was simple and relatively innocent: A cut made by its blade would always be straight and clean. This had come in handy when all she'd used it for had been cutting ingredients for her potions. For Tristan, it ensured he never cut himself too deep or jagged, and that his cuts never got infected. It wasn't a kindness on the hag's part. It was practical. Clean blood made a clearer signal, and a healthy bondservant was more useful to her than a sick one.

The first time he'd used the dagger, it had felt far too large and clumsy in his weak hands. If not for the stabilizing charm, he probably would've chopped off a finger. He didn't remember most of the people he had doomed with this knife, and that was by design. He had two rules: First, he had to choose the victims randomly. That was because he didn't trust his own sense of justice. Second, no children. That one was self-explanatory.

He hadn't bothered wrapping or cleaning the cut. His fingers curled over it but didn't touch.

Lately, his thoughts had been . . . dangerous. Rebellious. There was no hiding from the hag that he wanted out of the contract; she knew already from the torrent of emotion he couldn't withhold from the bond on every feeding night. But he had started to wonder whether there was a way to *un*make a hag. Every hag had been a witch once.

When a witch corrupted their magic with dark rituals—for eternal life, for beauty or youth, for power—then they ran the risk of becoming a hag. That was what she'd wanted: to live forever. She'd told him all that herself, with a self-satisfied air; she said she had ascended beyond the boundaries of her own craft. But could the process be reversed? Could a hag become a witch again? Was there another way out of this? If he could just think . . .

The lights had gone off without him noticing, and he'd slipped into a restless sleep.

But a sound woke him in the dead of night.

He lurched upright in bed, gasping for air. Whatever nightmare he'd been having, he couldn't remember it. But there had been a rustling noise—something moving, too close for comfort . . .

Some instinct made him turn his head to the right, where the other teenager slept in the bed next to his.

Had slept. The boy was gone. His pack was still there, though—all his worldly possessions, which he'd clung to so protectively earlier, and he'd just left it there on the foot of the bed where anyone could take it. At the other end of the room, the door to the dorms clicked shut behind someone who had just left.

Tristan followed. Out the dorm, through the halls, and into the night, where he found the boy walking unsteadily down the street. He lunged and grabbed him by the arm. It was the last thing he'd normally do—sneak up on someone so much like himself. Someone who was probably used to defending himself by any means necessary.

Sure enough, the boy swung around and threw a punch. Tristan ducked out of the way, releasing him.

"Where are you going?" he demanded, like it was any of his business.

The boy was practically trembling with suppressed energy, his eyes wide and alert. At Tristan's words, he broke into a smile so wide it looked painful.

"I'm going home," he said. "She's going to help me."

"No," Tristan blurted, even though helping the hag's victims was exactly what he *wasn't* supposed to do. "No, you—you're just hearing things. Come back inside."

"She promised. She can help me."

"Wait." Tristan snatched at the boy's sleeve, but he swayed out of reach, eyes clouded now.

"I'm going home," he said again, under his breath. "I'm going home. I'm going home."

He drifted away, uncertainly and then picking up speed, as if he'd already forgotten why he'd stopped. He would walk all night until he reached the forest, and then he would keep walking, not feeling his hunger or exhaustion, not feeling the moment he crossed into the hag's territory and sealed his fate.

Tristan watched him go, furious tears prickling behind his eyes. This was his fault. The hag had used the bond to find another victim—to show him that as long as he lived, no one around him was safe. That there was no way to unmake a hag. That he was powerless.

It was a warning.

Before he could think it over long enough to decide it was a bad idea, his legs were carrying him down the road to the train station. No one was around to see him jump over the turnstile and slip into an empty car. He got off at the end of the line, at Old South Cemetery, which was a ten-minute walk from the edge of the forest. That meant approaching the hag's territory from the east rather than northeast.

At first, he thought *that* was why he couldn't find the way.

He crashed through the underbrush, heedless of the noise he was making. He had to get to the gateway tree before the boy did. He'd beg for the boy's life. No, he'd bargain. He'd strike another deal with the hag if he had to.

The air grew cold and leaden with a bereft sort of silence: No insects disturbed the stillness, no birds or animals. The trees twisted grotesquely, their crowns tangled together so that the forest canopy became black and impenetrable. No moonlight disturbed the dark. No stars.

He wandered.

He wandered for a long time before the truth came to him—not a dawning but a drowning, the rising waters of the horrible realization slowly closing over his head. Normally, he could find his way through the hag's territory because of their bond. But she had changed the landscape of her world, and now he was lost. Trapped.

Later, he would learn that three days had passed before she released him.

It didn't feel like three days, though. It felt like forever. He stumbled through a world gone fractal and ghostly. There was no daytime, only a never-ending night. After a while, he stopped looking for the hag and kept his dazed face turned upward, desperate for a glimpse of the sky.

He was aware of the boy reaching the borderlands, too. He felt this other life—felt it, because the presence of life made ripples in time and space, which washed over him. But he never got anywhere near him. The hag wouldn't allow it. She twisted the world around him as easily as tying a knot in a length of rope, and Tristan went in circles and circles and circles. And then the boy was gone, through the borderlands and out the other side—the wrong side.

The borderlands shifted, expanding and contracting in a supernatural gasp.

The surge of energy she gleaned from the boy's life pulsed through the bond and washed over the borderlands. Tristan staggered and threw up the scant contents of his stomach. He'd barely had a chance to catch his breath and wipe the tears off his face before the bond tugged him onward. It was a command: The hag wanted him to keep walking.

So he walked.

Long after the boy was dead, Tristan fell on his knees before the gateway tree, shaking, fresh tears beginning to stream down his face. He didn't even know why. They weren't tears of sadness, not for the boy or for himself. He was beyond emotion.

"Why did you—"

It was a miracle the hag understood. He had to relearn how to shape his lips around the letters, had to rediscover where his voice lived in his body.

"Next time you think of disobeying me," the hag said. "Next time you think of cheating me. Think of *this*."

That was the last time he thought of rebellion, up until his foolish attempt with the hound that first night as a necromancer. He couldn't save anyone from the hag. Least of all himself.

HE USUALLY SLEPT outside nowadays. He'd found a ridge in the woods to curl up against; its overhang caught the snow and created a small nook. Good enough shelter for the night.

Under the coat and scarf he'd salvaged from his parents' house, Tristan's arms and torso were laden with bandages, which covered the marks of the hounds' teeth and claws. They'd done everything short of killing him; they *couldn't* kill him, not with his powers and his bond to the hag. But they'd fought him for every last shred of dominance.

He'd won that fight, though. His will had been stronger than their hunger.

Too bad willpower doesn't stop you from bleeding.

Every inch of torn or bruised skin screamed in protest as he sat up. Days ago, he'd managed to drag himself to the emergency room, not wanting the wounds to get infected; had the presence of mind to lie about his age; had been caught out as a minor anyway; and had ended up ripping out his own IV and fleeing before they could call social services. He'd been in and out of consciousness since then as his body had slowly healed itself.

All this because he hadn't been willing to steal a coat. Lesson fucking learned.

But even the hard-won respite of sleep was cut short. The pressure in the back of his mind, like an impending headache, deepened from a pang to a throb. Wasting no time, he climbed to his feet, checked his belongings, and set out to answer the hag's call.

Rain had softened the ground to sludge, and layers of fallen yellow leaves lay crumpled and mud-streaked under vacant branches. As he neared his destination, the forest darkened and the birdsong hushed, even though it was a clear, sunny morning.

The hag's territory existed in its own space, and Tristan had to cross a mangled, indistinct threshold to reach it. The first time, when the hag had lured a lost, grief-stricken, sixteen-year-old Tristan to her den, he wouldn't have made it through the borderlands and into her realm without her guidance. He had followed a voice in the woods all the way to the gateway tree; at first he had even thought the tree *was* the source of the voice. When the voice had finished making its promises, when it had laid out the terms of its magical contract, when it had gotten a shaky, whispered *yes* out of him, it had told him to let a few drops of his blood fall onto the roots of the tree to seal the deal—easy enough, as he'd scraped himself up stumbling through the forest. He had thought that the tree was drinking his blood, the way a plant drinks water.

Eventually he'd figured out that the tree wasn't sentient and couldn't speak. That there was something *inside* it. But it had been weeks before the hag had revealed herself.

After he had—symbolically—signed his contract, and as he made the journey over and over, he grew used to the wrongness, the confusion, the dark. He knew how to plunge through, single-minded, and fight his way to his destination without letting the un-world swallow him. If he got lost, he could turn inward and tap into the bond, using it like a map, finding where he was in the hag's web and following the dark signal of her magic to the center. As long as the hag let him.

That web stretched wider every day, a spreading disease. Her power encroached farther into the natural world, pushing against its borders. Tristan didn't know if she had a limit, or if she could theoretically become so powerful that her territory would swallow Blackthorn entirely.

Here in the borderlands, the forest arched over him like a ceiling, somehow both dizzyingly high and unbearably claustrophobic. When he brushed against the trees, he swore he could feel them move, as if they breathed with mammal lungs. Tristan's own breathing came too fast, and his heart galloped in his chest until its pounding was the only thing he could hear.

She wasn't happy with him. Even from afar, he could tell.

When he reached the gateway tree, he was panting; he couldn't tell if the burning in his side was a cramp or if he'd torn one of his stitches. He folded his arms around his middle and squinted up at the hag through eyes blurred with pain.

"You kept me waiting," she seethed.

"I'm sorry," he said dully.

She examined him, her foul magic feeling out Tristan's side of the bond. He bit the inside of his cheek until she withdrew.

The hag laughed. "Have you been quarreling with your siblings?"

Don't take the bait, he told himself, but the words burned the back of his throat.

"The hounds came after my mother," he blurted. "You didn't tell me they could do that."

"What mother?" the hag rasped. "The mother who threw you away like trash? I'm your mother now, child."

Tristan suppressed a shudder. "You didn't tell me they'd react if I got angry!"

"You should not have needed to be told. You should have mastered the hounds long before now. But why, my ward," she said, and her voice began to climb, "why, *why, why have you been wasting time?*"

Her mangled voice echoed around the clearing, as though the sky itself were howling at Tristan. It roused birds from the trees miles away and resounded through the dead borderlands. He flinched, ducking his head; the sudden shift from tranquility to bellowing rage took him back to his parents' house as effectively as being there in person. His stomach twisted itself up into a tight ball of fear.

"What do you mean?" he said to the ground, stalling.

"The girl," she snarled. "I told you to find her. *Where is she?*"

"I tried, but it didn't work," he said, trying not to sound as relieved as he felt. "I couldn't get through the gate. Neither could the hounds."

He'd thought he would have to lie. He'd practiced saying *I couldn't find her* to himself, over and over, trying to make himself believe it so that the hag would, too. He'd toyed with the idea of marking her home with blood from one of the hounds, hoping that the memory of performing the necessary actions would help him fake conviction in front of the hag, though of course hound's blood wouldn't help the hag find her victim. But he hadn't needed to do any of that. There had been some kind of . . . invisible barrier around Aziza El-Amin's home. When he'd touched the gate, it had burned him through his glove. He'd been elated.

The hag fell silent—a dangerous, calculating silence. He wanted to look up, feeling far too vulnerable there, on his knees with his head bowed and the back of his neck exposed. But he didn't dare.

"Maybe," Tristan said cautiously, "maybe I can find someone else. Another witch."

Promises like that were bound to backfire on him. He didn't want to find another witch for the hag to kill, not now, not ever.

"*No!*" she said. "It must be her."

"*Why?*"

"It is not your job to ask questions, bondservant," she said. "It is your job to obey."

"But if I can't leave the mark," Tristan pressed, making his voice as meek as possible.

Silence, again. And then:

"Ah. I see," she said, the words hissing out of her like vapor. "The old man must still be alive. His wards—"

"What?" Tristan said. He glanced up on instinct and glimpsed her long fingers stroking absently at the bough of the gateway tree, as though petting an enormous snake. But she ignored him.

"If you cannot lead me to the girl," she said at last, "then you must wait until she leaves the protection of the wards, and then bring her to me."

He had to run those words through his head several times before they made any sense. A stone dropped into the pit of his stomach.

"You want me to abduct her?"

"It is the only way. If you fail—"

Shakily, Tristan stood.

"You've never asked me to do anything like this. To physically harm someone," he said. "I've marked their homes, but I've never had to touch any of your victims."

The hag's laughter whipped through the clearing like a gale.

"Boy, I have never *asked* you to do anything. You are *bound*."

Tristan swallowed hard. His knees felt liquid.

"No," he said.

"No?" she repeated, so quietly her voice could have been mistaken for the grass whispering to itself. "Are you ready to forfeit your contract, then?"

Are you ready to die? she meant.

"Yes," Tristan said. His voice broke. "I'm done."

He braced himself for her next order, the one he'd always dreaded—to go and bring her his replacement. He would refuse, and then the pain would start. But he would have to withstand it. He'd thought before that he couldn't, but maybe he *could*. The part of Tristan that had clawed and bitten the hounds right back, the part that had snarled into their furious, bloodthirsty faces and hadn't flinched when they'd cut him open—that part of him could.

"You must not care, then, about what will happen to those you leave behind."

Tristan looked up at her, startled, breaking the first order she'd ever given him.

Her skin was wrinkled and sagging, lopsided, as if she'd ripped it off and then haphazardly replaced it. Ghastly scars cut through the folds of her shriveled face in the place where her eyes should've been. Compared to the gateway tree—a behemoth that could've swallowed a lesser tree whole—she seemed porcelain-white and doll-sized in her perch at the crook of its trunk. But she was not small; or rather, she was as slight or as great as she wanted to be. When Tristan had met her, she had made herself hunched and thin like an elderly woman. Now, even at a distance, she hung over him, the teeth in the gateway tree's maw. All at once, he couldn't breathe.

"Don't you want to know what will happen to them?" she asked. The words didn't match the movement of her jaw; it was like her body was a puppet and something else was speaking out of her.

Tristan forced his lungs to accept a gulp of air.

"What are you saying?" he managed.

"I am saying . . . that I do not reward failed servants with an easy death," she said silkily. "Those places I once spared, for your sake, will be my new hunting grounds. Your school. Every shelter that ever offered you a bed. Your house, and the parents who treated you so cruelly. Perhaps a part of you will even enjoy it when I feed on *them*." She cackled, a shattered-glass sound. Her next words were delivered with slow, rapturous delight. "But you won't like it at all, will you, when I come for precious, forgetful Leo Merritt—"

"Stop!"

Tristan hardly sounded like himself. It was practically suicide to interrupt her the way he just had, but he didn't care. The sound of this monster saying Leo's name was worse than anything he had endured so far: burying the bodies in Elphame, the hounds' teeth in his skin, even the hag's revolting magic inside his head.

"Have you had a change of heart?" she asked, with a vindictive pleasure he could feel through the bond.

"Yes," he said, and even to himself he sounded utterly, terrifyingly hollow. "I'll do what you want."

CHAPTER 11

AZIZA

THEY WERE IN Leo's car, parked under a streetlamp in the lot at St. Sithney's. A pair of half-empty paper cups holding their cold, three-hour-old coffee sat between their seats. Both of them were bleeding—Leo from the various cuts and abrasions he'd gotten stumbling through the woods with all those long, clumsy limbs and refusing to wear his coat because "we'll warm up once we've walked around a little!" and Aziza from throwing herself into a thorn bush to retrieve the *fucking* shade that had gotten away from her at the fair. She'd grabbed it without her gloves, and the goddamn oversized magical *worm* had bitten her, and Aziza had just clasped her hands tighter and squeezed like she meant to throttle it.

She couldn't, of course. Shadows didn't *suffocate*. If she'd really wanted to hurt it, she would've pinned it to a tree with her silver pocketknife. But she *didn't*, and did the shade have the decency to thank her for it? Of course not. But she had gotten it through the boundary and into Elphame, and the needlelike puncture marks all over her right hand were a small price to pay.

"I told you that would come in handy," Leo said. He was talking about the first aid kit that he'd stashed in the car last week. It was open on the dashboard now, his phone propped up against it, playing some sci-fi movie that involved a lot of incomprehensible made-up jargon about outer space and rocket ships. He'd learned that her pop culture knowledge was abysmal, and he'd made it his personal mission to fix that. Because it wasn't enough to be cursed. He was just desperate for another hopeless cause.

Aziza, who had wrapped her hand in a bandage and was sawing the end off the roll with her teeth, only grunted.

"Okay, *this* part—" Leo said, riveted, as if he hadn't seen whatever this movie was so many times that he could recite some of the lines by heart. "This is the *best scene*, look—"

"I'm looking." She watched from the corner of her eye while dabbing ointment over a cut on her cheek, the mirror in the sun visor open so that she wouldn't waste any by smearing it around. They were going to need every drop of this stuff.

Leo had been a bigger help than she could've anticipated when she'd agreed to let him join her on patrol. Aziza hadn't figured out what was disturbing the veil, but in the meantime, they did everything they could to minimize the damage. They stopped the kelpies from hunting on Blackthorn's shores, mostly by making sure no one was *there* to hunt. They walked the train tracks and roused the sleepwalkers who'd been led astray by sandmen. They salted the windows and doorways of the homes nearest to St. Sithney's, because salt repelled unwelcome visitors, like doppelgangers and even—though she hoped things wouldn't get this bad—fairies come to leave their changelings in human cribs.

She taught him about Blackthorn's spirits, like the Green Street Passenger, the Ash Witch, and the Man at the Bus Stop—the last of which had appeared before them when they were on their way back to the car one night in the middle of the rain. Leo, not recognizing him for what he was, had asked him if he wanted the spare umbrella in his car. Aziza didn't intervene—that would've annoyed the spirit and meant bad luck for both of them. She could only observe in silence as the Man at the Bus Stop had accepted Leo's offer. By the time they got to the car and Leo drove back around to drop off the umbrella, he was gone. That was when Leo had figured it out. But he had made a good impression. The spirit gave him a blessing of good fortune, and for the next week, stoplights were *always* green for him.

Nothing they'd encountered had scared Leo off yet. And this . . . irritated her.

She didn't exactly know why. It was good that Leo hadn't backed out. No one had died in front of her lately, and she also hadn't had to sprint to the train station while being chased by something carnivorous. And yet. Her own eyes in the mirror scowled back at her. No matter how she tried to talk herself out of it, the irritation was there.

On Leo's phone, something exploded to triumphant music.

"Why'd they blow up their ship?" she said distractedly. "I think I missed something."

"It's because we're watching in five-minute increments after patrol, how can you follow along if we keep getting interrupted?"

"I'll just read the synopsis online later."

"You *could* come over to my place and we could watch, like, the entire movie in one go," he said, wheedling. "Or another movie! You can meet Spot and everything. Take home a souvenir curse frog."

"We're not spending time together for the hell of it," she reminded him. "We're not friends. We have a job to do, and that's the *only* reason we're here right now."

She was brusque, as usual, and also as usual, Leo did not seem to take her seriously. She suspected that he had taken befriending her as a kind of personal challenge.

"What if I *promise* not to make laser noises during the fight scenes?" He held up a bandaged hand in a *wait* gesture. "Think carefully before you say no. This offer might never be on the table again."

"Tempting, but—" she began, and stopped, looking through the windshield.

"What?"

Through the windshield, the forest lay dreaming, blurred to obscurity in the dark. The rolling green lawns around the parking lot were silent. Cold moonlight painted the grass in washed-out, monochromatic tones, and Aziza could almost imagine that it was the source of the goose bumps breaking out over her arms. Nothing was obviously wrong, but . . .

"We have to go," she said.

Overhead, the streetlamp flickered and went out, plunging them into darkness.

And something outside growled.

Leo started the car, stomped on the pedal, and reversed out of the parking spot. As he yanked at the steering wheel, turning them, a hound stepped into the path of his headlights. It was bigger than she remembered, as if her mind had flattened the memory so that she'd be able to sleep at night. Its body loomed over the windshield, its fur so black they could not clearly make out its features—except for its eyes, aglow with reflected light, piercing and demonic.

"Mother*fucker*," she said eloquently.

Leo's eyes narrowed. "Seat belt?"

She clicked it into place. "Yup."

"Hold on."

Leo's car was a bucket of rust held together with duct tape and hope. It whined, it groaned, it sputtered threateningly every time Leo turned left—but as Leo put what must have been all his weight on the pedal and the car lurched into motion, it was a chariot of the fucking gods.

They sped toward the hound. Leo pounded on the horn, once twice three times, trying to scare it away. But it didn't move. It crouched as if to spring, teeth bared, eyes burning into Aziza's. Unconsciously, she pressed back into the seat, unable to look away.

Leo swerved seconds before they would have collided. They flew off the pavement and over the park trails, leaving tire tracks like scars in the grass. The car whined and coughed out fumes but obeyed, bumping across the lawn and then jolting over the curb. Then they were on asphalt again, accelerating down the road.

"Think it's gone?" he asked, glancing at the rearview mirror.

"Maybe," she said, and then: "Actually, no."

They were tracing the edge of St. Sithney's, shuttered storefronts on one side and the park on the other. There at the corner was the stop sign where Leo would normally turn; underneath it, the shadows clotted together, and a pair of luminous eyes blinked into existence.

Swearing vigorously, Leo made a U-turn, tires screeching.

"Can't go home," he said. "Not if it's following us."

"The library," she told him, obeying a sudden impulse. "Jiddo warded it ages ago, since he had to leave me there alone all the time."

Leo didn't object, and in about ten minutes, they were skidding to a halt as close to the library's entrance as he could get them. They leapt out of the car and up the steps, plowed into the wide double doors, and found them locked. Shoulders first, they shoved, banging against the entrance like a human battering ram, until Aziza's back ached and she could feel the bruises forming where she slammed against the old wood. But, at last, it gave way. They practically fell inside.

The hound emerged from the shadows at the base of the steps, as though crawling from the mouth of a tunnel. Its fur blended into the darkness, so that the shining eyes and the white teeth in its grinning snout seemed to hover disembodied, Cheshire-like.

They slammed the door and pushed one of the bookcases in front of it. She braced herself for the hound's body to crash through it, but nothing happened.

"But if it can get around by—by magic, how's this going to stop it?" Leo said.

"The wards. Otherwise it would be inside already."

"How do we know it's not?" he hissed.

She hesitated, and then—"Listen."

They both went silent, and she could tell when he heard it: a wet, animal panting from the other side of the door.

"This way," she told him. They ran for the emergency exit in the back, but when she touched it, it was hot—as if another hound was pressed against the door, waiting for them.

So much for their escape route.

"We can wait them out," Leo said. They both jumped as the thing on the other side of the exit moved; they heard a low thump, like a tail hitting the door as it turned away. She crept to the window between two bookcases in the mystery section. The hounds crossed the parking lot, loping along in that graceful, deceptively light way of theirs. Her heart lifted. They were leaving, they . . . they . . .

"What?" Leo said urgently. He'd heard her breath catch, or maybe he saw the look on her face and knew it meant bad news.

The hounds had reached the oak tree beside the entrance of the parking lot. The tree was the anchoring point of Jiddo's wards. And the hounds were attacking it viciously, trying to uproot it. If they did, they'd uproot the wards, too.

"They're going to get in." She sounded calm, and she felt it, too, the cool practicality that came of being in a situation that was so completely fucked that your mind tricked itself into not being afraid—like cold that was so cold it *burned*. Fear that ran so deep it became bravery.

They skidded down the hall to Meryl's office, which contained a desk and some filing cabinets and, against the back wall, an antique wooden chest. She shut and locked the door, as if that would help. With shaking fingers, she pulled out the secondhand phone she'd bought to replace the one the hound had broken at the fair.

"No signal," she said.

Leo was inspecting the chest. "You don't think there's a gun in here, do you? I can't shoot, but now seems like a good time to try."

"No way," she said. "Why would Meryl have a—"

He threw open the lid.

"You're right," he said. "That's not a gun."

"But this . . . this library doesn't have a basement!"

The chest was empty, the bottom was missing, and underneath it was a gaping hole in the floor. Inside, at the bottom of a short drop, was a staircase.

"We just came back from fairyland through an imaginary door in the forest," he reminded her.

"It's not imaginary."

"It's also not really a door, but you *imagine* it open and closed, so it also kind of is. And you're still somehow surprised by a secret tunnel? At least Indiana Jones prepared me for *this*." He paused contemplatively. "Hey, is your librarian a spy? Just wondering."

There was a crash. The wards were gone. The front door had either fallen over or splintered into pieces, and the bookcase was probably on the ground with books spilling off its shelves. Massive paws pounded against the tiles of the main hall; the hound's bass growl was audible already.

"Come on," she said. It was a tight squeeze, but she managed to slide into the chest, lower herself down with her hands clinging to the edge, and drop through the opening. The top stair was broad enough that she could land solidly on her feet. She moved aside so Leo could come in after her. He managed to close the chest on his way down while Aziza turned on her flashlight. She shined the light down the stairs.

A bang from above made them jump; the hound was trying to get into Meryl's office. Aziza glanced over at Leo, who wore a grim-faced look of determination. They didn't speak. Down the steps they went.

The staircase went on for what felt like forever. It was steep and slippery and terrifying, and there was no rail, only the smooth walls. The tunnel soon narrowed until she and Leo were walking single file. And then her light finally found the bottom.

"What the fuck," Leo breathed.

The staircase ended in water.

Another tunnel ran perpendicular to the one they had climbed down, and it was flooded. Cold water lapped at the bottom step and splashed Aziza's boots. There was no way of knowing how deep it was; it went rushing by, inky black, foaming and sloshing against the walls.

"I think this is the exit," she said. Her stomach clenched in dismay.

"What? We can't go in there."

"We can't go back, either. This has to be here for a reason. It's not natural—someone *made* it."

"And you think the reason is . . . to jump into it and probably drown?"

Aziza screwed her eyes shut. She knew what she had to do.

"Leo, I think I'm the one it's after," she said. "That first one looked at me like—I don't know. But if I go, maybe they'll leave you alone. You don't have to come with me."

"*Fuck.* Of course I do! Fuck, oh my god, it's going to be so cold."

A rustling noise made her turn around. Leo was already taking off his coat and boots.

She stared at him, bewildered. This whole time—not just tonight, but really since they'd met—she'd been waiting for the thing that would scare Leo off for good. How many times had she seen people close up and pull away at the first sign that something was *off* about her? Because, whether they knew they were doing it or not, people avoided things they didn't understand. She had never cared; she wouldn't compromise on who she was just to make someone stick around who wouldn't otherwise. So it was a given that they'd come and go. Nothing worth dwelling on. Maybe this was why it had irritated her so much when Leo had stayed. Part of her had been convinced it was only a matter of time before that self-preservation instinct kicked in and he would be gone. Only it hadn't happened yet. *This*, tonight, should've been the final straw, but somehow he was still here.

And she wasn't irritated with him anymore, but she didn't know *what* to feel.

So she looked away from him and didn't reply, not even to thank him. She eyed the water again and allowed herself a moment of intense self-pity before she peeled off her coat, too. They shed their sweaters and jeans, leaving Leo in an undershirt and boxers, and Aziza in a pair of leggings and a sports bra.

They squeezed onto the bottom step together, shivering already. The spray from the rushing water landed on her calves; it was so shockingly cold she almost decided to go back upstairs and throw herself on the hounds' mercy.

"It's fine," Leo was mumbling under his breath, more to himself than Aziza. "Just a little water. It's going to be fine."

She left her phone on the ground, the light shining up. The water crashed through their semicircle of illumination and vanished into the darkness of the tunnel. A current that powerful, she didn't even think they'd be able to swim. It would just carry them along to wherever it was going.

She still didn't know what to say. So she offered her hand, and Leo took it.

"Ready?" she asked.

"No. On three?"

"Yeah."

"One."

"Two."

They jumped.

The stream was beyond frigid, and it was only moments before her hands and feet went numb. The water ripped them down the tunnel at breakneck speed, even faster than it had looked from the stairs, and as rough as she'd feared it would be. She swallowed some almost instantly and tasted salt; they didn't have to work hard to stay afloat, but their hands clung together so tightly she was sure they'd both have finger-shaped bruises later. They kept bouncing off the sides of the tunnel, pinballing back and forth, and the water spun them around, and she could never be sure which direction she was facing because it was pitch-black, and the roar of the water echoed off the walls, and it was like being blindfolded in the middle of the ocean—

And then they *were* in the ocean.

Abruptly, the rushing water was replaced by the gentle push and pull of the sea as they were ejected from the tunnel. They ended up treading water under the vast open sky, releasing each other so they could swim properly.

In the first stroke of luck they'd had all night, the sky was clear and cloudless; she managed to orient herself by moonlight. They were at the base of the cliffs on Blackthorn's northeast shore. The tunnel had delivered them through a narrow opening in the rocks, which she was fairly certain would be submerged at high tide.

Leo stammered something that might've included the word *sharks*, though his teeth were chattering too hard to get a real sentence out.

"It's winter, there aren't any sharks here," she said, but *her* teeth were also chattering and her lips were numb, so there was no telling if Leo understood her.

She shook her wet hair out of her eyes and pointed. Leo nodded. They paddled through the icy black waters, around the bend in the cliffs, until they saw the pier jutting out into the sea before them. Their feet touched down on sand at last; they waded to the beach and climbed up to the boardwalk.

"We didn't drown," Leo observed, once he'd gotten the shivering relatively under control. "We didn't get eaten by sharks. We're not being chased anymore, probably. This is good."

"You don't have to be so fucking positive about this," Aziza said, folding her arms in a vain attempt to warm herself up. "We're soaking wet in our underwear at two in the fucking goddamn morning."

"One of us has to be positive, and we both know it's not going to be you."

"No phones, no clothes, no money—shit."

"Isn't that—*ohthankgod*," Leo said, and Aziza followed his gaze to the street, where Meryl was parking a minivan and stepping out. Leo headed straight for her and the promise of electric heating, but Aziza stopped in her tracks.

"What are you doing here?" she said, stunned. "How did you know to come get us?"

"I got an alert from my security system that someone was in the library. So I went to take a look—"

"Instead of calling the cops? Isn't that the whole point of a security system?" Leo said in disbelief, but Meryl only shrugged.

"I do live right upstairs."

"Since *when*?" Aziza said. "Why didn't I know that?"

"Since always. The hounds were gone by the time I got downstairs, but between the broken door and the bite marks on the chest in my office, I could just about guess what had happened," she said, and smiled at Aziza with a familiar combination of fondness and concern. "And I can only think of one person with a worrying interest in the hounds who comes to the library when she doesn't feel safe."

Aziza was too confused to smile back. And also, too cold. It felt like her facial muscles had frozen solid.

"Are those our clothes?" Leo said, bending to look in the back-seat. "I don't even care if you're an undercover CIA agent. You're my hero."

They took turns changing in the car, and then all three of them piled in. Meryl passed them the blankets she'd pulled out of the trunk and turned the heat all the way up.

"So . . . why *do* you have a secret tunnel to the ocean in your office?" Leo asked.

"I like to swim," Meryl said, without the faintest hint of irony.

"Are you a witch?" Aziza demanded.

"No," Meryl said.

"Then what—"

"Don't ask me that, because I can't say," Meryl said, in that gentle but firm tone of voice she used to tell small children to *only take one* piece of the candy from the bowl on her desk. Aziza couldn't find the words for another question—there was too much she wanted to ask—before Meryl spoke again. "Was this a random attack?"

"I don't know," Aziza said. "I don't think so. I think they were after me."

Meryl grimaced and did not tell her she was being paranoid. She flicked on her signal and navigated a U-turn in silence.

"Do you know anything about this?" Aziza pressed. "The hounds, the boundary—"

"I don't, not more than what you've told me. I was trying not to get involved," she said. "This changes everything, of course."

"Does that mean you're going to help us?" Leo asked hopefully. *Us*, he kept saying, and even though she'd accepted that *maybe* Leo wasn't going anywhere, she still had to try one more time to give him an out.

"Leo," she began, with great conviction, "you don't have to—"

But Leo gave her such an exasperated look—and was such a sorry sight, between the blanket pulled up to his nose and the clumps of damp hair half obscuring his eyes—that she decided not to finish that sentence.

"As much as I can, yes," Meryl said, answering his question. "I'm no expert on blækhounds, but if they're targeting Aziza, then someone is making them do that. And only necromancers can command blækhounds." Meryl peered at Aziza with her large, liquid blue eyes. "Have you offended a necromancer lately?"

"Wish you could've told me that last week instead of handing me a stack of library books on hellhound lore," Aziza grumbled.

"Last week, I didn't know you were a target," Meryl said, in that soft voice that made Aziza feel like a child, not in a patronizing sort of way, but in a *comforted* one. She fought that feeling valiantly, as she would have preferred to hold on to her righteous anger for a little longer. She'd always thought her only connection to the magical world was Jiddo. That she was alone in this. Meryl could've changed that, but she hadn't. Aziza *wanted* to be angry.

"If I'd known then," Meryl went on, "I would have done everything I could to make sure you never ended up in this situation."

Aziza looked away from her, but it was too late. The anger at Meryl's secrecy was . . . not gone, but on its way out.

"I don't even know any—" She fell silent, thinking, and then a memory came to her: "At St. Sithney's, when the hound attacked me and Leo, I saw a boy in the woods. I think he called it off."

"If he saved us back then, why'd he just try to kill us?" Leo asked.

She shook her head, lost, and tugged her borrowed blanket closer. Soon they pulled up to the library. Leo thanked Meryl profusely, promised to wash the blanket and return it later, and got out to start his car, leaving Aziza alone with her.

"Anything else you wanted to share?" Aziza asked stiffly. "Anything at all?"

"Nothing," Meryl said, with a sad smile.

"Fine." She turned away. Stopped. Turned back. "Did you at least have a good reason?"

Meryl bit her lip. "I can say, with complete honesty, that anytime I've lied to you, it was only because I had to."

That didn't make anything better, but she found that she believed her.

"Thanks for picking us up," she muttered, and left before Meryl could reply. She climbed into the passenger seat of Leo's car and found him warming his hands in front of the vent, looking through the windshield at the gaping hole where the library's front doors used to be, as if deep in thought.

"So how do we find him?" he said.

"Find him?"

He nodded at the damage to the library and shot her a sly grin. "Can't let him get away with that, can we?"

Not for the first time, and probably not for the last, they were on exactly the same page.

CHAPTER 12

TRISTAN

AT ELEVEN YEARS old, Leo was all curls and awkwardly long limbs and oversized glasses, because back then he only wore his contacts on the soccer field. You could hear his laugh from across the room. He was the most mesmerizing thing Tristan had ever seen.

That was his clearest memory of being eleven: learning what it was like to feel completely winded by the sight of another boy.

They had the same art elective. Leo couldn't draw to save his life. Tristan taught him about crosshatching; after that, Leo still couldn't draw, and Tristan was burdened with the knowledge of what his deodorant smelled like and what his laugh sounded like up close, as he leaned over Tristan's shoulder to watch his hand move across the paper. Once they started talking, they just never stopped; that first conversation spilled into lunch the next period, and then picked back up the next day seamlessly, and then they were trading numbers, and eventually the stretches of time they could go without talking shrank to nearly nothing.

That was how they ended up friends, even though Tristan was as different from sweet, athletic, popular Leo Merritt as it was possible to be. Leo was loved by everyone. Tristan was a loner at best and a loser at worst. But Leo never did get bored of him. Later, he'd look back and wish he could pinpoint when it happened—when he and Leo became permanent fixtures in each other's lives. What had he done to earn that? What had he said? If he could somehow recreate those conversations, would the rest of it follow as naturally, as effortlessly as it had the first time?

This was how he remembered being twelve, thirteen: sitting with Leo in every class they shared, or on the bus, or in Leo's room; study sessions and video games; walking Hazel around the neighborhood on Halloween, dropping her off at home, and sneaking out again; waiting on the bleachers for Leo to finish soccer practice so they could walk home together; Leo guiding his hands into signs when he'd started teaching him ASL and they had still needed excuses to touch each other: *Hello. Yes. No. Thank you. Please.*

Tristan was absorbed into Leo's core group of friends, who then—reluctantly—became Tristan's friends, too. He never totally clicked with them. He couldn't have even said why. It wasn't like they weren't nice to him. They talked to him when Leo wasn't around, invited him to all the same places. But it was like there was a glass wall between him and them, a distance he didn't know how to breach. They were all tuned in to the same radio frequency and he could never find the right channel. But he was always on the same wavelength as Leo. And Leo had this way of pulling things out of him that Tristan never would have thought he'd tell anyone, like the things his father said to him when he got angry, and why he liked charcoals best, and how he didn't know what he wanted for his future except to go someplace far away from here.

Their friendship survived the transition to high school, and by then people had started to view them as a set. They would play off of each other, Tristan filling in the gaps when Leo's stories went off on a tangent, Leo pulling Tristan back into conversations when he began to withdraw into silence, and they somehow tricked everyone into thinking that Tristan belonged with them when he really just belonged with Leo. And still Tristan managed to convince himself that Leo only saw him as a friend, all the way up until he was fourteen and Leo was leaning over the homework they'd spread out on the floor to kiss him.

This was how he remembered being fourteen, fifteen: learning what it felt like to bury his fingers in the soft curls at the nape of Leo's neck; movie nights with Leo's family, who were always happy to see him and never yelled; staying over at Leo's like he'd been doing for years, except one night Leo waited until everyone else was asleep and crept into the guest room, and after that they never slept apart if they didn't have to. On nights when Tristan wasn't supposed to be at Leo's place at all, sometimes he'd still end up biking there at midnight, needing to get away from home after the really bad fights with his parents. Leo would sneak him in through the back door and Tristan would go home again before dawn, feeling better, even if Leo hadn't said or done anything, had just let Tristan curl up in his bed and shiver against him.

No one knew about them. Not their friends, not even Leo's family. Leo swore he didn't mind the secrecy; he knew it would be a disaster for Tristan if his parents found out.

"I don't want you to be afraid when you're with me," he'd say.

And Tristan wasn't afraid.

But that silence was a greater sacrifice for Leo than he could've understood. At least at first. At least until he found out about the curse.

It was inevitable, spending more time at Leo's house than his own, that one day he'd be there when Maria slipped up, spoke aloud, and spat out a little Fowler's toad, which trilled happily into the sudden shocked silence around the dinner table. Then Leo told him about Spot, which explained all the "accidents" that happened around Greg. And then he made a third confession, about his own curse and what he expected to happen to him on his sixteenth birthday.

Tristan had never been happier.

It was like this: He believed in Greg's and Maria's curses. It was hard not to when he'd seen the proof croaking at him with its shrewd black eyes from the middle of the table while Maria covered her mouth in horror, Hazel laughed so hard she cried, Spot took advantage of the sudden chaos to flip Greg's plate into his lap, and Leo turned to Tristan with a look of utter dismay, as though his worst nightmare had come true. There was no way for Tristan to believe all that was anything but real. But he couldn't believe in Leo's curse, not in the same way. Leo's and Tristan's lives were so completely intertwined that for Leo to forget Tristan would mean losing most of his memories of the past four years or so. How could that be possible?

Maybe there was some arrogance on Tristan's part, too. No magic could be stronger than what he and Leo had. He never said it out loud, but deep down, that was how he felt—that love could conquer anything.

And Leo loved him back. That was all Tristan could think about, self-absorbed as he was. Leo thought Tristan was his "true love," in his own words. To hear Leo talk about the two of them with the same hopeless intensity that Tristan had always felt was kind of a revelation.

The night before Leo's birthday, Tristan had kissed Leo goodbye, for what he hadn't known would be the last time.

"If you forget me," he'd said, "I'll remind you."

"Promise?" Leo had asked, holding on to Tristan a little too tightly.

"I promise," Tristan had said, and he didn't move until Leo was ready to let him go.

He hadn't been prepared for what came next.

This was how he remembered being sixteen: He sat down next to Leo, like always, and Leo didn't look up. He said his name, and Leo turned around with no expression at all. Not a flicker of recognition. He could see him, hear him; the curse hadn't made Tristan *invisible* to him. But Leo didn't know him. Didn't remember being eleven, thirteen, fifteen together. Didn't love him.

It was like going back in time. He was the scrawny loner with ink stains on his hands, and Leo was the brilliant, charming jock, and they might as well have come from different planets.

"What?" Leo had asked.

And Tristan had mumbled, "Never mind," and slinked away.

He picked up on the "rules" of the curse quickly, that week, by watching other people interact with Leo. Everyone—friends, teachers, even people Tristan had never spoken to—wanted to know what had happened between them. *Why aren't you talking to Tris? Are you fighting? What did he do?* Leo would shut down, his face going blank, and never said a word in response, like he couldn't hear their questions. Because he really couldn't. Anyone who brought up anything related to Leo's lost memories, anything related to Tristan, went ignored. If they pressed, he'd end up with a headache, his brow furrowing in pain, his hand rising to touch the base of his skull gingerly, his eyes clouded with panic and confusion as the curse defended itself by ripping into his mind. Tristan rapidly grew to hate every person who tried to badger Leo about their "fight." He didn't know what would happen if he approached Leo again, or if someone reintroduced him to Leo as a stranger. Would the curse make Leo forget him over and over? And could Tristan survive that—*watching* himself be forgotten, over and over, by the only person who really knew him?

He was afraid to find out. So he didn't.

Tristan let people believe they'd had some kind of falling-out. He played at indifference. Inside, grief poisoned him. No one had known he'd been dating Leo, so there was no one he could talk to about what had happened, even if Tristan could've found a way to explain it without bringing up the curse. And—just as he'd always suspected—all of *their* friends were really *Leo's* friends, in the end.

Leo, for his part, had permanent bags under his eyes. He never took notes in class anymore. If a teacher asked him a question, all they got in response was a blank stare and a mumbled "Sorry, I don't know." Half the time he skipped school altogether. He was falling apart right before Tristan's eyes, and Tristan could do nothing to help him. Because Tristan *was* nothing to him.

Isolation and grief became anger and recklessness, and in a rebellious fit—convinced that nothing mattered, anyway, and he had nothing else to lose—he came out to his parents. Just blurted it out in the middle of a fight.

Turned out he still had a *lot* to lose, like a place to sleep at night.

The hag found him camping out in the woods. She made him an offer he couldn't refuse. Ten years of service in exchange for the thing he wanted most in the world: a broken curse. It had seemed like a bargain. What was ten years compared to the rest of his life? A life he could spend with Leo?

And this, Tristan knew, was how he would one day remember being seventeen:

Seeing Leo again in a snowy forest dimly lit by distant Christmas lights, not with his own eyes but through the cruel, starving eyes of a hound. Learning the hag wanted Tristan to hunt down the girl who'd saved Leo—the one who had protected Leo when he couldn't, protected Leo from *him*. It was like waking up *into* a nightmare instead of waking up out of it: There was no way to win, and every road led to himself or Leo or both of them dead. Every choice he'd ever made had brought him here, and he had now run out of choices.

For the blood of a bondservant was a signal—but so were other things, too. The hair he'd left on the collars of the uniforms still hanging in the closet at his parents' house. The fingerprints he'd pressed into his textbooks at school. The love he'd given to the only person he had ever loved. These were the marks he had made in the world, and they were all of them signals.

The hag didn't make empty threats. If he didn't obey, she would go after Leo.

What would Leo do? he asked himself, but it was a pointless question. Leo would never have put himself in this situation in the first place. Leo was *good*, and Tristan—

Tristan was bound.

CHAPTER 13

LEO

JUST THIS ONCE, he thought, as he slowly turned the house key and pushed the door open a crack, *just this once, please let me go upstairs without throwing a fit, and I'll never complain about you again.*

True quiet was rare in the Merritt household: Even when everyone was asleep, Spot liked to entertain himself by whistling through the vents or rattling the shower curtain in the upstairs bathroom. He used to knock things off the dresser in the master bedroom, waking Mom and Dad in the middle of the night, but they'd quickly learned not to leave anything out in the open.

Leo locked the door and paused, listening. He couldn't hear anything, which was bad, because if Spot wasn't making any noise, then that meant—

Something shoved him between the shoulder blades, *hard*. He stumbled, the keys flying out of his hand and landing on the floor with a clatter that was deafening in the silence.

"*Spot!*" he hissed, whipping around, but no one was there—no one he could see, anyway.

He scooped up his keys and trudged upstairs, running a hand through his damp hair. Even with the heat on, he shivered. His clothes were still wet and his underwear felt like literal ice. He couldn't get to bed fast enough.

But a noise stopped him outside his door. Not Spot, this time. A whimper from the room across the hall. Hazel was having another nightmare.

Her nightmares were about fire. That was all she ever told him. She was always ashen and shaky when he woke her, and it took her a long time to get back to sleep after. Sometimes he'd stay up with her, and they'd play card games until she dozed off or dawn came, whichever happened first. Or she'd reread her favorite comic books, a towel wedged into the gap under her door to hide the light in case their parents passed by on their way to the kitchen.

Tonight he barely had to touch her shoulder before she woke with a start. She sat up too fast, breathing hard.

"You okay?"

She twisted the blanket between her fingers and nodded.

"Want me to stay?" he asked, though he didn't think he'd make it through even one round of Go Fish before passing out.

She shook her head. He would've gone then, but her hand shot out and grabbed his sleeve.

"Why are your clothes wet? Were you with Aziza?"

Her voice was scratchy with exhaustion. Streetlight filtered in through the curtains and turned her eyes glassy.

"Yeah," he admitted, and stopped there, hesitating. He didn't even know where to start answering her other question, or if he should. One nightmare was enough for today; she probably didn't need to hear about the hounds right now.

He expected her to badger him for details anyway, but she had already moved on to more pressing concerns, it seemed. Because the next thing she wanted to know was: "Is she your girlfriend?"

"Uh, no," he said, startled. "Even if she was, why would that bother you? I thought you liked her."

He had regaled Hazel with the story of how Aziza had saved him at the fair, playing up some of the more dramatic details he'd softened for Mom and Dad's sake. Then he'd announced to the entire family that Aziza was a witch, and while his parents hadn't enjoyed the conversation that had followed, Hazel had been rightly impressed.

"I *do*, but what about your true love?" She picked at a loose thread in her blanket rather than meet his eyes. "You said you weren't going to give up on them."

She knows, he thought, not for the first time.

Hazel knew the identity of his true love, and had probably tried to tell him, but couldn't, because of the curse.

"I haven't given up," he assured her. "Aziza's going to help me break the curse."

"I could help, too," she said.

"We don't really have a plan yet. But when we do—"

"*Then* I can help?"

"Sure," he said. Hazel grinned, like she'd forgotten all about the nightmare already. "What would you have done if I *was* dating her?"

"Sabotage," she said, without hesitation.

"Okay. Good to know."

He left her to finally go to bed. As the line between consciousness and sleep blurred, a name rose in his mind like foam on the crest of a wave—a name closely guarded in his heart, haunting him as effectively as any poltergeist. But soon enough it slipped away again, and by the time he woke up in the morning, it was gone.

Saturdays meant sleeping in and waking up to an empty house.

His hand groped for his phone; he squinted at the screen. A text from fifteen minutes ago informed him that Mom and Dad had gone out for groceries—they always ran errands together, so neither of them would be alone if a curse-related mishap occurred in public. Hazel and her friends had biked to the park.

Leo flopped over in bed and buried his face in his pillow. He'd been too tired to shower last night, and now his body felt like one big clump of grime. His skin was dry and scratchy from the saltwater, there was somehow sand in his hair, and the smell of brine was lodged so deep in his nose he was pretty sure he'd dreamed it. To make matters worse, he had work today.

He had a part-time job at one of those counter-service build-your-own-meal restaurants spooning rice and salad into compostable take-out bowls. His parents had split the cost of a used car with him and paid for the insurance; Leo took care of the gas and any repairs it needed. That was mainly why he worked—to fund the car and the trips he'd taken out of state chasing magic. Funny, in retrospect, that he'd gone all that way only to wind up learning everything he could've wanted to know about magic right here in Blackthorn.

Almost everything, anyway.

He stumbled out of his bedroom, still half-asleep, his backpack slung over one shoulder. As he made his way to the stairs, a bang made him jump—but it was only Spot. He'd knocked the door to the master bedroom off its hinges again, and it had fallen. Dad was going to be *so* annoyed. He'd only just fixed it last week.

They had learned a few things about Spot and how to live with him, over the years. If Dad followed a routine—waking up and going to bed at about the same time, eating meals at about the same time, staying in the house as much as possible—Spot was almost tame. Deviations from the routine, new places and people, and moments of high emotion—like arguments—disturbed Spot and resulted in loud, aggressive reactions. He wasn't a spirit, like the Man at the Bus Stop or the Ash Witch; he wasn't really sentient, either, was truly an *it* rather than a *he*. He was nothing but magical energy carrying out the sole purpose it had been created for—like those robots that were just an arm, and all they could do was their one preprogrammed task.

Most furniture was too heavy for Spot to lift, but anything that he could've tipped over or dragged around was either mounted to the wall or nailed down. They had child locks on the kitchen cabinets and drawers to keep them from being opened and their contents flung at people's heads. They never left anything out in the open, not even a pen or a set of keys, because it would either disappear for days and turn up someplace inexplicable, like in a shoebox or the fridge, or it would be used as a weapon later on. But you couldn't Spot-proof the whole world. Once, in the early days of the curse, Spot had yanked the steering wheel from Dad's hands and driven him right off the road and into a ditch. He got away with nothing but a fractured wrist, but, for a long time after that, Dad had refused to get in a car with anyone else.

Leo lingered there, staring at the open doorway into Mom and Dad's room.

He shouldn't. He really shouldn't.

But did he have another choice?

They just left, he told himself. *I have plenty of time. I'll be in and out in a minute.*

He stepped over the fallen door. Morning light spilled into the room. His eyes went to the closet first. It was a walk-in with a shelf on top where they kept stacks of photo albums, and—he didn't really know what else. He'd never thought about it. Now seemed like a good time to start, so he cleared the shelf section by section, taking down boxes, checking their contents, and then replacing them just the way he'd found them before moving on. Mostly he learned that his parents hung on to every receipt and also every crayon drawing he or Hazel had ever made, which was sweet, and made him feel even guiltier about his snooping.

Just when he was about to give up, he came across something . . . unusual. It was a box of sketchbooks, and the drawings within were a far cry from the crayon scribblings he'd set aside with amusement before. They were mostly pencil and charcoal. Almost professional looking. And vaguely familiar, like maybe he'd glimpsed some of them over someone's shoulder one time or another. But his parents couldn't have done these. And he sure didn't, and neither did Hazel. He flipped through them, at first looking for a signature— there wasn't one—and then just looking. Entire pages of anatomy studies—eyes; shoulders; hands in different poses and from different angles, fingers curled and wrists flexing. Loose, sketchy figures in motion. Everyday objects—water bottles, bird feathers, cuffed sleeves—rendered with utmost care, over and over as the artist had practiced shading and perspective.

Most of the sketchbooks were full, except the one on top, which stopped halfway. All those empty pages gave him a weird sense of foreboding—like in a dystopian movie when the camera panned over the sad, crumbling remnants of the Before Times, a mug of tea abandoned on a counter or a car left haphazardly on the side of the road. Like someone's life had been interrupted. He shut the incomplete sketchbook and ran his hand down the cover, lingering over the faded spots on the spine and the corners where someone's touch had worried away the dye. There was a deep, empty ache in his chest, and, unaccountably, his eyes had started to sting. He scrubbed at them, surprised to find them damp.

He replaced the sketchbook and stood to put the box back where he'd found it. Who did those belong to? Why had Leo thought they looked familiar? Could it have something to do with . . .

He was turning off the closet light, wandering back into the hall on autopilot. There, he stopped. What had he come here to do again? Oh, right. Clues about the curse. He just had to figure out where to start, quickly, before his parents came back.

He stepped over the fallen door. Morning light spilled into the room. His eyes went to the closet first. Should he—no, he didn't think he'd find anything useful there. He wasn't sure why. Just a feeling. So he turned to the dresser instead.

Ugh. This is so wrong, he thought. But, still, he methodically opened and inspected the drawers. Socks, jewelry, a few folded bundles of cash, passports and insurance cards. A row of lacy bras—Leo slammed that drawer shut, nose wrinkled. Then down to the lower drawers—more clothes, folders of school and medical records.

Nothing out of the ordinary. He'd invaded his parents' privacy for no reason.

Then—in the bottom right drawer, the final one—he found a wooden jewelry box.

Gingerly, he pulled it out and set it on the floor. It was warm to the touch and had a flat lid with a hinge. He very much doubted it still contained jewelry. If it did, it wouldn't be hidden away like this.

Leo flicked open the clasp with his thumb and pushed the lid up.

Inside was an old picture of Leo. He was no more than six years old, with a curly mop of hair that half obscured his eyes. He held a toddler Hazel in his lap, his arms wrapped around her; they wore matching grins.

Leo squinted at the photo, turned it over, held it up to the light. There was nothing all that interesting about it. Sure, it was cute, but there was no reason for it to be in a box all by itself instead of filed away in one of the photo albums.

He checked the box again. That was when he spotted it: a scrap of something translucent, membrane-thin, about twice the size of a quarter. He had to lift it off the bottom with a fingernail. But he knew instantly it was not as delicate as it looked. Filmy and flexible, yes, but tough. Not easily torn. It warmed his skin, as if it'd been microwaved, and gleamed faintly in the light.

A noise startled him. The ice maker in the fridge, or the garage door grinding open?

He strained his ears. No footsteps downstairs, no voices in the hall. Ice maker, then. But his heart still raced. Forget the hounds. If Maria Merritt found her son going through her drawers, she would *end him*.

He replaced the photo but pocketed the unidentifiable fragment of warmth. His parents wouldn't miss it right away—and he had to show it to Aziza. Carefully, he slid the box back into the corner of the drawer, trying not to move anything else. He was tempted to skip work and go talk to Aziza right away, but if he missed any more shifts, he was going to get fired.

It could be nothing.

He could only guess, from the way it was hidden and the special box it had been placed in, that it was valuable. And he had to believe that the tools to find the truth and break his curse were within reach. He'd needed a lead. Now, he had one.

CHAPTER 14

TRISTAN

THE NIGHT AZIZA and Leo escaped from the hounds, Tristan passed out on a park bench again. The slats were hard and uneven beneath him, and he had to curl up to fit, the heel of his boot pressed to one end and his backpack wedged against the other. He had his head resting on it and an arm wrapped around it for good measure, and he'd pulled up his hood and collar to hide as much of his face as possible. In his layers, he looked bulkier, but he'd still been woken more than once by would-be thieves, people who were even more desperate than he was. His hands were tucked into his sleeves. The hounds had shredded his only pair of gloves during their brawl; it was a miracle the scarf had gotten away unscathed. Even with that and his coat, there was always a point in the night when he became so cold he went numb all over. When he woke up, he was unsurprised to find his bare fingers bone-white and rigid as the bench he'd slept on; later, when he warmed up, the ugly red blisters of frostbite would form on his knuckles. It wouldn't get any worse than that—the bond prevented him from sustaining more permanent injuries—but it still hurt like hell.

Images of the night before played on the inside of his eyelids every time he blinked. He'd sent the hounds after Aziza to capture, not kill. But given permission to hunt, given *encouragement* for the first time when all he'd done before was try and curb the worst of their violence, the hounds had gone almost completely out of his control. As he'd waited in the woods—watching everything unfold through the hounds' eyes—there had been a moment of pure terror when he'd thought they would go too far. He wanted to bang his head against the nearest wall when he recalled Leo's defiant glare, seen by the hound through blazing headlights and the windshield of his car.

The hag wasn't giving up on Aziza. He wasn't entirely sure why she had fixated on *this* victim. If any witch could, theoretically, become a hag, then maybe the hag didn't want competition. Or maybe there was a part of the hag that was . . . jealous. Because Aziza was what she used to be. Maybe, deep down, there was a tiny part of the hag that was repulsed by what she'd become.

Or maybe Tristan was projecting.

Regardless, if the hag was going to send him after Aziza again—and of course she was—and if Leo was going to be at Aziza's side the whole time—and of *course* he would be—then Tristan needed to be better. Twice now the hounds had almost hurt Leo. *Tristan's* hounds, whether he liked it or not. The hag had ordered him to take control of his new powers, but there was a part of him that had resisted, had refused to learn, because those powers disgusted him. That resistance ended now. To protect Leo, he had to become exactly what the hag wanted: a real necromancer and a true master of the hounds.

As Blackthorn woke, the shops rolled up their metal shutters and the coffee carts vanished. This was an older part of town, where the streets were winding and crooked, and clusters of shops and businesses staggered into neighborhoods full of sleepy row houses.

He'd grown up in Blackthorn, but there was a difference between the Blackthorn of his old life and the Blackthorn on the edges of society, the people and places no one looked at unless they had to. Late-night Blackthorn, when the trains stopped running. The Blackthorn of transient vagrant communities, people like him, huddling around small fires beneath the underpass to the north, only to flee in the morning because if they stayed too long, the cops would clear them out. Blackthorn at sunrise when its clay and sandstone cliffs practically glowed. Today he would be learning about the hounds' Blackthorn.

The hounds loved sunlight; they liked its shadows and the intriguing scents of all the waking things passing in and out of them. But daytime wasn't for hunting. It was for rest. The hounds didn't sleep, but they did retreat into the shadow plane until nightfall, existing just under the surface of the corporeal world: in the crook of a tree, beneath the scurrying of squirrels and insects, or in the cracks on the sidewalk, their shadow tongues occasionally swiping out unnoticed to chase the smell of fast food or sweat. But the two hounds from yesterday were still keyed up from their failed hunt, and he had to retrieve them before they were seen, or worse—before they murdered someone in broad daylight.

Every few days, the hounds killed for the hag. Where Tristan had delivered her one victim every week, the hounds had a bottomless capacity for murder. But the hag had learned from the fallout of the holiday fair massacre. People all over the city were on alert, investing in security cameras and guard dogs. Vigilante hunters stormed the woods, too near to her territory for comfort—and she could kill anyone who crossed into her land, but if she drew too much attention, eventually she would be fending off attacks. She liked how she lived now, eating her fill, slowly growing her strength, and she wanted no disturbances.

So the hounds made no more attacks on large groups. Instead, they picked off people they caught alone, especially at night and especially in or near St. Sithney's. Which meant mostly people like Tristan. The ones who had no choice but to be out alone after dark.

There were a lot more missing people in Blackthorn these days, but very few confirmed "wolf attacks." Just rumors.

One of the two wayward hounds was investigating a landfill, but the other was camped out in an alley between a 7-Eleven and a Chinese restaurant. As the street outside filled up with people, as the restaurant opened for lunchtime and the smell of grease and salt and ginger soaked the air, the hound bared its teeth, which dripped saliva. Tristan felt gravel under its paws, its tail brushing the wall behind it as it swished, its belly scraping the ground as it inched closer to the mouth of the alley.

He picked up his pace and took the train, ignoring the turnstiles and instead catching the emergency exit door as a woman with a stroller came out of it. By the time he got to the right 7-Eleven, the hound was almost close enough to the front of the alley to be seen, barely hidden behind a few stacks of empty shipping crates.

It started up a low growl when he stepped near. Its reflective eyes and white teeth gleamed through the darkness, a nauseating, violent grin. The bites and claw marks he'd gotten from them were still healing, and burned at the sight of it; he hadn't been this close to any of the hounds since that day at his parents' house.

There's only one of them this time, he reminded himself, *and you literally can't die unless she wants you to.*

Nor could he lose any of his ritual-knife-wielding fingers. But would the bond decide that he could do without some of his other body parts?

Footsteps, laughter, the rumble of traffic from the street behind him. The hound tensed as he drew even closer—and he felt that, too, the tightness in its muscles.

"You have to leave," he said, in an undertone. "Even *she* doesn't want you hunting like this."

He kept going, step by step, cautious but steady. Hands in his pockets, shoulders relaxed in a deliberate slouch. This wasn't a fight, not like last time. All the hound had to do was unwind itself into the shadows like it always did, and *behave*.

Almost level with it now, close enough to reach out and touch its snout if he wanted, which he didn't. It had ceased its growling, but it watched him like the woods watched an earthworm, like it was a measure of centuries more complex than he could ever fathom, and his existence in its presence was beneath its attention.

"Just *go*," he said, and then two things happened in quick succession.

First, deeper in the alley, a door clattered open and someone came out of the restaurant heaving a pair of trash bags. He probably wouldn't have paid Tristan any mind, only Tristan jumped, flighty as a prey animal, and the man looked up at him, and then his eyes traveled down, following the angle of Tristan's body. His eyes refocused, adjusting to the dimness of the alley, picking out the hound's outline. He drew in a breath, and Tristan *knew* he was going to shout and alert everyone on the street and inside the kitchen, and Tristan was in the middle of town and had nowhere to escape to—

Second, the hound lunged at Tristan teeth-first.

All he could think was, *Not again.*

But there was no pain. The hound's paws slammed against his

shoulders, and he fell flat on his back with the hound on top of him. His skull should've bashed against the concrete, but it didn't; he fell, and then he wasn't falling, but he wasn't on the ground, either, he wasn't *anything*. It was cold and pitch-black, and it was like the air had gone solid and was crushing closed around him. The only sensation he understood was the hound's breath in his face, its weight on top of him. It couldn't have lasted more than a moment or two. Then his body connected with something solid, at last, but it wasn't concrete. It was softer. And fucking freezing. The hound's weight disappeared—he flailed, hands still instinctively trying to catch himself, eyes screwed shut against an impact that had already happened. He opened them with a gasp, feeling—before he saw—that he was lying in the snow. Overhead, a web of bare tree branches told him he was in the woods. The hound sat nearby, eyeing this graceless display with disgust. Tristan shoved himself upright, staring at it, and then down at himself, needing to make sure he was all . . . in one piece.

"What just happened?" he asked aloud, as if he and the hound spoke the same language.

But he already knew the answer.

He'd wanted to escape, and the hound had obliged—not because he had commanded it, but because it had decided that this course of action suited it, too. So it had taken him and gone through the shadows—he had shadow-traveled *with* it.

He'd never imagined he could do something like that. It was the hound that had done it, technically, but it had done it in response to *his* thoughts and tapped into the bond to keep them tethered during the short trip. It was a disturbing thought. He was *human*, he wasn't a hound or a shadow, he shouldn't have been able to *disappear* from that alley and end up miles away in the space of a few breaths. But the worst part was—how much he had liked it.

He busied himself getting to his feet, dusting himself off, brushing his hands over where the hound's paws had landed on his shoulders to make sure it hadn't torn his coat—small blessings, it hadn't.

"I'm not going to thank you," he told the hound, petulantly.

Its lips pulled back from its teeth in that alarming fanged grin. In one swift, sinuous motion, it stood, dove under the jutting roots of the nearest tree as if into a pool of water, and vanished. Just a ripple of fur and the flick of its tail and then nothing.

He was halfway back to St. Sithney's before he realized that the hound, being not only a literal monster but also an absolute *asshole*, had left him in Elphame. He could feel it, Elphame's magic—warm in a prickly sort of way, like when he wrapped his freezing hands around a paper cup full of coffee and the heat seeped into him, pins and needles as sensation returned.

He hadn't been here since he'd buried those bodies.

Maybe it was that thought, and the subsequent lead weight in his stomach, that made the Ash Witch fall into step beside him. Her gait was light, almost inaudible, barefoot as she was. He didn't look at her.

"Rather cold out for a stroll through the woods, isn't it?" she said, with a tinge of wry humor. She wore only a thin dress that was all rags, so dirty it was hard to tell what color it was. But she never seemed to feel the cold, not even in the middle of a snowstorm. Her voice was smooth and refined—deceptively inviting. Rope had been tied around her ankles and wrists so tightly it cut into her skin, though she had long since been freed, the frayed ends of her bonds trailing after her.

He didn't reply, though he knew her, sort of. He'd glimpsed her once or twice. She normally ignored him as she paced along the trails that wound through St. Sithney's and into the nearby campgrounds in the woods. The Ash Witch was one of Blackthorn's spirits—the spirit of a witch who had been unjustly imprisoned and condemned to burn alive. In death, she had returned to dole out her own kind of justice as she saw fit.

Spirits were not exactly fae, the hag had told him, but they were an amalgamation of many energies and many magics, including the wild magic of Elphame. Thus they could move through the boundary at will. The hag had told him about the Ash Witch because she had suspected that their paths would cross sooner or later. He should never speak to the Ash Witch, the hag said, even if she addressed him first. This was different from how she'd counseled him to deal with fae, like the nymph, who would have been deeply and maybe even violently offended had he simply ignored her the way he ignored the Ash Witch now. And the hag said not to look her in the eye, either, for she could only pass judgment on those who faced her willingly.

Tristan hadn't wanted to ask what happened if she judged you guilty.

"I would pay much more than a penny to know what fascinating thoughts crossed your mind just now, Tristan Drake," the Ash Witch said, leaning over so that she spoke almost directly into his ear. If she had been alive, he would've felt her exhale.

"I don't use that name anymore," he said, meaning the family name that wasn't his because he had no family. Then he cringed. Had he *really* just done that?

He didn't look at her, but he heard the smile in her voice.

"Oh? Why not?"

Now that he'd spoken to the Ash Witch, her magic compelled him to answer again.

"It doesn't feel like mine," he said, the words digging themselves out of him.

He stopped in his tracks, unknotted his scarf with shaking hands, and tied it over his eyes as a blindfold. His heart hammered.

"Clever boy," she said. Her skirt rustled as she moved around him. "What name would you prefer, then? Just Tristan? Or maybe . . . Tris?"

"*Don't*," he said.

"What would he think of you?"

"He'd—" *He'd hate me,* he thought, but that didn't ring true, because he'd never known Leo to hate anyone. Not even whoever or whatever had cursed him. And since it didn't feel true, he couldn't say it to the Ash Witch. "I don't know," he said finally.

"You do," she said, her voice almost tender. "Look at me. The answers to this and many other questions are within you. I can help you see them, if only you let me."

He shook his head minutely, lips pressed together until it became painful, and at last he had no choice but to respond: "No."

The rustling, the scuff of her feet over the detritus. She spoke in a way that was almost maternal but prowled around him like a predator. He replied to her every question, her demands, her tearful entreaties, with a *No* that became weaker and more strained each time he repeated it.

In his makeshift blindfold, everything was darkness. He shut his eyes, though it made no difference either way; he couldn't shut out her voice. It had to be almost noon by now, or past, which meant he had no chance of finding an open fairy door until the next witching hour. He was stuck here for the next few hours at least. Unless he could get the hound to come back, and shadow-travel with it again . . . Of course, on any given day, the hounds obeyed his commands only a fraction of the time, and it usually took all his concentration. How many tries would it take to get even one of them to respond under conditions like these? And there was no guarantee the hound wouldn't just drop him someplace even worse.

But he had set out today wanting to work on his control. Here was his opportunity, then. His test. If he could focus with the Ash Witch in his ear, then he could do anything.

Ha. No, maybe not anything.

But at least he wouldn't have to stay with the Ash Witch until sunset.

"No," he said hoarsely, only half listening to the spirit now. He took a deep breath and began.

CHAPTER 15

AZIZA

SHE SHIVERED AWAKE, as if to the touch of sharp nails dragging down her spine.

Something was scratching at her window. Too persistent to be a branch scraping against the glass. Too deliberate. The jagged noise crept under her skin and licked at her bones.

Her first clear, waking thought was that there was nothing in reach she could use to defend herself. Her pocketknife was in her coat, hanging from a hook on the door. She could make a break for it, or she could turn around first and see what she was dealing with.

The scratching continued.

Aziza gritted her teeth. In a smooth, quick motion, she swung her legs over the side of the bed and sat up. Whatever was waiting for her, she wanted to meet it head-on.

It *was* a branch.

But the branch was attached to a wooden arm, which curved into a mossy chest, and above that, a pair of tree-sap eyes peered inside at Aziza.

Startled, Aziza moved to the window. She hesitated, her hand hovering over the latch, but then she knelt and opened a crack to speak through.

The nymph said, "I was starting to wonder if you were dead."

"How did you get through the wards?" Aziza whispered.

"I have something of yours," the nymph said. "A token freely given. A link, gatewalker, to you."

She held up the candy cane pin, glinting in the low light from the street. Viny tendrils wriggled under the crack between window and frame, forcing the opening wider. The nymph hoisted herself up and sat on the windowsill, unfurling against the ledge like a blossom.

"Why are you here?" Aziza asked.

"There are humans in the woods," came the nymph's breeze of a voice. "Not the little woods scattered through your metal and cement. The big woods outside your festering, teeming, disgusting collection of burrows and waste. The woods which are not yours, but which are *ours*."

Aziza shook her head, her braid starting to come loose with the motion. Impatiently, she combed the strands out with her fingers.

"Get to the point," Aziza said. "I can't stop people from going into the woods."

"Not people. *Hunters*," said the nymph. "They stomp around at all hours, leaving their stink everywhere. They kill. They cannot find the hounds, so they kill things that did not need to die, things before their time, and they leave the cadavers lying there like an insult. Their trash poisons the soil and the water. They are loud, and disrespectful, and careless—"

As the nymph spoke in shivery rustles and crackles, her voice snapped—like twigs breaking—over the words she emphasized. Vines crept over the walls. Dead leaves had begun to blow across the room, gathering in little piles against Aziza's shoes where she'd tossed them carelessly, her backpack, the foot of her dresser and nightstand, the textbooks she'd left lying open with pages of unfinished homework inside. Aziza watched, dismayed, as a squirrel dashed across the floor to take cover under the bed.

"Okay, okay, stop," she told the nymph. "You're saying you want me to do something about the hunters?"

"*Yes*," the nymph hissed.

"But why?" Aziza was baffled. "No, I know why you want them gone. I'm just shocked you'd ask me."

"You are a gatewalker," said the nymph. "Understand what that means: You do not only protect humans from fae. You protect fae from humans as well. It is your duty."

Aziza hadn't thought of it that way before. She'd never needed to.

"This is . . . It's beyond my power," she admitted, a little ashamed. "The hunters are there for the hounds, and the hounds are being controlled by a necromancer. I can't do anything about the hounds until I find him."

The nymph's eyes gleamed as she tilted her head. "You mean the boy."

"What boy?" Aziza said, too fast. "What did you see?"

"The hounds took their prey to Elphame to feed in peace, and the boy cleaned up after them," said the nymph. "He gifted one of the cadavers with deathlessness and then he took it away. I suppose he was amusing himself."

The necromancer. She'd seen him.

"What did he look like?" Aziza asked, breathless.

"Like a human."

"Yes, but—what color was his hair, his skin? How old was he, could you tell?"

She made a series of creaky whistling noises Aziza could only interpret as laughter.

"His skin and hair looked like yours: ugly. Humans are repulsive," the nymph informed her. "I suppose he was a young sort. He was younger than the fellow you live with."

"That's my *grandfather*. Everyone is younger than him," Aziza huffed.

"You desire information?" she asked, her voice low and calculating. "Knowing more about this boy . . . it would help you?"

Aziza bit her lip. This was a bad idea. "I do need information."

"And what if I could provide it?" the nymph asked.

"It would depend on what information you had," said Aziza lightly.

"He sleeps in the woods some nights."

"He *sleeps* there?" It was *January*.

"He stinks of death. I could find him from a mile away," said the nymph. Her bark-skin creased and whorled as she wrinkled her nose.

"Are you saying you would take me to him?"

"For the right price," said the nymph.

"*Price?*" Aziza gaped at her. "You came here demanding favors from me!"

"Performing your duty is not a *favor*, gatewalker," said the nymph. *Fucking fae. I wish I'd been a hearth witch instead.*

"What do you want?"

The nymph shifted, as if she meant to crawl down off the sill. She wasn't even fully inside, but it was startling how much space she took up. Aziza forced herself not to step back.

"Your hand," rasped the nymph.

"That's your price? Are you serious?"

"You have two," she reasoned.

"No! Absolutely not!" Aziza said, voice rising before she remembered Jiddo sleeping down the hall. "I'm not letting you cut off my hand."

"If you are not ready to bargain, perhaps I should not waste my time."

"Oh, cut it out. You know damn well that flesh and bone are far too high a price for simple information."

"Then give me a counteroffer, gatewalker."

"I'll give you a secret," she said. Secrets were an old staple of bargaining with fae, and she kept a mental cache of them for situations such as these. "A secret no one knows about me."

"What if I leave the flesh, but take the skin? A hand's worth of skin is a good price."

Aziza's stomach turned over. "No."

"It will grow back."

"I'll give you my firstborn child," said Aziza. As long as she never had children, she wouldn't have to pay this debt.

"Five fingernails. Those grow back, too, you know," the nymph countered.

Giving the nymph a piece of her body was akin to giving away some of her magic. A witch's magic wasn't a finite resource, but that didn't mean you wanted just anyone to take bits of it from you.

But she badly needed this information. Needed to know why the necromancer was after her and what he'd done to the boundary, *if* he was the one responsible. And there was no one else who could help her. The day after their narrow escape from the hounds at the library, she had realized that Jiddo, like Meryl, must have known the blækhounds were tied to a necromancer. But he hadn't told her. She had *asked* if the boy in the woods was a witch. Jiddo had said he wasn't sure. Maybe that was true in the most literal sense, but he could've told her about the *possibility*. He had withheld information from her on purpose.

And if she couldn't turn to Jiddo, then she had to turn to those who *would* help her. Even if that help came at a cost.

She sighed. "A lock of hair. To be given *after* you've held up your end. Take it or leave it."

"Done," said the nymph. The jagged seam of her mouth curled up in a nasty smile. "I can take you to him now."

"In the morning. I'm bringing an ally."

"Very well," said the nymph, prying herself away from the edge of Aziza's window. She left bits of bark behind, as if she had fused partway into the wood of the frame.

"Wait," said Aziza. "What name should I call, if I need you?"

"I answer to Eirlys," said the nymph, withdrawing.

"Just take the damn squirrel with you."

Eirlys slipped away down the side of Aziza's house. Aziza spent the next thirty minutes scraping leftover bark off her window frame so that she could close it properly, and when she'd finished, the squirrel was indeed gone, but the rest of it—leaves, vines, fungi—remained. Without her noticing, a ring of mushrooms had sprouted around her textbooks, and patches of moss coated her bedposts. Aziza sighed as she bent to brush the grit off her backpack; she plucked a snail off the zipper.

When at last she fell into bed to seize a couple more hours of fitful sleep, the scent of the forest found its way into her dreams.

As dawn crystallized into the rose-tinged gold of a Blackthorn morning, Aziza and Leo met Eirlys at the southern edge of St. Sithney's Park.

"Hurry," she rasped. "He never stays in one place for long."

She took them even further south, in a winding route that required them to fight through tangles of brittle underbrush and clomp through sticky patches of mud, striped with half-melted ice from last night's snowfall. Finally, she stopped and gestured with her spiny fingers through a gap in the woods, where the trees skirted around a bend in a stream.

"Follow the water for as long as it takes a hummingbird's wings to beat twenty thousand times, and you will find the one you seek." She held out her hand. "Pay your debt, gatewalker."

Aziza dug in her pocket and withdrew a lock of hair, tied together with a rubber band. Eirlys's fingers closed over it. A greedy light flared in her eyes. Aziza grimaced, wanting nothing more than to take it back.

But a bargain was a bargain; a hedgewitch's word was unbreakable, or it was worthless.

"Hummingbird wingbeats?" Leo repeated under his breath, as Eirlys vanished into the woods. "Didn't we *just* give her a watch the other day?"

They set off, tracing the bank of the stream. Their footsteps were inaudible in the soft, damp soil, and after a few minutes, she could make out the crackle of a fire and the sizzle of cooking meat. They took cover and peeked into a small clearing, where a bed of flat stone jutted into the stream.

And there he was—the boy she'd seen at St. Sithney's, huddled between the water and the trees, using a stick to prod at a lump of probably-rabbit as the fire licked up its sides.

His hair was platinum blond, almost white, with papery skin to match. A backpack rested on the ground nearby. Like his clothes, it was faded and frayed, with a quarter-sized hole in the side.

Leo drew Aziza back, out of earshot. "That can't be him."

"It's him," she insisted. "I saw him at St. Sithney's."

"But he—he looks like he needs help." Leo ran a hand distractedly through his hair. "I don't want to—I don't think we should—"

He trailed off, brow furrowed in what could've been either confusion or distress.

"What are we supposed to do—wait for the hounds to come back for us?" she hissed. "What's your problem?"

"I don't know," he mumbled.

She stared at him. They were *so close* to getting answers, and now Leo—who'd been downright courageous in every other absurd situation she'd put him in—was backing down?

"Are you all right?" she asked, suddenly concerned.

"I just . . . When Meryl said we were dealing with a necromancer, I was picturing some powerful, hotshot jerk," Leo said. "Not a homeless kid living in the woods."

"I'll try and talk to him before anything else," she promised. "Stay behind. Let him think I'm alone."

"This is a bad idea!" Leo whispered as she walked away.

The woods were quiet as she crept up to the boy's campsite, as if the world was holding its breath. Daylight filtered through the canopy, glinting off pockets of frost between roots and patches of ice in the stream. With the boundary as unstable as it was lately, any gleam could be a lesser fairy camouflaged in the sunbeams and yellow leaves; any twitch of a branch could be a wood nymph stretching its limbs or a wind sprite taunting the birds.

She inched into the clearing; but she wasn't careful enough, because the scuff of her boots made the necromancer snap to attention. He shot to his feet, leaving his meal burning in the fire.

"What are you *doing* here?" he said.

Of all the reactions she'd expected, that hadn't been one of them.

"What am *I* doing?" she said, outraged. "I saw you at the park! I saw you call off that hound, and—and then you sent them after me! What are *you* doing, asshole?"

"We are right on the edge of—" he began, and stopped. Something like anguish twisted his expression. "You need to leave before she realizes you're here."

"Who?"

The tightness in his shoulders and the subtle shift of his boots warned her he was on the verge of fleeing. She clenched her fists, preparing herself to give chase.

"*Fuck,*" he said, and flung out his hand in a deliberate gesture, like he was signaling to something out of sight—

She tackled him.

They went down in a heap, narrowly avoiding the fire. He struggled, rolling them over, but she twisted under him until she had enough leverage to shove him off and into the stream. She grabbed his arm, dragged him out—swearing and shivering so hard he couldn't even resist—and held him down with a knee against his back.

"Don't call the hounds," she snarled, pinning his wrists to his spine. His cheek ground flat against the dirt, his wet hair falling into his eyes. Up close, there was no mistaking him for a normal teenager. Black magic poured off him. It felt like decay, like a depression in her heart, like death.

"You shouldn't have come after me," he gasped. "I don't have any other choice."

A shadow fell over them. That was her only warning before a massive body slammed into her, knocking her clear off the boy's back. She skidded on the ground. Winded, her whole flank feeling like one giant bruise, she had no time to recover before the hound planted a paw on her chest, immobilizing her.

She couldn't see the boy, but she could hear him pacing.

"*Don't* come here again!" he said, somewhere in between angry and terrified.

Aziza squirmed, and the hound pressed down on her chest so hard she couldn't breathe; its strength was crushing. A growl rumbled in its throat. The tips of its claws caught in the weave of her sweater.

She froze. Her fingers dug into the ground; staying still was a struggle when her instincts wanted her to fight.

"As long as you're in Blackthorn, I'll find you," Aziza told him, gasping for air. "Anywhere you go. So you can either tell me why you sent the hounds after me, or you can expect to see me again *real* soon."

The hound's hot, stinking breath puffed over her face. She swallowed down the urge to gag. But it hadn't killed her. Hadn't even seriously harmed her. She frowned up at it, into its searing black eyes and vicious snarl. It clearly would've loved to tear her throat out, so why hadn't it?

Her anger ebbed slightly.

"Don't come after me," the boy said, voice rising, sounding halfway unhinged, "or I'll—I'll let the hounds kill you next time!"

His boots crossed into her line of sight. A scarred hand swiped up his backpack by the strap. He was going to run now, while she was pinned.

"Who's *she*?" Aziza said. "Is someone making you do this?"

The hound snapped its jaws inches from her nose, but she didn't flinch. She couldn't let him leave without telling her who was really responsible for all of this.

"I know you're still here!" she said. "Let me up. Maybe I can help you."

"No one can—"

A strangled scream in the distance cut him off.

"Was that—" he began.

"Leo?" Aziza called. "Leo! *You*—get your mutt off of me!"

The hound withdrew; she rolled over and got to her feet.

"Leo!" she shouted. "Are you okay?"

No response.

"You brought him here?" the boy said.

"Did you think I'd come after you alone?" She couldn't stop a hint of defensiveness from creeping into her tone. It was something about the boy's expression—the sick fear in his eyes. He became, if possible, even paler.

"We have to find him," he said. "*Now.*"

CHAPTER 16

LEO

HE COUGHED OUT a lungful of dirt and sat up, sore all over.

"Zee?" he called. "Hey! A little help?"

But there was no response.

Leo had heard the unmistakable sounds of a scuffle, had abandoned his hiding place to go help her—and had only made it about two paces before his boot pushed straight through the ground, and the place where he was standing didn't exist anymore, and he'd fallen.

A short fall, at least. Behind him, a gap in the ceiling showed where the ground had caved in. Green-tinged sunlight poured down. But everything else was darkness.

He pulled out his phone to light his surroundings. He wasn't in a pit, like he'd first thought, but a tunnel, its packed dirt walls laced with roots. Here and there, earthworms squirmed away from the glare, and a beetle startled into flight, buzzing past his face and scaring him half to death.

How far does this go? he thought. It ran in the same general direction Aziza had gone. He pointed his flashlight that way, but the tunnel made a gentle curve; he couldn't see where it ended.

If he stayed put, Aziza would come looking for him—unless she was in trouble. Sounds from above were muffled down here. He couldn't hear her fight with the necromancer anymore, or any voices. He had no idea if she was okay or not.

Nothing for it. He'd have to look for another way out.

At least there wasn't any water in this one.

He brushed off his clothes, found his bag a few feet away, and slung it over his shoulder. Flashlight pointed ahead, he walked. The tunnel wove back and forth, snakelike. As he left the window of sunlight behind, the darkness came alive; it pressed down on him, his flashlight a weak defense against it. He kept passing its beam over the walls just to remind himself that the shadows *didn't* go on forever. That there was nothing down there with him, lurking on the outer edges of his vision.

But then why did it feel like he wasn't alone?

He stopped, breathing hard. He hadn't gone far, he was certain. But he was *warm*, almost sweating under his coat. The air was humid, as though he'd climbed inside the throat of some great beast.

There were no worms or beetles in the walls anymore. Every now and then, though, his flashlight passed over other things half-buried—a shoe, a rusted keychain, a clump of something fuzzy that, when he dug it loose, turned out to be a teddy bear. Strange, sad, abandoned things. Like he was walking under a pauper's grave. Despite the warmth in the air, when he pressed his hand to the ground, it was so cold it numbed his fingers.

And as he knelt, the back of his neck prickled with the sense that he was being watched.

Calm down, he told himself. *You're too old to be afraid of the dark.*

If Aziza were here, she'd tell him to turn back.

The tunnel was suffocatingly warm by now. His scalp tingled, as if a breeze had stroked through it; that *not alone* sensation washed over him again. It kept him rooted to the ground, unable to take another step forward *or* back.

And then:

"*Leo!*"

Aziza's voice.

It was like a spell had been broken; he hurried back the way he'd come, back into cool winter air and in sight of the sunny gap in the ceiling.

"Zee?" he called. "Over here!"

He jogged into the sunlight and waited until she appeared, kneeling over the edge, her tangled hair falling over her shoulder and her face drawn with worry.

"What happened?"

"The ground was there, and then it, uh, wasn't," he said. "What is it with this town and secret tunnels?"

"A *tunnel*? How far does it . . ."

"No idea. But, god, it's *weird*. When I went that way"—he pointed—"it got all warm, and . . . I think there's something down here."

Her jaw set, and her lips pressed together. He knew that look. That look never meant anything good.

Great, he thought.

"Let's get you out," she said.

She leaned down as far as she could and held out her hand. He reached up and managed to grab hold when he stood on his tiptoes—but they couldn't get a solid grip. Their fingers slipped apart.

Sitting up, she looked over her shoulder. "A little help?"

As soon as her eyes were off him, that sensation came again: a prickling under his hair, like sweat drying on his scalp. He pointed his flashlight into the dark. Nothing moved, but a gust of warm air blew up from the shadows like a desert wind. It brushed over his cheeks and made his eyes sting.

Not a wind. A breathing.

"Stand back," said another voice from overhead. A huge black shape blocked out the sunlight—a hound leapt through the hole in the ground and landed gracefully in the tunnel. Its claws scored the dirt; its black eyes regarded him with something like scorn as he backpedaled, instinctively putting space between them.

That heat was at his back again, like now it didn't want to leave him alone. The air was so thick and humid it was hard to breathe through it, and the hound towered over him—

He didn't even notice its rider until he'd dismounted. It was the necromancer, shaky and breathless as he pushed in front of the hound. The color of his eyes was startling, a green so pale it was almost silver.

"Leo," the boy said; a shock jolted through him, something sparking in his mind—

And then the heat engulfed him; he took a gasp of breath, and shutters fell within him, and he couldn't see couldn't hear couldn't think—

There was nothing.

Except for the voice.

CHAPTER 17
TRISTAN

He and Leo had started dating freshman year, and Fairview High had made it easy to be secretive. It was an old brick building with a pompous air to it, with its colonnades and its dormer windows, but it was also a place full of quiet, tucked-away spaces. There were a dozen empty classrooms at any given moment. On the roof, if you picked the right spot, you'd hear someone coming long before they ever saw you, because footsteps always echoed up the stairs and the push bar on the door made a resounding metallic clang. Their relationship had unfolded in between the places and blocks of time that segmented their daily lives, in sidelong glances and small touches when no one else was looking.

Now, as he half fell off the hound's back and turned to Leo, it was like a warped echo of a song he knew by heart. For a second, this tunnel could've been any one of the empty, sunlit hallways where they'd stolen a few seconds together here and there. And Leo—standing half in the dark, scruffy and dirt-streaked, frowning nervously up at the hound and then down at Tristan in confusion—was still the person he always missed, whether he'd gone an hour without seeing him or a year. All the grief and longing came flooding back, the pain of losing him as sharp as if it had happened yesterday.

"Leo," he said, his voice weak, his knees weak. Leo's eyes caught and held on his. His molecules and the cosmos and all things in between ground to a halt. Nothing else could stop time the way Leo could for him. Not magic. Not even the hag.

The bond stirred in the back of his mind.

No, he thought, but it was too late. Her magic wrenched at the bond, clawed its way through his mind, and all at once she knew everything: where Tristan was, who he was with, how close they were to her territory. Her magic lashed out at Aziza and was repelled—something was shielding her, like her house had been shielded. But Leo had no such protection.

His eyes went hazy and unfocused. He turned, unsteady, and drifted away into the dark.

Tristan lunged for him, latching on to his arm and forcing him around.

"Come here!" he snapped at the hound. It growled at him; he bared his teeth and pushed the full force of his fury at it, until it relented, kneeling before him. He wrestled Leo onto its back and climbed on behind him, holding him in place with one arm wrapped around his waist and fisting his free hand in the hound's fur. In one smooth leap, it carried them aboveground and bent down again so that they could dismount.

"What's wrong with him?" Aziza asked, helping him guide Leo off the hound's back. Calmly, Leo shook them off and walked away into the trees. Tristan caught him by the sleeve and reeled him backward.

His head throbbed. *To me*, the hag was saying through the bond. She couldn't use her powers to make Aziza come to her. But if Aziza just stepped into the hag's territory, the borderlands around the gateway tree, then the hag wouldn't need to get into Aziza's head. She could bend reality around her, could contort the world so that every direction Aziza walked would lead to her. Just a few yards *that* way, and Aziza was hers.

As if to drive the point home, Leo strained against their grip, trying to throw himself into the borderlands. Because the hag knew Tristan would go after him. Because the hag guessed Aziza would, too.

To me, said the bond in the language of pain.

Tristan squeezed his eyes shut and clung to Leo's arm, mind racing for a solution. Distantly, he heard Aziza pleading with him:

"Leo? Can you hear me? Leo!"

Tristan opened his eyes. He knew what to do, but it had to be done *fast.*

Then the hound was there, its huge snout pushing against Leo's chest, crowding him backward until he was pressed against a tree.

Aziza whirled around, furious. "Tell me what's happening to him."

There were patches of mud and dampness on her clothes from scuffling with Tristan by the stream; her hair was tangled on one side and falling into her face so that she had to shove it distractedly away. She was almost as much of a mess as Tristan was, and he found that weirdly comforting. He didn't want to be the only mess here.

Calmly, he drew the ritual knife from his pocket and held it out handle first. "Stab me with this."

"What the fuck?"

"We don't have *time,*" he snapped. "Take it!"

"No!" she said. "Tell me what's going on!"

"He's listening to a voice in his head, and you can't let him do what it wants," he said. "Don't let him out of your sight until you snap him out of it. But it can't *look* like I let you get away. You stab me. You get him out of here. You help him."

"I don't want to hurt you," she said, and it sounded like she really meant it.

"You have to." The pain was so sharp his eyes blurred. The hag didn't know what he was doing—only that he wasn't getting any closer. If he brought Aziza into the borderlands, she would let Leo go. Her sick promise was poison-sweet in the back of his throat.

It need not be both of them, said the bond in the language of hunger.

Tristan pointed at a spot on his lower abdomen. "Here. Nothing vital. As long as you don't twist it or anything, I'll be *fine.*"

Aziza hesitated, glancing between him and Leo.

As the hag's impatience grew, the bond seemed to swell, until it filled his head and pushed at the inside of his skull.

"It has to be now!" Tristan said.

The urgency in his voice must have convinced her, because Aziza took the knife from his outstretched hand. She looked down at the blade, thumb smoothing over the hilt.

"Do it," he said. "And then run. As fast as you can."

She nodded.

Then she dropped the knife and shoved Tristan hard, not like how a kid pushes another kid on the playground, but shoulder-first, like she meant to break down a door. He stumbled, tripping over a tree root, and sprawled on the ground. She hadn't even hit him that hard. It was the shock more than anything that got him.

He spat out blood from where his teeth had cut the inside of his cheek. The hag *always* knew when his blood had been spilled.

That works, he thought.

To Aziza's credit, she didn't hesitate. By the time Tristan even understood what she'd done, she had already taken off, dragging a dazed Leo by the hand, their footsteps fading quickly as they fled.

The hag's fury was like an axe splitting his skull open; pain exploded within him, flooding his senses, blinding and deafening him. He didn't recall shutting his eyes; he didn't notice the strangled scream that fought its way out of his throat.

Hours later, the hag relented: not out of mercy, but to give him time to be afraid before she tortured him through the bond again. He lay on his back, grateful even for this unkind respite, panting and shivering.

It was going to be a very long day.

But for the hag to be this furious meant only one thing: Aziza and Leo were long gone.

And so, as every inch of skin burned like it was on fire, as the hag's rage howled in his mind—through the dread of the coming hours and through blood and tears—Tristan smiled.

CHAPTER 18

LEO

LEO COULDN'T TRUST himself.

His mind was full of dark corners, dead ends, tripwires. He had stray thoughts that didn't make sense because the context was buried in a memory he no longer had access to. He had photos he couldn't look at because his eyes went blurry when he tried, planners full of days he'd lost and notes that made no sense to him. He had dizzy spells, headaches, blackouts, like he was sick, from chasing reminders to their root memories and running up against the curse's walls. But sometimes the thing that scared him most was the overwhelmingly powerful impulse to keep fighting when he didn't really know what he was fighting for.

He would think, *I miss you*, and know it was true, know it in every part of himself, a crushing, bewildering pain that sat on his chest each night so he couldn't breathe and perched on his shoulders so that sometimes just taking a step forward required a monumental effort. That part wasn't the curse. That part was Leo. But it came from a side of himself that was as much a stranger as his true love.

He couldn't trust the person he was now, because he didn't know who he used to be. He couldn't trust his own mind.

But he could trust the voice. He just knew it.

Come find me.

The voice was all things soft and soothing. It was made of rain pattering on a window, and the growl of his car's ignition coming to life, and the satisfying *thunk* of his foot connecting with a soccer ball at the perfect angle for a goal-scoring kick. It was Mom's voice those rare times she spoke, hoarse and scratchy, but always safe.

Come back to the forest, it said.

He tried, but someone kept stopping him.

Aziza?

Distantly, he was aware of her hand in his, her voice calling to him. She sounded afraid. But there was nothing to fear.

She'll understand, the voice said. *I'll help you break the curse. Come find me.*

A tug within his mind showed him the way, south through the woods until the world went gray as dove feathers and summer storm clouds.

No more unanswered questions, no more stolen memories, no more loss and sorrow, the voice said. *Come find me. Let me help you.*

Aziza was going to help him, though. Aziza had promised.

She said she can't break a curse. She said so herself.

Was the voice fae? They'd say anything to get what they wanted. They couldn't lie, but they twisted their words so well it was just as good as lying.

The voice chuckled, a sound so warm and pleasant that he couldn't hold back a smile.

I am no fae.

Still, a tendril of suspicion snaked through his pleasant daze.

Tell me, Leo Merritt . . . why hasn't your true love come back to you? What happened to them? What if they're in trouble?

The voice was right. He had to find them. Anxiety pinballed off the inside of his skull, doing its best to instigate a headache, but the voice soothed it away before the pain could come.

I will make it right. I will set all of it right. Come to the forest.

He tried to take a step, but something was strapped across his chest.

A . . . seat belt?

When had he gotten to his car? How had he forgotten that? His car was supposed to be safe. He didn't usually forget things there.

The anxiety bubbled up within him again, and this time, the voice couldn't suppress it.

The voice . . .

What voice?

What the hell was he talking to?

Don't you want to break your curse? You can't give up. You don't just give up on true love.

The pull grew stronger, compelling him to return to the forest.

Last time he'd had a strange voice in his head, it had been the voice of the curse. *This* voice was different, but it didn't belong there, either. It wasn't a gap in his memory, but an intrusion into his heart. It camouflaged itself within the landscape of Leo's mind, using his own desires and fears against him.

He fought it as fiercely as he'd fought the curse. But it buried him, and he was lost.

CHAPTER 19

AZIZA

I'VE SEEN LEO do this a million times, she told herself, sliding the key into the ignition. *It's going to be fine.*

The necromancer's screams had followed her as they'd fled—as if he'd been attacked. But she couldn't go back, not with Leo in this state. It had been a struggle to get him strapped into the passenger seat when he'd kept trying to squeeze past her and wander back into the forest. If he'd used any force at all, he could've knocked her over. But it was Leo. Even now, there was no aggression in him. Finally, she'd gotten his seat belt on and slammed the door.

Hands locked tight around the steering wheel, she inched out of the parking lot and onto the road, which was blessedly empty. Leo's face was angled away from her, watching the trees blur past his window as though it was the most fascinating sight in the world.

His phone went off in his pocket. She ignored it, focusing on the road.

"You'd better be okay," she told him sternly. "I don't want to be the one to explain it to Hazel if you're not."

Moments after Leo's phone went silent, hers rang. She yanked it out of her pocket—the car swerved dangerously—but it wasn't Jiddo. Or any number she recognized.

They left a voicemail. She pulled up the message and put it on speaker.

"Hi, Aziza. This is Greg Merritt, Leo's dad. I can't find—that is, he wasn't in his room when I checked on him this morning. He didn't tell us he had plans today, and he's not picking up his phone, and, well. It's not like him. He's taken off like this before, but—but he always texted us at least so we knew he was safe. We're a little concerned," he said, in a strained tone of voice that made it clear he was actually a *lot* concerned. "So we wanted to see if he was with you. Could you give me a call when you get this? Thanks."

Guilt stabbed at her chest. She veered around a corner, skidding into the library's parking lot and slamming on the brakes. The library didn't open until noon on Sundays, so no one was around to see Aziza's laughable attempt at parking. Meryl threw the doors open; she'd probably heard the screech of the tires. She hurried to the car, where Aziza was trying to maneuver Leo out of the passenger seat. Aziza slung one of his arms over her shoulders, and Meryl took the other, and together they got him up the stairs and into Meryl's office.

They set him down on the couch. He wasn't struggling anymore. At some point, his eyes had fallen shut. His forehead was creased in what might've been pain. While they got him settled, Aziza filled Meryl in, starting with Eirlys's midnight visit and ending with her encounter with the necromancer.

"He said, 'It can't look like I let you get away,'" she recalled. "There's something in the forest that he's afraid of. But I've never heard of anything that could do this to Leo. Except *maybe* a sandman."

"I don't think it's fae," Meryl said. She looked guiltily at Aziza, and then away. "There's something I should have told you. I was hoping I wouldn't need to . . . There were no hounds last time . . ."

Her voice trailed off into a whisper, and then to nothing.

"Last time?" Aziza repeated.

"There *is* something in the woods," Meryl said. "But it was supposed to stay asleep. It—" Her hand flew to her throat as if she were choking. Aziza reached out to her, alarmed, but then Meryl shook it off—whatever it was—and inhaled shakily. For a moment, Aziza almost didn't recognize her; it was as if all these years Meryl had been only a shadow of herself, but Aziza had never known it. Now Aziza could *almost* see the fullness of Meryl's self, but before that person could materialize, she retreated back into her shadow, quiet, restrained, and weary to the bone. Meryl sighed, her hand dropping to fist in her skirt. "I'm forbidden to speak of it."

Forbidden. In magical terms, that word held a lot of significance.

Before, Meryl had said that she couldn't tell Aziza certain things, but Aziza hadn't realized that meant . . . she *literally* couldn't.

"Meryl," Aziza said. "What is going on with you?"

Meryl avoided her eyes. "Let's just get Leo through this first."

They got him to drink some water while he blinked up at them, eyes glassy. He soon fell asleep curled on his side, his arms over his face, like he was hiding from something. Meryl left when the library opened; Aziza stayed with Leo, taking the necromancer's warning to heart: *Don't let him out of your sight.*

But Leo was fighting. She was sure of it.

She sat on the ground in front of the couch, fists clenched in her lap, increasingly furious. Leo didn't deserve this after what he'd been through with the curse. She'd known going after the necromancer was dangerous, but she hadn't thought she would be exposing Leo to *this* kind of risk.

Aziza had spent years pushing people away before she could scare them off, because if she was going to be alone, it would be on her terms. But she couldn't blame anyone for being afraid of magic—for being afraid of *her*. Magic was dangerous. Leo hadn't been afraid, and look what had happened to him.

Only, she couldn't convince herself that Leo had been wrong to stick around.

She didn't *want* him to be wrong.

But the only way to prove him right was to fix this.

The library closed at five in the afternoon, just before sunset, and Meryl came back with more water.

"Can you stay with him?" Aziza asked. "I'm going to Elphame. If I can find a sandman and pay for a favor, it might be able to wake Leo up."

"He's not dreaming," Meryl said quietly.

"We don't know that," she argued. "We need to do something."

The one thing she did know was that she couldn't stand to sit there and watch him fight this alone anymore.

She couldn't risk her perilous driving at this hour, when the roads were packed, so she called a cab. Night had fallen by the time she reached St. Sithney's. It was deserted. With the hounds still on the loose, people were afraid to be near the woods after dark.

Swaying crowns of elm and ash saluted her. The streetlamps were hazy gold spotlights that she avoided out of habit as she jogged toward the tree line, her eyes adjusting to the dark. Her magic probed at the boundary, seeking one of the tiny cracks that she could pry apart to make a door.

But before she ever got that far, something pulled itself apart from the natural stirring of the woods under night breezes barely felt; a pale and slender figure, somehow familiar. Waiting for her.

CHAPTER 20
TRISTAN

THE HAG WAS still angry.

He woke up into her restless fury; it was the first thing he felt. The rest came in short order. His face was pressed against the base of the gateway tree, the bark scraping his cheek and his body nestled between two of its roots. Instinctively, he recoiled—*bad* idea.

Everything hurt, a raw, scalding pain. He swallowed and tasted blood.

Slowly, this time, he told himself. He pushed himself up. Sweat broke out on his forehead. The proximity of the gateway tree was nauseating; he would have thrown up if there had been anything in his stomach to expel.

A blurry recollection of the past day surfaced in his mind. He had to assume the only reason he was alive right now was that his ploy had worked: The hag didn't know he'd let Aziza get away on purpose. She had punished him for weakness, for inadequacy, but not for betrayal. It had been the most painful few hours of his life. At some point, she'd forced him to return to the gateway tree, but that journey had taken the last of his strength, and he'd passed out.

But he'd saved Leo. For the first time in over a year, he had done something right.

She was beyond speech; her wrath was such that she had regressed to the thing that was just a voice, the thing that was just a pull to a cold gray hell. The bond ached like a bruise, still, a low-level ambient pain. Understanding what she wanted, he picked his way around to the front of the gateway tree, where he could kneel before the hag. Every step made his legs seize up and threaten to give out; the effort of lowering himself into a kneeling position almost sent him sprawling to the ground again.

He wanted to sleep. He wanted to get away from here, find someplace to be alone, and nurse his many wounds in private. A glance down at his clothes told him he'd bled through his bandages, but he would worry about that later.

"*Beg for my forgiveness,*" she said, the words carried to him in the groan of the gateway tree's branches, in a rumble from the sky like distant thunder, in the hammering of his own heart.

"I'm—sorry," he said, his throat still in tatters from screaming. "Please—forgive me."

He was not forgiven, but his cowering was satisfactory; her attention shifted to something else in the clearing. Tristan looked around until he found it, a contorted shape he would've mistaken for a tree root if she hadn't pointed it out. He heaved himself to his feet again and approached.

His stomach clenched in horror. It was . . . alive.

The creature was a wrecked, twisted thing made of wood, its limbs burned away to charred nubs and sap running down its torn body like blood. Its bark had cracked open in places to reveal its pale interior. Tristan could still make out a half-burned face, one tree-sap eye, a gash of an open mouth. It twitched, and Tristan's face screwed up in either disgust or sympathy; he couldn't have said which.

"It's a wood nymph," Tristan said, in answer to the hag's unspoken question. "Or . . . it was."

A memory returned to him, then. A burial in the woods; the nymph, *this* nymph, at the fairy door; talking his way out of Elphame. The hag had told him once that fae were petty. They held grudges and they never forgot the debts they were owed. The nymph had come here to demand the payment he'd denied her. But she had *known* she couldn't stand up to a hag—what had changed?

Then the hag held up, between two clawlike fingers, a lock of hair.

Tristan's heart sank. The nymph must have gotten that from Aziza.

It caught fire, burning into a small flame of pure white. The hag's jaw dropped open, impossibly wide, and she swallowed the flame whole. It lit her up from the inside, her scarred eye sockets and blackened mouth and every fold in her deadened skin showing dark against the bright white of Aziza's magic.

As the hag consumed it, the light faded away. The gateway tree shivered; its branches stretched as if yawning, and its roots unfurled a few inches farther into the clearing. She didn't look any different, but there was an air of renewed energy about her, an awakeness.

The hag had gained the gift of hedgecraft, a drop of it, just enough to send Aziza her regards. And she was sending Tristan with it. He was meant to go after Aziza right now, as the hag made her move. Whatever she had done would make Aziza vulnerable.

"I understand," he said. He folded an arm around himself, in a defensive gesture, and discreetly pressed the heel of his hand into one of his wounds. The pain chased away all his other thoughts. He couldn't let the bond pick up on what he intended to do next.

"*Are you afraid?*" the hag said, and she might have spoken aloud or she might have let the woods speak for her; here, it was all the same.

It took him a second to process the words. How was there any question? Of course he was afraid. "Afraid" was a permanent part of his being, fused into his body like an extra limb. He had two arms, two lungs, a few ribs, a network of veins, and this cold lump of fear he carried around everywhere. That was how he lived now.

"Sometimes," he said. "But not too afraid to do what I have to do."

As he left the hag's clearing, he prepared himself for death. The hag had tried to snare Leo and failed. That meant there was nothing holding Tristan back from betraying the terms of his contract. The moment the hag detected his rebellion, he'd die. She had seen that he could withstand torture, so there would be no point in delaying his death, not even to try and make him find another bondservant to take his place. But that didn't matter; he had been ready to die for some time now.

He would pay back the debt he owed Aziza while he still had the chance. This was the second time she'd saved Leo's life. Whatever the hag had sent after her, Tristan would help her stop it, and maybe make up in some small way for all the harm he'd done.

As soon as he'd cleared the hag's boundarylands, he called on one of the hounds. The twilight shadows rippled; two obsidian eyes blinked into existence near his knees, and then rose and rose until they were peering *down* at him. It circled him, a sinuous, winding motion, so close its fur skimmed his coat. Its breath puffed against the back of his neck and ruffled his hair.

He could see himself through its eyes, could feel its deep-seated urge to sink its teeth into his throat.

He waited, unmoving.

At last, it shook out its fur, regarded him disdainfully for a moment, and knelt.

He climbed on its back. Together, they sank into the dark and vanished.

CHAPTER 21

AZIZA

HER SIDE FELT like a trellis of bruises from where roots and stones had dug into her flesh, her coat offering little protection; her palms burned from struggling to push herself up, from the pathetic half crawl she'd adopted; and her scalp ached as she was pulled and dragged by the hair, deeper into the woods. But Aziza didn't make a sound. You weren't supposed to speak to the Ash Witch.

The Ash Witch was a local spirit, a little like the Man at the Bus Stop. Less benign. But she had never bothered Aziza.

Until now.

Aziza twisted around, trying to swipe at the Ash Witch's heels, but the hand in her hair gave a yank that threatened to wrench her skull off her spine.

You got yourself into this mess, Aziza told herself sternly. *You'd better get yourself out.*

She had been careless. The Ash Witch hadn't even snuck up on her; it wasn't strange to see her wandering the woods. And the park, the nearby streets, the hiking trails—always trying to trick people into speaking to her. Most mistook her for a homeless woman and ignored her or wordlessly handed her change. But she would taunt them, or cry, or flirt, anything to catch them off guard and get them to look into her eyes. Given an opening, her magic would compel them to answer her questions, and from there, she'd make her judgments. Those she deemed innocent walked free, often with a small blessing—they'd get a piece of long-awaited good news or heal from a minor ailment. The others, Aziza would usually find tied up in the woods, terrified out of their wits, with only fragmented memories of what had happened to them and a deep, gut-churning sense of remorse.

In life, the Ash Witch had been a kind of mind reader, or a psychic. That was an umbrella term for one of the broader categories of witchcraft. There were hearth witches and healers, oracles and rooks—which was what Jiddo was, and her parents, people with protective magics whose spells were walls, chambers, and locks. These gifts could manifest in a variety of ways, depending on the witch. Psychics had telepathy, sometimes, or the ability to sense emotions, to spy on dreams, even to influence the mind if they were really powerful. The Ash Witch had had only a minor form of the gift: She could tell when someone was lying. Now she was dead, and all that was left of her was a little bit of energy, a little bit of magic, and a scrap of the person she'd once been. That was all a spirit really was: not a monster, not fae, and not a person. Just energy and emotion.

"Hello, hedgewitch," the Ash Witch had said, when they'd come across each other at St. Sithney's. "Did you leave this gift here on the boundary for me?"

What gift? Aziza had wanted to ask, but she didn't.

"Oh?" the Ash Witch had said, as if she'd heard the question anyway. "Is this not your doing? But it's *your* magic, Aziza. The boundary was bloated with it; it was like you intended for someone to pluck it off the vine, and who better than myself?"

This was when Aziza had finally clued in to the fact that something was very, very wrong with the Ash Witch. Spirits collected magic from the world like foragers. Even the urban legends that tended to form around such spirits generated a kind of energy that nourished them. But they spent as much as they took just by existing, so when they became as real as the Ash Witch, the Man at the Bus Stop, and others like them, their power tended to plateau. Except in the rare case that something happened to give them a magical boost.

Aziza's hand had gone to her pocket; her fingers had closed around the handle of her emergencies-only silver knife. She didn't draw it, but the Ash Witch had seen, and her face had twisted into an expression of rage.

And then she'd vanished.

A hard shove had knocked Aziza to her knees. She caught herself with both hands, still holding the knife, and then the Ash Witch was there again, stomping down on Aziza's wrist, and Aziza had dropped her only weapon. The Ash Witch had kicked it away, taken a fistful of Aziza's hair, and twisted it around her own hand. There was no fire, but Aziza smelled smoke anyway, felt it thick in her lungs, and had coughed uncontrollably as she'd fought against the Ash Witch, who dragged her into the woods.

She had spent a lot of time in the woods, but not like this. Hands scraped up. Throat raw from the coughing that had only just ceased minutes ago. Scalp burning. As she struggled on her knees to keep up with the Ash Witch's languid strides—at odds with the iron grip she had on Aziza's hair—her mind conjured the image of Leo as she'd seen him last, unconscious in Meryl's office because Aziza had refused to listen to his sensible warnings.

Her heart was lead in her chest, an impossible weight. Maybe the Ash Witch had already judged her, speech or no speech, and this was her rightful punishment.

"Where are you taking me?" Aziza rasped, finally giving in.

A jolt as she was pulled over a small ridge in the ground, like a stair, concealed under heaps of dead leaves. They'd hit one of the hiking trails. And Aziza had a bad feeling that she knew where they were going.

"You haven't judged me," Aziza said, desperate to be wrong. "You can't bind me yet."

"You think you know everything," the Ash Witch snarled, "because you have your rules and your rituals and your tokens. Don't you know, when it comes to magic, how quickly the rules can change?"

Overhead, the forest canopy dropped off suddenly, and the night sky gaped down like an audience, silent and breathless. Aziza craned her neck around, as much as she could. It was as Aziza had suspected—they were in the campgrounds about half a mile into the woods, which many of the hiking trails fed into. Off-limits for now, thanks to the hounds. Which meant they were alone.

"Stop," Aziza said, struggling with renewed urgency. Her chest was tight, as if she really had inhaled smoke.

The Ash Witch let go of her hair long enough to take her by the arm instead, and then Aziza was half shoved, half thrown. She landed hard, turned over, and pushed herself up on her hands so that she could reorient herself.

The fire pit. The Ash Witch had tossed her into the fire pit.

Aziza looked up at her. "What did I *do*?"

The Ash Witch resembled a woman in only the loosest sense of the term. Her limbs were skeletal, shriveled, her eyes burning with a hellish light, and her wan face hollow—a face that didn't suit her voice, the voice of a highborn lady from an era long past. Dark hair hung in matted chunks around her neck. Aziza's eyes went, as they always did, to her wrists and ankles—still bearing the ropes that had been used to keep her on her pyre however many years ago.

"I don't exactly know," the Ash Witch said. "But there was a voice, you see. When I took the gift of your magic. And the voice told me *everything* wrong in Blackthorn is *your* fault, and *I* must fix it. The gift was conditional upon my fixing it."

Fixing the problem of Aziza's existence, she meant.

Aziza's knife was back in St. Sithney's. Her bag had slipped off her shoulder somewhere in the woods. And spirits weren't fae, so her craft didn't work on them.

She flung herself away from the Ash Witch and over the stones around the edge of the fire pit, scrambling to her feet and propelling herself forward at the same time. But then the Ash Witch was abruptly before her, shoving Aziza back, her hand hot as a brand and surprisingly solid again where just moments before she'd had the weightless swiftness of any ghost. And Aziza was down again in the soot and the dirt, inhaling it, coughing it back up as pained tears stung her eyes.

"That voice lied to you," Aziza croaked.

"No one can lie to me." The Ash Witch knelt beside her and yanked Aziza's wrists together. This was the first time her skin had touched Aziza's, and her touch burned like metal left outside in the sun all day. Aziza shrieked, writhing, but the Ash Witch's strength was unyielding and final.

She tied Aziza's wrists with rope from her own body; a pull at the shorn end of the bindings around her arm, and it came loose and long as if being unspooled, even though there was no less of it on her. When she'd tied off a knot, leaving Aziza tightly bound, she cut the end with her teeth and went for Aziza's ankles next.

Aziza was dizzy with pain. Everywhere the Ash Witch touched, Aziza's skin burned and blistered. She may have blacked out for a second, because she blinked and the Ash Witch was straightening again, and Aziza couldn't kick anymore because her legs were cinched tight together.

There was a pile of kindling beside the fire pit. The Ash Witch scooped up an armful of it and let it rain down on Aziza, who winced and turned her face away. The last piece she kept, a switch of pale stripped wood, and blew on the tip. It caught fire instantly, despite the cold.

The Ash Witch dropped it into the fire pit. Aziza couldn't see it, but she smelled the smoke, felt the slow-growing heat climbing around her knees.

Is this really it? she thought, more stunned than afraid. It felt like mere seconds ago she and Leo had narrowly escaped death, and now she'd blundered right back into it, like any one of the hapless victims of fae mischief she was so accustomed to rescuing. And she hadn't figured anything out. Hadn't solved the mystery of what was in the woods. Hadn't saved Blackthorn. Hadn't even saved Leo. She would die here, burned to death by the spirit of another witch. Die even younger than her parents had.

She had never dwelled on their deaths much, or wondered what dying had been like for them, what their last moments had been like. Had they been afraid? Had they thought of her, the way she was thinking of them now? But, to her, they were less than ghosts. They were photographs in dusty albums, could-have-beens, and anecdotes in Jiddo's voice.

She was going to leave Jiddo all alone, just like they had.

And then a streak of darkness leapt over her, colliding with the Ash Witch in a whirl of black fur and wicked claws. It was a hound, sinking its teeth into her throat.

The Ash Witch shrieked with fury and flung the hound off of her with more strength than her slim frame should have contained. It sprawled on the ground, two handprints burned into the fur on its chest. But it rolled to its feet and faced the Ash Witch again, growling, bent to strike.

Someone was cutting Aziza free, kicking away the low flames, and pulling her to her feet. She cooperated purely out of instinct and noticed only distantly the paleness of the hands that had rescued her. She was up, knees shaking; stepping out of the fire pit; running into the woods with the boy—the necromancer.

"What are you—what are you doing here?" she said.

"Helping," he panted. "But I'm too weak to call more than one hound at a time right now. We have to get away."

The screams she'd heard as she'd left the woods with Leo earlier still rang in her head; she was almost surprised to see him alive. As it was, his face was hollow and bloodless, and she had to slow her pace or else he'd have fallen behind.

"What happened to her?" Aziza asked, voice low. "She said she absorbed my magic—she mentioned a voice."

"My master," he said. "A nymph came to her with a lock of hair—"

Eirlys, Aziza thought. A sense of foreboding washed over her. She opened her mouth to ask a question she probably didn't want the answer to, only then he staggered as if he'd been struck, rocking sideways, his shoulder slamming into a tree, his hands flying to his neck. She stopped running and turned back to him in confusion.

"The hound." He swallowed as if his throat hurt. "I felt—"

Then she heard it: the silence.

The hound's snarls in the near distance had ceased.

When the Ash Witch caught up with them, it was instantaneous. Gone was the Ash Witch's limping, subdued walk, her wander; where before she was smoke, now she was spark and flame. She made no sound. There was only a rush of stinging heat chasing away the cold, and the shine of her eyes appearing out of the woods.

"Stop," Aziza told her, backing up. The Ash Witch vanished, as if the wind had blown her away. Aziza spun, searching for her, turning in circles. She saw the hound still in the campground—it had been ripped in half, and its torso lay about five yards away from its hind legs. Its front paws were dragging it steadily toward its lower half, leaving a bloody trail behind; its tongue lolled out of its panting mouth. In the fire pit where Aziza had been minutes before, a full-blown blaze had lurched to life.

That heat again, the smell of smoke. Aziza leapt to the side just as the Ash Witch snatched at her, and then the spirit had vanished again, leaving Aziza to choke on her next gasp of air. Her eyes watered, making the world go blurry.

"Aziza!" the boy said. Something slid across the ground, scattering leaves, and struck the side of her boot. She swiped it up instinctively. It turned out to be a dagger—the same one he'd offered to her when he'd begged her to stab him earlier. A hilt of onyx, a blade of silver. Fancy. And old. A ceremonial tool. Not something he'd just picked up at random.

And then hands clamped down on Aziza's arms; she felt the deadly heat of that grip through the material of her coat, and the shocking strength, the new power that had warped the Ash Witch the way water pressure at deep enough levels could warp a human body. Without stopping to think, Aziza thrust the knife up between the wings of the Ash Witch's rib cage. Up close, the Ash Witch reeked of sulfur and radiated heat, as though she was still burning after all these years. She let out a scream that was pain and wrath and defiance. But she didn't bleed. Light spilled out from the edges of the wound, where the blade met her flesh. Spirits were made of magic, and it was magic she bled now, draining from her like an infection.

Aziza yanked the blade out and stabbed in again, putting all her weight behind it—but the Ash Witch caught her wrists, still burned from her touch before. Aziza let out a strangled scream.

The hound, recovered, leapt onto the Ash Witch's back, its teeth clamping down on her throat. The Ash Witch released her to grab at it; Aziza staggered back and ended up sprawled on her ass. Her hand was empty. She'd lost the blade. It was still embedded hilt-deep in the Ash Witch's chest.

The boy appeared at her side as she struggled to her feet, still walking unsteadily, arms wrapped around his chest. "Let's go."

"If I could get her one more time—"

The Ash Witch caught the hound by the snout and forced its mouth open—and open, and open, until she ripped its jaw clean off. The boy shuddered, hand flying to his mouth, clutching his jaw as if to hold it in place. He was in bad shape, and she wasn't much better. They had no chance of outrunning the Ash Witch.

When the Ash Witch turned back to Aziza, she seemed downright ecstatic to see the two of them, huddled together helplessly.

"You again! Tristan Drake. Tristan No-Name," she said mockingly. She tugged at the hilt of the dagger, as if testing it, and then she gave it a merciless wrench and pulled it free, grimacing with her blackened teeth. The blade clattered to the ground. Her hand covered the two stab wounds, the light of draining magic shining through the cracks between her fingers. "You left, last time, before we could finish our conversation. But I have seen enough to know your heart."

She disappeared. The stench of smoke was all-encompassing, and it could've been the fire in the campgrounds, climbing higher, but it wasn't. It was the Ash Witch's magic, dispersing from her wounds.

And then the Ash Witch had Tristan by the throat. There was something blurry in her outline now, like she was a figure out of an old photograph, caught mid-motion. But her hand was tight around Tristan's neck, and Aziza's stomach twisted in horror as she smelled charred flesh.

"You are guilty," the Ash Witch said. Tristan's mouth was open in a silent scream. The hound had been halfway back to its feet, but it dissolved now like a shadow in the sun. He'd lost control.

Aziza went for the knife, a side-step and a lunge at the ground behind the Ash Witch. But the Ash Witch caught her by the hair again, a fistful of it, and she slammed Aziza's head on the ground. White spots exploded in Aziza's vision. The world spun. She groaned, shifting, trying to get her arms under her to push herself upright, but too dizzy to manage it. A body landed next to her, and it was Tristan, but he wasn't screaming anymore, and she didn't even know if he was alive or not. The Ash Witch had Aziza's wrist again, and she was being dragged—

And then light poured over them, half blinding her. The Ash Witch dropped her, whirled around, screamed—

Aziza managed to lift her head, and there was Leo—he'd fought off the enchantment, he was *all right*. And he had a flashlight in one hand, an emergency flare from his car in the other; it was ignited, hissing and spitting flame, and he had it shoved into the Ash Witch's belly. The Ash Witch knocked it aside, and it landed on the ground— the flashlight fell, too, and Leo swore—there was movement, a struggle, a shout from Leo, and Aziza was fighting her way to her feet but she didn't have the slightest goddamn clue what was happening—

"*No*," someone rasped. Tristan. He raised a hand and, with a twitch of his fingers, summoned back one of the hounds. It cut through the beam of the flashlight, leaping on the Ash Witch, knocking her away from Leo and to the ground. Another twitch of Tristan's fingers, and a second hound was there, emerging from nowhere, right behind the Ash Witch's thrashing head.

"Tristan," she said, concerned. Sweat beaded on his forehead.

"You did the hard part. I just have to finish it," he wheezed.

They latched on to the Ash Witch's arms, the two hounds, and dragged her back, away, deep into the woods. She grew weaker by the second. Their teeth tore into her, making more wounds for her to bleed even more magic. It struck Aziza that the Ash Witch might lose more than just the power-up she'd gotten today; she might lose all of the magic and energy she had gathered over the years, the force that made her a spirit. There might not even be an Ash Witch anymore after this.

Aziza had never wanted that. The local spirits were part of what made Blackthorn magical, and she would no sooner get rid of them than she would tear down the woods and cut Blackthorn off from Elphame entirely.

But there was nothing to be done now. In moments, the hounds and the Ash Witch both were gone. Tristan fell over in the grass, unconscious. Leo stomped the flare out before its flames could spread.

The night was dark, quiet, and peaceful, as if nothing unusual had happened at all.

CHAPTER 22

LEO

THE NECROMANCER—TRISTAN—WAS OUT cold, so Leo carried him to the car. Without the coat, he would've weighed nothing. He crumpled in Leo's arms as readily as paper, and his breathing had an alarming wet rasp to it. Leo maneuvered him into the backseat, where he lay on his side and did not stir.

"Why'd he help us?" he asked Aziza, after he'd started the car and she had filled him in on what he'd missed. He could hear that labored breathing over the hum of the heater.

"He didn't say. Do you remember anything from earlier? It's like—you were conscious, but you weren't aware."

"I was *kind of* aware," he said. "There was a fog over everything. I could see and hear, but not clearly. And then there was this voice."

Aziza scrubbed at a smudge of dirt on her cheek. "The Ash Witch mentioned a voice, too."

He told her what the voice had said to him. How trustworthy it had sounded. How comforting and right it had felt, how desperately he had wanted to keep listening to it. He'd only managed to shake it off because it had started to remind him of the curse, and he'd had more than a year of practice in trying to fight the curse off.

Even then, it had been a back-and-forth, a stalemate, Leo's resistance against the voice's allure, equally matched. He had known he couldn't outlast the voice. Sensed it, somehow, that it would wait until he'd exhausted himself and then it would have him. And he had thought: *I'm never going to see you again, am I?*

You, who Leo missed in this thoughtless, essential way—like breathing, like falling asleep, his body needing no instruction in the matter. *You* who Leo had sketched out in his mind like a contour drawing, just an approximation, an outline around emptiness—*I don't remember turning fifteen, so I must have spent that day with you*, he'd think, or *Maybe I snuck out to see you, that's gotta be why I keep trying to sleepwalk out the door*, or *Pretty sure I've never seen this book before in my life, so what's it doing on my shelf? Did you lend it to me?*

And then, as he prodded at the gaps in his memory the way he could never quite stop himself from doing, the curse had swept in, hitting reset on his brain like Leo was a faulty hard drive, and that—that had given the voice some kind of a jolt. Kind of funny, when he thought about it. What was it like to experience someone else's curse secondhand? Like the hot water shutting off when you were in the shower, maybe. Like someone sneezing in your face. A sudden, unpleasant shock. So then Leo had done it again, on purpose this time, triggering the curse's mind-wipe response, and the voice got quieter and quieter until finally it withdrew. He'd pitted the curse and the voice against each other, Godzilla-versus-Kong style—"What?" he said, at the incredulous look Aziza shot him. "It's true."

He hated to admit it, but the curse had saved him from the voice.

No, screw that—Aziza and Meryl had saved him. His true love had saved him.

He'd woken up in Meryl's office. She'd told him Aziza had gone to St. Sithney's to look for a way to help him. Only she hadn't answered when he'd texted her, which meant either she was in Elphame or something was wrong. So he'd followed her.

"Good thing you always start your patrol in the same place," he said. If he hadn't known exactly where to go, he wouldn't have seen Aziza's bag lying there where she'd dropped it, or the smoke from the campgrounds. And then who knew if he'd ever have found her.

"And a good thing Tristan decided to help," she added. "I want to know what changed."

"Maybe he was being controlled."

"But he didn't seem . . . hypnotized, like you were. And the Ash Witch said he was guilty."

A strangled laugh escaped him. "Sorry, what? Are we taking her word for it? Between the stabbing and the burning, I don't think she's our biggest fan, either."

"We're not taking her word for it. I just think it's interesting."

In the rearview mirror, Tristan was a pale, motionless heap. Ice blond hair fanned over the seat, and a hand curled in front of his face, as if even in sleep he was trying to hide. Leo felt another pang of sympathy, despite Aziza's perfectly justified wariness.

"I'm just saying that whatever was in my head, it was powerful. Pretty sure at one point I was willing to do anything it told me to," he confessed. "If you hadn't bought me time to fight . . ."

A strained silence fell over them.

"What's wrong?" he asked, unable to let it be.

"You told me it was a bad idea to go after him, and I didn't listen." Her arms were folded, and she wasn't looking at him. "And you got hurt because of it. I'm . . . sorry."

"If we hadn't done it, we still wouldn't have any answers."

"Wouldn't have been worth it if something happened to you," she muttered, glaring at the dashboard as if it had offended her.

He allowed himself the smallest grin, counting on the darkness to hide it. They'd come a long way from Leo having to bargain for her time.

I care about you, too, he thought, but knew better than to say it out loud. It'd only embarrass her.

At the library, Aziza went inside to give Meryl a heads-up while he collected their passenger. He slid an arm behind Tristan's shoulders and got the other under his knees, only then realizing—as he gathered up all those long, bony limbs—that he was about Leo's height. His frightening thinness and baggy clothes made him look smaller than he was. Leo's chest ached with something that . . . must have been pity.

Tristan mumbled a sleepy, pained protest at being moved.

"Sorry," Leo whispered, lifting him out of the car and kicking the door shut. It was after hours, so the place was empty. He ferried Tristan into Meryl's office and deposited him on the same couch where Leo had apparently spent the better part of the day.

"Maybe we should've taken him to the hospital instead," he said, as he joined Aziza and Meryl by the door.

"And say what?" Aziza asked. "He's magically exhausted?"

"He's got those burns." Pretty bad ones, too, a band of welts and blisters on his neck where the Ash Witch had grabbed him.

"I'm afraid he'll disappear again if we leave him in the hospital. We can't let that happen, not before we talk to him."

"So you think whoever he's working for is the same person who messed up the boundary."

Aziza rubbed at her arm just above the burns the Ash Witch had given her, nearly a matched set with Tristan's. "I don't know if it's a person. It *used* my craft. It didn't just take my magic and channel it into raw power; it put my magic *into* the boundary so that the

Ash Witch could find it. That's hedgecraft. But a hedgewitch can't borrow magic."

It sounded like the setup for a riddle: *I steal like the fae and act like a hedgewitch, but I'm neither. I'm underground and in the woods and in your head. What am I?*

But all they could do for now was leave Tristan in Meryl's care until he woke up.

HE CHECKED HIS phone distractedly as he plopped down in the driver's seat, did a double take at the number of missed calls and texts, and groaned.

"Maybe now's not the best time," Aziza said, "but I need to talk to you about this."

From her bag, she produced the vial containing the scrap of mystery material that Leo had stolen from his parents. "I'm almost positive it comes from Elphame."

He grabbed the first aid kit from behind his seat, and they swapped. "How can you tell?"

"If you look at it really close, you can make out a network of thin veins. I compared it to pictures of insect wings, and it's not exactly the same, but it's pretty close. What can you think of that's insect-like and magical?"

He'd been carrying around a piece of *wing* this whole time? God. *Gross.*

"And you said fairies are the only kind of fae that can cast curses."

"Maybe this doesn't have anything to do with your curse. There could be another explanation."

He glanced over at her skeptically. "Like what?"

"Like any other explanation that doesn't involve us looking for fairies."

She looked nervous. He'd never seen her nervous before.

"It can't be that bad," he said hopefully. "I mean, compared to kelpies? What, do fairies eat people, too?"

"No, but they have the kind of power that can destroy you. A fairy can craft illusions so real you could cut yourself on them, or coax you into trading away whatever matters most to you with a few words and a dash of magical charm. They have strict laws of etiquette that they treat like a game—until you offend them, and then they'll cut you down with a smile. They're stronger than humans, and live a lot longer. But they don't live near boundaries. You'd have to go deep into Elphame to come across them." She had the first aid kit open in her lap while she dabbed burn cream over the marks of the Ash Witch's touch. "So before we do anything else, there's one question you really need the answer to."

"What's that?"

"What did your parents do to piss off a fairy?"

Son of the wicked, the curse called him. He'd never really considered what that meant. Or rather, in the same way that he didn't view the Ash Witch as an objective judge of Tristan's character, he didn't much care what the voice of the curse had to say about his parents and their alleged wickedness. Whoever had cast the curse had to have a pretty skewed moral code. Now, though, he wondered. He'd known they'd done *something*, but . . . had it really been something bad? Something *wicked*?

He dropped Aziza off at her place, and then he was out of excuses to put off going home. When he pulled up in the driveway, Hazel was biking up and down the block. She wheeled over to him as he got out.

"How bad is it?" he asked.

"Bad. They filed a missing person report," she said. "But the cops said you probably just ran away, especially since this wasn't the first time they reported you missing when you were just . . ."

When he was chasing rumor and hearsay around the country in hopes of finding a way to break the curse.

"I forget to tell them where I'm going *one* time and they hold it against me forever," he complained. Usually he was only gone for a few days, and even when he'd left for the whole summer, it wasn't like he'd *never* texted them. "So I didn't answer the phone for a few hours—talk about an overreaction."

He headed for the front door. Hazel hopped off her bike, leaned it against the wall, and followed.

"It wasn't just them. I was worried, too," she said reproachfully.

"I'm sorry," he said. "If I could've called, I would've, I swear."

"You always say you're sorry." Hazel's eyes welled up. "I don't believe you anymore."

"Then *don't*," he said, more harshly than he'd intended. He opened his mouth immediately to take it back, to apologize again, but Hazel had already thrown the door open and vanished inside.

Things did not get better from there. The next hour would be filed away under "memories he'd happily let a fairy zap out of existence." It was a million times worse than when he'd lost the scholarship. Dad wasn't the type to yell, so he mostly paced, and rubbed his forehead, and gave Leo wounded looks while he tried and failed to extract the truth about what he'd been up to since before dawn this morning. Mom *was* the type to yell, but she hated the shrill coqui frogs that poured out of her mouth when she did. They were small and fast and hard to find later, and they kept everyone up at night. And if Spot caught any of them, they ended up in pillowcases, underwear drawers, the Brita filter . . .

So Mom didn't scream at him, but she clearly *really* wanted to, standing there red-faced and tight-lipped and signing so rapidly and shakily that Leo could pretend he didn't understand her, and half the time it wasn't even a lie. At last, Mom threw up her hands, stopped Dad as he made another circuit around the living room, and took several deep breaths until she could sign, slow and deliberate, "No more car." Fists curled a little too tightly. "Give me the key." Knuckle jabbing into her palm.

He tossed it to her. He'd already made a copy.

Mom turned redder and glared harder. "No more allowance."

"Okay," he said. Maybe she didn't realize that Aziza had been pitching in for gas money and that he'd been picking up more shifts at work; they'd be fine.

He and Mom stared each other down, equally stubborn. He could almost see the gears in her head turning, see when she realized there wasn't much more she could do to him.

He'd have felt guilty if it weren't for the vial in his pocket and the voice of the curse echoing in his memory as always, whispering the word: *wicked*.

His parents weren't bad people. He'd never believe that. But neither were they the victims of a random evil, a haunting that had picked on their unlucky family for no apparent reason. The voice of the curse was someone with a grudge. And he had to find out why. How his family had wronged this fairy, if they could fix it, and most importantly, where the fairy was now.

At last, Mom signed, "Go to your room," and stomped away.

Dad sank onto the couch, head in his hands. "I just don't understand what you were thinking," he said, for the fifth time. "Or why you won't tell us what happened."

Leo sat next to him, trying to figure out where to start. Mom was safely out of earshot. Hazel was in her room. Dad was already mad, and this conversation would make things even worse, but Leo just . . . didn't care. Earlier today, whatever was in the woods had used the curse and the promise of breaking it as bait to lure him into danger, and if Aziza hadn't been there, it would've worked. It had reminded him of just how vulnerable his mind was, and how, even when the curse wasn't *actively* wiping his memories, it still had so much control over him. His parents lost their shit if he didn't text back, and they expected him to tell them everything, but they couldn't be honest with him in return. For once, he didn't want to be the one to back down in the name of keeping the peace. Dad would have to back down this time, because Leo wasn't giving up until he had answers.

"I keep running the possibilities through my head," Dad said, dropping his hands at last and facing Leo, his forehead wrinkled with stress. "Like, what are all the alarming things my teenager could be getting up to? But I know you. You're a good kid. So if you're not keeping secrets because you did something wrong, then you're keeping secrets because you did something that would scare me. Something dangerous."

Leo didn't reply. He couldn't.

"Am I getting warmer?" Dad asked.

"You can't tell Mom," he began, which was definitely the wrong thing to say. Dad went white.

"That bad?"

"Not in the way you're thinking."

He took the vial from his pocket and knew exactly when Dad recognized the object inside. The look in his eyes, as he stared at the vial, was the closest Leo had ever seen Dad come to hatred.

"How did you get that?" Dad asked hoarsely.

"I stole it from your room."

"Leo Merritt, I cannot believe the nerve of you right now—"

Dad cut himself off, shut his eyes, and took several deep breaths. He removed his glasses and let them drop onto the coffee table with a clatter.

"Put it away," he said. "You didn't have the right—"

"I do have the right!" Leo hissed, conscious of Hazel and her too-sharp ears upstairs. He returned the vial to his pocket. "Aziza says this belongs to a fairy. And I *know* it has something to do with why we're cursed."

"I am *begging* you to let it go," Dad said.

"Let what go? My *true love*?"

"The idea of breaking the curse! Don't you think we *tried*—"

"If we could find the fairy who did it—"

"Don't even *say* that word—"

"What, *fairy*?" Leo gave a strangled laugh.

"This isn't something to joke about," Dad snapped.

"I'm *not* laughing!" His voice was climbing, and he couldn't stop it; but this whole day had showed him how much he had zero control over, so what was one more thing? He didn't care if Mom or Hazel heard anymore; he didn't even care that there was something monstrous in the woods, something bigger happening in Blackthorn than one little curse. The events of the day had left him overwhelmed; he felt detached from the world around him, almost like he was watching himself from outside his body, but even now the gaps in his memory felt so real he could've walked into them and disappeared. This nameless, faceless person that he'd loved once— that he *still* loved, somehow, because his heart remembered what the rest of him didn't—they were real.

"Sit down," Dad said tiredly. Leo hadn't even realized he'd shot to his feet.

"You told me my true love is the one I choose," Leo said. "Then I must have chosen."

"What about their choice?" Dad said.

"What?" The question caught him off guard; he felt himself falter. And even though Dad was still sitting and Leo was standing, he no longer felt like he had the upper hand in this conversation at all.

Dad replaced his glasses and gave Leo a hard, serious look. "Where has your true love been all this time?" He spread his hands out, as if to indicate the empty room around them. A chill ran through Leo as Dad unknowingly echoed the words of the mysterious voice in the woods. "This person *left* you. You're fighting for someone who isn't even here."

"Did they leave, or did the curse *take* them?" Leo argued, but there was no heat to it. It wasn't like the thought had never occurred to him. Maybe his true love hadn't loved him back. Maybe they hadn't loved him enough. Maybe they'd already moved on. Maybe, at the first sign of trouble, they'd decided that Leo wasn't worth it. He struggled to regain the energy that had propelled him just moments ago, but it was gone. He said haltingly, "The words of the curse . . . it said—"

"It's a memory curse. It's not a—a vanishing curse. It doesn't make people disappear," Dad interjected, in the reasonable tone he always used when he was trying to defuse an argument. Only the tightness around his eyes and the lingering edge to his words betrayed him. "I don't know what happened to . . . I don't know, but I honestly don't believe the curse is what's keeping them away."

"Do you know *who*—" Leo started, but Dad was already shaking his head.

"I have a guess. But don't ask. You've tried before, and you never remember my answers." He stood and, hesitantly, put a hand on

Leo's shoulder. "I'm sorry. I know it doesn't seem that way, but . . . I really am."

He retreated to his office then, and it was only once he was long gone that Leo realized how effectively Dad had derailed the conversation. All to avoid talking about the contents of that vial and what had happened the night they'd all been cursed. Dad hadn't backed down after all. He'd gone on the offensive. He'd lashed out at Leo— something Dad never did, not once in Leo's memory.

You're fighting for someone who isn't even here.

But true love, Leo thought, probably required a little bit of faith. He wasn't ready to quit. Not yet.

WITH EVERYONE AVOIDING each other, it was almost as if he had the house to himself. So he began his search. His parents had kept a clue about the curse—the fairy wing—hidden in their room; who knew what else he might unearth if he looked?

Instead of clues, though, all he found were superstitions. Rows of iron nails hammered into the top of every window frame. Rowan switches tucked in with the potted plants. Stones with a hole through the center, hidden near all the doors and windows. The shrubs with the tiny yellow flowers that Mom had planted along the edge of the house, which turned out to be St. John's wort.

"That's weird, right? All this stuff?" he asked Aziza quietly over the phone, while he balanced on a stepladder and worked the nails out of the living room window using the hammer he'd fetched from the garage. He'd told her what he'd found so far, and she confirmed his suspicions.

"Those are protective charms people used to use to ward off fae,"

Aziza said. "Your parents must really be afraid that something will come looking for them."

He paused, his hand gripping the hammer tightly. "I know I'm asking for trouble here. But . . ."

There, he faltered. But what? Aziza spent all her time trying to protect people from fae, and here he was, doing the opposite. Stripping the protections away. Deliberately making himself and his whole family vulnerable. Would this be the point where Aziza told him his curse-breaking obsession had gone too far? Where he'd be on his own again?

But all Aziza said was, "Look for the salt."

He closed his eyes for a second, more grateful than she'd probably ever know.

"By the doors?" he asked.

"Yeah. It might be in a container. You'd have noticed it otherwise."

That was all he needed; he knew exactly where to look then. He moved the stepladder to the front door and took down the wooden cross nailed above the entrance. He turned it over, examining it, until he found it—the latch. It was *hollow*. His fingers worked clumsily at the latch—it stuck a little, like it hadn't been opened in years—until it came free all at once, the back of the cross sliding off and salt spilling everywhere. He cursed under his breath, but inside, he felt grimly victorious. He threw out the rest of the salt and cleaned up what had spilled.

By the time he'd found the other hollow crosses and done one more sweep of the house, making sure he'd missed nothing else, it was late. No one had eaten. He shuffled into the kitchen and then shuffled out a few minutes later with a marshmallow-fluff-and-peanut-butter sandwich on a plate, which he took upstairs. He knocked lightly on Hazel's door.

"It's me. I brought, uh . . . dinner. Kind of."

The door opened a crack. A brown eye glared sullenly down at the plate, and then up at him. It was her favorite. He suppressed a grin at the internal struggle he could almost see taking place. At last, the crack widened so that Hazel could stick a hand through it and accept the plate.

"Were they mad at you?" she mumbled.

"So mad." He gave her his most pitiful look. "I thought Mom was going to *literally* explode."

"Good," she said, through a mouthful of peanut butter. "What really happened today? Why didn't you call?"

He gave her a version of events that was both heavily edited—she didn't need to know about the necromancer and the hounds, or how close the voice in the woods had truly come to snaring him—and heavily exaggerated, turning the Ash Witch into a twenty-foot-tall colossus. By the time he was done, they were both sitting on the floor, Leo leaning against the door frame and Hazel's clean plate abandoned at her side. Her eyes were huge with awe.

"Let me go with you and Aziza next time!" she begged.

"Maybe when you learn to drive. Or do magic."

She pouted, which still worked on Dad, but hadn't worked on Leo since she was, like, six. "But you said I could help."

"With the curse," he said. "And only when I had a plan for breaking it."

He felt a twinge of guilt at his lie of omission. But sabotaging his parents' anti-fairy protections on the house was not really a *plan*. The word *plan* suggested a course of action that had been crafted with thought and care, after considering alternatives and accounting for possible setbacks.

What he'd done tonight wasn't a plan. It was an act of desperation.

CHAPTER 23

TRISTAN

TRISTAN WOKE BECAUSE whatever he was lying on was too soft, and it felt like a trap.

He opened his eyes to an unfamiliar ceiling. Gauzy blue curtains softened the sunlight.

He shot to his feet too fast, went light-headed, and caught himself on the arm of the couch—so that's what he'd been lying on. *Everything* hurt. Breathing hurt—he pulled up his shirt to check, and sure enough, bright red blood spotted his bandages. He brushed his fingers against his neck and winced at what felt like raw wounds.

There on the ground was his bag, with the hilt of his ritual knife sticking out of the side pocket. So he hadn't been robbed. That was something, at least. The sight of the knife pinged in his mind as important, somehow—what was the last thing he'd done with it? But his head was full of clouds, full of pain and the aftertaste of the hag's fury.

He glanced around the room, which turned out to be an office. The desk in the corner was empty, the door was shut, no one else was around. Swiftly, he put himself back together, gathering up his bag, checking that nothing had been taken from it, and tucking his ritual knife away in his boot. He didn't know where he was or who had brought him here, and he didn't like that at *all*. He had to get out.

He checked the window first—locked. But the door wasn't. He inched it open, checking to make sure no one was around to see, and slipped out. By the time he had crept down the hallway outside and found himself in a library, his memories of last night had sharpened into awful clarity.

He'd done it. He'd betrayed the hag. For good, this time.

Weak in the aftermath of the hag's torture, he'd used up the last of his energy in the fight against the Ash Witch. He'd passed out. Mostly. He must have drifted in and out of consciousness, because he had vague recollections of being in a car, of being carried inside—

Carried?

He searched his mind for a clearer memory. Had he dreamed the sensation of Leo's sweater against his cheek and Leo's arms around him . . . or had that been real? A split second of intense longing was swiftly replaced by a horrifying thought: *When was the last time he'd showered?*

He cringed. Humiliation made his face burn.

It must've been Leo and Aziza who'd brought him here, then. But this revelation made his leaving even more urgent. If he was alive, it was because the hag still thought he could be useful. Despite his clear and willful disobedience. Being around the two of them would only put them in danger.

He crept past a circulation desk and into the stacks. The vaulted ceiling arched overhead, segmented by ivory support beams, like the inside of a whale's rib cage. Stained glass windows threw geometric patterns of colored light over the study tables. Through gaps in the shelves, he glimpsed Aziza talking to a petite black-haired woman wearing a name tag he couldn't read from this distance—the librarian, he assumed. She held open a thick tome, and Aziza had bent close to read over her shoulder.

Then the woman looked up sharply, and Tristan ducked out of sight, heart pounding.

"Did you hear that?" she said, though Tristan was certain he hadn't made a sound.

"What?" Aziza asked.

"I think . . ."

Aziza figured it out at the same time she did. "Shit. We didn't lock the door."

Footsteps as they headed back in the direction of the room Tristan had just abandoned. He hurried through the stacks, staying low, ears strained for the sound of their return. By the time he heard them coming back, he was pushing the double-door entry open just enough to squeeze through and get outside. It was early morning, so early the library couldn't have been open yet.

He took the steps two at a time, evaluating his limited options for escape. Around the back, or straight ahead, onto the road? But before he could make a decision, he stopped dead in his tracks.

There was only one car in the parking lot, and it was Leo's.

Leo was just getting out, phone pressed to his ear and a paper bag in his hand. Their eyes met. He broke into an easy smile, as if he and Tristan had planned to meet here. With nowhere to hide, the breath knocked clean out of him, Tristan froze like a fucking rabbit.

"Actually," Leo said into the receiver, "hang on. I'll see you in a bit."

He hung up. Shut the door. Placed the bag on the hood of his car, which he then leaned against, watching Tristan but making no attempt to come nearer.

"I won't stop you if you want to go," he said. "But we'd really like it if you'd at least talk to us first."

"You—you don't want me here," Tristan said, his mouth dry, stumbling over the words. "You don't know what I've . . . and it's dangerous if I'm here . . . for you—I mean—for all of you—"

"Just hear us out. Please?" he said hopefully. Tristan was silent. Leo must have taken it as hesitation instead of what it actually was—resignation—because he added, with an offhand gesture at the bag, "I brought food. Meryl didn't have much on hand, so I went and picked this up just now. You've been out of it since yesterday, you've gotta be hungry—you can leave right after you eat if you still want to."

As if he needed to be persuaded. Leo couldn't know this, not anymore, but Tristan could never say no to him.

That was how he wound up going right back the way he'd come, trailing meekly along after Leo and the heavenly smell of greasy food. Aziza and the librarian were waiting; they looked startled when they caught sight of Tristan, and Aziza said, "Why did you—"

And then she met Leo's eyes. A look was exchanged, the kind where Leo's said, *See? No problem*, and Aziza shook her head and didn't bother finishing her sentence. They convened at one of the study tables, with the librarian—Meryl, the name tag said—making half-hearted protests about how they technically weren't supposed to eat in there, until Leo bribed her with a bacon-egg-and-cheese, and Meryl said, "As long as it's all cleaned up before opening hours . . ."

Just like that, Leo had charmed everyone in sight. And then the four of them were sitting awkwardly around the table over half-unwrapped breakfast sandwiches: Tristan, his ex-boyfriend, a librarian, and a witch. Somehow, the librarian was the most unsettling part of the equation, her eyes a dark, abyssal blue that made Tristan's neck prickle with foreboding—or maybe he was just rattled because she'd overheard him when he'd thought he was being so careful sneaking away.

Leo had sat down first and patted the back of the chair next to his, indicating that this was meant to be Tristan's seat; Aziza and Meryl were opposite them. This was the first time he'd been this close to Leo—without either of them being in mortal danger—since he'd dropped out of school. His hands ached with the need to reach out to him. He still recognized the rhythm of Leo's breathing. His own chest rose and fell in time, an old habit. He used to match his breathing to Leo's when he had trouble falling asleep.

"I'll go first," Leo said.

Tristan jumped, only then realizing that while he'd been pining away, an uncomfortable silence had fallen over the rest of the group. When he looked up, Leo was smiling at him. Not the smile Tristan was used to, though. This was the sort of smile you gave a skittish greyhound, reassuring but detached. A stranger's smile. But then Leo started talking—going over everything he remembered from yesterday—and Tristan forgot all about his pathetic broken heart.

"Wait," he said. "You fought her off *yourself*? Aziza didn't—didn't use magic to save you, or—"

"I think the curse made it hard for her to hang on to me." Leo frowned thoughtfully. "Once it figured out it wasn't getting anywhere, the voice went away on its own. I just had to hold out until then."

Tristan was stunned.

And *proud*.

He'd severely underestimated Leo. He'd done terrible things because he'd been afraid the hag would hurt Leo if he didn't obey. But Leo hadn't needed Tristan to protect him. He hadn't even needed Aziza. He'd fought the hag off all on his own.

"The voice told me she could break the curse," Leo said. "She knew things about it that she shouldn't have known. Can she read minds?"

"Sort of. She uses people's desires and wishes to prey on them." He hesitated. "What kind of curse is it?"

"I lost my true love," Leo said, unabashed. Tristan's heart constricted painfully. "I have to get my memories back and find . . . whoever they are. But she couldn't really break a curse, could she? It was a trick, right?"

"I don't know," Tristan admitted. It was almost funny. She'd promised him and Leo the exact same thing, only Leo had been smart enough to say no.

It struck him then, how badly he'd misjudged Leo. He knew Leo better than almost anyone, but he hadn't believed in him. Leo had never expected Tristan to break the curse for him. He'd planned to fight it himself, and if he failed, he'd just wanted Tristan to *be there*. He'd wanted Tristan to remind him of what he forgot. He never cared if they had to start from scratch, as long as they could still be together.

Leo had faith in them.

Tristan had been the one who'd thought Leo wouldn't want him anymore. *Tristan* had been the one who'd let his insecurities get the better of him. *Tristan* had been the one to self-destruct.

If you forget me, I'll remind you. That was the promise he'd made to Leo and promptly broken. He'd been so afraid of rejection that he hadn't even given Leo a chance. He'd just left. And he was supposed to be the one who loved him. So then what was Tristan's love worth?

"There are very few beings that can break someone else's curse," Meryl said, startling him; she'd been so silent he'd almost forgotten she was there. "The ones that can—it wouldn't be worth the price you paid for it. Otherwise, only the caster of a curse or its victim can break it."

"The victim?" Leo said, sitting up. "*I* can break the curse?"

Meryl shrugged one dainty, cardigan-clad shoulder. "Curses usually have loopholes."

If Leo did break the curse, Tristan wondered, would he ever forgive him?

"Tell us what we're up against," Aziza said. "Who or *what* is the voice Leo heard?"

She leaned forward, her cloud of dark hair falling over her shoulder. Her magic had a force to it that was impossible to ignore, even when she wasn't using it. He could sense it, a can't-put-your-finger-on-it quality that made someone magnetic, the way some people had charisma or charm. Aziza wasn't charming, but she *was* magical.

There were too many overwhelming people in this room. He addressed the table.

"I don't fully understand what this means," he said, "but I know that she's a hag."

For some reason, Aziza looked at Meryl, gauging her reaction. Meryl's eyes were down, and her voice was almost meek when she said, "I see. It's just—she was supposed to be dormant."

"But what's a hag?" Aziza asked. "You mentioned a *last time*."

"She was asleep, and someone woke her," Tristan said. "I don't know who. That was before I . . ."

"Before you what?" Meryl said softly.

All eyes landed on him. Only then did it sink in: If he wanted to help Aziza and get rid of the hag, he had to start with something scarier than a dozen Ash Witches. He had to tell the truth. Shame choked him so he could hardly speak. He would've given anything for Leo to not be in the room just then.

"September before last, my parents kicked me out," he said haltingly. "I thought I could camp in the woods. And then I heard the voice."

The same voice Leo had heard. With the short-lived flare of power she'd gotten from being newly woken, she had cast the net of her magic wide, seeking a suitable target—and found Tristan, devastated and vulnerable. But once he'd reached the gateway tree, she lifted her enchantment. She didn't want him for prey. She needed a bondservant. He had to be clear-minded and able to consent in order for the contract to take.

"Why did she need a bondservant?" Aziza cut in. "She found you without any help."

"It takes a lot of energy to spread her magic all over the city like that," Tristan said. "She can't do it all the time. With a bondservant to guide her, she can aim her magic at a target."

Her hands curled into fists where they rested on the arms of the chair. The disgust was clear on her face.

Once he'd started talking, it was easy to keep going; the sooner he got to the end, the sooner he could stop. But when he tried to gloss over the terms of the contract, Aziza had more questions:

"Ten years of servitude for a magical favor?" she repeated. "What favor would be worth that?"

"It's personal," he said shortly.

He couldn't tell them what the hag had promised him. The curse would kick in and put Leo into that dreamlike state where he couldn't hear what was being said, where he lost time and didn't even realize it. Tristan couldn't stand seeing him like that. And Leo was the only person who *needed* to know; Tristan wasn't interested in baring his soul to two strangers.

He had nothing but this secret. He was keeping it.

"Then when you figured out you weren't going to make it ten years, what did she have against you to keep you obedient?" she pressed. "What finally made you decide to help us instead?"

"If I tried to quit, she would've killed me," he said. "I was afraid to die. But I'm not anymore."

Even leaving out the most important thing—her threats against Leo—that much was true.

"Can she still do that?" Leo asked, alarmed. "Kill you, even if you're nowhere near her?"

"She can, and I'm not sure why she hasn't yet," Tristan said. "She knows I've betrayed her. She knows she's lost the only thing she could use to control me. So the fact that I'm still alive right now . . ."

"She thinks she can still use you," Aziza finished.

"Yes," he said. "You should stay away from me. I want to help you, but I—I don't know what she's planning."

Meryl bit her thumbnail and stared off into the distance. "Hags are created when a witch is corrupted by power. They can take many forms, depending on what their original craft was, and they grow more powerful over the years as they hoard magic. This one is a couple of centuries old, maybe more."

"The only thing she ever admitted to being threatened by is . . . something called the Fair Folk," Tristan said. "Could we get them to help us?"

"That's an old term for fairies," Aziza said. "And no. It would take a long journey into Elphame to find them; even if we did, they wouldn't help us for free. They're not borderland fae and nothing the hag does affects them. We don't want their attention anyway, trust me." She straightened up in her seat. "Meryl, if she was dormant before, how do we make her dormant again? Can she be killed?"

Tristan held his breath. Even the possibility of such a thing—*killing the hag*—was more bewitching than any spell.

"The last time she woke was about twenty years ago," she said. "The one who woke her—"

Abruptly, she stopped, like her voice had been snatched out of her throat. She swallowed hard, looked at Aziza, and shook her head apologetically.

"You know who woke her, but you can't say," Aziza guessed, and she sounded angry, but not at Meryl.

Meryl nodded.

"Do you think the same person woke her again?"

She hesitated. "It's possible. But . . . that person . . . is not in Blackthorn right now. I . . . Wait." Her hand touched her throat, as if in response to the tightening of an invisible rope. "I can tell you that when a hag rises, it takes an immense magical effort to bring her back down. I can tell you that . . . about twenty years ago . . . no, more like seventeen years ago, there was only a small handful of witches in Blackthorn." She gave Aziza a significant look. "Of those, the only ones willing to take their chances with the hag—"

This time, when she stopped, it didn't seem to be because she'd lost her voice. The ensuing silence between Aziza and Meryl grew thick with tension as the seconds passed.

"What were you about to say?"

But it sounded like Aziza already knew.

"Your grandfather never mentioned—"

"No."

"I'm sorry," Meryl said.

"So . . . my parents, then."

"I wish I could tell you more," Meryl said, wringing her hands. "It's not just that I'm forbidden. Some of it I don't even know."

"Zee?" Leo said, after the silence had stretched painfully long.

Aziza exhaled slowly, like she'd made a decision. "Thanks, Meryl. We can figure it out from here. Tristan, does any of that help?"

"If your parents had something to do with locking her up in the first place, that would explain why she wants to get rid of you so badly," Tristan said, gathering his thoughts, trying to figure out how the pieces he had fit in with Meryl's. "And she said—her powers didn't work on you because of *the old man*."

"My grandfather. He made me carry a spell pouch in my backpack," Aziza said. "Meryl, I'm guessing you don't know how they stopped her."

"No."

Without missing a beat, Aziza turned to Tristan. "You're a necromancer."

"Yes, but—" he said, and then he fell silent as he figured out what she was getting at. "You can't be thinking—"

"We don't know how to stop a hag," she said. "The only people who do are dead. My grandfather might know something, but he threatened to send me away from Blackthorn if I didn't stay out of trouble—what do you think he'll say if I ask him about *this*? But if we could talk to my parents—"

Leo and Meryl erupted with protests.

"I don't know if that's the best—"

"That is *super fucked up*—"

"Does anyone have a better idea?" She swept out her hands in a go-ahead gesture.

No one did.

"Leo, she tried to kill you. And she's coming after me next," Aziza said.

"Aziza's right," Tristan said. "But I tried to wake someone from the dead once, and—it didn't go well. I think I have a better handle on my powers now, but are you prepared to see your parents . . . like that?"

He didn't elaborate on what *that* meant, and to his relief, she didn't ask.

"I was still a baby when they died," she said. "They're strangers to me. I'll be fine."

Tristan nodded, taking her word for it. "I'm willing to try."

Meryl sighed and sat back, giving in. Leo looked around at the three of them, evidently unable to believe what he was hearing.

"*This* is the plan? This is seriously the plan?"

"It's not a big deal," she said.

"They're your parents!"

"So?" Aziza and Tristan said, in unison.

But Tristan preferred it when Leo was on his side, so he made a stab at winning him over.

"If this means we can kill the hag, all of Blackthorn will be safer," he reasoned.

"Exactly!" said Aziza, who clearly was going to do whatever she was going to do, whether or not Leo approved, but also seemed to be aligned with Tristan in not wanting Leo against her if it could be avoided.

Outnumbered, Leo relented.

The bond was worryingly quiet in the back of Tristan's mind, but he tried not to dwell on that.

CHAPTER 24

AZIZA

OLD SOUTH CEMETERY was a hundred-acre stretch of scraggly grass-land, crowded with stubby granite headstones and dotted with rick-ety trees.

Aziza hadn't visited her parents' graves in years. Jiddo used to take her every few months when she was little, but they'd fallen out of the habit, in part because it was a long trip—about two hours on public transportation. They didn't have a car, since Aziza could walk to school and Jiddo could take the train to the university. And on her own, Aziza had little motivation to go. Any sentimental feel-ings she'd had about her parents had faded a long time ago. It had been many years since she'd pored over pictures of her mother, trac-ing the yellowed lines of an arched nose, brown eyes, and waves of frizzy hair that were just like hers.

"We can still call this whole thing off," Leo said.

It was after hours; there were no streetlamps past the cast-iron gate, but the moon laid a silver glaze on the field.

"If you're scared, you can stay in the car."

"No way," he said, with a forced laugh. "Whoever stays behind gets picked off by the bad guys first, everyone knows that. I just think, you know, as far as team-building exercises go, graverobbing wouldn't be my top choice."

She grimaced. Not at the graverobbing comment. Her objection was to Leo referring to the three of them as a *team* in the same tone of voice with which he'd once insisted that he and Aziza were going to be *friends*, and, yes, he'd been right back then, but he wasn't right this time. This wasn't a team, it was her and Leo and a temporary alliance with someone who might or might not turn on them at any moment. But she let it pass without comment.

"We're not robbing them," she said instead. "We're going to put them right back where we found them."

"Maybe I should've brought something. Mom says, uh, you don't go to anyone's house empty-handed—I guess this isn't really their *house*, but—"

"And these aren't really my parents," she reminded him. "They're just bodies."

Leo's tight-lipped expression seemed to say, *I hope you're right, but I don't think you are.*

They pulled the shovels out of his trunk, hopped the gate, and crept out into the field. Tristan lagged behind them, pale and thin as a wraith. The hand not carrying the shovel was tucked in his pocket, and his head was bowed. His walk had a tinge of the blækhounds' movements, a lightness to it that made his footsteps silent. It was unsettling. And his refusal to say why he'd signed the hag's contract made her uneasy. When it came to dealing with the fae, half the battle was figuring out what they wanted; once she had that, nine times out of ten, she had the situation under control. Not knowing what Tristan wanted felt dangerous.

"Are you sure you're feeling strong enough for this?" Leo called softly over his shoulder.

"Doesn't matter," Tristan said. "The hag could strike me down at any moment. We have to do this now."

She knew the general area where her parents' graves were located. An old memory unburied itself: She was maybe nine years old, and she had wanted to know what happened after death. If Mom and Dad were in heaven. Or if they'd been reborn. Or if they were ghosts.

"I don't know," Jiddo had said. "No one does. Not even witches."

"But what do you *think*?" she'd asked.

"I don't see the point in thinking anything," he said. "I'll find out soon enough, won't I? The only thing I believe in, habibi, is doing right in *this* life. I believe in family. You and me." He'd kissed the top of her head. "You are the answer to every question that matters."

Jiddo's peaceful acceptance of the unknown had comforted her. She didn't need to be afraid of death if he wasn't.

They trudged down three rows of graves before they found the right pair, marked with her parents' names—Ahmed and Leila El-Amin—and the years they'd lived. That was all. No inscription. Not even a *beloved daughter* on Leila's marker, though she had been. Jiddo still couldn't say her name without his voice breaking.

Leo tilted his head as he read the names. "Isn't your grandpa your mom's dad? But your last name . . ."

"When they died, he changed his name so we'd have the same one," she said. Jiddo was so quick to give things up, to sacrifice. But sometimes she just wanted him to *talk* to her.

Aziza's family history was a patchwork stitched together from the stories Jiddo occasionally let slip, the photos in albums in drawers where Jiddo never looked but didn't mind if Aziza did, and the questions Aziza sometimes dared to ask, only when it was late at night and if Jiddo grew sad he could go to bed soon and it would be okay in the morning.

She had learned that if she asked about events—like how her parents had met or what had happened the day she was born—she'd get the bare minimum response. The facts and nothing else. So she began to come at the matter sideways, surprising him into giving away details that didn't fit the script he'd prepared. He wanted to teach her about their family the way he taught his students about ancient civilizations, creating timelines around events of significance, structuring it like he'd structure a curriculum. But a timeline wasn't what Aziza wanted.

So she had hoarded bits of information like the shiny little tokens she collected for Blackthorn's fae and saved until she needed them. Things like the way Ahmed had been nervous to hold Aziza when she was born, but once he got the hang of it, he hardly ever wanted to put her down. And the way Leila started reading picture books with Aziza as soon as Aziza had gotten big enough to be able to sit up and look at the illustrations, even though at that age she was still too young to understand them. And before he met Leila, Ahmed hitchhiked to the West Coast and back, and Jiddo only half remembered some of the stories Ahmed had shared about that time in his life, but Ahmed had always said he'd tell Aziza all about it when she was old enough to start dreaming of adventure. And Leila whistled back to the robins every morning. And Leila always caught the spiders and set them free outside. And Leila's first word, when she was a baby, had been *Baba*.

Years of asking and that was all she had, just bits and pieces. But maybe there was no amount of secondhand information that would have satisfied her curiosity. In the end, it was never going to be the same thing as truly knowing them.

Their shovels broke the hard, frozen crust of soil and sliced down into the soft earth below. Hours passed to the rasp of their blades scooping up mouthfuls of dirt and then dumping them into growing mounds off to the side. The graves hollowed out, slowly but steadily, under a rising moon. By the time Aziza's shovel struck something hard, she was drenched in sweat, and it was close to midnight.

They brushed the final layer of dirt off the coffins. Aziza and Tristan heaved Leila's open, while Leo uncovered Ahmed's.

She'd expected a stench, but there wasn't one, not really. The skin and flesh had decomposed a long time ago; even the hair was mostly gone. All that was left were Leila's bones and the dress they'd buried her in, a modest floral thing gone faded and moldy.

"Still want to do this?" Tristan asked under his breath.

"Don't waste your energy worrying about me."

"I'm not worried. I just want to make sure you're not going to back out before we get the information we need." He looked at her directly for the first time all night, his eyes more haunted than any grave. "We have to get rid of the hag. No matter what."

"You don't have to remind me," she said. "She's the one who put them here, remember?"

Leo reached down to help her climb out. Tristan hoisted himself out on his own before Leo could offer his hand. They stood before the two graves, dirt-streaked and sweaty, gulping in the crisp night air.

"Stay back," Tristan said. "Last time I tried this, he was— dangerous."

Nothing happened at first. If not for his white-blond hair, Tristan would've disappeared against the dark sky. Despite the clarity and brightness of the night, he wore the shadows like a cloak; the moonlight itself seemed to shy away from his slim shoulders. He clutched the shovel in both hands, like a club. She was on the verge of asking why when a harsh cold spread from the point where he stood, freezing the words on her tongue.

The oppressive pall of dark magic followed. Beside her, Leo's breathing came too fast, as if the magic was so potent that he could sense it, too. She reached for him automatically, a hand on his arm, and his hand flew up to cover hers.

A noise disturbed the tense silence: the rattle of bone against wood, the crack and snap of old joints shifting, the scrape of thin fingers scrabbling up dirt walls. The yellowed, animated skeletons of Leila and Ahmed El-Amin emerged from their graves.

They slumped over the ground, grasping and straining for purchase. Ahmed's grinning skull turned at an unnatural angle to regard Tristan, and he stretched out his hand, reaching for the hem of Tristan's coat.

Leo twitched forward as if to intervene, but Aziza held him back.

"Don't," Tristan snarled, raising the shovel threateningly.

"*Help me,*" the skeleton rasped in a voice that was almost, but not quite, human. "*You who woke me. Help me, please.*"

Tristan was unmoved. "You can get out on your own."

A hollow sound emerged from the skeleton, the ghost of a laugh. But Ahmed and Leila did indeed pull themselves up on their own, with surprising strength. Ahmed knelt beside his grave; his head turned a slow circle, rotating a full 360 degrees as if to take in his surroundings, before his eyeless gaze settled on Tristan again.

"*Why have you woken us, summoner?*" he said.

Leila's skeleton pushed itself upright and then, with a heave of effort, stood. Her legs beneath the tattered floral skirt were twisted grotesquely, her spine arched back, her jaw hanging open—as if her body was a tool she'd forgotten how to use.

When Leila spoke, it was a single word: "*Aziza.*"

"Don't look at her," Tristan ordered. "Talk to me."

Leila's skull bobbed atop her spine in a rough shake, a deathless *no*. "*I will only speak with Aziza.*"

"It's fine," she said, stepping forward until she stood level with Tristan. Leila and Ahmed tilted their faces toward her. Their empty eye sockets were bottomless black pits. Nausea crawled up her throat; she forced it down.

"*So my daughter spends her days with a summoner and a curse bearer,*" Ahmed said, teeth clacking, the words billowing from his skull like a cold wind. "*I would have raised you to keep better company.*"

She searched their unreadable faces for something that would resonate with what she knew about her parents. Something of the father who'd wanted to tell her stories and the mother who rose with the birdsong each morning. But there was nothing there, nothing recognizable.

She didn't know if that was a disappointment or a relief.

"*How old are you?*" Leila asked, her jaw barely moving. Her voice had a whispery undertone to it, earthy and textured, like the *shush* of a hand sifting through loose soil.

"Seventeen," Aziza said. She pretended she was talking to one of the borderland fae, and kept her tone neutral and polite. "That's about how long you've been gone. Do you remember how you died?"

"*Did you wake us to ask what comes after death?*" Ahmed asked bitterly.

"No. Do you remember the hag?"

Leila took a jerky step forward, like a marionette being handled by an inexperienced puppeteer.

"Stop," Tristan ordered. She stopped.

"*I remember,*" she said.

"*I remember,*" her husband agreed.

"She came back, and now she's coming after me. I need to know how you beat her."

The skeletons considered her in silence. Did they have thoughts to gather? Did they have emotions to suppress?

"*We used our craft,*" Ahmed said at last. "*How else?*"

"*My gift of locking and unlocking,*" Leila said.

"*And my gift of building hidden spaces,*" he finished. "*Did you inherit one of our gifts?*"

"No. I'm a hedgewitch."

"*Hedgecraft runs in my family,*" Leila said. "*It is a valued but dangerous skill.*"

"*It won't help against a hag,*" Ahmed added. "*Run, hayati.*"

She shuddered at the sound of the endearment—one she'd only ever heard from Jiddo—mutilated in the corpse's mouth.

"I can't run. Blackthorn is my home."

"*Starting over is a privilege.*"

"I don't want to!" she snapped. "There has to be a way. What exactly did you do?"

"*Ahmed made a world below the world, a place to bury her in the woods,*" Leila said. "*And shaped a path underground to her territory, that we may approach her unseen and take her by surprise. She guards her borderlands well, sensing all that enters or attempts to leave, but only aboveground.*"

"He made a tunnel," Aziza said. She glanced over her shoulder at Leo, who grimaced. That explained the underground passage he'd crashed through—but the hag had evidently learned from her mistake. The warmth he'd felt had been her magic. There would be no sneaking up on her this time.

A picture formed in her mind, replacing the memory of Leo in the tunnel: Leila and Ahmed in his place, the way they looked in their photos, creeping in the dark and silence to confront the monster that would kill them. Aware of the danger but pressing on anyway. Not knowing it would be the last night of their lives.

It had been brave of them. Jiddo had never told her that part, how brave they were.

"*I bound her power to a tree and buried what couldn't be bound,*" Leila continued. "*Even if she's woken up again, what we did can't be undone; the gateway tree is the core of her power. If you destroy the tree, you might destroy the hag.*"

"*Or you might not,*" Ahmed said.

"*Are you alone?*" Leila asked, before Aziza could form another question. "*Where do you live? Who takes care of you?*"

"Jiddo does," Aziza said impatiently. "The gateway tree—"

"*Baba?*" Leila sounded suddenly very alive and very young. "*Is he here?*"

"No. He doesn't know—"

"*I want to see him,*" she said plaintively.

"You can't."

For some reason, her eyes burned. Maybe because, for an instant, she finally recognized the skeleton as the woman from the photos she'd memorized. Or maybe because, if her and Leila's positions had been switched, Jiddo would be the first person *she'd* want to see, too.

She took a deep, steadying breath. "The hag has done something to the border between our world and Elphame. I have to fix it."

"*Hags carve out their own space in the world,*" Leila explained. It was as if talking about Jiddo had reminded her whose daughter she was. She spoke in the same measured, placid tones Jiddo had always used to teach Aziza about magic. "*Her territory is not in Elphame, and not in Blackthorn. It exists on its own plane, and that existence disrupts the natural world. There is always a small amount of crossover between our realm and fairyland, but when a hag rises, we see levels of magical activity that are unusual and dangerous, even for a place as close to Elphame as Blackthorn is. Last time, we had pixies huddling under our neighbors' windows, wind sprites tugging at my skirt each time I stepped outside, goblins playing music on street corners and train platforms. The fairies stole a child every night and left behind a changeling. I couldn't let you out of my sight for a minute. They would have taken you, too.*"

"I told Leila and Khaled we should leave," Ahmed said. "Get as far away as we could."

"*I wanted to stay and fight,*" Leila said serenely. "*This is my fault.*"

Aziza didn't know how to respond to that. So she didn't.

"Tell me how to defend myself. Tell me how to defend Blackthorn."

"*She wants revenge for what we did to her,*" Ahmed said. "*We're not there to face her retribution, so you have inherited it. The moment she identified you, you were doomed. A hag never lets her prey go. Never.*"

"What do I do?" she pressed.

"*Run,*" he said again, and toppled backward into his grave with a chilling crash.

Tristan gasped. "They want to go back—I can't hold them."

"Leila, *please!*" she begged. "I need your help. Please . . . Mom, I just need this one thing from you—"

Leila extended her hands, palms up. "*I have given you all I can give. Your gift most of all. Your gift can save you; I know it can.*"

"Wait—"

"*Tell Baba—*"

A shiver racked her aged, ruined frame, cutting the words off.

"She's tired," Tristan whispered.

Whatever had animated Leila's bones went away. The unnatural blackness faded from her empty sockets, so that they were no more than dusty hollows again; the skeleton went limp, and she, too, collapsed into her grave without another word.

CHAPTER 25

LEO

LEO WAS CHECKING his backpack for his wallet and keys when Hazel burst through his door. He opened his mouth to remind her that they had talked about knocking, but he stopped when he saw the look on her face.

"There's a *voice*," she said breathlessly, and he raced after her, thinking of the hag. Somewhere in between skidding down the hallway, deftly sidestepping the bathroom door as Spot flung it open in his face, and careening into Hazel's room, it struck him that, if it *was* the hag, Leo wouldn't be able to hear her voice. It would be inside Hazel's head. So he was relieved when he found Hazel standing uncertainly beside the open window letting in the cold winter night, hair and clothes rustling under what must have felt like a light breeze, and heard the soft whispering that accompanied it.

"*Curious child,*" the whisperers said, and then, at Leo's arrival, they flitted to him, pulling at his sleeves like they were children themselves. "*We know you, gatewalker's companion.*"

"Yeah, hi," Leo said, feeling nervous and victorious in equal measures. Their first visit from Blackthorn's fae. Getting rid of the salt and the nails had worked; the house wasn't protected anymore. To Hazel, he added, "Don't be scared. They're just wind sprites."

"What's that?" she said eagerly. "Are they magic?"

"They're elemental spirits. If you want them to like you . . ." He looked around and found a rose-scented tea light candle on her desk. He picked it up, half paying attention to what he was doing and half listening to the sprites, which shared with him stolen snatches of conversations they had picked up in passing, the voices of countless strangers tuning in and out of clarity as if coming through a broken radio. "Light this," he told Hazel, handing her the candle and digging a lighter out of his backpack. He didn't smoke; it was just one of the supplies he'd taken to carrying around, like the first aid kit and the coffee thermos in his car, or the flashlight he had as a backup in case their phones stopped working.

Hazel lit the candle, and the whispers ceased. The sprites still moved around them, gently now, like a current of air from a fan that was slowing to a stop. The tiny flame stirred as the wind sprites investigated it. Soon the scent of roses was all around them. The sprites murmured their thanks in a voice that wasn't theirs, and then they swept back out the window, and the air was still again.

Hazel looked amazed, like all the holidays had come early.

"You pay them in scents," he told her, gratified by her reaction. It was normally *him* responding with that wide-eyed awe every time Aziza introduced him to something new, some strange being that had coexisted with Blackthorn all this time and he'd never noticed. "And sometimes they'll tell you secrets. Aziza says they're harmless."

Hazel's smile faded a little. She looked down at the candle still burning in her hands, and then up at Leo, dressed to leave for the night, his backpack slung over his shoulder.

"You're going out *again*?"

He shrugged. "Why are you even up this late? I thought you went to bed hours ago."

It was her turn to evade, dropping her gaze so that she could put the candle back in its place on her desk and shut the window. "I don't know. I just am."

He waited until she had crawled back onto her bed before he said, "What's wrong?"

She wrapped her arms around her knees and peered up at him through a curtain of frizzy curls, which hid most of her face. When Mom didn't braid her hair, she went around looking like the girl from *The Ring*. "Just nightmares. That's why I opened the window."

Because she had dreamed of fire and had woken up wanting to be cold.

He sat on the edge of her bed. "Think you'll be able to go back to sleep?"

"'M not tired anymore. Can't I go with you instead?"

"It's not safe," he told her.

"But you're *always* out, and I'm stuck here, and it's not fair!" she whined. "You're never home. It's just like . . ."

She fell silent, fuming, her face scrunched up angrily.

"Just like what?" he said, bewildered.

"Someone almost found out about Mom the other day, did you know that?" she said. "When she was picking up the groceries. No one really believed the lady who saw, but she made a scene and Mom got banned from the store for bringing animals inside. And last week Dad slipped on ice and hurt his shoulder, and he could barely pick anything up with that arm for, like, two days. Did you even notice?"

He hadn't. Hazel saw the guilty look on his face; she nodded once, in a there-you-have-it sort of way. She was right—between all-night border patrols with Aziza, school, and work, he *hadn't* been paying attention to what was going on with his family. Forget grocery store bans and bad shoulders; he was so exhausted the house could've fallen down around him, and he wouldn't have noticed. Maybe he was avoiding their parents, too, partly because he was still a little mad about their fight the other day but mostly because he didn't trust himself not to confess to tossing out the salt and the rowan and all. He somehow felt completely justified and also horribly guilty about it at the same time. So he found excuses to stay away. Before, Aziza would come over on the weekends to study sometimes—and, yes, to watch sci-fi movies that she was terrible at pretending not to be invested in—but now it was him doing his homework at Aziza's place more often than not. He ate his breakfast while walking out the door, and when he had to be home, he was usually in his room taking a much-needed nap.

"I'm sorry," he said at last. "You're right. I haven't been around. And I can't promise that I'll be home more, not yet. I'm helping Aziza with something important. Something serious."

"The thing in the woods," Hazel said, in hushed tones.

"Yeah. We're going to get rid of it." He paused and added ruefully, "Somehow. But—I'll make it up to you. This weekend. Sherlock Holmes marathon—whichever one you want to watch—and triple chocolate-chip brownies."

She eyed him suspiciously.

"What if I wanna watch BBC *Sherlock*, and the Guy Ritchie movies, and season one of *Elementary*? And the Granada version, we have to start with that one. That'll take us, like, all weekend probably."

"Is that a challenge?" he asked, with feigned outrage. "I'm the binge-watching *champion*. Bring it on."

He managed to convince her to at least try going back to sleep. As he turned off her desk lamp and backed out into the hall, she said, "What happens if you can't get rid of it?"

"We will." He was holding the door handle, the hallway light casting his shadow into the room. Then an uneasy thought occurred to him. "Uh, I know I said the wind sprites won't hurt you. But if you hear any other voices, come get me right away, okay? If I'm not here, go to Mom and Dad. Don't listen to any voices unless you know where they're coming from."

This earned him the sort of look he only received when he was being particularly dense. "Obviously."

"Okay, okay. Good night."

"Night."

As he shut the door quietly behind him, he considered what Hazel had said. And what she hadn't said. She thought he was acting the same way he had after his sixteenth birthday, at the curse's onset. The way he took off all the time, making them worry. They didn't know the half of it, how he'd volunteered himself as Aziza's assistant and getaway driver, throwing himself headlong into dangerous magical situations. How he'd gone out of his way to make his house, the house his *whole family* lived in, vulnerable to fae. On the off chance that a fairy who evidently *hated* them would come back. This wasn't the healthy way to deal with his parents' secrecy, he knew that. But doing the unhealthy thing was better than doing nothing.

And even though Hazel was kind of right, she was kind of wrong, too. There was a difference between what he was doing now and what he'd done before. This time, he wasn't alone.

It was their first night patrolling as a group of three, and he could tell Aziza was on edge. Since the cemetery trip—which he'd *known* was the worst idea ever—there was a restless urgency to her that worried him. Like hearing her parents' story, what they'd gone through get-ting rid of the hag, had made it personal to her in a way it hadn't been before. He was afraid of the risks she'd take, in her desperation to fight back and end the chaos.

And it was chaos. The wills-o'-the-wisp were no longer confined to the woods; they drifted through tiny neighborhood parks and jogging trails, ghostly and hypnotic lights that kept leading people into ditches. They had found a tangle of shades in an antique shop, hiding inside gold lockets and behind dusty mirrors. They broke into someone's basement to coax a marsh nymph out of it; she had flooded the place and filled it with cordgrass and sea lavender.

But they couldn't be everywhere at once. Anytime he turned on the radio and heard the news talking about yet another missing per-son, he wondered—and he knew Aziza wondered—if it had been something from Elphame that had gotten them.

They didn't listen to the news anymore.

Tonight's catastrophe involved a poor woman they found bur-ied up to her neck in an insect swarm. Beetles the size of Leo's fist seethed around her, some of them with opal-colored shells, brilliantly patterned, others sleek and black as roaches, with curving horns. Underground, hidden from view, the imp yanked at her ankles, dragging her down into the earth. Aziza and Tristan lit matches and held them over the mound. A cloud of flies startled into the air, and other indistinct squirming things scuttled into the shadows.

"I'll set your whole burrow on fire if you don't let her go," Aziza said, addressing the imp.

The woman had her eyes screwed shut and was mumbling, "*Pleasepleasepleaseplease.*" Leo knelt down next to her, since Aziza and Tristan had the matches and the threats covered.

"Hi," he said. "I know this sucks, but you're going to be all right."

She whimpered.

"Uh, would it help if I held your hand?"

She opened her eyes a crack. Something skittered over her tearstained cheek, and she squeaked and clamped her mouth shut, as if afraid it would crawl in. But she managed to free a shaky hand and reach out. Leo plucked a couple of slugs off her knuckles and took her hand.

"What do you do? Got any kids? . . . Okay, no worries, you don't have to talk. I'm Leo, and these are my friends—" At Aziza's glare, he broke off. "Um, never mind. Maybe it's better if we don't do names."

Sticking to safe topics, he chatted with—or rather, *at*—the woman until Aziza got the imp to release her. Then the three of them dug her out; it took a solid hour or two before she could clamber free.

"Will you be all right?" Leo asked. "We could walk you—"

Half-hidden in the shadows, Aziza turned her most forbidding glare on the woman.

"Go through that arch," she said, pointing at the fairy door she'd made back at the tree line. "If you stray, you'll be lost forever. I will not come after you." (Leo knew for a fact that was a lie.) "Don't ever come back."

The woman fled.

"You didn't have to be so harsh," Leo said.

"We can't have people recognizing us," she told him, crossing her arms. "No one will believe her about what just happened, and she didn't get a good look at me or Tristan, but if she sees *you* on the street someday—"

"Come on. She was being tortured. What was I supposed to do, ignore her?"

"For her own good. *And* yours."

"Are we going after the imp?" Tristan hung apart from them, examining the remains of the mound, which was slowly breaking up as the insects scattered.

"It probably tunneled away," Aziza said. "Anyway, we're already in Elphame, which is right where I want it to be. The only thing I can do is keep patching up the boundary so it doesn't escape into Blackthorn again."

Tristan dragged his fingers through his hair, dislodging a spider. He shuddered and inspected his clothing for more stragglers. "Why don't you kill it? I could send the hound after it."

A nearby patch of shadow, which contained the hound in question, released a low, intrigued growl.

Aziza's expression darkened.

Uh-oh, Leo thought. He'd spent the whole night trying to keep the peace between Aziza and Tristan. Aziza didn't trust him, and she was annoyed that he insisted on bringing a hound with them on patrol—but probably even more annoyed, Leo guessed, that she didn't have a good reason to tell him not to. Because if a hound had been there that time with the kelpies, no one would've died. But that didn't mean she had to like it. If she'd been a little grumpy with Leo when they'd met—which was her default with new people—that was nothing compared to how she was responding to Tristan's company.

To be fair, he *had* spent a year working for someone who wanted her dead.

That wasn't even the part that bothered her the most, though. It was his continued secrecy about *why* he'd signed the hag's contract—what the hag had promised him in exchange for his years of service.

She said he had to be hiding something truly awful, because what could be worth concealing from them at this point, when they knew everything else?

"I don't know," Leo had told her. "I just don't think it's that black and white."

But Tristan wasn't going out of his way to win their trust, either. He was aloof, defensive. And sometimes a little bit prissy, which Leo found kind of endearing, but Aziza—who ran around in the woods all night chasing pookas and wrangling pixies and not caring if there were spiders in her hair—definitely did not.

"If I killed everything that annoyed me—" she began, but Leo coughed loudly before she could finish that sentence.

"Over there," he said, pointing above the trees.

A flock of lesser fairies wriggled from the canopy and poured into the sky like a flurry of golden bats. Aziza's groan told him they'd crossed through the veil and into Blackthorn.

"Nothing we can do about that right now." Aziza sighed. "We'll round them up later this week. They'll fall asleep in bushes and window boxes, assuming the cats don't get them first."

"I haven't seen anything here that can help us kill the hag," Tristan said, a shade of haughtiness sneaking into his tone.

"You have a better idea?" she snapped. "My parents said to use my gift. *This*"—she flapped her hand in a vague gesture—"is my gift. The answer is *here*, somewhere."

"We can't wander around aimlessly until we stumble into something helpful."

"We're not wandering. We're patrolling, so that *I* can fix the damage *your* master has done to the boundary," she said. "I think our best bet is to find reinforcements. Get the fae to help us."

"None of them stand a chance against the hag," he said. "Except the Fair Folk."

Leo perked up at the mention of fairies, but before he could chime in to agree with Tristan, Aziza said, "That's out of the question. You don't know what you're talking about."

"So you're saying fairies are worse than the hag?"

"I'm saying when you've got a problem, you don't go, *Hey, know what would make this better? Pouring gasoline on it and lighting it on fire.*"

"When the problem is a *tree*, maybe gasoline is exactly what we need."

She started to deliver a heated response, but broke off and tilted her head, listening. "You hear that?"

They fell silent, letting the sounds of the night wash over them.

"Water?" Leo whispered.

"We're not near any water," Aziza said, and walked away without another word. Leo and Tristan hurried after her. Soon, they broke through the thickets and found a broad stream. It ran clear over a bed of smooth, flat stones. The bank was lumpy and cracked, scrunched up where it met the stream, as though a giant pair of hands had dug into the ground and parted it roughly to make room for the water.

"Did I somehow miss this?" Aziza said.

"No," Tristan said. "This wasn't here before."

She and Tristan exchanged meaningful glances.

"What? What's wrong?" Leo said, lost.

"The landscape of Elphame is changing," Aziza said. "Which means things are getting worse."

Then—Leo barely saw it happen. A whip of water lashed out of the stream, snaked around Aziza's ankle, and dragged her in. She fell over with a slew of curses and a splash.

"What the hell just—" Leo stepped into the knee-deep water to help her up, but something shoved his back—and Tristan grabbed his arm, and they both went down, landing halfway on top of Aziza.

As they struggled to disentangle themselves from each other, weighed down by their coats and boots, the currents reshaped themselves into faces that peered out at them from the surface of the water.

"Sprites," Aziza said, getting to her feet.

"Are they . . . attacking us?" Tristan asked. He tried to get up and slipped. Leo hauled him up with one hand on his arm and the other on the back of his coat.

"No," Aziza said. "It's just mischief."

"*Not mischief,*" said one of the faces, in the bubbling voice of the stream. "*Retaliation.*"

"What for?" Aziza demanded. "I've done nothing to you."

"*Yes. You have done nothing,*" said another one of the sprites. "*Fix this, gatewalker.*"

"Don't you have anything better to do?" Leo shouted. He scooped up a handful of pebbles and hurled them into the water; the faces dissipated. "If you can't be helpful, then lay off the one person who's *trying!*"

But no liquid voices responded. The stream was just a stream again—as much as anything was *just* anything in Elphame.

Once they'd gotten a short distance away, they stopped to peel off their coats. Leo turned to Aziza, expecting her to be upset, but— despite the fact that she was soaking wet, teeth chattering, scraping her clinging hair out of her face, and had just been reprimanded by a school of sprites—she was grinning.

"I know who can help us," she said. "I know what kind of fae might have strong enough magic to stand up to a hag."

"What?" Tristan said, sounding dubious and hopeful in equal measures.

"*Meryl.*"

CHAPTER 26

TRISTAN

Leo dropped Aziza off at home first, and then it was just him and Tristan, alone on streets growing slick with a sudden predawn rain. The ghosts of spattered raindrops wafted from the asphalt, and the streetlights made blotchy gold reflections on the windshield.

Leo had given Tristan the spare set of clothes he kept in his trunk, since Leo was going straight home anyway and Tristan didn't have anything else to change into. A simple gesture that probably took Leo no thought at all had left Tristan a conflicted mess. Embarrassed that he had to accept someone else's clothes because he didn't have his own. Deeply comforted by this too-large sweater that smelled like Leo. Vaguely guilty, like he'd gotten away with something, because Leo didn't realize that Tristan was all too accustomed to wearing his clothes. The scarf he'd taken from his parents' house belonged to Leo. He'd sent Tristan home with it once because Tristan had left his own in his locker, and Tristan had forgotten to give it back the next day. And Leo's birthday had been later that week. So he couldn't give it back now.

Wouldn't do it even if he could, if he was being honest.

He couldn't help sneaking glances at him. Leo was gorgeous—

always had been, but it was more true now than ever. He wasn't a gangly kid anymore. His shoulders had broadened; he'd filled out a bit. His curls had grown out—Tristan had always liked them like this, long enough to run his fingers through, not that he had that privilege anymore. He was winter-pale, but come summer, his tan skin would darken almost to gold, and freckles would show up on the bridge of his nose and across his shoulders.

Pull yourself together and say something, he told himself. *You don't have that much time left.*

It had never been difficult to talk to Leo before. They used to talk all day and then stay up late texting. They could be in public and still have a bubble of space around them because, just from their body language and the subtle way they angled themselves toward each other, anyone who even thought of coming up to them would've felt like they were intruding. He used to be able to tell how Leo was feeling on any given day from the way he said hello. There came a point when you were so close to someone that half the time if you were speaking aloud, it was almost for show, for the benefit of the other people in the room, but the real communication took place in fragmented exchanges indecipherable to anyone else, in raised eyebrows and suppressed laughter, in late-night whispers when Leo had snuck Tristan into his room.

And now they were . . . awkward silences and uncertainty. When Leo stopped at the intersection where he would've turned toward the library, and didn't move when the light turned green, Tristan couldn't have even begun to guess what he was thinking. It made him feel completely lost.

"Leo?" he said tentatively.

"Look, what if . . ." Leo hesitated. "Come stay at my place instead."

"I can't," he said, though it hurt to refuse. The Merritt household was more his home than anywhere else had ever been. And he would've given anything to go home.

"Why not?" Leo said. "It's better than camping out at the library."

"It's dangerous. The hag could follow the bond and find your house—your family."

That was true, but also a moot point—Leo's house was already full of Tristan. He'd grown up there. His happiest memories were there. The hag could use the bond to find it anytime she wanted. Tristan had stationed hounds all around the property to alert him if anyone other than Leo tried to leave in the middle of the night. With the hounds' help, he'd be able to intercept them and then warn Leo. He also had the hounds guarding his parents' house, Fairview High, and the handful of shelters he'd stayed at semi-frequently. But nothing had happened yet. Maybe the hag was saving her energy for Aziza.

No, staying away from the Merritt household wouldn't make them any safer. He just couldn't face Maria and Greg, not after everything he'd done.

"I didn't think about that," Leo said, deflating. "But are you sure you're all right?"

"I'm fine," he said. "I just wish Aziza would've told me what Meryl actually *is*, so I wouldn't have to imagine her sprouting tentacles."

That earned him a surprised laugh. He tilted his face toward the window to hide his own grin.

"Meryl's nicer to you than Aziza is."

"At least I know what to expect from Aziza. You don't think Meryl's a little creepy?"

Leo took a hand off the wheel to rub distractedly at the back of his neck. "Never really thought about it. Aziza loves her, so—"

"Aziza has an unusually high tolerance for creepy things."

"I just watched you raise the dead the other night."

"Sure, but I've only been a necromancer for a few months. I'm not used to it just yet." He grimaced. "I'm not sure I *want* to get used to it."

Leo went quiet for a second, making a U-turn. They'd yet to see another car. Tristan could almost believe there was no one else in the city but the two of them.

"Hey, Tris," he said at last. "How come you won't say why you signed on with the hag?"

"It's—it's personal," Tristan stuttered.

"You don't have to tell me what she promised you. I guess I'm just . . ." Leo paused, choosing his words carefully. "Are you not telling because you're scared? Or is it something else? I just need to know you didn't sign on for the hell of it."

Leo was giving him a chance to defend himself, and Tristan almost couldn't stand it. He'd just about rather fling himself out of this moving vehicle than let Leo feel sorry for him. But he was accustomed to being more honest with Leo than he was with himself, and that instinct made him capable of answering without the words sticking in his throat, made it so he could tell the whole truth unflinchingly—as much as he could without Leo's curse rendering his efforts pointless.

"I lost—I lost my best friend. Then my parents kicked me out for being gay," he said. "I had no clue how to survive on my own. I didn't have anywhere to go or anyone else to turn to, and then the hag called out to me. What she offered—I had nothing to lose and everything to gain. I didn't know what I was getting into, but that's no excuse, because I was desperate enough that I might've said yes anyway."

"I don't believe that," Leo said quietly.

Tristan gave a jerky shrug. "I don't want to believe it. I just don't know."

A tense silence fell over them until Leo said, "Thanks for telling me."

His voice carried no judgment at all, and his smile was so kind it almost made Tristan feel ashamed, because it was far more than he deserved. Tristan nodded awkwardly.

"I'm bi," Leo added, offhand. "You know. Since we're sharing."

For the first time in ages, Tristan smiled back, tremulously. Out of the two of them, Leo had always been the one with pride. "This is the first time I've talked about it since I told my parents," he said.

"I'm sorry they—" Leo shook his head, cutting himself off. "I haven't told mine. They wouldn't kick me out, but I think they're happier not knowing."

That was the last thing he'd expected Leo to say. Greg and Maria had always been kind to Tristan—leagues above his own parents, which admittedly was a pretty low bar. When they'd pulled all-nighters studying for exams, Maria would kiss them both on the forehead before she went to bed. Greg would ruffle his hair and make idle conversation about whatever he'd read on the news that day, and he'd ask Tristan about his end-of-term art projects and sound genuinely interested in the answer. Maybe they were just being decent in the most basic way possible, but it had felt like they cared about him. They'd felt like *real* parents, people who *liked* being parents and weren't just going through the motions. And even though he and Leo had never told them the truth about their relationship, Leo had never let on that he was worried about their reaction.

"You really think so?" he said carefully.

"Mom's family is pretty old fashioned. When her cousin came

out, it was a big deal—her parents disowned her, she moved out of town, everyone had something to say about it. Mom didn't agree with that, but she didn't stand up for her, either. It wasn't worth fighting about, I guess." Leo shrugged one shoulder. "Dad's side of the family is like that, too—appearances are more important than anything. Mom and Dad would have to choose between defending me, cutting ties, or just . . . saying nothing. I think I know what they'd pick, but . . ."

"But you don't want to find out if you're wrong."

"Yeah. Thing is," Leo said, "maybe I'm *already* out to them. I was probably out to Hazel. But I don't know for sure. I'd have to ask, and I don't *want* to have to ask. I hate that the curse took something as personal as coming out from me. It's bullshit."

Tristan's fingers clenched hard in the fabric of the borrowed sweater he was wearing. Now he *really* couldn't go back to Leo's place. Once his family realized that Leo didn't remember him, they'd know that Tristan was his true love. He'd out Leo to his parents just by *existing*.

So he'd made the right choice. He couldn't go home. Not ever.

"Tris?"

He blinked and found Leo smiling at him, a little perplexed, brown eyes crinkling in that way that always made Tristan melt. He was still reeling at the fact that he got to be *Tris* again. It was like a gift Leo didn't even know he was giving him.

"Yeah," he said hoarsely.

"Forget what I just said. My parents are good people. You'd be welcome at our place. So, after we get rid of the hag . . ."

Tristan bit his lip. He had one last secret to keep: There was no *after* for him. Death was the only way to get out of the contract early, and nothing could change that. Once the hag died, the contract would take him with her.

But he couldn't tell Leo that. He and Aziza were too noble to sacrifice him for the greater good. They'd want to *save* him.

He wasn't going to let something like that get in the way of killing the hag.

But he said, "I'll think about it," and was rewarded once more with Leo's smile. All he wanted was to get Leo to look at him like that as much as possible in whatever amount of time he had left. That would be enough for him.

THE NEXT MORNING was thick with fog, clammy like a cold sweat, and unpleasant in a way that seemed appropriate for what he was about to do.

Leo and Aziza had school today, so he wouldn't see them until later. Meryl had recruited him to be her assistant in exchange for room and board—or rather, he had all but begged to be allowed to help in hopes that if he made himself useful, she wouldn't be in any hurry to get him out of her office. ("You don't have to *earn* anything here," she had said, but those were just words, and he couldn't survive on words any more than he could've bought groceries with arcade tokens.) But the library wouldn't open for a few hours yet. So he'd taken one of the hounds and shadow-traveled back to the woods at St. Sithney's, bringing nothing but the ritual knife, which he still carried with him at all times, even though he hadn't used it since he'd turned against the hag. And he hoped that wasn't about to change.

"Can you track her?" he whispered to the hound. Its reflective eyes were only a dull, glassy black in the sunlight, like chunks of volcanic rock polished smooth. The noise it made in its throat sent plumes of steam leaking out from the cracks between its teeth. It led the way, lithe and oddly fluid in motion, and no, he soon came to understood by probing at its mind; the one they were tracking had no scent. Even the smell of smoke that Tristan had perceived so strongly the first time he'd met her was more a product of her spiritual energy than a true scent. But the hound would find her. If there was anything left to find.

It took a couple of hours. He was just starting to think he'd have to head back soon when the hound raced ahead. It took him to a shallow ravine with a creek running through it, brown leaves floating through its murky waters. He climbed down carefully and brushed his hands off on his jeans after. The muddy banks of the creek stuck on the soles of his boots, so that each footstep required a bit of a tug to get free. The strip of earth between the water and the wall of the ravine was too narrow for the hound to walk beside him, so it trailed behind, emitting a low, warning growl.

If the Ash Witch hadn't spoken then, Tristan might have walked right past her. Or possibly through.

"Come to finish me off?"

The voice at first seemed to come from the water; then he saw the shimmering, vaguely human shape hovering over a cluster of stones that marked a bend in the creek.

"Is that you?" he whispered, and then felt foolish.

"Or maybe you've come to gloat."

It was hard to keep his eyes on her; was that the hem of her dress, or a stray beam of light reflecting off the water? Her voice was how he remembered, but fainter than he'd ever heard it, a wisp of itself.

"Do you want to keep guessing, or will you let me get this over with so I can leave you alone?" He drew his ritual knife and then, quickly so that he couldn't overthink it, sliced off a lock of his hair. He placed it on the ground near to where he thought the Ash Witch stood. "Take it."

At full strength, Aziza's magic had made the Ash Witch monstrously powerful; now, depleted as she was, maybe a piece of Tristan's magic would be enough to restore her to what she'd been before. Hopefully. He didn't really know why he was doing this. He hadn't told anyone before he'd come, not even Leo, which probably meant it was a terrible idea.

The Ash Witch must have moved, because her voice was closer when she spoke again. "I suppose you think you're saving me."

"If it works, then yes. That would be the result." He inched backward, one hand reaching for the hound. "What happened to you was . . . wrong."

Maybe, though he wouldn't have dared admit it to her, he felt a kind of twisted kinship with the Ash Witch. She'd died a prisoner. That was part of the essence of who, *what*, she was now. He understood her, he thought, much better than he wished he did.

The Ash Witch's laugh came practically right in his ear. He jumped, his hand fisting tight in the hound's fur. It bared its teeth at a spot slightly to Tristan's left.

"You don't care about saving me. I'm not really a person. You just want to pretend you can fix what you've done. And you can't, can you?" she said. "People have died. You can't bring them back with good intentions and a little magic."

"I know that," he said, his voice betraying him in its roughness.

"Is this enough for you?" the Ash Witch went on. "Make an offering to an unfortunate spirit, wait until you see me once again haunting the trails I used to haunt, and feel satisfied that you struck one thing off your master's long list of ghastly accomplishments. Is that enough?"

"No," he snapped. "Of course it's not."

"Then *try harder*."

The leaves in the creek stirred, and so did the end of his scarf and the hound's fur, as if a gust of cold wind had blown through the ravine. When the air settled, the lock of hair he'd given to the Ash Witch was gone, and so was she.

The Ash Witch had been right; what he'd done today had little to do with saving *her*, specifically. He'd just wanted to undo something the hag had done. He had been thinking about the imp and Aziza's refusal to use force against it. The way imps were part of Elphame's borderlands, the Ash Witch was part of Blackthorn. She *belonged* to Blackthorn. He knew better than most people that Blackthorn was ugly and dangerous sometimes, and its magic was ugly and dangerous sometimes, but the ugly parts of Blackthorn had a right to exist, too. The hag was the one that didn't belong. She was slowly transforming Blackthorn—cutting people's lives short, wrecking its magical boundaries—and it seemed the height of unfairness that the hag, who was confined to the woods and could never know Blackthorn the way he did, could make the whole city hers in this way.

"Saving" someone who was already dead was truly bottom-of-the-barrel heroism. But what else could he do?

What else *could* he do?

He thought about that as he went back to the library, returning in time to help Meryl open. Turning on the computers and bringing in the contents of the book drop outside kept him distracted, but there was this itchy restlessness under his skin. Persistent enough to catch the hounds' attention. He didn't call on them, and they didn't appear, but they were watching him. His shadow went misshapen, appearing, at times, to have four legs instead of two, a tail, a snout.

Better get that under control before the patrons get here, he thought. And then he paused, there next to the cart of books he was replacing, eyes stuck on the ripple of not-quite-there shadow fur across Bishop Library's mosaic tiles.

Since he'd left the hag, he had been testing the limits of the hounds' obedience to him. They hadn't killed a single person since the day they'd battled the Ash Witch. Not the man sleeping on an empty train. Not the woman scurrying home from some graveyard shift somewhere. Not any of the people who passed nights alone and vulnerable in abandoned lots and under scaffolding. People like him, the ones who had been the hounds' favorite targets because they could be picked off without raising any alarms, and Tristan had looked away because he'd told himself that the only way to be fair was to be neutral. He didn't have the right to choose who lived or died. But his inaction wasn't neutral *or* fair, really, because it meant the hounds had taken, disproportionately, the poorest and most helpless people in Blackthorn.

The hounds weren't eating anything but animals now, and he certainly wasn't blood-marking any more houses. The hag had no victims, no food source. He was starving her.

But the Ash Witch thought he could do more. And she always told the truth.

It came up on him slowly, a droplet of an idea that spread like dye in water. He didn't have to wait until Leo and Aziza figured out how to kill the hag. He could fight back right now, a hundred tiny battles, weakening her bit by bit. The hounds were, after all, the only beings that could move freely through the human world, through Elphame, and even through the hag's territory, unaffected by the disorienting nature of her magic. They could infiltrate. They didn't even mind the stench of the gateway tree. And while the hag slept hidden in her den under the earth, preserving her energy now that she had nothing to replenish it, biding her time for the retaliation that he knew was inevitable—the hounds could rise from the shadows the way they had that first night when she had bound him to them. They could do what he'd tried and failed to do then. *Attack*. Not the hag. But the gateway tree, which was the heart of her territory and connected, in ways he didn't fully understand, to her own twisted, poisoned, monstrously overgrown magic.

If they could dig up its roots, starting from the outside and working their way in so that they'd go unnoticed for a little while . . . then maybe he'd chip away at her defenses. And maybe, in the end, that would make a difference. He might not be around to fight with Leo and Aziza when the time came—the hag could put him down anytime she wanted—so he would have to do his fighting right now, while he still could.

You have a vicious streak. I intend to nurture that, the hag had told him once.

She had nurtured it well, and she would see that now firsthand.

CHAPTER 27

AZIZA

MONDAY MORNING, AZIZA came downstairs earlier than she needed to make it to school on time. She would be making a detour before class. It was earlier, too, than Jiddo left for the university. He shuffled into the kitchen a few minutes after she did and raised a bushy white eyebrow at the sight of her.

"Are you feeling all right? I don't think I've ever seen you up at this hour."

She could barely look at him. He'd lied about her parents' deaths all these years. He'd given her the spell pouch that had protected her from the hag but refused to tell her that was what it was for. He knew the blaekhounds had to belong to a necromancer, and he'd withheld that information from her. She kept uncovering new deceptions, and it made her question everything about him, about their whole lives.

"I wanted to go to the library before school," she said.

Jiddo grunted in acknowledgment as he sat beside her, at the table where she was forcing herself to eat half a bowl of cereal. He sorted through his bag, checking for his lesson plans.

Leila's voice followed Aziza everywhere, even into her dreams.

Tell Baba, she'd said. What had she wanted Jiddo to know? But that was, in part, the tragedy of death. Sometimes there were no last words and no goodbyes.

But Aziza still had a chance to talk to him. She was lucky to have that, and maybe she owed it to herself, to both of them, to try one last time. He'd said he'd take them both away from Blackthorn if he couldn't trust her to stay out of trouble, but that had been over winter break when the university was closed; he couldn't just drop his classes now that they were in session. Not except as a last resort. So as long as Aziza didn't admit to him that the hag was after *her,* specifically . . .

She dropped her spoon, which clinked against the rim of the bowl, and said in a rush, "I found out what the spell pouch is really for."

Jiddo's wrinkled hand stilled on the zipper of his bag. "And what's that?"

"Something called a hag," she said quietly.

They looked at each other, his gaze heavy for someone who seemed so thin and frail at a glance. It wasn't only his gaze she felt, either, but his wards all around her, a protective presence she'd known all her life and taken for granted. These wards he had poured magic into day in and day out for seventeen years, draining him, aging him before his time.

"It's not fae," he said at last. "It has nothing to do with you. Some-one else will take care of it eventually."

"And who took care of it last time?" she demanded.

This pause was even longer than the last. Through the window, the sunlight intensified. Aziza watched it, the light in the overgrown garden, and waited.

"How did you figure it out?" he asked.

"Does it matter? *You* should have told me."

"Why? What good does it do you to know that your parents were murdered?"

"You say that like they were passive victims. They died fighting. They died *heroes*."

Jiddo made an angry noise in his throat. "There's nothing heroic about getting yourself killed in a battle you had no chance of winning and leaving your infant daughter an orphan. People they thought they could rely on to help them abandoned them to a miserable fate."

"People like who?"

"Like the ones they called their coven. But there is no loyalty in American witchcraft. They learned that the hard way."

"You never told me they had a coven," Aziza said, and for some reason, this bothered her almost more than his lies about how they'd died. She'd always assumed that, like Jiddo, they had wanted no coven but the coven of family they'd had in Lebanon. It had never occurred to her to wonder if they, as younger witches, would have been more motivated than he was to seek out friends. A community.

Would they have wanted her to be the way she was? As isolated as she was, and not even realizing—at least not until she'd met Leo—that things could be different?

"Because, when it really counted, they *didn't*." Jiddo zipped the bag closed with more force than necessary and set it down on the floor, leaning it against the leg of the table. Without looking at her, he said, "What they did wasn't heroism. It was a *mistake*. A mistake that cost them their lives. And for what? They didn't even kill her."

"Calling it a mistake makes it sound like they didn't know what they were doing," Aziza argued, suddenly angry not for herself, but for Leila. "They were there because they cared about Blackthorn— *Leila* cared."

"You don't know why she was there."

"Yes, I *do*!"

"You do?" Jiddo said, quiet, questioning.

"I found the necromancer who was controlling the hounds. He was being forced to . . . never mind," Aziza said. "I went to the cemetery with him, and I asked him to wake my parents up. I had so many questions, I . . ."

She stopped. The story was a tangle in her head, and she couldn't remember what she'd just decided was safe to tell him and what wasn't. Already she knew she'd said too much, knew it with the sickening remorse of someone who could see a crash coming but had too much momentum to stop. All she could do was grit her teeth and brace herself for the impact.

"Wake them up?" he said. There was a faint, deceptively harmless shake to his voice, like the tremors preceding an earthquake. "You dug up their bodies?"

"I needed answers," Aziza said.

He shot to his feet, the chair scraping against the floor. "What were you thinking?"

She got up, too, fists clenched. She could count on one hand the number of times in her entire life that he'd raised his voice at her.

"I was thinking no one else would tell me anything," she said. "You never talk about them, and you *lied* about—"

"You disturbed their graves!" he roared. "You let someone perform dark magic on them—death magic—"

"They're already dead, it's not like it can hurt them," she said, too loud, just short of a shout, and the only reason it wasn't a shout was because she was so taken aback. Jiddo was thoughtful, reserved, always measuring his words and using only precisely the ones that were needed. They butted heads sometimes, and he could be stern, but he didn't get *mad*, not like this.

"How do you know if it hurts or not?" He didn't have the energy to keep shouting at her, so this came out as more of a wheeze.

She didn't have the words to explain to him that those things in the graveyard weren't really her parents—just hollow, decayed vessels with faint scraps of energy still clinging to them like a residue. There was enough of them left to talk out of their skulls with the help of necromancy, but not enough to make them *real*.

Only, Leila had been real enough to miss her father, to try and send him one final message. And Ahmed had been real enough to want to save his daughter's life, even if he'd delivered his advice and his warnings in a prickly, uncompromising sort of way that reminded Aziza a little of herself.

The truth she'd tried to ignore, because it was inconvenient and it was uncomfortable, was that she didn't *know* if being raised from the dead hurt. Even Tristan didn't know. If a trained witch wielded her craft like a scalpel, Aziza was a cudgel. The hag was not only infinitely stronger, but infinitely more *skilled*. The way Aziza had barreled into this fight against a threat she only halfway understood, collateral damage was all but guaranteed.

It felt like she had been quiet for a long time, but it couldn't have been more than a moment or two.

"I didn't know where else to go," she said, the words clipped as she struggled to control her volume, to find that place of calm determination that she'd retreated to every time she'd had to lie to him over the last several weeks. She was doing what she had to. *Everything* she'd done, even the graveyard—it was because she had to. And that was a good enough reason. Wasn't it?

He leaned heavily against the table, one hand rising to rub at his brow, as if he had a headache. To her horror, when his eyes opened again, they glistened with tears.

"Get out of my sight." He said it so calmly she didn't understand at first. Then she got it, and the guilt came again, followed quickly by shame, and then anger that burned everything else away, and then . . . nothing. Suddenly, all she felt was defeated.

Nothing she said mattered. If she lied. If she told the truth. If she asked for help, or didn't—it made no difference. There was no getting through to him. There never would be.

She left. Grabbed her backpack from the front hall. The door slammed behind her as she escaped into the struggling morning light.

AZIZA BANGED ON the library doors until a harried Meryl threw them open. Her round glasses slipped down the end of her nose; she cradled a bucket-sized cup of coffee, and her usually pristine bob was creased and snarled at the ends.

Sheepishly, Aziza lowered her raised fist. "Can we talk?"

Meryl's eyes flicked over her shoulder.

"Just me," she said. "Leo's at school."

"*You* should be at school," Meryl chided her lightly, but stepped aside so she could come in.

Nearby, Tristan had been put to work shelving books. Passing him, Meryl pointed at another cart parked at the end of the circulation desk.

"That one next," she said. When he nodded, she turned back to Aziza. "What's wrong?"

"I was thinking about how I've never actually seen you leave the library after closing, or seen you come in before it opens. You're *always* here."

"I do work here."

"You're the *only* librarian. I've never seen anyone helping you out—this is the first time you've had anything like an assistant," she said. "All the extra hours you must have put in over the years—"

"I'm lucky enough to love my job."

"And I bet it helps that it's closer to the sea," Aziza said. "I bet you can sense the water flowing underground."

Meryl's expression went blank. "Let's go to my office."

"Fine," Aziza said, and followed her down the hall, leaving Tristan to stay behind and pretend he hadn't been listening.

"What gave me away?" Meryl said, shutting the door.

"We had a run-in with a few water sprites yesterday, and I finally made the connection. All those things you know about magic, even though you're not a witch. Those hints you keep dropping about answering to someone you can't disobey. You're a selkie."

"I can't talk to you about this," she said. "I want to. But I'm not allowed."

"Who stole your sealskin?"

Meryl shook her head and busied herself sorting out the sheaves of paper and stacks of books behind the desk.

Whoever possessed a selkie's skin *owned* her. She would be magically bound to obey their every command, even harmful ones. If they ordered her silence, then she had to be silent. If they told her to throw herself off a cliff, her body would move without her permission. She became a puppet with only as much free will as her captor allowed her to have. It was one of the cruelest things anyone could do to another person. And it explained why Meryl hadn't been worried about the hag trying to get inside her head when Tristan had started staying overnight at the library. She'd insisted she would be fine. And she was right, because the control exerted over her by the one who held her sealskin trumped even the hag's magic.

On any other day, this would have been a crisis to eclipse all others; Aziza wouldn't have been able to rest until she had found the culprit and taken Meryl's freedom back. But—though she hated having to let Meryl remain in the trap she was in for even a second longer—it needed to wait until the hag was dead.

"I need your help," Aziza said, dropping the subject of Meryl's stolen skin. For now. "Selkies are more powerful than almost any other kind of fae. They could help me kill the hag."

"I can't—I wouldn't be allowed."

"Not you," she said. "Your pod. Those selkies I always see by the cliffs—they're your family, aren't they?"

Meryl set down the stack of paperwork she was clutching to her chest like a shield, but didn't speak for a long moment.

"They won't stray far from the ocean," she said at last. "What happened to me was a lesson for all of them."

"My parents said the core of the hag's power is sealed underneath the gateway tree. If the selkies could use their magic to flood the place, I bet that would be enough to kill her."

"Maybe." Meryl sighed. "But it won't be easy to convince them. I can't talk to them directly. I'm not allowed."

Not allowed. Aziza was beginning to hate that phrase. When she found out who'd done this to Meryl, she would skin them alive.

"Then you haven't talked to them in . . . years?"

"About twenty years, yes," Meryl said, her voice carefully neutral. "But when I dip my hand into the river, I can hear them singing to me. Sometimes I even sing back, though it's harder, with human vocal cords."

Meryl's grief felt more real than anything Aziza had ever felt or thought about her own parents. She had been curious about them, but that curiosity didn't connect to some well of feeling inside her. Her parents were long gone. She couldn't miss what she'd never had.

Talking to them in the cemetery hadn't changed that, exactly. Maybe she'd never mourn—but it *mattered* that they had died defending Blackthorn. Learning what they'd done was the first time she'd ever felt connected to them. She put her life at risk for Blackthorn every day. Without even knowing it, she'd made a choice that echoed theirs.

If Aziza failed to stop the hag, then it would mean they had failed, too. Maybe she didn't feel the way she was supposed to feel about her parents, but at the very least, as a witch, she was determined to preserve the good work of the witches who'd come before her.

To do that, she needed Meryl. What could Aziza say, though, to get through to her now? If Aziza grieved like Meryl did, what would *she* want to hear?

And Leila gave her the answer. *Tell Baba—*

"I could take them a message from you," Aziza said, at last.

Meryl bit her lip. And then, hesitantly, she nodded.

Sea spray doused the narrow wooden slats until they were slick and dark. Aziza ran her hand along the rail, her footsteps slapping dully over the bridge's damp surface. Leo and Tristan followed close behind. She didn't turn on a flashlight for fear of scaring the pod away, so they waded through brine-scented shadow. Moonlight glinted off the water below.

"We're close," she said.

"How can you tell?" Leo's voice was hushed. She almost couldn't hear him over the waves bashing themselves open against the base of the cliffs.

She pointed to where, ahead of them, a rocky shoulder jutted out, and the bridge disappeared around its curve.

"Under that part of the bridge, that's where the river from the library lets out," she said. "Past that, there's a spot where I've seen the selkies resting during the day. Some of them sleep there, too."

The cliffs cut Blackthorn's coast in half. To the north was the harbor, where mostly fishing boats docked. To the south were sand and pebble beaches, and the pier, which branched off into the narrow boardwalk they traversed now. If they followed it to the end, it would let them out at the wharfs.

Past the bend in the bridge, she could look down and see where the base of the cliffs curved up and jutted into the water like a half-submerged boot. She stopped and leaned over the rail as far as she dared.

"There," she said. "See them?"

"Those rocks?" Leo asked. Tristan inched up to the rail next to him, squinting against the wind. Then one of the rocks made a snuffling sound and rolled over. Leo jumped.

"Oh," Tristan said, standing on tiptoe to get a better look. "Now what?"

"Wait," she told them, and shut her eyes. The low roar of the ocean and the taste of salt on her lips faded out of focus as she felt for the veil with her magic. Selkies, like hedgewitches, guarded Elphame's boundary. They were the ones who kept the sea serpents and the sirens at bay, not to protect humans, but for the sake of peace and balance. Their magic wove through the boundary here at the cliffs like a length of rope, magic that had the give of sand and the will of the tide.

They would recognize her magic, too. In theory.

She sent a tendril of it shooting through theirs like a minnow: small and harmless, but noticeable.

Dawn broke sluggishly, with a first sliver of sun like the horizon cracking open an orange eye. Its rays streaked across the water and grazed the hides of the selkies as they stirred, their mottled furs smooth and supple, their silhouettes limned in gold. They were indistinguishable from normal seals.

Then they spotted her. She stood with the boys at a safe distance on the bridge, both hands visible on the rail. Still, some of them dove into the water instantly, vanishing with a plunk; others hesitated, looking to a bull selkie near the center of the congregation. When he began to change, so did the rest of them.

She'd been right. They knew her.

Their fur peeled away to reveal skin, angular human frames pushing past layers of blubber, snouts being shoved aside in favor of human noses and jaws. They stood, some of them tying their furs around their waists and others draping them over their shoulders like cloaks. Their human forms were muscular but soft, all of them with comfortable rolls of fat, and it struck Aziza how skinny Meryl was in comparison—practically emaciated for a selkie.

"Whoa. That's, uhhh, a lot of naked people," Leo said, averting his eyes. If Tristan turned any redder, his eyebrows would burn right off.

"They're selkies," she hissed. "What, you thought they wore swimsuits under the fur?"

"I don't know! Maybe!"

The bull selkie that the rest had deferred to stepped to the front of the congregation. He looked a strong, healthy human sixty, which put him probably in his late hundred-twenties. A mane of iron gray hair was slicked back against his skull, and his braided beard clung to a square jaw. His nose was crooked, and his blue eyes were the same as Meryl's.

"Gatewalker," he called. "You trespass."

"I come with a token," Aziza said, drawing it from her pocket. "And I come to make a bargain. Will you grant me an audience?"

"What token?"

She tossed it over the rail, and he caught it: a lock of black hair tied around a rolled-up note. He examined both briefly, his mouth thinning to a grim line.

"This is from my daughter."

"Yes. She said you'd talk to me."

Some of the others crowded closer to him, peering over his shoulder at the note, reaching out to touch the lock of hair with their fingertips.

"Only you," he said, giving her companions a hard glare. "The men must leave."

"What? *No*," Leo whispered.

"They're my . . . coven," she said, hesitating for only a moment. Her fight with Jiddo and what he'd revealed about her parents' coven was still fresh in her mind, but this wasn't the same thing. They weren't a real coven. It was just the most convenient word to use, because fae understood the concept of *coven* better than they'd understand *friend and temporary ally*. "We stick together."

"They stay where they are. You come down here."

"*No!*" Leo said, again. She put a quelling hand on his arm.

"Selkies don't trust human males," she said in a hurried whisper. "They're usually the ones who steal their skins. It's *fine*. We can't blow this."

Leo frowned worriedly but didn't argue. Aziza slid under the rail, lowered herself down with her hands clinging to the side of the bridge, and dropped. It was only a seven-foot fall, give or take, but the rocks were damp and uneven. She almost slipped. Luck saved her from humiliation, and she turned with relative composure to face the selkies. The overpowering smell of fish assaulted her; only years of staring down the easily offended woodland fae kept her from wrinkling her nose.

"We haven't spoken to Meryl in many years," the Chief said, holding up the note. "She is forbidden from seeing us, and we fear she would be sent away if we approached her. Her words are a gift. Tell me why you've come here."

"I have an enemy, one who wants me and many others dead," Aziza said. She told them everything she knew about the hag, and her plan to flood the underground chamber where her power was sealed.

"You ask for a great deal of magic," the Chief said. "And if the hag does not die, my people risk her vengeance."

"The hag has put you in danger already," she countered. "Or haven't you noticed the state of the boundary this year?"

He scrutinized her. "It's unstable. It used to be constant and predictable, like the phases of the moon, but now . . . Is this the hag's doing?"

"We think so," she said. "I know I'm asking a lot of you. But maybe there's something I can do to help you in exchange."

He looked around at his people, wordlessly consulting with them. One of the women leaned in, still half dressed in her sable pelt, flippers folded modestly over her breasts and her human eyes sitting above the rounded nose and whiskers of her seal form. She whispered in his ear. But the Chief shook his head.

"She's barely grown. Still a pup."

"I'm grown enough," she said, stung. "I can handle whatever it is."

The Chief eyed her with faint amusement, the way you looked at a precocious child.

"Are you certain?" he said. "You may regret it once you hear what we require in return for our aid."

She heard a strangled noise that was probably Leo, and knew—without even having to look at him—that he was willing her not to do or say anything reckless.

But there was only one way forward, and this was it.

"Tell me everything I need to know."

CHAPTER 28

LEO

IN THE DAYS following Aziza's meeting with the selkies, they spent all their nights patrolling up and down the coast. Leo was sick of the taste of brine on the air, the algae-sunscreen-fish smell of the beach. But their diligence paid off, because—after nearly a week—they made a breakthrough.

He crouched under the pier, helping Aziza dig out a small, wiggly creature that'd gotten tangled up in a set of plastic soda rings and then stuck in the mucky wet sand at the base of the posts. Tristan kept watch nearby for cops and kelpies alike.

"Are you sure it's not an octopus?" he asked. Another swipe of his fingers wiped away enough sand to reveal rubbery skin.

"Positive," she said. "You can tell because—"

She freed one of the wormlike tentacles and flipped it over. The suckers were ringed with tiny, vicious spikes.

"Ouch." He recoiled.

"See how it's moving its tentacles in circles?"

"Yeah?"

"It makes whirlpools. Fine when it's this size. Less fine when it's grown."

She tried to maneuver the creature's tentacles out of the plastic rings, but it was squirming so persistently it took a while to get anywhere. Its bulging eyes were luminous gold with rectangular pupils, and its skin had a dark blue scaly pattern. The lattice around the scales flashed neon blue whenever Aziza tried to move it.

The kraken let out a gush of ink, and Aziza whipped her hands away.

"Acidic," she told him. To the kraken she added crossly, "How am I supposed to help you if you do that?"

They took their gloves off long enough to pour handfuls of water over the kraken, to clean the ink off of it. Between the two of them they managed to get the plastic off—though not without having their gloves shredded in the process—and dug it out of the sand. His hands stung like they were covered with paper cuts, from where those insidious little spikes must have just managed to nick his skin.

It lunged toward the ocean as soon as it was free, squirming over the ground with surprising speed. Aziza scooped it up in a glass jar full of seawater and screwed the lid on. Leo bent down to get a better look at it, wincing as it scraped at the sides of the jar with its spiked suckers.

"Normally I'd let it go. Whirlpools are fairy doors, so it would find its own way back home before it got big enough to be a problem," she said. "But its mother must be desperate if she's followed her hatchling out of Elphame. It must've been lost for a decent amount of time. We're just lucky it washed up on shore, or we'd never have found it."

"So lucky," Leo said weakly.

They had needed this win; last week, three students had gone missing from Towne High, and Aziza was angry with herself because she hadn't figured out what was doing it yet. It was probably a sandman keeping their classmates trapped in an endless sleep so that it could feed on their dreams, Aziza said, and they would need to find them before they starved to death.

So it was great that something had gone right for them, and they'd figured out why there was a kraken stalking Blackthorn's shores and harassing the selkies. Less great was—later that very same night—having to climb into a dingy little fishing boat captained by Meryl's dad. They were calling him by his title, Chief, because they hadn't "earned his name." He looked at Leo and Tristan like he was barely restraining the urge to toss them overboard. Into freezing February waters. Which contained *a real, live, full-grown kraken.*

"How big do krakens get?" Leo asked Aziza as they got on the boat.

"Don't worry about it," she said shiftily. "We probably won't even see her."

"Of course," Tristan said. He half fell into the boat, staggered, and then righted himself with as much dignity as he could muster. "Just a kraken. Easy to miss. Bet it happens all the time."

"It does," Aziza said. "In the ocean, your worst nightmare could be inches away and you'd never know it. Not unless it wanted you to know."

She gave Tristan what Leo had mentally started referring to as her *witch look*, a penetrating stare that made you feel like you couldn't hide anything from her, like she knew things about you that even you didn't. Tristan lost that staring match, no contest, and busied himself finding a semi-dry spot to sit down.

Leo gave her a *look* of his own until she hissed, "What?"

"Go easy on him," he said, under his breath, not wanting Tristan to hear.

"I don't know what you're talking about."

"You're freaking him out on purpose."

"Me? I would never."

Aziza joined the Chief at the helm, and Leo retreated to the stern, where he sat beside Tristan on the narrow bench. Just two unwelcome human males. As if he'd overheard Leo's thoughts, the Chief glanced back at them, one glaring eye framed between the shoulder of his yellow rain slicker and the brim of his hat.

"Um, where are the life vests?" Leo asked, while he had the Chief's attention.

"Don't have any."

The motor rumbled to life. They pulled away from the shore, bumping over the moonstruck waves. The ocean had looked smooth and placid from the docks, but that was an illusion. Out in the deep, the sea was all ridges and valleys. The night had smudged the horizon out of existence, like a great ink-stained thumb rubbing away an errant line.

When Blackthorn was nothing but a glimmer of faraway lights, Aziza said, "Wait."

The Chief cut the motor, and she pressed up against the side of the boat.

"*There.*"

Leo followed her gaze to where foam spun out in streaks from a spot maybe fifty feet away, unspooling like thread. Something long and thin poked up out of the water; it could've been a bit of driftwood or a reed, but then it kept going, up and up and up. It thickened to the width of a tree trunk, the width of a cargo truck, large enough to wrap around a battleship and crush it. Its skin flashed neon blue in slashes and spots like glaring eyes. When it twisted, Leo could make out spikes the length of his forearm ringing bloodred suckers.

"*Ohhh my god,*" Leo said, in what was definitely not a squeak.

Tristan shrank back in his seat. "She said we wouldn't see—"

The ocean heaved, and he and Tristan were thrown off the bench.

They sprawled across the deck as seawater sloshed over the hull and soaked them. He caught a fistful of Tristan's sleeve before he could slide away, and they scrambled upright, clinging to the portside rail. The tentacle loomed over them, reaching up into the yawning night sky.

Aziza leaned over the starboard side, *closer* to the angrily writhing tentacle. Her back was to them—all they could see was her mane of dark hair whipping about in the wind and her hands where they clung to the rail, spectral under the light of the kraken's markings.

Over the roar of the sea, Tristan said, "Is she—talking to it?"

"I don't know!" Leo yelled back.

If she was, it wasn't listening; the waves frothed, tossing the boat about like a marble in a washing machine, and when Leo looked down into the water, its depths flashed electric blue. Only then did he understand that the thing connected to the tentacle fifty feet away was *directly underneath them.*

Aziza pulled the jar from her bag and unscrewed the lid. With the same mildly annoyed expression she'd worn when she was untangling it from the plastic rings, she said something to the hatchling that Leo couldn't hear. He had no idea if it could understand her. Then she leaned perilously over the side of the boat, one hand holding the rail and the other reaching down toward the water with the jar. Leo jumped forward and grabbed the back of her jacket, holding her steady against the frenzied rocking of the boat, while she dipped the open jar into the water. When she straightened, the hatchling was gone. She turned back toward the Chief, holding on to Leo with one hand and the rail with the other.

"They're leaving!" she shouted. "She'll make a whirlpool—the water might suck us down—can you get us clear?"

"Hold on!" the Chief bellowed, and threw himself on the helm.

The motor must have come on, because the boat jolted into motion again, but Leo couldn't hear it. There was nothing but the howl of the wind and the waves booming like thunderclaps.

As the tentacle withdrew, as the furious blue lights in the waters below faded and the dark shape sank away into the deep, the Chief slowly turned the boat around. Its prow pointed at Blackthorn's distant, light-speckled shore. But even as they sailed for home, the currents changed. The water churned behind them. The sea dragged them backward.

"Aziza!" Leo said. "You can close the door. Right?"

"Once she's gone," Aziza said placidly. Her eyes had the distant look she got on patrol, when she worked her craft and her mind was halfway in Elphame. There was no trace of fear in her, and though she hung on to the rail as tightly as the rest of them, there was a weight to her presence, as if something more than gravity anchored her to the world.

He was forcefully reminded that, despite all the ways they were alike—despite spending every spare minute in each other's company, splitting their homework, taking 3 A.M. power naps in his car; despite everything they'd been through together and the fact that he felt like he'd known Aziza his whole life—the two of them were different. He was pretty sure he understood her better than anyone else on the planet did, but there were some things about her he could *never* understand, not really. She was a witch. *This* was what that meant.

The boat lurched. Behind them, the currents swirled into a vortex, as if the ocean was trying to inhale the sky.

The Chief swore profusely, putting his whole weight against the helm, and the boat inched away from the whirlpool. But they crested the next wave too fast; they were airborne for a heart-stopping second, crashed back into the sea with a surge of freezing seawater dousing them all—and the boat tipped dangerously to the side. Leo hooked one arm around the rail, clung to Aziza with the other, and then the whole world seemed to slow down as—on the opposite side of the boat, too far for Leo to do anything but watch in horror— skinny, sodden Tristan lost his grip and tipped overboard.

Tris can't swim.

He didn't know how he knew it. He just did, and there was no time to wonder why. He lunged at the spot where Tristan had disappeared, not thinking, fully intending to throw himself after him. Aziza beat him there, blocking him at the rail.

"You can't!"

"He can't swim!" he told her, trying to shove past. That one, unbidden thought filled his whole mind, crowding out everything else. Even his own name might've escaped him in that moment.

But Aziza held him off with surprising strength.

"Leo—*stop*—"

"We have to help him—"

He was trying to get past her without hurting her; Aziza had no such qualms. She shoved him so hard he fell on his ass. He scrabbled for purchase on the slippery deck, shoulder aching where he'd banged it, but he could barely feel it. The image of Tristan disappearing blazed in his mind. Before he could make another move, though, the Chief was shucking off his boots and jacket, haphazardly pulling on his sealskin.

"Take the helm!" he ordered, and dove overboard in a blur of rippling muscle and sleek gray fur.

The screech of panic in his mind quieted: Someone far more capable than he was had gone after Tristan. Still, he was shaken. His heart beat so fast it *hurt*, like it was bruised. He tried to get to his feet but fell again as the ship bucked.

Aziza held out a hand, and he took it. She pulled him up, and together they did what they could to steady the boat. The console was studded with an array of switches and buttons, but they just grabbed on to the wheel and tried to keep it straight, which took all their strength. The seconds dragged on for an eternity as they were buffeted on all sides by wind and water. A cloud must have passed over the moon, or maybe the lashing sea had swallowed it, because there was no trace of light, nothing but black on black and three different kinds of cold smacking them in the face.

At last, the Chief returned. He pushed Tristan up the ladder first and then crawled in awkwardly after him, flopping around as a seal until he managed to wriggle out of his skin. Tristan was barely conscious—just enough to roll over and cough out half the ocean.

Aziza gave Leo a hard glare. "Stay here and hold the wheel. I've got him."

She went to check on Tristan, holding on to him so that he didn't fall overboard again. Leo stayed at the helm, even when the Chief returned, helping him as best he could. Under the Chief's guidance—with Leo's assistance—the boat cut through the waves and into calmer waters. Behind them, the ocean quieted. The moon reappeared, and the boat bounced steadily over tiny foothills of water, nothing like the towering waves they'd endured just minutes before. The Chief waved him away.

He sank down next to Aziza and Tristan, who had stirred and sat up but still looked petrified and faintly nauseous. Aziza looked at Leo, her face pinched, like she was more worried about him than Tristan—which, yeah, of course she was. He pressed his shoulder against hers, and gave her a sheepish look that he hoped she interpreted as, *Sorry I'm a mess, thanks for not letting me drown.*

She'd saved him. And he was grateful. But for a lightning flash of an instant, as they'd struggled, he had been *furious* with her for stopping him. Furious because she hadn't wanted him to dive headfirst into kraken-infested waters.

What was wrong with him?

CHAPTER 29

TRISTAN

TRISTAN HAD NEVER been more grateful for the sight of Blackthorn's grimy port, with its creaking docks and the stench of fish guts. He staggered off the boat and clung to a post until the ground stopped seesawing.

Leo threw an arm over his shoulder.

"I'll be honest," he said, in that cheerful way Tristan could always tell meant he was faking. "You kind of scared me back there."

I did? Tristan thought, dazed. Leo was so warm, and so *close*. The whole world narrowed down to the weight of his arm wrapped around Tristan, the gleaming droplets of seawater clinging to the ends of his hair, the tiny wrinkle between his eyebrows. Tristan resisted the impulse to lean into his touch.

"Sorry," Tristan mumbled. "I thought I was holding on, but—"

Leo gave him a friendly squeeze and released him, to his dismay. "I'm just glad you're okay. Aziza is, too, by the way. I know she doesn't *look* like she cares, but she always does."

His eyes drifted over Leo's shoulder, to where Aziza was conversing with the Chief too quietly for him to hear. The Chief pressed something into her hand.

"Looks like it worked," he told Leo.

"I never even wanna *see* the ocean again," Leo said as Aziza came over to them. "Starting right now, I'm not going near any body of water bigger than a bathtub."

But her only response was a distracted "Hmm? Oh. Yeah," and a worried glance at Leo. She didn't say a word to either of them as they left the Chief with his boat; she fiddled with whatever the Chief had given her and frowned at nothing, seemingly lost in thought.

They had almost gotten back to the road before she said, "How did you know Tristan couldn't swim?"

"What?" Tristan said, too quickly.

"When you fell overboard," she said, jerking her head at Leo, "he knew you couldn't swim. How?"

"Um," Leo said. "I don't actually know."

His hand rose to rub at the back of his head. Tristan was certain a headache was forming, the one he always got when someone tried to talk to him about the curse.

His heart flipped over at the thought that Leo had remembered something about him, however small. But it was a short-lived victory. A fluke, brought on by urgency and adrenaline. It didn't matter, not really. The only thing that mattered to him right now was making sure Leo wasn't in pain.

"I mentioned it the other night," he said.

"Did you."

It wasn't a question. She knew he hadn't.

"I did," Tristan said anyway. "After we dropped you off, on our way back to the library."

"That's right!" Leo said, with evident relief. "I just remembered."

His hand dropped. The headache must have subsided now that the curse had installed the false memory. But it was too late: His

I don't know had tipped Aziza off that something was wrong. Her eyes narrowed. Tristan cast about desperately for a way to change the subject.

"What's that in your hand?" he asked.

After a last, lingering look at him, she held it up for them to see. It was a clamshell, smooth and dry, its exterior a light sandy brown. The hinge was intact, but the front slightly open, frozen in a desiccated half smile.

"We have to get this into the gateway tree and break it open," she said. "That'll send a signal to the selkies and trigger their magic. They'll send a flood that will uproot the tree, wash it away, and drown her."

Tristan stopped short. "That's it? All we need to do is get that thing into the tree?"

"And break it, yeah."

"The hounds can do that," he said, his heart kicking up into a gallop. "They can be inside the hag's territory in seconds."

He didn't know if their quiet attacks on the gateway tree had made any difference to anything. Either the hag hadn't noticed what they had been doing yet—in which case he knew they could sneak past her defenses—or she didn't care because she thought they were no threat to her. She wouldn't know what the clamshell token was, either; by the time she figured it out, *if* she did, it would be too late.

"This could be over right *now*," he said.

Aziza and Leo traded glances. Despite everything, Tristan couldn't suppress a pang of jealousy. He missed being the one Leo checked in with. But it didn't matter anymore, did it? If Aziza agreed to this plan, he had minutes to live.

"I don't know," Aziza said. "Handing this token to a hound after what we just went through to get it . . . If the hound doesn't obey you, if *anything* goes wrong, we don't have any other options. We'll be stuck."

"It *will* obey me. Please," he said, looking only at her. He might lose his nerve if he met Leo's gaze now. Hopefully, she'd put the tremor in his voice down to his wet clothes and the chill night air. "I can do this. *Let me.*"

"You're *sure* this will work?" she asked.

"Yes!"

She glanced again at Leo, who shrugged.

"I . . ." The conflict was plain in her expression. "Fine."

They'd left the wharfs behind and stopped amongst the warehouses, cranes, and repair centers of the inner port. Boxed in on all sides, they couldn't see the ocean anymore, but its thunderous voice carried to them on the wind. A lone streetlamp on the far corner lit the way to the parking lot. In this density of shadow, it took hardly any effort for Tristan to reach through his bond to the hounds, nudge the nearest one to attention, and summon it.

The sulfurous stench of the hounds wound around him; Aziza and Leo caught a shiver as the temperature dropped. Where Tristan stood, though, the air grew so hot his clothes steamed, and then the shadows before him solidified into a snout. The hound stepped up and out of the darkness. Though it was taller than him, it bowed its head so that its black eyes were level with his.

Tristan held out one hand to Aziza, so that she could pass him the token, and gripped the scruff of the hound's neck with the other. Its eyes snapped toward Aziza when she inched nearer, but Tristan tugged at his fistful of fur, hard, until it returned its gaze to him.

He didn't need to speak his orders aloud; the hound would understand anyway.

Token. Tree. Bury. Shatter.

Obey.

Aziza's hand hovered over Tristan's. Pausing to study him one more time, wan and tight-lipped and distrustful, she seemed on the verge of changing her mind and snatching the token away again. But she didn't. She dropped the clamshell token into his palm with a barely audible sigh. Tristan's fingers closed around it.

The hound shivered. Instinctively, he tightened his grip on its ruff, soothing it through the bond, but then—

The bond that tied him to the hound *snapped*.

It was a total and instantaneous severing; he couldn't feel the hounds at all, and it left him bereft. All this time he'd been aware of them even when he wasn't actively paying attention, their sharp senses and instincts making the world around him more vivid and full—he hadn't noticed what a difference it made until it was gone. All that was left was him, emptier and weaker than he had felt in a very long time, and the other bond, the one to the hag, the one that now was taut with her attention. *She* had done this.

"Tristan," Aziza said. "What's happening?"

The hound whirled around to face him. A growl tore from its chest, its lips curling in an enraged snarl. And in the back of his mind, cold laughter echoed out from a starless gray place in the woods.

The hag had taken back the gift she'd given him. He wasn't a necromancer anymore, and the hound had no master at all.

It let out a howl of fury, confusion, bloodlust—and leapt at him.

CHAPTER 30

AZIZA

WHEN THE HOUND lunged at Tristan, Aziza did, too.

She didn't know what had happened, but there was one thing she was sure of: She had to get to the token before the hound did.

It pounced on Tristan, sending him crashing to the ground, its huge paws pinning his shoulders down. Aziza threw herself on top of it, wrapping her arms around its neck and trying to drag it away. Tristan struggled underneath it. The hound fought to hold him down and buck her off all at once, and then it rolled over and everything was pain and confusion—hot black fur in her eyes and mouth, her elbow banging into the asphalt, Tristan shouting at it in a voice choked with desperation—she was going to kill him herself if the hound didn't manage it—

She ended up on her back, both hands shoving up at the hound's throat, its teeth snapping inches from her face. It snarled, and a gust of putrid breath nearly made her gag.

Something metallic bashed into its face: Leo had found a crowbar somewhere and shoved it between its teeth. It yelped and bit down, and the metal crumpled between its jaws. Then Leo's hands were yanking at Aziza's arms, dragging her out from under it, while it dropped the crowbar with a clatter and swung around, seeking its attacker.

Its eyes landed on Tristan, who stood hunched and panting, but unharmed.

"Stop," he commanded. The hound padded closer, chest rumbling with one long, continuous growl, every muscle in its considerable frame tensed.

"Tristan," Aziza said, her voice low and steady. "Throw me the token, and run."

If the hound only wanted the token, then Tristan would be fine. If the hound wanted revenge on its old master, well—then Tristan wouldn't be fine, but at least the token would be.

They were about to find out, either way.

"But if *you* have the token—" Leo whispered, but Aziza shook her head. She knew.

Tristan drew back his hand—the hound's eyes snapped to his closed fist, and it crouched to spring—and flung the token into the air.

The hound leapt for it but missed, its jaws clamping down on nothing. Tristan's aim was true: Aziza caught the token, its cool, smooth surface against her palm sending a rush of triumph through her. She clutched it to her chest and sprinted away, back toward the wharfs and the sea, hoping that hounds couldn't swim—

Its great paws slapped over the pavement, the sound growing louder and louder as it ate up the distance between them. The air went hot—it was bearing down on her—

It sprang clear over her head and landed in front of her, blocking her path to the ocean.

She froze with indecision. Her breath came in harsh pants, and she was sweating under her damp clothes. Part of her mind went back to the clearing where she'd faced another hound with the certainty she wouldn't survive; she could almost see the fairy lights through imagined tree branches and hear the police sirens. But this time, she had nothing to defend herself, not even her backpack, and Tristan couldn't wave his hand and make it go away.

The hound lunged, and she dodged, staggering backward. Her arms flew out for balance, and that was her final mistake. It snapped its jaws and caught her right hand between its teeth.

Someone was screaming.

Aziza's throat went raw, and the hound's burning smell choked her, and only then did she realize the anguished voice was hers.

Her bones crumpled like paper. Muscle and skin shredded to ribbons around it. The bite must have been quick, but her mind recorded every millisecond, every tiny fraction of fang sinking into her flesh and ripping her hand open. The pads of her fingers registered the searing wet heat of its mouth—and then that was gone, and the only sensation left was agony. She screwed her eyes shut, and her knees went out from under her.

The hound released her.

Her hand was mangled—and empty. The token shone dully between the hound's grinning teeth. Looking directly at Aziza, it threw its head back and swallowed the token whole.

It dove into the shadows with the same careless ease of a selkie slipping into the ocean, and was gone.

SHE'D NEVER SEEN Leo break so many traffic laws.

In the passenger seat, she hunched over her towel-wrapped hand—the blood had already soaked it through—and tried not to cry from the pain.

"You're gonna be fine," Leo said, his knuckles white on the steering wheel. He ran a stop sign and didn't even seem to notice. "Zee? You still with me?"

Talking took *so much* effort. Everything that didn't involve clutching her ruined hand to her chest and counting her breaths seemed like a monumental task. Still, it was Leo asking, so she summoned a response.

"It's just a little blood. Relax."

She hadn't told him that she couldn't feel her fingers anymore, couldn't even make them twitch.

"I'm—I'm so sorry," Tristan mumbled, finally breaking his stunned silence. "I don't know what . . ."

Forcing the words out through gritted teeth, she said, "Does the hag know what we were planning?"

"I don't think so," he said, after a pause. "But she must have felt that I was getting ready to make a . . . a last stand against her."

"Then how come it went for the token?" Aziza shot back. "If she didn't know—and if she can't command the hounds, like you said— then how come it was so set on taking it away from us?"

"It was the last order I gave before she took my powers away. Maybe it somehow stuck. The hound has no master now, so it just . . . clung to the last thing I told it to do."

"How convenient," she said. She forced her chin up, so that she could look at him in the rearview mirror where he sat stricken and shamefaced in the backseat. She should've known not to trust him. He was all secrets and strange, loaded silences, and his reek of black magic and creepy psychic connection to the hounds had put her off from the start. How much of this confused, pitiful reaction was an act? What if his "betrayal" of the hag had been a ploy all along?

Fury simmered under her skin—under the all-encompassing

pain—but she had to tackle one problem at a time. First, make sure she didn't bleed to death. Then, deal with Tristan. Then, figure out a new plan to defeat the hag. Maybe the selkies would trade another favor for another token, though she'd be shocked if they trusted her with a new one after she'd lost the first.

And she'd have to call Jiddo. No, the hospital staff would probably call him, since she was still underage. He was going to lose sleep worrying about her.

Her mind must have wandered. She lost track of time; the night blurred away as Leo raced through at least two red lights and screeched to a halt in front of the emergency room. Before she had even begun to reach for the door, Leo had thrown it open and was helping her stagger out of the car. He half carried her through the hospital's entrance, shouting for help.

As the nurses swept her away, Leo's phone rang. She looked back over her shoulder in time to see him glance at the screen, frown, and answer. He met her worried eyes for a split second before the nurses guided her around a corner, and then he was out of sight.

Who would call him in the middle of the night? There weren't many options. She just hoped, whatever the reason for the call, that it wasn't important.

The last thing they needed now was another emergency.

CHAPTER 31

LEO

HE'D EXPECTED DAD to be angry, so the staticky sigh of relief that met him when he picked up the phone was borderline unsettling.

"Leo." Dad's voice was hoarse, either from exhaustion or worry. "Where are you?"

"Hospital," he admitted. "But I'm fine! Aziza's a little—"

"Come home now."

"I can't just leave—"

"Is Hazel with you?"

"No," he said slowly. "She's not at home?"

A hand touched his shoulder. Tristan had followed him into the waiting room. At his questioning look, Leo shook his head.

"Maria heard something and woke up. She checked on Hazel, and . . . Was she here when you left?"

"Yeah. I heard her sleep-talking."

At least, he *thought* she'd been asleep. Maybe she'd been on the phone with someone.

"Come home. Help us look. I'll call the police and her friends, but you're always the one who finds her when we can't—"

But this was different from Hazel wandering outside when their backs were turned, or getting distracted by something on the street and falling behind while they walked on, or crawling into cupboards as a toddler. Still, he was right. Leo was the best at finding her.

"I'm on my way."

Tristan hovered close by, those pale green eyes watching Leo with concern, arms folded over his thin chest—of course, he had to be freezing in his damp clothes. Leo sure was—or he had been, a minute ago. He couldn't really feel the cold anymore. He couldn't really feel anything.

"What's going on?" Tristan asked.

"My sister's missing." Leo pocketed his phone and dug out his keys. "I have to go. She probably just—snuck out to see her friends, or something. Is thirteen too young to start sneaking out?"

Tristan didn't meet his eyes. "Probably not. I was sneaking out at fourteen," he said to Leo's collar. "But she's not—I mean, does your sister seem like the type to do that?"

"Maybe. I haven't exactly been setting the best example for her."

Inwardly, he winced at the memory of their argument the other day.

"She's fine," he said, as much to himself as Tristan. "She can't have gotten far. You can stay here with Zee while I track her down."

Tristan flinched. "I—I don't think—Shouldn't I go with you? I could help you look."

"You said the hag could follow you to my place. Right?" Leo reminded him.

Tristan's mouth opened and closed again.

"She . . . she could," he said, sounding as if he'd forgotten that.

"So you have to stay here. I'll come get you guys as soon as I find Hazel."

He went back to his car, Tristan trailing along after him, and retrieved his spare set of clothes for Tristan to change into and Aziza's bag to return to her when they let her out. The lights in the parking lot were bright as daytime, but the sky was a pitch-black ceiling above them; the dissonance was jarring. Leo had never wanted so badly for a night to end.

"Wait," Tristan said, sounding oddly panicked. "I don't think you should go alone. Just stay here for a bit, and Aziza will come with you. Since I can't."

"Aziza's hurt," Leo said, shoving down a wave of remembered fear. The sight of all that blood, and the way Aziza had slowly started to drift on the drive to the hospital—it had been terrifying. "I don't want her to worry about anything except recovering. I told you, Hazel's probably fine. She's not a baby anymore. She snuck out, and I just have to go get her."

"What if—what if something's really wrong?" Tristan said, voice dropping to a strained whisper. "What if somehow . . ."

"The hag?" he asked. He closed the trunk of his car and turned to face Tristan, studying him. His hair was a slightly darker blond when wet, a soft buttery color, and his lips had a purple-blue tinge. In this light, his eyes were unreadable; Leo's own tired face reflected back at him. "But she couldn't. She can't find my place if you don't mark it for her. Right?"

Tristan said something strained and fearful, but Leo didn't catch it. His head throbbed; he closed his eyes for a moment, and the pain ebbed.

"It'll be okay," Leo said. "Stay here. I'll call Aziza's phone and let you know when I'm on my way back."

"*Leo.*"

Halfway through yanking the door open, Leo froze.

"Please," Tristan said. He drew closer, so close Leo could see the fine, almost invisible tips of his eyelashes. "Don't go. Not by your-self. Not without me."

It was too easy to be close to Tristan. Leo's whole body burned with the need to reach out for him.

He took a step back, needing to put distance between them so that he could think again.

"It's Hazel," he said. "I have to."

Without giving Tristan time for any more protests—without giv-ing him a chance to change Leo's mind—he climbed into his car. He felt Tristan's gaze on him as he pulled out of the parking space, but he didn't look back.

BY THE TIME he got home, Dad had called all of Hazel's friends, her friends' parents, her teachers, and the cops. No one answered except the cops, since it was nearly three in the morning. Mom was locked in the master bedroom, trying to cry silently but inevitably hiccup-ping tree frogs, which scattered at her feet. He thought he even saw a salamander disappear under the nightstand.

"Mom," he said, closing the door behind him and then wrapping his arms around her. She tucked her head under his chin. When had he gotten so much taller than her? "Calm down. We'll find her."

Mom shook her head frantically and pulled away to sign some-thing he interpreted as, "They took her back," but that didn't make any sense. Maybe he'd misunderstood. He still got his signs mixed up sometimes; she'd probably said, *They took her away.* So she thought Hazel had been kidnapped. But that couldn't be true. It just couldn't.

"I'm going to go drive around and see if I can find her bike at any of the neighbors' places," he said, grabbing a tissue from the dresser and pressing it into her hands. He nudged her over to sit on the bed. "Don't cry. It's going to be okay."

She blinked out a few more tears. With shaky hands, she signed, "I'm sorry. My fault. I'm sorry."

"What? No, you didn't do anything. It's *my* fault. Hazel knows I sneak out all the time, and she decided she wanted to give it a try, too." He draped the throw blanket over her shoulders and placed the box of tissues next to her. "Just stay here. I'll be right back."

The cops insisted on speaking to Leo. When he'd shaken them off, he checked Hazel's room, even though of course everyone else would've already looked there. He expected to give it a cursory look and then leave again, finding nothing useful—but when he came through the door, he froze. Hazel's room was littered with candles and spent matches, and sticks of incense she must have nicked from Mom stuck inside empty soda cans she was using as make-shift burners. Tea bags. Scraps of paper, which—when he examined them—turned out to have been sprayed with their parents' perfume and cologne.

Scents for the wind sprites.

He had expected her to be curious about magic, but this wasn't curiosity. This bordered on obsession. What could she possibly have been talking to the wind sprites about?

Whatever it was, if that was the reason Hazel had left tonight . . . then it was all Leo's fault. Leo and this unbelievably selfish thing he had done, thinking—no, telling himself—that Hazel wouldn't be affected, only him. Who had he been kidding?

He felt sick.

Shakily, he picked up a stick of incense, lit it, and went to the open window.

"Hey," he said, into the night. "Are you still there? If you are, then please—tell me where my sister went."

Wisps of smoke curled away into the darkness; the tip of the incense turned to ash and flaked off, and its sandalwood scent filled the air.

A breeze picked up, catching the ash and flinging it away.

"Please," he said again.

The whisper carried through the window belonged to Hazel, and she sounded so close she could've been in the room with him.

"*No, you're wrong.*" The words had a tremble that could've come from the distortion of the wind, or could've been fear. "*Stop saying that.*" The breeze tugged at his collar, and the next message came a little clearer, from another conversation maybe. "*Before, you said I should go, and now you think I should stay? Make up your minds.*" And: "*They wouldn't even know I'm gone until morning.*" And then, in a dreamy voice that hardly even sounded like her: "*You're liars. She told me not to trust you. If I ask her, she'll tell me everything.*"

An eerie calm settled over him. He knew where Hazel was now.

Mechanically, he made his way back outside. Dad caught up with him in the hall and followed.

"Leo, there's something you should know about your sister," Dad said. From the upstairs bathroom, there came the telltale crash of Spot knocking down the shower curtain rod. He wasn't happy about Hazel being gone, either.

"Will it help me find her?"

"Not—not exactly."

"Then I don't care." He threw the front door open. The drive home, the brief once-over he'd given the house, talking to the cops—it felt like he'd wasted *hours* even though it hadn't been anywhere near that long.

"But—"

Leo cut him off. "Forget it. I know where she is."

He got into his car. Dad caught the edge of the door before he could close it.

"*Where?*" he demanded.

"Doesn't matter," Leo said. "I'm going. You're not."

"Leo, I need you to listen to me right now—"

"No," Leo said. His voice came out flat and emotionless. "Now you want to talk? Now you have some big secret to tell me about Hazel? Save it. I don't care anymore."

He slammed the door and drove away, leaving Dad in the driveway.

Just one more thing left to do. Steering one-handed, he grabbed his phone and called Aziza.

Tristan picked up. "Leo?"

"You were right," he said. "I don't know how, but the hag got to Hazel. She's been in her head, telling her . . . I don't know what. I'm going to the forest to find her."

"Come get us. We'll go with you," Tristan said, frantic.

"There's no time. She could've left hours ago. She's probably in the woods by now."

"What do you think you're going to do against the hag?" Tristan said, his voice rising. The part of Leo that was strangely calm hoped he'd had the sense to go outside, and wasn't shouting in the middle of the waiting room. "You're powerless."

"If I can get to Hazel before she makes it into the hag's territory, we'll be okay. I'll drag her back home and then we can snap her out of it."

"And what if you don't find her in time?"

Leo didn't bother responding. Tristan had to know the answer already.

If the hag already had Hazel, he was going in after her.

"The hag probably got to her through me," Leo said. "When she was in my head, that's how she must've found out about Hazel. Maybe a piece of her magic followed me home."

"That's not how it works," Tristan said. "Her magic can't stick to her victims like that. If it could, she wouldn't need a bondservant."

"Then how'd she do it?" He didn't know why he was asking; he didn't really care about the answer. However it had happened, the hag had found a way into his home. And Hazel had been vulnerable to her influence. He had told Hazel it was okay to talk to the wind sprites as long as she didn't listen to strange voices, but he hadn't been around to notice when she started doing nothing else *but* talking to the wind sprites, going by the state he'd found her room in. What had they said to her that had upset her enough to make her listen to the hag?

"She must have used me," Tristan said, sounding miserable. "Because I used to . . ." He hesitated, and then said, "Because I've been around you so much lately. If she found out where you live, she must have done it through me, okay? This is my fault, so please— please come back. Let me go with you. I know that after what happened tonight, you must think—But you can trust me, I swear, I'd never hurt you—"

"Hey. I know you wouldn't," he said, his voice softening by a fraction. "I'd go back for you if I could. I know splitting up is exactly what the hag probably wants us to do. But every second I waste, Hazel's in danger."

"This isn't about you or Hazel!" Tristan burst out. "You get that, right? The hag is doing this to get to Aziza. And it's going to work. Because Aziza will follow you, even if she knows it's a trap."

"Not if you stop her," he said, because it was worth a try. All he knew was that he'd rather die than live with a version of himself that hadn't gone after Hazel.

"You can't ask me to do that!"

"Then I guess I'll just have to be faster than you."

He hung up.

CHAPTER 32

TRISTAN

HE STOOD MOTIONLESS outside the hospital, the light through its glass doors spilling out on either side of him. The line had gone dead, but he still held the phone pressed against his ear, as if Leo's voice might come back if he just wanted it badly enough. But it didn't.

Tristan had failed.

After everything he'd done to keep the hag away from Leo, she'd taken him anyway. And he couldn't do anything about it. Not anymore. Not without the hounds.

But there was one person who could.

He dropped the phone into his pocket. He'd already changed into Leo's dry clothes and stuffed his wet ones in his backpack, which he'd then hidden. The only thing he took from it was the ritual knife. He'd come back for the rest later, if he lived through the night.

Now, he went back inside, slipped past the desk while the receptionist took a call, and found the corridor where they'd led Aziza away. He poked his head into rooms where the doors were ajar, knocked on the ones that weren't, calling her name and ignoring the irritated woman in scrubs that was making her way toward him. He was nearing the end of the hall when the next door flew open and Aziza came out.

Her hand was bandaged and secured in a sling. Pain and exhaustion showed in the tightness around her eyes and mouth, the way she leaned against the door frame as if she'd collapse without it. Her sweater was spattered with blood, the right sleeve soaked halfway to the elbow.

Tristan froze where he stood, unable to speak.

This was it. This was why the hag had kept him alive: so that he could do exactly what he was about to do. So that he could ask Aziza to die.

Maybe she'd started planning this from the very first moment he'd seen Leo again, in that tunnel in the forest. And Tristan should've known. Part of him *had* known, had registered the bond's silence—and simply ignored it. It had felt good to be doing something to stop the hag, and he hadn't felt anything resembling good in so long. But he should've stayed far away from Aziza and Leo. He should've buried himself in the ground and waited for the hag to decide he wasn't worth the effort of keeping him alive. He should've done anything other than what he *had* done: make everything worse, play right into her hands, and incapacitate the one person who had a hope of standing up to her.

Even when he thought he was doing the right thing, he wasn't. Maybe he wasn't capable of it. Maybe he was too selfish.

The nurse caught up to him, but Aziza shoved herself off the door frame and stepped between them. He observed—distantly, as if overhearing a conversation someone else was having over the phone—as Aziza argued with the nurse until she left them alone. Then she grabbed his wrist and towed him into the examination room.

"What's wrong?" she said, closing the door. "You look . . . Where's Leo?"

"The hag got Hazel," Tristan said. He had to scrape the words out of the vast empty space inside of him. "Leo is going after her. We have to—"

"No."

His head snapped up. "What?"

"*We* aren't doing anything," she said. The look on her face made him reel back a step. She followed, stalking toward him. "You did this, didn't you?"

It should've been impossible to hurt this much and not bleed.

"Not on purpose," he said, his voice cracking like sugar glass. "I swear."

"Enough with this fucking wounded act," Aziza hissed. She got right up in his face, until his back hit the examination chair and there was nowhere else for him to go. "You pretended you were done with the hag, but you were working with her all along."

"What? *No!*"

"Stop lying!"

"I'm not!"

She grabbed him by the collar and tugged him roughly down so that their eyes were level.

"When you fell overboard," she said, "Leo tried to go after you. But it was just like when the hag was using her powers on him. He didn't know what he was doing or why—like something was *forcing* him—"

Tristan shook his head rapidly. "It's not what you think—"

"And then he didn't remember why he knew you couldn't swim. He didn't remember until *you* told him what to remember! You did something to him—I don't know what—"

She released him with a shove and turned away, disgusted.

"I'm going after Leo. *Alone.* If you come anywhere near me . . . if you try to interfere in any way," she said, her back to him, "I will drag you into Elphame and sell your life to the fae."

She reached for the door—if she left, he wouldn't get another chance—

"I signed on with the hag because—because she said she could break a curse."

Her hand fell away from the doorknob, and she faced him again.

"You're . . . cursed?" she said incredulously. It was less a question and more a prompt. From her tone, he knew she had guessed what he really meant. He also understood that she needed to hear him say it, all of it, before she could even start to believe him.

You can still back down, said the part of him that shamefully, jealously guarded all his secrets. *Make something up. If you tell her, she'll hate you even more. She'll say you never deserved him anyway. She'll be right.*

"No," he said. "My true love was cursed. To forget me."

She was silent for so long he started to worry he would have to repeat himself, and there was only about a fifty-fifty chance he could bring himself to do that.

"Am I hallucinating," she said at last, "or did you just say that you signed away *ten years of your life* to save your relationship?"

"I know you thought I was harboring some nefarious secret, and this must be such a letdown in comparison. Sorry to disappoint."

He prepared himself to argue his case, to beg, to do whatever it took to convince her that he could help. Or that, at least, he couldn't possibly make things any worse.

"I'm just grateful the crossroad demons were unavailable." She took a deep breath and blew it out slowly, regaining her composure.

"You really *didn't* do anything to him, then. On the boat. He remembered on his own."

Braced for a fight that no longer seemed to be happening, he faltered and had to collect himself.

"Yes. But if you talk to him about the curse—Well, you can't," he said. "He mishears, or doesn't hear anything at all. Or he gets a headache. There's no point—it just hurts him."

"You betrayed the hag for him." Aziza stared at him with that piercing gaze of hers, like she could see down to his foundations and unmake him with a thought. "She went after him, and when she failed, she didn't have anything to use against you anymore. You didn't care if she killed you, because you knew he was safe."

Thought he was safe. How shortsighted he'd been.

"Let me come with you. You can trust me—"

"I *can't* trust you, but it doesn't matter. The only thing that matters is getting Leo and Hazel back." She looked away from him to blink furiously at the ground. "He's my best friend."

"Yeah," Tristan said. "Mine, too."

Their eyes met, and in that moment, they understood each other perfectly.

CHAPTER 33

AZIZA

THE HOSPITAL HAD already called Jiddo. His insurance plan from work had covered her treatment tonight. She'd told him Leo would be giving her a ride home and not to wait up. But she knew he'd wait up anyway.

The last thing she wanted was to call him again and tell him what she was about to do. Ever since they'd fought, they could barely be in the same room together. He would take this as another betrayal.

But the only thing worse than telling him now would be *not* telling him . . . and not getting a chance to say goodbye.

She left the hospital without checking out—all she'd been waiting for was the doctor to return with a prescription for painkillers, which she didn't plan on using, anyway. Painkillers would cloud her mind. She booked a cab; at this hour, the trains would take too long. She and Tristan didn't speak, just waited side by side in silence.

Once she couldn't delay it any longer, she lifted her phone again and made the call. He picked up on the first ring.

"Aziza?"

"Hi, Jiddo."

"What did the doctor say?"

The doctor had winced at the sight of her hand, so Aziza had braced herself for the worst. With the aid of a nurse, he'd cleaned her wounds, bandaged her up, set the bones, and maneuvered her into a brace, as a stopgap until the swelling went down enough for a real cast. There would be nerve damage, he said, and a loss of mobility that could be permanent; at the moment, she couldn't move it at all past the wrist. He mentioned the possibility of surgery, but there was no guarantee that would get her hand back to the way it had been before.

And he'd given her a rabies shot. It had taken all of her energy to hold back a hysterical laugh.

"He said, uh . . . we'll have to wait and see how it heals."

"Are you coming home now?"

"Jiddo, the hag took Leo."

He knew immediately what this meant. What she was really saying.

"No. *No.* I don't care. Come home right now!"

"I can't. She took him because of me. Because she knew I'd come after him."

"Aziza, no. Please. If you never listen to me again, listen to me now, just this once."

She swallowed past the lump in her throat, unable to respond. But her silence told him everything he needed to know.

"You're just like Leila," he said, his voice choked with tears. Aziza closed her eyes, willing herself to stay composed. "She never listened, either. She thought being a witch made her invincible."

"I don't think that," Aziza said, and it was true. Of the witches she knew, two of them were her parents, dead in their twenties. One was Jiddo, who had put his craft away like a rusting tool in a garage, to be dusted off only when necessary. Another was Tristan, not a born witch but one created by someone else to be their pawn. Another was the Ash Witch, a vengeful spirit unrecognizable from the person she'd been once. And one was the hag, a former witch corrupted.

Death and destruction everywhere she looked. These were the only examples of witchcraft she had.

"You gave up magic because of what happened to my parents. And you don't trust other witches because Leila's coven didn't help her when she needed them," Aziza said. "But you made that decision for both of us. I had to figure out so much of my craft on my own because I didn't have a real teacher. I never questioned it because I thought what I had was enough."

"Stay at the hospital," he said. She heard movement on his end of the line, like he was grabbing the house key, putting on his shoes. "I'll come and get you."

But their ride was minutes away. By the time Jiddo called a cab for himself and got here, she and Tristan would be long gone. She didn't try to stop him, though. He didn't understand this choice, not then and not now. For Aziza, it was hardly a choice at all.

She was Blackthorn's hedgewitch, and Blackthorn was her home. This was how she'd defined herself and her connection to Blackthorn: in terms of the purpose she served, the role she played here. But she'd been wrong. Blackthorn wasn't her home because she was useful to it. It was home because of the people she cared about. Jiddo and Meryl. The people at the fair who got to keep all their fingers because she caught the shade. The woman she and her coven had dug out of an imp's den, and the taxi driver she still thought she could've saved somehow if she'd just been a little better. The spirits and the fae. And because of Leo, maybe him most of all.

Their ride pulled up, and Tristan climbed in.

"I have to go now," she said. "I love you, Jiddo."

"Aziza!"

"Goodbye."

"Please—"

She hung up and followed Tristan into the car.

"Anyone you want to call?" she asked, and held out her phone.

"No."

It was a very quiet drive.

CHAPTER 34

LEO

WHEN HAZEL WAS four or five years old, she almost drowned in the pond out back.

She wasn't supposed to be outside on her own. But Hazel had always been too curious and too crafty for her own good. If she wanted out, she was getting out.

Leo had been the first to notice her missing. Leo, at eight-ish years old, had been the one who went outside as if called there by intuition—or God, Mom later said, but he didn't think God had anything to do with it. He was Hazel's big brother. It was only natural he'd know when something was wrong with her. The sky was blue, water was wet, and Leo would always be there for Hazel.

He found her facedown in the pond, hands scrabbling at the water for purchase. Drowning was soundless, he'd learned that day. She hadn't been able to lift her head long enough even to scream; the frantic motion of her hands made only the tiniest of splashes, no louder than a tadpole slipping into the water. He'd waded in and plucked her out by the wrist, as easy as anything, and carried her back inside while she wailed against his shoulder. Part of him still saw that Hazel whenever he looked at her: chubby, four-year-old

Hazel with her face all red and screwed up, her wet clothes and hair plastered to her skin, howling plaintively as if she'd been wronged.

In the dark, the woods were velvet. The moon had disappeared behind a veil of clouds, so Leo held up his phone's flashlight and followed the path Eirlys had once taken them down—or close to it. Weeks of tramping through the woods with Aziza made him sure-footed on the uneven, root-laced ground. He ran at full speed, heart tripping over itself, already losing hope of finding her. She had to be way ahead of him, and he couldn't even be sure he was going in the right direction—

Then his light fell on a small figure, barefoot and dressed in thin PJs despite the late-winter frost. He came to a halt, panting. She stood there mannequin-like, not even shivering in the cold, not even breathing; she stared back at him with waxy, unseeing eyes.

"Hazel?" he said, inching nearer, not wanting to startle her. "It's okay. You're okay."

He reached out his hand—

Hazel turned and bolted. He chased after her, but she was unbelievably fast—unnaturally fast—flying through the woods with the reckless grace of a fawn, and Leo was somehow certain she could go even faster. That she was holding back for his sake, staying just close enough for him to see but too far for him to catch. She flickered in and out of sight, disappearing beyond the trees until he caught up enough for his light to shine off the ends of her braids, or the soles of her feet flicking up paler than the rest of her, almost white against the darkness.

"Hazel!" he shouted, his voice violently disruptive in the quiet of the deep woods, like he'd disturbed something sacred. "Don't listen to her!"

Because he knew with a dreadful certainty that Hazel was only half-aware of what she was doing. The hag's voice was in her head, commanding her. If he could just catch up with her—just pick her up by the wrist, prop her against his shoulder like she was still four years old, and carry her back home—everything would be okay again, he would *make it okay again*—

But the woods were changing around him. The gray rolled in like a fog, like the place where a dream shifted into a nightmare, the light and the darkness twisting together until he couldn't tell one from the other. The clouds cleared and the moon came out again, but the world dimmed, and the sounds of the forest dropped off behind him so all he could hear was his own breathing—

Hazel disappeared past the reach of his light. He went faster, sprinting, but just as he glimpsed her again, his luck ran out—his foot caught on a root, and he went sprawling. The wind was knocked out of him. He groaned, shoving up onto his knees, expecting Hazel to be gone—but no. She was still there, frozen in place, staring down at her outstretched hands, which—what was wrong with her hands?

She screamed, a shrill cry of shock and pain. Then she caught her breath and screamed again, longer and louder, with pure terror. Leo scrambled to his feet and ran to her, caught her by the shoulders and pulled her around to face him, scared to death she was hurt—

"Hazel—are you okay? Look at me!"

Slowly, she tilted her tearstained face up into the moonlight.

She was changing.

Her skin turned a pale green, and her ears grew long and pointed. Two sets of translucent wings, like a dragonfly's, unfurled on her back. His hands flew away from her like he'd been electrocuted. And still she was changing. Her brown eyes had gone shimmery and silver, pupil-less. Her cheekbones grew sharper, more defined, and her chin narrowed to a point.

"Leo?" she choked out. "What's happening to me?"

She held up unnaturally long-fingered hands, and her knees gave out. Leo couldn't move, couldn't speak. The tail end of a memory floated to the front of his mind: Back in the house after Hazel's almost-drowning, while Mom had scrubbed at Hazel's hair with a towel, Dad had knelt in front of her and asked her what she'd been doing in the pond.

I was talking to the water, she'd said. They'd put it down to four-year-old babbling, but now Leo thought of sprites and wondered if the signs had been there all along.

Hazel was a fairy.

"It's okay," he said, kneeling down and putting an arm gingerly around her shoulders. Her wings fluttered anxiously, but she didn't pull away. She was still wearing her braces; they fit all wrong on her new teeth.

"I knew it," she whispered. "I knew there was something wrong with me."

"No, there's *nothing*—"

"The wind sprites said . . . They said all these weird things, and I didn't want to believe them, but . . ."

"Forget what the wind sprites said—"

"Mom and Dad lied to me." Her tears flowed pearly and bright. "Did you know?"

"No," he said, tightening his grip as her eyes grew clouded again. "I didn't know, but we can go home and figure this out together—"

"I'm not going back. *She* promised she'd tell me everything. She'll help me."

Her voice hardly even sounded like her own. He got up and lifted her to her feet, trying to tug her back the way they'd come, but she resisted, with surprising strength to match her speed.

"Hazel, *don't*—"

She ripped out of his grasp and fled deeper into the woods. The shadows quickly swallowed her, and Leo followed. His mind raced, trying to solve the riddle before him. The scrap of fairy wing in the vial. The photo of him and Hazel he'd found with it in the box. Mom and Dad's obstinate silence. And the way Mom had said, *They took her back.* All the pieces were in front of him, but he couldn't put them together. As they delved deeper into what had to be the hag's territory, it became harder to hold on to his thoughts. The woods were wild and dark, and Hazel's unearthly cries lingered in the air like stardust. Her grief blazed a trail through the forest, or maybe it was her newfound fae magic; his flashlight curved strangely through the gray nothing, at times slicing through the shadows and at other times bending around them.

Then Hazel vanished. There for a breath, gone by the time he exhaled.

Frantic, he kept going to the place where she'd disappeared. The ground rolled up like a wave to meet him; the soil was soft and warm like a living thing, and it swallowed him up; there was no sky, no moon, no light since he'd dropped his phone—he tried to breathe and tasted dirt—

The world stopped tumbling around him. He was underground.

Another tunnel? No. This was a pit—not even a pit, but a cell, a space so cramped he couldn't stand up. A hitching, wet breathing came from somewhere close by.

"Hazel?"

"Leo?"

He shuffled forward on his knees, one hand steadying him against the dirt wall and the other feeling around in the dark until it connected with Hazel's shoulder. She scooted toward him; her eyes almost glowed. He pulled her close, and she sobbed against his shoulder.

"What's happening to me?" she choked out. "Where are we?"

"Shh. I've got you. It's okay."

He tried to think, his mind sluggish and clouded. Tristan had said the magic of the hag's borderlands was disorienting, but he'd gotten used to it, and so could Leo.

The hag didn't want them, not really. She'd probably kill them later, but they weren't her priority right now. They were bait. Aziza would come after them; until then, the hag was making sure they couldn't leave. She'd folded the world around them like a pocket, tucking them away for safekeeping.

Eventually, Hazel's breathing slowed, and her sobs died down. He released her and started feeling out their surroundings, trailing his hands over the walls. The darkness wasn't total—there was light filtering in from *somewhere*. Sure enough, his fingertips caught on a slight gap over his head—a seam where the hag had opened and then closed the earth again. He couldn't see it, but he traced its length with his fingers.

He scratched and clawed at the opening, widening it bit by bit, shaking off the clumps of dirt that fell into his hair. But each time his hand broke through the innermost layer of soil, and he thought he could feel the cool night air on the very tips of his fingers—the ground shifted and closed up again.

He gritted his teeth and kept digging.

CHAPTER 35

TRISTAN

"I'll go to the hag," Aziza said, "and you find Leo."

On edge of the hag's borderlands, the woods had the uncanny not-quite-rightness of a clay doll. The boughs of the trees stretched ghoulishly in the hard light of their phones; the crooning of the katydids was faded, ghostlike.

And Aziza's face was carved stone, betraying no emotion.

"You want to split up?"

"If I distract her, you might have a chance to escape."

"But you'd be alone."

"Can you get Leo out or not?"

That was assuming he and Hazel weren't already—No. He wasn't even going to think that. Past the thrum of fear, he considered her question as objectively as he could. He was still bound to the hag, and his sense of her territory was intact, his sense of the things that came and went. "Yes," he said at last.

She nodded once, like that settled the matter.

"How do I get to the gateway tree?"

"Just start walking. She'll show you the way."

He touched her shoulder before she could go. But when she turned back to him, the words wilted in his throat. What could he even say to her? He had been so afraid to die. It had taken him a year to get to the point where he would've killed himself to escape the hag. But Aziza was about to go fearlessly to her own probable death with no more than an hour's preparation and the faint hope it wouldn't all be for nothing.

"Take care," he managed, as inadequate a goodbye as there ever was.

"You too."

A few steps, and she was gone; the glow of her flashlight was swallowed by the woods as easily as a drop of water disappearing into oil. Very soon, the hag would know Aziza was coming. This was the chance—the distraction—Aziza had given him. He plunged into the hag's territory for what would likely be the last time, knowing he would not be coming back out. Either Aziza would somehow kill the hag, and Tristan would die with her—or the hag would kill Aziza and then finally dispose of Tristan. Someone would win, but it wasn't going to be him.

That was all right, though. He'd spent six years of his otherwise shitty life in love with Leo. For about three of them, he'd even been loved back. How miraculous was that? How lucky was he? He clung to those memories—the memories he safeguarded for himself and Leo both—and let them guide him like a light through the darkness.

Inside the hag's territory, the illusion that space and time were quantifiable things—concepts that could be measured and predicted—was gone. Seconds were eternal, and as fleeting as a wingbeat. Everything that crossed in and out of the hag's threshold made ripples in the gray nothing. *There*, the hag. *There*, Aziza, her warm-bright magic washing over him even as she moved farther and farther away. *There* and *there* and *there*, small helpless lost things, birds that had flown into the hag's territory by mistake and couldn't find the way out anymore, foxes that had burrowed too far.

And *there*. Two lives, halfway to the gateway tree. Trapped.

That was where Tristan went, racing through the woods with abandon. In the hag's borderlands, distance wasn't real, not in any way that mattered. He concentrated on being with Leo, and that was what closed the space between them, more than the steps he took or the time that passed.

Just get to Leo, he told himself, as he half dissolved into the gray dust.

Leo.

Leo.

Leo.

He'd often wondered what Leo's last thought of him had been, before the curse set in. He hoped the very last thing the curse took from him was the knowledge of how much Tristan loved him—that Tristan loved him completely, unwaveringly, *truly*. And if Leo broke the curse one day after he was gone, he hoped that was the first thing he'd remember—and that it would matter to him still, despite all the things Tristan had done wrong.

He was so close to Leo and Hazel he could feel the way their breaths disturbed the atoms of the air, the way their pulses made low vibrations in the stillness of the borderlands. They were straight ahead, past the ridge in the ground—like the spine of a dragon rearing up out of the earth. Tristan sped up, heart pounding, eyes sweeping his surroundings for any sign of them—

Then the dead thing in the corner of his senses *moved*.

He stopped short, panting.

A hulking, bearlike shape stepped into his path—taller than him even on four legs, so black it blended with the shadows, except for the gleam of its eyes. A hound. Not just any hound, either: the same hound that Tristan had ordered to come here before the hag had taken his powers away.

The hound that had the token.

It bared its teeth, a flash of white in the dark. Tristan drew his ritual knife.

No time to think. He couldn't turn back when he was so close.

Its snarl tore through the air, magnified and echoing, as if it carried the voices of a hundred hounds in its throat. He didn't need to be a necromancer to know it was afraid and confused to find itself so suddenly with no master, no anchoring presence—and a hound reacted to fear and confusion with violence. He charged it before it could make the first move. This time, there was no magic for him to lean on, no reason for it to yield to him. All he had was this: the desperation to duck under its jaws and take its claws down his arm instead; the fury to shove his shoulder into its chest and send it rolling off him with a pained whine; the madness to jump on top of it, stabbing wildly, until it rolled over again and pinned him down and—

Its eyes landed on his face, and it hesitated for the briefest instant, its growls quieting. As though it had recognized him, and something deep in its feral mind still remembered when he was its master.

That second of hesitation was all he needed. He plunged the silver knife into its belly and dragged it up, forcing it through the hard muscle of its chest. Blood spilled out over him, so hot he could've sworn it burned. The hound collapsed onto the ground on its side.

It wouldn't stay dead for long. He had to run—had to get to Leo and Hazel—

But not yet.

He pushed himself to his knees and bent over the hound's corpse.

Its stomach was already knitting itself back together. He sliced it open again and thrust his hand inside. All he could feel at first was slick-warm softness; the iron-sulfur-dog smell of its blood choked him, so he had to take deep, gasping breaths through his mouth once he could bear it no longer—

His hand closed around something smooth and compact, but when he pulled it out and wiped the blood off on his jeans, it was only a piece of bone from whatever it'd eaten last. He stuck his hand into its guts again, digging around, and then his fingers brushed another small, hard object—this one with a familiar rounded shape and ridges on one side.

He withdrew it and, with trembling fingers, wiped it clean.

The clamshell token.

The shock of victory roared through him, so powerful it made it to the bond. As he staggered to his feet, a sliver of the hag's attention turned away from Aziza and toward him.

She didn't know what he'd done, but she knew enough to be sure she didn't like it.

Hurry, he told himself.

He left the hound's body behind, climbing the ridge where he'd sensed Leo and Hazel. When he glanced backward once, the hound was struggling to its feet; it glared up at him before slinking away into the woods.

"Leo?" he called, when it had vanished.

A muffled voice responded. But where *was* he?

He turned in place, probing again at his bond-given awareness of the hag's territory. Before, he'd felt them *in* the ground, but how—

The bond yanked at his thoughts. *Turn back,* it said, not with words, but with feeling: a foreboding that ate at his stomach and clouded his mind.

"*Leo!*" he shouted at the top of his lungs. He was running out of time.

"*Tris?*"

His voice had come from practically right under Tristan's feet. He dropped to the ground, clawing the soil aside; a layer of mud soon coated his blood-soaked hands.

Turn back! the hag howled at him through the bond. Her fury blazed through his head like fire and carved a line of agony down his spine; it crackled and roared in the voice of a fire, too, so that he couldn't even hear himself calling to Leo again, couldn't hear if Leo replied. Even the thump of his galloping heart was gone. He kept digging. All he had to do was finish this one thing, and then nothing else would matter, not even the pain.

His hand broke through a gap in the earth; he widened it, and there, two pale faces streaked with sweat and dirt peered up at him, one with strange, mirrorlike eyes—*Hazel?*—and one familiar. They were trapped in some kind of pit—Leo was digging from his side, but his hands couldn't breach the surface. The ground itself was working against them, closing over the gap and hiding Leo from view. They reached for each other over and over, only to be torn apart again.

Tristan lay flat on the ground and shoved his arm through the gap, using his other hand to keep the opening clear, desperate to keep Leo in sight—and as he did, he could feel the ground rumbling, as if the hag meant to make the earth cave in on her captives.

The bond pressed down on him like a weight, like the hound's body pinning him to the ground. Tristan strained until he thought his spine would unravel, stretched his arm out until every joint ached. Leo's eyes were huge and dark, his sweat-damp curls sticking to his forehead; he clutched Hazel to his side with one arm and reached up for Tristan with the other.

With a final gasp, his fingers breached the remaining millimeters between them, and Leo's hand clasped his. Even as his strength drained, even as the pain mounted in his chest, even as the bond began its final, lethal assault—he pulled Leo and Hazel up, helping them break through the ground and clamber out of the pit.

Leo's lips formed the shape of Tristan's name. He shook his head, unable to hear, unable to speak—unable to breathe—

He sank to his knees. Leo followed him down, steadying him with his hands on Tristan's shoulders—his hands sliding up to cup Tristan's jaw—

Tris? he said, soundless. *Tris, please!*

He was so close his fringe brushed Tristan's forehead. Tristan's hands rose instinctively to clutch at Leo's wrists. Through pain-blurred eyes, he took one last look at Leo's face, wanting him to be the last thing he saw—

The hag withdrew.

He breathed.

"Tristan!" Leo's voice, Leo's rough palm against Tristan's cheek—all he could do was blink in response. "Jesus, fuck, tell me what's wrong—"

"I'm fine," he wheezed.

Why was he fine?

And then he knew.

The hag's triumph resounded through the bond. She didn't care about him anymore; his punishment could wait. She had more pressing matters to attend to.

Because Aziza had reached the gateway tree.

CHAPTER 36

AZIZA

IN THE END, Aziza was alone.

Nothing moved except for her. The forest had an undead quality, like true death would have been more peaceful than whatever this was—the ash trees gone white and uncertain as ghosts, the silence tense as if the world was waiting with bated breath for an unfinished song to pick back up. Everything aware of her—aware in a way that felt real enough for her to touch, like a collar around her throat.

The threshold to the hag's territory is indistinct, blending into the natural world, Tristan had explained, *so passing through her borderlands is disorienting. You're not really there, but you're not really in the human world or in Elphame, either. Reality . . . bends. Time bends.*

As she drew deeper into the hag's borderlands, the world grew cloudy and confusing. The pain shooting up her arm from her limp hand made it hard to focus. She'd ditched the sling but kept the brace, not wanting to have her hand pinned down, but its deadweight and alarming numbness threw her off balance.

You'll find the way if you will *it to be so,* Tristan had said. But it felt as if she walked an endless, winding road. Through the daze, she hoped Tristan, Leo, and Hazel were together. Hoped she could distract the hag long enough for them to get out.

Hoped, most of all, that Leo wouldn't do anything foolish.

She didn't know how far she walked before something wrenched itself from the woods and staggered into her path. It was emaciated and long-limbed, jerking around like a giant spider in its death throes, and Aziza flinched and swore and backed away—

And then she recognized it.

Recognized *her*.

"Eirlys?" she whispered, and moved hesitantly closer.

Eirlys was dead. There was no denying it. Her magic was gone; she was an empty husk. Her body was burned and torn and missing great chunks. One of her eyes had been carved out, leaving a ragged pit behind. Her chest gaped wide open, so that Aziza could see all the way through the sap-crusted hole in her torso.

"*Gatewalker,*" Eirlys rasped, the word mostly air. "*Help me.*"

"What happened to you?"

"*Trapped,*" she said. "*The hag killed me and took my magic. I can't return to Elphame without it.*"

"Return? But, Eirlys . . ."

Did Eirlys think she could come back to life?

"*When a nymph dies,*" Eirlys said, "*Elphame's wild magic consumes us. We go back to where we came from. Please, gatewalker. I want to go back.*"

Aziza swallowed hard against a surge of guilt. If she hadn't given Eirlys her magic, Eirlys would never have approached the hag, and she'd still be alive.

"I can't do anything," she said. "I'm sorry."

Who else had she hurt when she'd thrown herself on a collision course with the hag? Jiddo. The Ash Witch. Leo. And it would amount to nothing in the end. She hadn't wanted to admit it to Tristan, but she was outmatched, even though she was the strongest she'd ever been. Ever since the hag woke up, Aziza had been putting in extra hours on patrol. She dealt with more unruly fae in a week than she had in the rest of her life combined. She'd pacified a kraken, its magic ancient and complex beyond her ability to comprehend. Each new trial had pushed her abilities farther. By any measure, she was a better witch now than she had been a year ago.

But she still couldn't save Eirlys from *this*.

"*Are you not a gatewalker?*" Eirlys demanded.

"Yeah, and what good does that do against a hag?"

Eirlys lurched forward. Aziza reached out to steady her, but her hand passed through her shoulder. Eirlys's frame distorted around the intrusion, as if melting, but Aziza felt nothing. Just air. She whipped her hand away.

Eirlys pinned her with a one-eyed leer, as if Aziza's discomfort amused her even now.

"*You mend gates,*" Eirlys said. "*You can also break them.*"

Aziza mulled this over. Wasn't that exactly what she was doing when she opened doors into Elphame? Breaking the gate, albeit in a controlled way, and repairing the damage after?

"And you're saying that this place has a gate, too," Aziza said, feeling the faintest twinge of hope. "One that can be broken."

"*It does. I can show you,*" said the thing that was once Eirlys. "*And in exchange, you will help me. You will end this.*"

"Deal."

The apparition grinned with vengeful delight.

TRISTAN HAD DESCRIBED what she would find in the clearing, but she still wasn't prepared for it. Something inside her wanted to recoil, a response that felt deeper than fear, felt like a primeval impulse wired into her biology, as if she were looking at a human corpse.

It was a monstrous, alien *thing* trying to pass itself off as a tree, with veins of gleaming black sap and a system of branches so complex and expansive they were a forest all on their own, a tangled, self-contained world. Aziza caught the stench of death that emanated from it and suppressed the urge to gag. The bones of an old cottage cradled the base of the trunk like a nest, the stumpy, decayed remnants of the walls all but buried under yellow-caped woodlovers and white-brown dollops of wet rot. At the crook where branches met trunk, the tree was split wide open, peeled apart to reveal an impenetrable darkness within.

That was it—the source of the hag's power. In *there*.

Aziza's magic rippled out from her, sinking into the earth and weaving its way through the clearing. It was like swimming through mud, filthy and slow going; she breathed through her mouth and willed herself not to throw up. She had never worked her craft in a place like this: somewhere not human and not fae. But that tree was a boundary of *some* kind, a threshold, not like a doorway but more like a web. Black magic flowed to the surrounding woods in elaborate networks and pathways, feeding into itself, into the swirl of pure power at the center. That swirl lay directly under the gateway tree, like a whirlpool, like a portal.

This was why the hag's borderlands had no clear perimeter. Her own magic was the foundation for this pocket realm. As the hag had fed and grown stronger—first with Tristan's help, and then through the hounds—her realm had encroached farther into the natural world, pushing against Elphame's boundary, warping it. It wasn't that the hag had done something to the boundary on purpose. She destroyed things simply by existing.

Aziza had only ever strengthened and reinforced magical boundaries before. This time, she'd have to do the opposite: tear the boundary open with no intention of putting it back together. Uproot it.

"Come closer, witchling," said a ragged voice that might've come from the bowels of the earth itself.

And the ground opened up beneath Aziza, swallowing her.

She was underground, the earth churning. It tossed her to and fro, too soft for her grasping hand to find purchase but hard enough to knock the air out of her. She couldn't see, couldn't breathe, couldn't hear anything but the world shattering around her, a sound that was more than a roar: It was the train grinding to an agonizingly slow stop while a kelpie bore down on her, the ocean ripping itself open under a far-too-small boat, her parents' bones crashing back into their graves. A gap overhead, a reprieve—she clawed her way back to the surface one-handed, coughing out dirt, muddy tears streaming from her stinging eyes. But then another pocket opened in the ground, and she was sucked back under, into a space that quickly collapsed on top of her—it was a concentrated avalanche, a violent burial—she was going to drown on dry land—

Again, she fought her way to the surface. This time, she managed to climb to her feet, but then something slammed into her side. She landed *hard*, wrenching her shoulder; her whole flank ached, and a searing pain made her certain she'd broken a rib. On her back, gasping for breath, she twisted around to see what'd struck her—the hag?

No—she rolled over in time to avoid another blow from a whipping tree branch. The trees that ringed the clearing were lashing out at her, their boughs writhing and straining. Their roots groaned as they slithered from the ground, as if preparing to chase her—

She took my magic, Eirlys had said.

She stumbled away from the tree line and deeper into the clearing, her lungs burning, until she was walking over the roots of the gateway tree. Every time she stepped between them, pockets opened up in the soil, sucking her down—so she had to balance with her feet on the roots, treading unsteadily closer to the trunk where they were thicker and easier to stand on.

She was being herded closer to the gateway tree.

And if the moving trees were nymph magic, then . . . the gift of hidden spaces, the gift that the hag was using against her now . . . that gift belonged to—

She reached for her own craft again, trying to turn inside of herself and slip into that state of peaceful concentration. She had to at least *try*. If only because she'd made a deal with Eirlys. A hedgewitch's word . . .

But her magic hit a wall. It was being blocked—being *locked*—

There was no denying it. The hag was using the gifts she'd stolen from Aziza's parents against her.

Fury burned her up inside. At last, she looked up at the hag.

Perched in the crook of the gateway tree, the old woman reclined as if on a throne. Her skin was gray and spotted, practically falling away from her bones, as if she'd been boiled. Her hair, a scraggle of oily tendrils, half hid her face. She didn't have eyes, only two knots of scar tissue where her eyes had once been.

"What is it?" said the hag. "Have you never seen true power before, witchling?"

"I'm going to kill you," she told the hag, and her magic ripped through the hag's lock and struck again at the core of her power; there was no peace and no balance in her craft just then. It carried all the venom and rage in Aziza's heart. That was exactly what she needed. She wasn't here simply to close a gate; she was here to rip its foundations up from the ground, to topple it, to leave the gate so mangled it would never stand upright again.

As her magic warred with the hag's, she dragged herself another step forward over the gateway tree's roots. And another. If her magic wasn't enough, she'd climb the fucking tree and rip this fucking monster apart with her bare hands—

"Quite the unladylike temper you've got there," said the hag. "That's enough."

Iron wrapped around her heart—a lock turned inside her—

And her fury was snuffed out.

Without it, she was empty, drained. No, not empty. The hag was there, in her head, riffling through her mind as if browsing a magazine, unlocking memories and feelings Aziza had buried— Jiddo's tearful voice on the phone, Leila's bones begging to see her father again, Meryl's wistful voice when she talked about her family, Leo in the throes of an enchanted sleep—herself, screaming as the hound's teeth crushed her hand, making reckless deals with nymphs, dragging Leo into danger night after night, lying to her grandfather, watching a kelpie ride off with its victim, letting the shade get away—every failure, everything she'd ever done wrong in her life, a whirlwind of guilt and shame and fear and doubt—

The roots of the gateway tree jerked underneath her. She fell hard onto her knees, her face inches from its trunk, the hag looming over her. Tears streamed down her cheeks, but she hardly felt them.

"Yes," said the hag. "Very interesting gifts your parents had. But I was a witch, too, once. Would you like to see *my* gift? My very own gift, the one I was born with?"

She dropped to the ground behind Aziza, a graceless and abrupt fall, like an insect being knocked off a wall. Her body shouldn't have been capable of standing; upright, she was hunched and lopsided, her legs twisted awkwardly like the bones had melted out of shape. Her scarred, eyeless face and predatory leer were revolting up close. Aziza pressed her back against the trunk, unable to think, unable to gather the strength to attack or run or do *anything*—

The hag's skin came off in flakes and blew away like ash, but there was no flesh beneath; there was only roiling flame, the dark red and orange of hellfire. This was what had become of her hearthcraft, a simple and practical gift warped beyond recognition. She shed her wrinkled exterior, and the flames grew, and grew, and grew into a towering inferno. She was a demon, a devourer, blazing above the treetops to scorch the sky. The roar of the flames was deafening. The gateway tree did not burn at her touch, but she left smoldering black footprints in the grass.

A fiery hand reached down for Aziza. She threw her arms over her head, uselessly, as the air grew so hot she felt like she was being cooked alive—even if she ran, she wouldn't be fast enough—

A shadow fell over her; past the roar of the fire came another sound, a chorus of snapping and creaking. Something brushed her cheek—a leaf.

She lowered her arms and looked up. The trees had uprooted themselves again, had swarmed into the clearing, and now stood between Aziza and the hag, a living wall. The hag swept a flaming arm across them—ash rained down on Aziza—but even as they crumbled away to nothing, another row of wooden soldiers replaced them.

The forest was protecting her. No, not the forest. Nymphs—recruited by Eirlys. They were buying her time. Time that made all the difference, because it was then that she found it: the wounds in the hag's magic where Tristan had sent the hounds after the gateway tree, gnawing away at its roots while she slept and conserved her strength. In a web of magic so vast, these wounds must have felt like tiny nicks, cracks so fine as to be invisible. But they were weaknesses. And a weakness was all Aziza had needed. With one last burst of energy, she sent her magic crashing down on the hag.

The gateway tree cleaved in half.

As if invisible hands were pulling it apart, the fissure at the crook of its branches grew, until finally its trunk crashed to the ground in pieces. Aziza stood there in the wreckage, breathing hard, dripping sweat under her coat and squinting against the firelight.

The hag screamed—except it wasn't a scream, it was a *boom*, and the acrid smell of sulfur rose into the air, smoke smothering the gray sky. Her fiery form swelled and swelled, eating up more of the clearing; there was nothing humanoid about her anymore, no limbs, no taunting voice. The hag was a wildfire.

She swallowed up Aziza's protectors, burning them to cinders. Their branches blackened like spent candlewicks and disintegrated, the trunks following suit moments later. No more could even come close without igniting. The flames encroached on Aziza, surrounding her on all sides, licking at her boots. Her skin stung from the heat, and sparks jumped up on her coat—

But she couldn't waste this chance. If she went down, she was taking the hag with her.

With no way out, she turned inward. She dug the hag's metaphysical roots from the ground, ripping up the hag's magic with her own. There was no subtlety or grace to what she did. Her magic was feral and merciless, only barely responding to her directions. She let it sweep her away, tearing down everything in its path, and then—

She found the center of the web, old and freezing cold and slimy to the touch of Aziza's mind. The hag's original power. It was what she had been, mutated into something evil and deathless.

"ZEE!"

She couldn't see through the fire, could barely even hear. But the warning made her look up. Blisters had opened up on her bare hand, the hem of her coat had caught fire, and the hag was everywhere: a cyclone whirling around and around Aziza, searching for gaps in the magical barrier she'd hastily erected around herself, a flimsy thing she'd never attempted to use against anything larger than a shade. Aziza's concentration faltered, and the flames surged in—

No. She *had* to live long enough to finish this.

There was only one place for her to escape to.

The wildfire crashed over the spot where Aziza stood, an explosion of heat and light, but Aziza dove—

She dove into the hollow where the tree had once stood—an opening in the earth, concealed before, surrounded only by splinters and shrapnel now. *This* had been the gateway all along. As she crossed the threshold between *above-* and *below*ground, Aziza felt a faint, familiar crackling, as though she'd passed through a thin layer of static—but she couldn't have said *why* it was familiar. Suddenly it was so dark and cold she couldn't imagine ever being warm again; fire was less than a memory, it was a half-lost fairytale, and the icy-dark went on forever—

She saw and knew nothing for a very long time as she pushed into the hag's den.

CHAPTER 37

LEO

LEO AND HAZEL climbed out of the pit, muddy and winded; he clung to Tristan's hand until they were on solid ground again. Tristan's cold fingers slipped out of his, then, and he let go of Hazel's shoulders. He doubled over, catching his breath.

"I thought we were done for," he said. "Thanks."

Tristan stood apart from them, hands clutching at his throat. His expression was grim but unsurprised.

"Tris?" he said, drawing nearer.

Tristan shook his head, his throat working. He tried to take a breath and visibly *couldn't*.

And then he was sinking to his knees.

"Hey, no," Leo said, dropping to the ground and reaching for him. "No, no, it's okay—Tris, what's happening?"

His hands were huge and clumsy on Tristan's shoulders; he held on tight, too tight probably, feeling the shape of Tristan's bones under his fingers, feeling the faint spasms as he tried and failed to draw breath.

Tristan ducked his head as if he was too weak to hold it up anymore, and Leo caught his jaw in his hands, needing Tristan to keep looking at him.

"Tris," he said. "Tris, please—"

Tristan didn't look afraid. His hands rose and clung lightly to Leo's wrists, and his expression was very calm as he met Leo's eyes, as if to say, *It's going to be all right.*

His mind raced, eyes darting around for a solution, for something he could *do*, but there was nothing: just the voiceless woods and green-skinned Hazel with her hands clapped over her mouth, tears welling up.

Tristan gave another weak spasm, trembling in Leo's hands—his eyes fell shut—

And then, a gasp. And another.

He was breathing again.

Heart hammering in his chest, Leo shifted so that Tristan could lean against him, not yet trusting him to stay upright on his own. Tristan blinked rapidly, as if shocked to find himself still alive.

"Tristan—" His voice broke with relief. "Jesus, fuck, tell me what's wrong—"

"'M fine," he mumbled.

"What just happened?" Leo said. Already Tristan's energy was returning; he moved as if to get up, so Leo helped him to his feet.

"The hag tried to kill me, but then she stopped," Tristan said, casually, as if he almost died in Leo's arms all the time. "Because of Aziza."

"The hag has Aziza?" he repeated, his head spinning.

"I wouldn't say she *has* Aziza," Tristan said. He was brushing dirt off his knees, but it wasn't doing much good, because his hands were covered in what Leo had thought was mud, but—he now realized—was actually blood. "Aziza went there herself. She wanted to distract her long enough for us to get away. I guess it's working."

Leo was going to have a fucking heart attack at this rate.

"That's the worst plan I've ever heard in my life, including the one with the kraken—"

"Don't worry. I'm going to help her."

"What?"

A wide, oddly devious smile broke over Tristan's face. He reached into his pocket and held up the clamshell token.

Leo's jaw dropped. "How—how did you get it back?"

Despite the fact that he was blood-soaked and half-dead, Tristan seemed stronger than he'd ever been, reinvigorated by this impossible victory. He'd been so hesitant and so quiet with them before— Leo had thought him almost fragile at times. Not anymore.

"You don't want to know," Tristan said. "I'll take this to Aziza while you get out of here."

"That's not going to happen, and you know it."

"You can't come," Tristan said, with a faint air of triumph, like he thought his argument was bulletproof, "because you have to take Hazel home."

"I can't go home like this!" Hazel wailed. Leo jumped; she'd been so uncharacteristically quiet he'd almost forgotten she was there. Tears welled up in her eyes again, like *she'd* forgotten her own predicament but now it was rushing back to her all at once. Guiltily, Leo held out an arm, and she practically threw herself at him. She wept into his shirt.

"It's all right," he told her, trying to figure out how to hug her around the wings. He ended up settling his arms over her shoulders.

"What happened to her?" Tristan asked hesitantly, like he wasn't sure he was supposed to bring it up.

"She's a changeling." He was growing accustomed to the borderlands, and his head was clearing. Memories surfaced of the stories

Aziza had told him as they left lines of salt at the windows of those houses that were situated a little too close to the forest.

Changelings were fairy children who were swapped for human ones, she'd explained, with a glamour to disguise them until their mothers returned to take them home. The switch would've happened a long time ago—when Hazel was a toddler. But the fairies *always* took their young back.

Why hadn't Hazel's mother come back for her?

"Then where's the real Hazel?" she said, her voice muffled against Leo's shoulder.

He wished she hadn't asked that. Not yet. He didn't think she could stand to hear the truth right now: that the girl she'd replaced was probably dead. Aziza said that human children never survived in Elphame for long. If something in Elphame didn't kill them, they wasted away in a matter of weeks from overexposure to its magic when their bodies weren't strong enough to handle it.

"*You're* the real Hazel," he told her instead.

She sobbed something else, so garbled it took Leo a second to interpret it. He sighed.

"You're not a freak, sis," he said. "You're magical."

He peered down at the top of Hazel's head, studying her pointy ears, the dragonfly wings, the dark green-black hair still braided the way Mom did it for her before bedtime.

"Take her and get out of here," Tristan said. "There's no point in us both going after Aziza. It only takes one of us to give her the token."

"I'm not leaving her."

"She wants you to be safe!"

"Too bad."

"But Hazel—"

"She can come with us."

Tristan sputtered. "She *can*?"

"I can?" Hazel pulled away, wiping her eyes on her sleeve.

"She's right—she can't go home like this," Leo said. "Anyway, I promised her she could help."

"You promised her *what*?"

"Not with the hag, exactly, but, like. Generally."

"You *did* promise!" Hazel put in.

"And if I don't let her come, she'll follow us anyway."

The truth was, Leo had shut Hazel out and that was why the hag got to her. He'd learned his lesson, and he wasn't going to make the same mistake again.

"Hazel, are you—" Tristan began, and then stopped. "Um, hello, by the way. I'm Tristan."

Hazel stared at him in confusion for a second. Then she glanced at Leo, and her eyes widened. "Right. Hi."

"Are you *sure* you don't want to go wait in the car?" Tristan said, a pleading note in his voice.

"I'm sure!" she said, almost before he'd finished speaking.

As far as Leo was concerned, that settled it.

A GUST OF heat slammed into them as they neared the gateway tree, so powerful Leo instantly broke into a sweat. They abandoned their coats and pressed on. Soon he glimpsed an orange glow through the trees; a faint rumble in the distance swelled to a roar.

"A forest fire?" Leo said.

The gateway tree's clearing was consumed by an inferno; the heat was so overpowering they almost couldn't get close. They made it to the edge and stopped, Leo throwing his arm out in front of Hazel protectively, as if that would make any difference in the face of a blaze that reached higher than the forest canopy.

If Aziza was in there—

"It's not a normal fire," Tristan said. "It can't be. It would've spread farther by now."

"Wait—I see her—"

Once his eyes adjusted, he could make out a figure—Aziza, standing stock-still as the unnatural flames whirled into a tornado.

"ZEE!" he shouted, and would have thrown himself into the clearing, but Tristan grabbed his arm and hauled him back into the relative shelter of the trees.

It was too late, anyway.

Aziza leapt *into* the ground and vanished. The inferno poured into the opening after her, a fiery, twenty-foot python; the earth swallowed all the light and heat and noise, and when it was gone, nothing was left but darkness and silence. His ears rang in the aftermath.

"Where did she—"

"The gateway tree," Tristan breathed. "It's—in pieces. I can see where it used to be, but it's gone now."

Leo blinked until the spots cleared from his vision and ventured into the clearing. He took a breath, got a mouthful of soot, and coughed into his sleeve. As he neared the center, he had to pick his way over the protruding roots of what he assumed was once the gateway tree—which now was nothing more than a pile of ugly, stinking debris around a hole in the ground.

He peered inside but saw only blackness. No firelight. No voices.

"Zee?" he called.

No response.

He looked up at Tristan. "Any idea what's down there?"

Tristan shook his head. "I guess we're going to find out."

"Hazel," Leo said. "Stay here."

"No, I—I want to come with you," she said, though she didn't sound very sure about that anymore. "I want to help."

"You can. We're going to need someone to get us out of there," he said. "It looks pretty deep. Can you fly?"

Her lips parted, but no sound came out. Her silvery eyes widened. "I don't know."

"Try it," he said.

She tilted her head, and her wings fluttered tentatively. They beat faster and faster until she began to rise into the air. She laughed, delighted, and Leo managed a smile in return.

"When I shout, come down and get us," he said. "Till then, stay here and practice."

She landed unsteadily, staggering. "But what if—"

"If you don't hear anything for an hour," he said, "get out of here and call Mom and Dad. *Don't* come back here. Go to Bishop Library and talk to the librarian. She can help."

He prayed she wouldn't argue, and she didn't. Instead, she threw her arms around him and hugged him tight.

"Please come back," she whispered.

He hugged her back, unable to speak. To his surprise, she threw herself at Tristan next, nearly bowling him over. Then she let go, and he and Tristan stood together at the precipice, the darkness yawning at their feet.

No point in putting it off.

"I'll go first," Leo said.

And before Tristan could object, he lowered himself into the pit, half sliding and half falling down the tunnel within. It narrowed as he descended, like a funnel into the earth's core, and then the world spun dizzyingly until he wasn't falling anymore but crawling, climbing, not understanding what was happening or how, only knowing that he had to keep going. The air was hot and thick, the dirt walls searing, like sand at the beach in summer.

"Tris," he said, shakily pulling himself up a slope that was danger-ously close to vertical.

"I'm here," came Tristan's voice from behind—below?

The darkness softened; above him was a gap, a place where the tunnel widened out. He grasped the edge, heaved himself up—his feet braced against the wall, hoping he wasn't kicking dirt into Tristan's face—and gasped for breath as he cleared the mouth of the tunnel.

He crawled out into the crook of *another* gateway tree.

This gateway tree was the reverse of the other: bone-white, its veins glowing red-hot like magma showing through cracks in the earth's crust. Its branches—or roots?—spiderwebbed up and met the far-off ceiling of the cavern.

He reached back down and helped Tristan up. They balanced on the boughs of the tree, catching their breath. The cavern was so dark he couldn't tell how wide it was, how much space existed beyond the reach of the gateway tree's limbs. He couldn't see the floor, not without leaning precariously far over the edge of his perch. He could only tell where the ceiling was because of how the thin outermost branches flattened against it and spread out like fingers; where he and Tristan sat, it was like being inside a cage of bones.

Then something above and to the left of him moved—

"Zee!"

He climbed, slipping and pulling himself up again. Around her, the branches had come alive. They had wrapped around her torso, pinning her arms to her sides, and crisscrossed down her legs. One twisted around her throat, and even as he watched, another few coils moved sluggishly over her, bindings on top of bindings, a slow mummification.

Her hair fell over her face, matted with dirt and sweat. Her eyes were wide and unfocused. He would've been alarmed if he hadn't known what she looked like when she turned inward to reach for her magic. Suspended as she was in the air, he had to stand up, balancing precariously, so that he could reach her. He worked his fingers under the tendril that wrapped around her neck, but it was too tight, and he was terrified of hurting her even more.

"Zee," he said. "Come on, snap out of it. You've gotta tell me how to help you."

She blinked, once, twice, three times, as if waking up.

"Leo?" she managed, a choked-off gasp.

"Yes! Yeah. I'm here," he said, and clutched at her uninjured hand. The brace on the other one was probably ruined now, bent out of shape under the unforgiving grip of the gateway tree. Her fingers twitched weakly in his.

"Shouldn't . . . have come," she said.

"Don't start," he told her, scowling. "I'm gonna check your pockets, okay?"

Nothing useful in her coat, but she had her small silver knife tucked in the front pocket of her jeans. He pressed the flat of the blade to the wooden coil around her neck. It squirmed, loosening just enough for him to slip the blade underneath and slice through it. She gasped for air. But already another tendril was creeping up her collar.

"Where's the hag?"

"*Everywhere,*" Aziza said through a cough.

"I saw the other gateway tree—it's wrecked. Did you do that? Can you do it again?"

"That wasn't the real gateway tree. *This* is," she said. "I'm holding her back, but I don't know how long I can last."

She struggled weakly against her bindings; the branches creaked as they tightened around her chest, and she made a pained, strangled noise.

"What do I do?" Leo asked.

Aziza looked up, and he followed her gaze. There, suspended in the dead center of the gateway tree, was a glowing black *thing*. Except it didn't glow, not exactly. It seemed to suck the light away, instead. Gleaming veins stemmed from it, ribboning sleekly into its cradle of white branches and dangling off them like strands of saliva.

"The core of her power," Aziza said. "Her heart. It needs to die."

A branch caught around her throat again, and Leo pried it off her. "If I leave, can you hold on?"

"Leo," Tristan said. He jumped; he hadn't even heard Tristan come up after him. "Take this."

Tristan pressed the clamshell token into his hand. Aziza's eyes widened.

"Cover me?" he said. Leo had no idea what he meant, but Aziza must have, because she nodded.

Then Tristan left them and climbed up, heading for the hag's heart. He was going to try and kill it himself, Leo realized. Aziza's eyes went unfocused again, picking up her fight against the hag—and as she worked, Leo didn't fail to notice that the branches pinning her down tightened and grew more vicious, more resistant to the silver, harder for him to cut off . . . but Tristan remained untouched, the boughs quivering around him, some twisting as if to reach for him, but then stopping, as if an invisible hand held them back. Aziza's hand.

And while Aziza shielded Tristan, Leo shielded *her*, fighting for her when she couldn't fight for herself. He couldn't do much, but at least she wouldn't be alone.

No matter what happened next.

CHAPTER 38

TRISTAN

THE BARK WAS slimy-smooth under his hands, notched with old scars. It was warm to the touch, not like fire, but like flesh.

He suppressed a shudder of revulsion. Aziza had given him something vital: a *chance*. He couldn't waste it.

Wedging his boot into the fork between two branches, he heaved himself up. High above him, a pulsing un-light absorbed the glow of the fire that streamed in rivulets under the bark. He'd known what it was the moment he laid eyes on it: a physical manifestation of the dark power that weighed down the other end of his bond to the hag. He had recognized it the way someone else might recognize a long-lost sibling.

The branches shivered underneath him as if to buck him off; their sharp leafless points curved around like teeth, poised to bite into him. But they didn't. They shook with suppressed energy.

He looked down, just once. Aziza followed him with her eyes, forehead creased in concentration. Leo, from his perch, leaned precariously over the gap between them, hooking his fingers around a thick branch crisscrossing her torso from her left shoulder to the right side of her rib cage. He pulled her in until they balanced on the same bough. When he peeled a rubbery limb off her neck, a collar of red welts showed. The hag was wringing the life out of her.

Tristan faced forward again and kept climbing until his hands were sore and he had to blink the sweat out of his eyes. He took a gulp of dry air that stung the back of his throat. Had it been this hot down here a moment ago?

The next handhold was a fork in a branch over his head; he grabbed for it and then whipped his hand away, swearing. It *burned*. His muscles ached, and it was so hot he could barely breathe and the branches beneath him seared like soldering irons. His head spun as the heat grew unbearable. The world rocked wildly around him.

Don't fall. He rearranged himself on his perch, one knee pulled up to his chest and the other leg dangling down. Both hands clutched the tapering end of the bough. He wasn't imagining the rise in temperature, but the movement was in his head. He knew it was; Aziza was covering him.

The hag is counting on the fact that you're a coward.

Carefully, he brought his other knee up. Above him, the branches grew narrower. They wouldn't bear his weight for long. Once he moved, he wouldn't be able to stop.

He reached up again for the next handhold, and flame lashed out of it from the veins in the bark, billowing over him. It reshaped itself until the hag's hunched figure loomed over him, horribly familiar, her eyeless face recognizable even through the flames.

"*Failure,*" the hag thundered in the voice of the fire. "*Traitor!*"

"You should've killed me when you had the chance!" Tristan howled at her.

He reached straight through the scorching red void where her torso should've been and hauled himself up. The hag's burning form broke apart, not dissipating, but unable to hold its shape. Fire whirled around him like a vortex, screaming at him in the hag's voice. His hands were raw with burns and blisters; the ends of his hair were singed. But the fire didn't touch him—*couldn't* touch him. It ran up against an invisible barrier. A boundary.

"*If you do this,*" the hag hissed into his ear, "*you are mine forever.*"

The hag's heart was right *there*, just ahead of him, oozing with the same black sap that once ran down the trunk of the aboveground gateway tree. Wordless screams of rage rang through his head, and the heat choked him as surely as a pair of hands around his neck. Moving as though in a dream, he drew the silver ritual knife from his boot. The same knife that had left scars all over his palms; the same knife he'd used to mark the hag's victims.

He gripped the onyx hilt tight, raised the blade high over his head, and stabbed it deep into the hag's heart.

The screaming reached a fever pitch, no longer enraged, but fearful and desperate and *dying*. He dragged the blade down and yanked it out. That sticky black saplike substance gushed out over his hand and onto the white branches, waterfalling down the trunk and into the nothingness of the cavern floor somewhere below. Deep in his mind, the bond was on fire, incinerating him from the inside out.

The branch under Tristan gave out with a snap he *felt* more than heard.

He fell.

CHAPTER 39

AZIZA

He really did it, she thought, astonished.

Her bindings loosened and fell away. Leo steadied her as her muddy boots slid perilously underneath her. Together, they sank down and knelt on the shuddering bough. Pinpricks of pain burst into existence all up and down her legs as feeling returned to them. But she couldn't tear her gaze away from the crown of the gateway tree, where Tristan was pulling out the knife with a spatter of black ooze—was wobbling—was falling.

"Leo," she said, but she was closer. She lunged with her good hand extended, trusting Leo to anchor her—he did, arms locked around her middle and swearing directly into her ear—and managed to catch Tristan's wrist as he plummeted past them. His weight almost jerked her and Leo clean off the bough—

"Oh my god oh my god oh my god," Leo said.

"Just hold on."

"I'm trying!"

He had his legs clamped tight around the branch; Aziza was on her knees, only Leo's grip keeping her from sliding off. Tristan dangled from her hand, completely limp. Her arm ached with the strain of supporting his weight, and her fingers dug too tightly into his sleeve.

"Tristan!"

He blinked up at her, dazed. His lips twitched, almost but not quite forming her name.

"Give me your other hand!" she said.

It took him a second to comply, as if there was a lag inside his head, but his other arm rose jerkily, groping for purchase, and she got him to grab on to her forearm above the brace. Slowly, she and Leo hoisted him up.

Above and below and around them, the gateway tree withered to nothing. Its extremities crumbled to ash and drifted away; the air was cloudy with it, the smell thick and hot and rancid. The firelight veining the gateway tree dimmed, and the cavern grew darker and darker.

"The token—" Tristan wheezed. His hand was pressed against his chest, as if he'd gotten injured somehow.

"She's already dying," Leo said, but Tristan shook his head.

"Not—not enough."

"He's right," Aziza said. "Come on."

They crawled, slid, and climbed gracelessly back down to the crook of the trunk. There, on the brink of escape, they paused. Tristan leaned against her, his fingers curled into a claw over his heart, and she propped them both up with her good hand, though her arm shook—catching him had jarred her shoulder badly. Leo dug in his pocket for the clamshell token, coughing into his sleeve against the ash-choked air, an apocalyptic heat and darkness closing over them.

Then he had it in his hand, leaving sooty fingerprints on its surface, and it looked like nothing, worthless, no more magical than any other piece of junk you could've picked off the beach. At her nod, he broke it in half and let the pieces fall away.

Nothing happened for a second.

Then, a sound: a low growl that crescendoed into the thunderous bass of rushing water.

The cavern walls broke open as great streams of water flooded in. It pooled around the gateway tree, eating up its distant roots and the base of its trunk at alarming speeds. Leo ushered Aziza and Tristan into the opening first, and then followed. They fell down the shaft, limbs knocking into each other, unable to see a single thing—and the world flipped over horribly and they weren't falling anymore, they were crawling, clumsily and desperately, and then they weren't crawling but climbing—

Cool air blew up the tunnel, a sea breeze urging them onward, but they weren't fast enough. *She* wasn't fast enough, with her broken, aching, torn-up hand—she was slowing them all down—

"HAZEL!" Leo shouted.

Light, above. Moonlight. Maybe the first moonlight to touch the hag's territory in a year.

Then a long-eared, silver-eyed shape blocked out the light. Wings fluttering, the fairy dove down into the tunnel and grabbed Aziza's hand. Tristan hooked his arm over her elbow, and reached back to grab hold of Leo, and the fairy dragged them all unsteadily out and into the light.

As they cleared the surface, Aziza registered again that familiar crackling of energy—and this time, she recognized it. But before she could parse what it meant, the fairy dumped them unceremoniously on the ground.

"Thanks," Leo said, panting.

"Are you okay?" said the fairy, who had Hazel's voice and Hazel's clothes and rushed into Leo's arms the second he got up.

A changeling. Poor Hazel.

She opened her mouth to ask what she'd missed, but the words slipped away from her as she sensed . . . something.

The hag was almost gone. Drowning. She could feel that much with her magic. Already, a not-too-distant chirping of crickets could be heard. A tentative wind ventured through what had once been the hag's borderlands. The changeling's skin began to lose its green tinge as her glamour—doubtless stripped away by the hag— reasserted itself.

But something was wrong. There was something else, something nagging at her, if she could only put her finger on what it was.

The gateway tree was nothing but a pile of kindling now. The woods sighed with relief as the gray receded; stars peeked out of the night sky, igniting one by one, cautiously at first and then with abandon. The smell of rot had dissipated, even though the charred black footprints remained.

And Tristan was—

Tristan was on his knees, hunched over with his arms folded tight around his chest, breathing raggedly. His face, what she could see of it, was screwed up in pain.

That was it. *That* was what was wrong.

She shuffled over to kneel in front of him.

"The contract?" she asked. Her voice came out rough. The welts the gateway tree had left around her neck stung when she spoke.

Tristan squinted up at her, streaked with sweat and dirt and blood.

"Yes," he said hoarsely.

"Did you know—"

"Yes. Didn't—didn't want you to hesitate."

"I wouldn't have," she lied reflexively. His mouth twisted in what might've been an attempt at a smirk. Awfully cheerful for a dying boy. In fact, if she wasn't mistaken, he even looked a little relieved.

"Wait, what's—what's going on?" Leo said, drawing nearer.

Tristan shot him an agonized look, and then Aziza, as if to say, *Please don't let him see this.*

Aziza sighed. "Can you give us a sec?"

"What?" Leo said, face clouded with worry.

"Please."

And in the end, that was all he needed to hear. With a lingering look back, he and Hazel retreated to the far side of the clearing, just out of earshot.

"Thank you," Tristan said, ducking his head, like he was content to roll over and die now.

Honestly.

"I've decided," she said, "that I want the contract."

"You . . . what?"

"So you'll need to tell me what your terms are."

"What? What are you—"

"I'm taking over the contract, and you're going to live. But I can't have a *bondservant*." Just saying the word made her want to gag. "My craft is about balance. This will be an equal bond. But you have to say what you want from me."

"I—you—there are nine years left," Tristan argued weakly.

"I said tell me your *terms*, not tell me shit I already know."

He gaped at her. But some long-neglected self-preservation instinct must have taken over, because at last he whispered, "I just want Leo to be safe."

"I can't promise that," she said. "I can't control accidents, disease—Ask me for something else."

"I . . ."

He seemed on the verge of collapse, like that one question might be the thing that broke him.

"Tristan. It's okay. Just breathe."

He breathed.

"My terms are, don't make me get on a boat ever again," he said.

She nodded solemnly. "Okay. And in exchange, you must promise to make no more deals with hags. Agreed?"

He nodded.

"How do we . . ."

"To seal a contract with a witch—" She held out her uninjured hand. "We shake on it."

He clasped her hand, and they shook.

Tristan gasped, but Aziza barely heard him. She had stepped into Tristan's bond, which connected her—briefly—to the hag, too. It was like unlocking a sixth sense, a sudden onslaught of new information. There, underground, a wounded, fading evil, too weak to hurt her any longer even with a direct link to her magic. There, in the clearing all around, the web of power Aziza had sensed, unraveling. *There* and *there* and *there*, trapped within the web, all the gifts and souls and lives the hag had hoarded over the years. Aziza inherited them, and if she had wanted to, she might've held on to all that power and started the slow transformation into a hag herself. She had a moment of vertigo, of that swooping existential fear you'd feel standing on the roof of a very tall building and knowing how easy it would be to step over the edge and fall.

But Aziza did not hold on. She let go and felt it all slip away:

Eirlys returning to Elphame, leaving ripples of gratitude in her wake; all the other trapped spirits the hag had kept for her own amusement; the magical gifts, mostly unfamiliar, except for the two that belonged to her parents—shining bright points that Aziza recognized intuitively. These she released with some reluctance. She couldn't have used them, but—that magic was the very last trace of Leila and Ahmed that existed in the world. And now it was gone.

Then there was only one gift left. Her hand tightened on Tristan's.

"Do you want to be a necromancer again?"

He stared at her. He wasn't in pain anymore—she *knew* he wasn't, because she could feel, with this new sense of hers, the difference between Tristan-hurting and Tristan-not-hurting.

"You can do that?" he said, his voice small.

"It's there, in the bond. I can let it go, or I can return it to you. But only if you want it."

He hesitated.

"I can't hold on to it for much—"

"Yes!" he blurted. "I don't—I don't want to be powerless again."

And she eased the necromancy gift through the new bond to Tristan. That bond anchored itself in the back of her mind, a taut rope that led from her magic to another presence. When she finally dropped his hand, that bond wasn't the hag's anymore, not even a little bit, because the hag was dead.

"I can't believe you did that," Tristan said, and she both heard and felt his shock, and his relief, and the fact that a part of him really *didn't* believe it, because being saved was not an outcome he'd considered possible.

"All clear," she called out to Leo. He jogged back to them, Hazel fluttering along after him—and then touching down as the glamour hid her wings away again. That was it, the last sign of her fairyhood;

no one who didn't know better would've suspected she was anything other than human.

"What did you just do?" Leo said, looking down at the two of them.

"I'm not one hundred percent sure," she admitted.

All she really knew was this: She had promised Leo she would help him break his curse and find his true love. No Tristan meant no true love. No true love meant she'd broken her promise.

And she was not about to break a promise to Leo.

With Leo's help, they got to their feet. Between her and Tristan, it was a toss-up as to which one of them was worse off. But they both refused the hospital, unanimously and without hesitation.

"Let's just go home," she said.

No one argued with that.

CHAPTER 40

LEO

LEO AND HAZEL opened their front door and stood in the gold-lit threshold. She hesitated—but before Leo could persuade her to go in, Mom was there, gathering Hazel up into a hug.

"Where did you go?" she wept, forgetting to sign. She pulled back an inch so she could scrape Hazel's muddy hair out of her face. "And why are you so filthy? Do you have any idea how worried—"

Toads rained down on the floor. Hazel pushed Mom away, roughly. Mom looked between her and Leo, and understanding dawned on her face. She dabbed at her tears with a tissue, folded it up, and tucked it in the pocket of her sweatpants. Then she crossed her arms and waited with a sort of grim resignation, like she'd been expecting this moment for a long time.

Leo didn't know where to start. He couldn't think; he was too tired. But Hazel found an untapped vein of energy within herself. The nightmare was over for him. For her, it was just beginning.

"Why didn't you *tell* me?" she demanded, looking at Mom.

Dad had picked up a red-spotted toad; now he fumbled and dropped it again, and it hopped away, trilling smugly.

Neither of them asked what she meant.

Mom raised her hands to sign, and they hovered in the air for a few moments before she managed, shakily, "I was protecting you."

"You were lying to me!"

"Can we at least sit down?" Dad said wearily.

They migrated to the kitchen, a painfully awkward procession, but no one actually sat. Mom turned her back and busied herself making coffee. Hazel huddled in the doorway, arms folded. Leo would've liked to sit down, but he already felt guilty about all the dirt he and Hazel were tracking in, and he didn't think any of the furniture really needed a mud-print in the shape of his ass. So he picked a part of the counter Mom wasn't using and slumped against it.

Dad looked at them all, shook his head, and sat down at the table by himself. "All right. I'll tell you about her."

"About me?" Hazel said.

"You, and our . . . other daughter," he said, his voice already rough.

It took a few starts and stops. Mom cried, and then Dad did, and so did Hazel, and Leo just clung to the counter and tried to keep it together. But eventually the whole story came out.

It went, more or less, like this: When Leo was six and his sister was two, she'd—transformed. Overnight, she changed from a bouncy, giggling baby into a solemn, silent shadow of herself.

"The look in her eyes changed," Dad said, which didn't make any sense to Leo. Toddlers didn't have *looks* in their eyes, did they? They were *toddlers*. But the color and texture of her hair, the shape of her nose and chin, were off by degrees, too. The differences were so imperceptible they could've gone unnoticed. But Mom and Dad noticed.

As far as the doctors were concerned, she was perfect. There wasn't anything wrong with her.

But Mom and Dad did some digging—and Leo's heart sank as they described the steps they'd taken, so similar to the painstaking magic research he'd done after his curse set in and before he'd met Aziza. They figured out their daughter had been kidnapped by one of the Fair Folk and a changeling had been left behind in her place.

They tried to get her back. They hired everyone from private investigators to priests. They walked through fairy doors and performed rituals learned secondhand. They contacted folklorists at the world's top universities, begging for advice.

Nothing worked.

And then pretty soon it was too late anyway, because they found out—what Leo already knew, what he'd hoped Hazel would never have to learn—that their daughter was probably dead. Too much time had passed.

"They said the mother would return," Mom signed. Her eyes were red and swollen, but the tears had dried. She went to say something else, gave up, and wrapped her hands around her mug. Dad took over again.

"Right. The fairy was going to come back for . . . for you, Hazel," Dad said. "So we waited for her."

What he meant was, *Mom* waited for her.

Mom was the one who hid in the nursery every night, guarding it. Mom was the one who saw the fairy slip inside through the window and bend over the crib. Mom was the one who stepped out of the shadows and ripped the wings off the fairy's back with her bare hands.

And then she doused her in oil.

And then she set her on fire.

Hazel's hand rose to cover her mouth. Leo wondered if she was thinking about the nightmares she'd had all her life about fire, or if she hadn't even connected those dots yet.

"But she cursed us," Mom signed. "With her final breaths."

As she burned, the fairy executed a retribution that would outlive her:

A curse for silence.

A curse for chaos.

A curse to break a heart.

Fae hate to be constrained, said Aziza's voice in Leo's head. *Their language has no word for* forbidden.

The fairy had punished them in the fairy way, by setting limits on their lives.

Hazel was pale and speechless. But Leo had one more question. One thing he couldn't rest without knowing. He dug the vial from his backpack.

"What's this?" he asked, holding it up.

Mom wasn't surprised that he had it, or maybe she just didn't care at this point. "Her wing," she signed. "I found it in the ashes. A memento."

A memento, or a trophy?

He thought back to the photo he'd found in the box alongside the scrap of wing. If he had to guess, he'd bet that photo was the last picture ever taken of the other Hazel. In hindsight, it was pretty embarrassing that he'd just assumed the presence of the photo meant that the secret Mom and Dad were keeping had something to do with *him*. He'd overlooked the most obvious clue of all.

"You should have *told* me," Hazel said, her voice breaking.

"Not important," Mom signed, trembling fingers splayed open. "You're my daughter. Not hers. Mine."

"I thought there was something wrong with me!" Hazel half shrieked. "I'm different from everyone else. I thought—and if you'd told me, I could've—"

"What?" Mom signed, tight-lipped, every bit as angry as Hazel. "Go back? To where they steal children? They are evil. Dangerous."

Dad sighed. "We didn't know how to take you back, even if we could've. Hazel, we love you. I know this is . . . scary and confusing, but I promise, we were trying to do the right thing for you."

"I don't believe you," she said, echoing words she'd said to Leo once. They'd all failed her, badly. She wiped her eyes on her sleeve and fled upstairs.

Leo stared blankly at the two of them, Mom burying her face in her hands and Dad looking at the ceiling rather than back at him.

"You could have told *me*, at least," he said. "You let me drive around half the country looking for answers. Chasing rumors and fake leads. You could have just—"

"You would've gone after them," Dad said. "At least when you were chasing fake leads you weren't in fairyland. You would've been convinced that you could talk them into helping you, but you don't want their kind of help. The enchantress is dead, anyway, and none of the others can break our curses—"

"Yeah, she's dead because you *killed* her!" Leo said. It was just hitting him, the enormity of that. "You literally murdered someone. Holy shit."

It wasn't like killing a hag, which was just . . . a monster. A fairy was a *person*. A person like Hazel.

Mom looked up, wiping her eyes. And it almost scared him, the total lack of remorse in her. She was still just Mom, in the old T-shirt and sweatpants she wore around the house, her hair in a messy bun. But her expression was both hollow and somehow electric, all thunder and lightning, as she said with steady hands, "I'd kill a thousand fairies for what they did."

"You're not even sorry," he said bitterly. Not even sure if sorry was what he *wanted* from her, if it made any difference at all.

"I'm sorry about something," Dad said. Mom jerked around to glare at him, looking almost betrayed, but he touched her shoulder in a calming gesture. "I'm sorry we lied to you, even if I'm afraid of what the truth would have done to you before. And I'm sorry you lost your true love. I swear I am." He approached Leo cautiously. When Leo didn't move away, he wrapped an arm around him, a hand settling on the back of his head. Leo couldn't bring himself to hug him back, but he didn't fight the embrace. He got one more glimpse of Mom's face—she was beginning to tear up again, and he didn't know if it was for him or Hazel or the whole sorry lot of them—before his head dropped, his forehead hitting Dad's shoulder lightly. "We already lost one kid to the Fair Folk. We can't lose you or Hazel."

Leo closed his eyes. In his earliest memories of Hazel, was that Hazel-the-changeling or Hazel-the-human? The loss of that other sister didn't feel real to him, not yet. But if someone had taken the Hazel he knew away from him, and then she'd died before he ever saw her again, all alone in some strange place . . . Yeah, okay. He got it. He got Mom's rage. And Dad's fear. And why they'd thought telling him the truth would've all but guaranteed he'd do something extreme. Hell, extreme decision-making apparently ran in the blood.

They'd protected him, but they'd hurt him, too. And the confusing thing was that he had no idea if he'd have done anything different in their place, but he still couldn't shrug off the hurt or the betrayal. It was like he was caught in some kind of emotional bear trap, gnawing off his own arm to get free, just wounding himself worse in the process.

There was probably more he could've, should've asked. But all he really wanted to do was go to his room and pass out.

Hazel didn't answer when he knocked, but the door was unlocked, so he opened it tentatively and peeked inside. She was the picture of desolation, sitting on the floor amidst her spent candles and torn-open tea bags and soda can incense holders, lights off and face turned toward the moonlit window.

"Hey," he said quietly. "You wanna shower first?"

She looked up at him. Maybe it was the light and shadow, or maybe it was his tired eyes, but he thought . . . for a second, that Hazel's glamour didn't fit quite right. Like it had been put back on crooked. Something in the glossiness of her hair and the angles in her face, a strangeness that was there and gone again when he blinked.

Just his imagination, he told himself.

"What am I supposed to do now?" she croaked. She must have just stopped crying minutes before he got there.

"Take a shower," he told her firmly. "And sleep. And then we'll take everything else one step at a time."

"Easy for you to say." She sounded like she wanted to be furious but had depleted the fuel she needed for it downstairs, so all she could muster was a quiet, choked imitation of rage. "I don't want to take things one step at a time unless I can walk backward. I don't want to—to be like this, I want to go back to how I was—"

Her chest was heaving, and she broke off into these horrible, dry sobs that were somehow even worse than tears. He came in and knelt down hesitantly next to her.

"I know," he said.

"It's your fault," she said, with all the conviction in the world. "Because you couldn't just—deal with the curse like Mom and Dad did, you had to blow up *everything* to try and break it."

"I know," he said again.

"I w-wanted you to break the curse, too," she said miserably. "But I mostly just—wanted everything to go back to normal—and now it never will."

He could say nothing to make this better. So he just sat with her, waiting to see if she would ask him to leave or lean against him for comfort like she had in the woods. Neither of those happened; eventually, they both passed out there on the floor, Hazel curled up with her arms wrapped around her knees, Leo leaning against the side of her desk. He woke up a few hours later, sore all over, and he managed to lift her up and onto her bed without rousing her before slipping out.

He showered, finally. He went to bed. He lay awake for what felt like ages with the story Mom had told stuck in his head on repeat, until he dozed off while trying to recall the exact shade of green Hazel's skin had been when her glamour was gone.

He woke again maybe an hour later, heart racing from nightmares where he set Hazel on fire.

"Your mom *burned* one of the Fair Folk alive," Aziza said.

"*Your* mom bottled up a hag like leftover wine," he reminded her wearily.

He sat with Aziza and Tristan at a coffee shop where the music was too loud to hear any of the conversations going on at neighboring tables and you could get a twenty-ounce drink for less than the cost of one-way train fare. Tristan kept glancing furtively around as if he expected to be kicked out.

"How was the sleepover?" Leo asked, wanting to talk about anything but dead enchantresses.

Unwilling to send Tristan back to the library—"It's safe for him to stay with us now," she'd pointed out—Aziza had brought him back to her place. Leo could hardly believe it. Five minutes ago she could barely stand the sight of him, and now—

The fact that he'd almost died helping them kill the hag must've won her over. It *had* been pretty outrageously brave of him.

Leo found himself fighting back a smile, his first in what felt like days. Tristan had been amazing. Unstoppable. Selfless. And now he just huddled in the seat next to Aziza, head bowed a little, like he was nothing special at all.

But Leo knew better.

"It was fine," Aziza said. "Jiddo was so angry with me, he didn't even have time to worry about the fact that we had a necromancer sleeping on our couch."

"He was nice," Tristan mumbled.

"He didn't want to make a scene in front of a guest," Aziza said. "Anyway, you can't stay at the library forever, and I don't think my couch is that much of a step up, so—"

The barista called their names. Before he could get up, Aziza shot to her feet.

"I'm getting the drinks," she said. "*You* tell him."

"But," Leo said, and stopped. He figured he didn't have to remind her she only had one working hand to carry three drinks with. She walked away, leaving the two of them alone.

CHAPTER 41
TRISTAN

"Tell me what?" Tristan asked.

Leo propped his elbows on the table. "First, *you* tell *me* something. Are you okay? You've barely said a word since we got here."

"I . . ." he said, and couldn't continue.

Last night, in the immediate aftermath of the hag's death, he'd been numb. He hadn't spoken, hadn't argued as Leo had driven him and Aziza back to her house. He couldn't have made a decision just then if his life had depended on it. Aziza had taken charge. She'd pushed him into the bathroom with orders to shower. She'd given him a change of clothes out of her own closet—a baggy pair of sweatpants and an oversized sweater, which were a few inches too short for him in the sleeves and ankles, but otherwise did the trick. She'd offered him food, and when he couldn't form a response, she'd shoved an apple and an energy bar into his hands, insisting he eat as much as he could and nodding with satisfaction when he managed a few bites. She'd piled what must have been every spare blanket and pillow she owned onto the couch, marching down the stairs with great armfuls of them. God. How had she even had the *energy*?

Tristan had barely had the willpower to mumble a "thank you" every now and then.

And then somehow the longest day of his life was over. The hag was dead, he was alive, Leo was safe, and the moon had risen without fanfare, as if the whole world hadn't upended itself. Even the hounds—tethered to him once more—did something akin to sleeping, as if being torn away from him and then abruptly reconnected had left them as much in need of rest as he was. Once Aziza had turned off the lights and left him alone on the couch with a mountain of blankets, he'd lain there for a long time, until the numbness that wrapped around him like a shell had cracked, and he'd wept. Quietly.

Her charity had extended into the morning. She made sure he ate again before they left her place. Then she bought him a coffee even though he'd tried to refuse—he didn't *need* it—and she'd assured him he wasn't going to have to sleep in the library anymore. Or the shelters. Or a park bench. Or in the woods. Not ever again. It seemed as though she would've liked to be comforting but didn't know how to do it, so she was brisk and practical instead.

Neither of them mentioned the magical bond between them. They came to a mutual, silent agreement to discuss it another time.

And now? *Was* Tristan okay?

"Better than yesterday," he settled on. "How's Hazel doing?"

"She's . . . I don't know," Leo said. "Last night she was coping. Then this morning she locked herself in her room and wouldn't come out."

"Oh."

"I guess it explains why my parents got so mad every time I brought up the curse," Leo said. "They were protecting Hazel. And I ruined everything."

"It's not your fault," Tristan said. "The hag did this."

"The hag only got her because of me."

"No," Tristan said. "The hag is an expert at using whatever you love against you. It wasn't your fault. Trust me."

"It's not just that," Leo said to the table. "I've been obsessed with breaking the curse. I was willing to put my whole family in danger over it. And for what? My true love's probably long gone. The curse said they'd be *lost*, but that doesn't mean they were taken away by force. Locked in a tower or something. Maybe they just left."

Tristan swallowed hard. He wasn't wrong; Tristan *had* just left. But he didn't like the flat, hopeless way Leo said it. *Hopeless* was not in Leo's vocabulary. "Do you really think that?"

"Who falls in love at sixteen?" His expression was scarily blank. "For real, I mean. I probably had a crush and blew it way out of proportion. As soon as the curse kicked in, they went running—"

"That's not true!" Tristan said, without thinking.

"What?"

"The—the point of the curse is to take something of value," Tristan said, flushed and irrationally upset. "You weren't cursed to forget your *crush*. You were cursed to forget your true love. And anyone who gave up on you that easily *wouldn't* be your true love."

No one who ever had half a chance with you would walk away without a fight, he thought, but did not say. *I regret so much of what I did, but I won't ever regret that. Even if you never love me back again.*

Unconsciously, he'd started twisting a napkin between his hands, crumpling it up and flattening it again and then slowly, mercilessly shredding it. Leo placed his hands over Tristan's, stilling the anxious movement of his fingers.

Tristan stopped breathing. His lungs just up and quit on him.

"Relax," Leo said gently. "You're okay now."

Tristan nodded, unable to speak. Leo pulled away, and relief warred with crushing disappointment in Tristan's mind.

"The thing Aziza wanted me to tell you," Leo said, offhand, "is that we think you should come and stay with me now. Like we talked about before, remember?"

Tristan sat bolt upright. "Stay with you?"

"You said you'd think about it."

"I did. I think it's a bad idea."

"Why?" Leo said. "We have a guest room. You won't have to crash on the couch. And my parents already okayed it. I think they feel guilty about the whole 'lying about our curses and killing the only one who can break them' thing."

Leo leaned in a little as he made his argument, like he was going to try and touch him again, and if that happened, Tristan would shatter into tiny pieces right there all over the table, and his resolve would blow away like silica dust, and he'd do anything Leo wanted him to do. Tristan hid his hands under the table and slouched in his chair, trying to put space between them.

"I'll—I'll stay at a shelter," Tristan said. "They have—programs for teenagers—"

"Tris."

That fucking nickname. Tristan was the weakest person alive, and Leo didn't even need to touch him—if he kept looking at Tristan with those eyes and saying Tristan's name with that voice, Tristan was *done*, there was no hope for him—

And then Aziza returned, balancing all three drinks between her uninjured hand and her brace, cutting off whatever Leo was about to say.

Tristan shot to his feet.

"Excuse me," he said, and walked shakily in the direction of the restroom.

He may have blacked out, because the next thing he knew, he was clinging to a chipped white porcelain sink and trying to breathe. His reflection was ghastly under the harsh white light, which threw the bony planes of his face and the bags under his eyes into sharp relief. The burns and gashes on his palms stung when his grip tightened.

What the hell was he doing here?

He hadn't expected to live. Hadn't planned for it. The whole concept of a future as something he still had was outlandish, over-whelming, and even—to a dark part of his mind—unwanted.

But you get to go home, said a small voice in his head. His stomach lurched. He closed his eyes and pressed his forehead to the cool mirror.

He was going back to the Merritt household. With Leo.

Home.

But even this thing he had wanted desperately for so long was frightening now that it was reality. He was going to have to face Maria and Greg. If Leo had mentioned him by name, then they prob-ably already knew everything—

He abandoned the sink and stumbled to the toilet to throw up.

It was like every emotion he'd had to suppress in order to sur-vive the last year and a half was now crashing into him all at once. Every vulnerability he'd locked away so that he could command the hounds and withstand the hag came screaming back into the open, raw and painful and demanding attention. And now he was hav-ing a breakdown in a public restroom because something *good* was happening for once, and all he could do was imagine all the ways it could go horribly wrong.

Eventually, the tide ebbed. He just couldn't sustain that level of feeling for long.

You've been through the worst already, he told himself. That was the first step to truly calming down.

He flushed the toilet and went back to the sink to rinse out his mouth. His eyes strayed to his reflection again; he didn't recognize himself. The person in the mirror didn't match up to the version of himself he saw in his head. Maybe because the Tristan he saw as his true self was sixteen, happily in love, and convinced he'd get to stay that way forever.

He took a long, hard look at his reflection. *This* was who he was now.

Aziza had given him a second chance. He knew that. He was *grateful.* But he'd never expected a second chance to feel so much like standing on the brink of an abyss, alone.

He wasn't alone, though. He had a place in Leo's life again. He had Aziza's tentative trust. He had a . . . coven.

It was a start.

CHAPTER 42

AZIZA

SHE SET THE drinks down without spilling anything, though it was a near miss. Luckily, Leo was too busy staring morosely at Tristan's retreating back to notice.

"I don't get it," he said. "I told him he could stay with me rent-free, and he acted like I gave him a death sentence."

She kicked her chair back and sat down. "He has a lot to get used to."

"So do you."

That was a given. Having to do everything left-handed was already driving her up the wall. But everything had a price, and this was the price she paid for going up against a hag.

She shrugged. "And I *will* get used to it. So. Aren't you going to ask?"

"What?"

"About Hazel."

He stirred his drink—which was little more than whipped cream and ice, as far as she could tell—until it was mostly slush. "Which one?"

"Up to you."

"Okay." He blew out a breath. "Can Hazel stay in the human world?"

Aziza wrapped her good hand around her coffee, feeling the warmth seep in through her palm and steeling herself for what she had to say next. "For now, yes. But I don't know how much longer. Glamours only work on children—as she matures, it'll wear off."

Fairies were known and feared for their illusion magic. But most of their illusions were created by enchantments that required constant upkeep. Once a fairy stopped pouring magic into their illusion, it would dissipate. A glamour was different, less an illusion and more a costume. It had a lasting quality, withstanding the changeling's separation from the fairy parent that had crafted the glamour; more than that, it had to grow *with* the changeling, who might be left with a human family for weeks or months. This one had survived for *years*, which was a testament to the formidable power of the enchantress who'd made it. Still, it had been made for a child; once Hazel was no longer a child, whatever that meant in fairy terms, it would break down.

"So she has to go back," Leo guessed.

"Not right away. Not unless she wants to."

"She *doesn't*." He frowned. "I don't think she does. Why would she?"

"Maybe she doesn't," Aziza conceded.

"Can you talk to her? About, uh. Fairy stuff?"

"I can try. But I don't know much about them. I've only ever seen one in person my whole life. I had the good sense to run away."

"*You* ran?"

"Yeah."

"Wow." He shoved his drink aside and propped his elbows on the table. "What about Meryl? Would she know anything?"

At this, Aziza had to look away to compose herself.

"Meryl's missing," she said.

"*Missing?* What do you mean?"

"I went to the library earlier—I wanted to tell her what happened. But she's *gone*. Her office was cleared out. The entrance to the river is boarded up. There was even a—" She was almost too outraged to get the next part out. "A *new librarian* working there!"

"Did she leave, or . . ."

"Whoever has her sealskin must have ordered her to leave. She wouldn't have gone without saying goodbye, not willingly."

Maybe Aziza had no right to say that so decisively—to speak as if she knew Meryl well enough to make proclamations about her *would have*s and *wouldn't have*s. Their relationship was built on several years of lies Meryl had been forced to tell and assumptions Meryl had never corrected. Aziza hadn't even known Meryl wasn't human until recently. How was she supposed to know what Meryl was thinking? How could she be so sure Meryl would've wanted to say goodbye to the hedgewitch who had not only failed to save her, but hadn't even noticed she needed saving? How—

"How do we find her?" Leo said, and while she had spent the morning working herself up over that precise question, it sounded different coming from Leo than it had in her head. She hadn't even needed to ask for his help. To him, it was a given they were going to look for Meryl—that they were *all* looking for Meryl.

But as for how—she didn't have the slightest clue about that.

"We . . ." She sighed. "I'm working on it."

That, and a dozen other things. The sudden disappearance of the hag's territory had disrupted the boundary almost as much as its initial intrusion. Aziza would have to do a complete circuit of the city, and fast, to repair the damage. After that, the boundary would stabilize, now that the hag wasn't around to screw up her hard work—but it wouldn't happen overnight.

Then there was her bond with Tristan. They'd have to figure out how it worked and how it would affect them. She would have to learn as much as she could about the Fair Folk, too, so that they could help Hazel. If Hazel wanted to stay in the human world, then there had to be a way to make that happen for her. Something that could replace her glamour when the time came.

And she had to find a way to make things up to Jiddo. Because she'd figured out what that strangely familiar magic at the entrance to the gateway tree had been: Jiddo's wards.

It wasn't just her parents who'd fought the hag. Jiddo had been there. He'd fought, too, and finished the job of sealing the hag into the prison her parents had made. He had been the sole survivor. All this time she'd blamed the house wards for draining him of energy, but really it had been the strain of maintaining the ward over the hag's den. At least in part. Because that was a far more complex, far more powerful piece of magic, and one he'd held up for *years*. It made her sick when she thought about it for too long—her parents had been killed by the hag, a swift and immediate death, but Jiddo had been dying for it, too. Just much more slowly.

Had he dragged Leila's and Ahmed's bodies out of the woods himself?

She understood now—too late—the things he couldn't talk about, and why, and forgave him for his silence. But she missed how things had been between them before. He looked at her like she was Leila's ghost.

"Zee."

She blinked up at Leo, who had that look on his face he always got when he was reading her mind with startling accuracy. A few weeks ago she would've found it unnerving. Now it was a relief to have someone else around who knew exactly what she was going through. Who was going through it with her.

"We're not going to fix everything at once," he said. "I think we can take a day to celebrate Coven Blackthorn's first win. Just *one* day."

Oh, no. This was what she got for letting it slide when he'd called them a "team." She leveled her fiercest, most implacable glare at him. "We are not calling ourselves that."

He grinned tiredly at her, and for a second, it felt like maybe everything would be okay after all.

By the time Tristan returned, not meeting anyone's eyes, they'd moved on to mundane topics—homework, plans for spring break, a new album that some band had just released. Tristan sat between them and listened. Like this, Aziza could almost pretend they were just a group of unremarkable teenagers with nothing more pressing than SATs on their minds, and nothing ahead of them but summertime.

Far away to the west, the forest breathed freely, settling into its old ways and its old magics. Many long nights awaited them there. But she was secure at least in the knowledge that there was nothing in the woods, now, more terrifying than the three of them.

ACKNOWLEDGMENTS

I STARTED WRITING *The Buried and the Bound* before I knew anything about writing. I set it aside, worked on other projects, and returned to it over and over. I learned to be a better writer for this book, and learned to be a better writer *from* this book. Along the way, I benefited from the support and friendship of too many people to count, probably, but I'll try my best.

I would first like to thank my agent, Erica Bauman, for being a tireless champion of my work; I'm eternally grateful for her enthusiasm and insight on everything from character arcs to the ins and outs of the publishing industry.

Working with my amazing editor, Mekisha Telfer, has been a dream come true. She truly understands this book, both what it was and what I wanted it to be; she helped me dissect it and bring the best out of it. A trilogy is an exciting venture, but a daunting one. I could not be more thankful to be tackling such a huge project alongside someone who is as passionate about it as I am, and to be able to put my work in her capable hands.

I don't actually have words to express how grateful I am to my Pitch Wars mentors, M. K. England and Jamie Pacton—the first people, other than myself, who really believed in this book. Thinking back on the state it was in before they got their hands on it, I'm even more amazed that they were able to see what it had the potential to be. They weren't afraid to give me the kind of feedback I needed—the kind that said to take the story apart and rebuild it starting from the foundations—and allow me the chance to rise to the challenge. Their wisdom, then and now, has meant everything to me.

Thank you to the incredible team at Roaring Brook Press/ Macmillan, including Kathy Wielgosz, Jennifer Healey, Ana Deboo, Nicole Wayland, Peter Mavrikis, Celeste Cass, Raymond Ernesto Colón, Leigh Ann Higgins, Sara Elroubi, Molly Ellis, Mariel Dawson, Gretchen Fredericksen, Taylor Armstrong, Jennifer Edwards, Beth Clark, Mallory Griggs, Jordan Winch, and Kristin Dulaney. Their hard work has shaped every part of this book, from the smallest details in the editing process to the massive undertaking of putting it into readers' hands. Huge thanks especially to illustrator Helen Mask and designer Samira Iravani for their brilliant work on the cover, which exceeded my wildest hopes, and for indulging me when I sent over notes like "can Leo have a fluffy mop of curls" and "Tristan should be pointier." You two are the absolute best.

To anyone who took the time to read any part of this book— especially in the early stages, five or more years ago, when it was a very different story—I can never thank you enough. In particular, I'm grateful to Rachel Morris and Meg Long for their feedback, support, and company throughout all the ups and downs of the publishing journey. The two of you are at least 90 percent of my common sense and emotional stability on any given day. Thank you as well to Mary Roach and Jessica Froberg, whose notes and encouragement helped me and this book move forward.

I am forever inspired by my many friends in the writing community, especially my Slackers, whose humor and advice have been invaluable—thank you for being there through the long drafting sessions, for the IRL and virtual hangouts, for the celebrations and commiseration. I'm thankful to my family for their continued support and excitement, especially my parents and sisters, who have suffered through the endless clacking of my keyboard on FaceTime calls and during holidays.

And finally: Thank you to every reader who will pick up this book and spend time between its pages, and to the booksellers and librarians who will help put it into their hands. None of this would be possible without you.